# JUSTICE
# BETRAYED

# JUSTICE BETRAYED

## PATRICIA BRADLEY

Revell

a division of Baker Publishing Group
Grand Rapids, Michigan

Published by Revell
a division of Baker Publishing Group
PO Box 6287, Grand Rapids, MI 49516-6287
www.revellbooks.com

Printed in the United States of America

Library of Congress Cataloging-in-Publication Data
Names: Bradley, Patricia, 1945– author.
Title: Justice betrayed : a Memphis cold case novel / Patricia Bradley.
Description: Grand Rapids, MI : Revell, [2018] | Series: Cold case ; 3
Identifiers: LCCN 2017053933| ISBN 9780800727161 (softcover) |
    ISBN 9780800735142 (print on demand)
Subjects: LCSH: Cold cases (Criminal investigation)—Fiction. | Murder—
    Investigation—Fiction. | GSAFD: Suspense fiction.
Classification: LCC PS3602.R34275 J87 2018 | DDC 813/.6—dc23
LC record available at https://lccn.loc.gov/2017053933

This book is a work of fiction. Names, characters, places, and incidents are the product of the author's imagination or are used fictitiously.

18  19  20  21  22  23  24       7  6  5  4  3  2  1

To Erin, who was the inspiration for the
character of Erin Ballard in the story.
You go, girl!

When you pass through the waters,
I will be with you,
or through the rivers,
    they will not overflow you. . . .
For I am *ADONAI* your God,
    the Holy One of Israel, your Savior.
                    Isaiah 43:2–3

# PROLOGUE

Shirley traced her finger over her mother's image in the photo, then shoved the picture into the backpack with her other possessions. Every night, she promised herself she'd leave as soon as her father parked himself in front of *All in the Family* and fell asleep. A band squeezed her lungs, making it impossible to breathe.

*You do it tonight.*

She clenched her jaw. It wasn't that she wanted to stay. But what if he came after her and found her? Or what if the law found her? She was only fifteen, and they would drag her back to him.

After all, they'd bought her father's story that her mom had fallen down the basement steps as she'd carried a basket of clothes to the washer. If the sheriff suspected her father had pushed his wife, he'd kept it to himself. No one wanted to get on the bad side of Big Al in their small community, not even the law.

She flinched as the back screen slapped against the doorframe. "Shir-lee! Shirley Irene, I'm hungry. Get supper on the table."

Shirley shoved the backpack under her bed and hurried to the

7

kitchen, stopping at the doorway to take a deep breath. "Evening," she mumbled.

He ignored her and turned on the television. The actor Ronald Reagan filled the screen in one of his election ads, and he snapped the set off.

"Washington's never going to stop spending our money," her father muttered, then he turned and laid his John Deere cap on the red Formica table.

Shirley wanted to snatch the dirty thing off the table her mother had been so proud to get from a neighbor after she updated her kitchen. She sidestepped past him to the avocado-green refrigerator to take out a package of pork chops. The sour odor of beer and sweat made her want to gag.

"Where were you this afternoon?"

She averted her eyes. "The teacher asked me to stay and help with cleaning up."

"Look at me when I ask you a question."

Shirley pulled her gaze past the beer gut hanging over his belt to his ruddy face and dead brown eyes.

"That's better. You aren't worth anything to me helping somebody else. I needed you to help load logs. Next time you tell her you have other jobs to do."

"Yes, sir," she said, rubbing her thumbs over the calluses on her fingers. He worked her like a mule.

"Now get supper on the table."

Shirley grabbed an apron and tied it around her waist. At the sink, she scrubbed her hands with the pumice soap until they were almost raw. Green sink, green stove, green refrigerator. She *hated* green. Her heart leaped into her throat as her gaze settled on the straight razor on the counter and then traveled to the leather strap hanging on the wall. She'd forgotten to sharpen his razor. That meant another beating if she didn't get it done before morning.

Or maybe not. She wouldn't be here by then. She would be gone.

With her spirits lighter, she lit the fire under the pot of beans and set a skillet on another burner and fried the pork chops, not even minding when the grease popped out, burning her arm. In twenty minutes, she had supper on the table and held her breath as he tasted the food.

"Girl, can't you do anything right? You got the beans too salty." He shoved away from the table and stood.

Her heart plummeted. But this time she wasn't going to take it. "You're not going to beat me again."

"I wouldn't have to if you didn't mess up all the time." He yanked the leather strap from the wall and marched toward her. "Any fifteen-year-old should be able to cook a simple meal without ruining it."

"I won't do it again." She backed up against the sink.

"This is to make sure you don't."

She screamed as the strap came down and barely turned in time to protect her face as the strap stung her back.

"I told you not to scream. Now you've gone and done it, and I have to correct you again. Turn around and face me."

"No!" The straight razor lay on the counter waiting for her to sharpen it. She grabbed it.

"You always say that." His fingers closed on her shoulder, and he yanked her back.

She came around swinging the knife at his throat. Blood spurted from his neck.

He grabbed his throat and staggered back. "What have you done, girl? Call an ambulance!"

With every heartbeat came more blood.

"No." He'd beat her for sure if he lived. Shirley sucked in air. "You shouldn't have made me do it."

"Girl, I'm sorry." His breath came shorter. "I won't do it again. Now call that ambulance."

She pressed her fingers against her mouth. He couldn't die here. The law might not believe her. "I'll drive you to the hospital."

"You . . . better . . . hope I don' . . . die." His voice grew weaker. "Haunt you . . . never get away from me."

*Can he do that? No. When you're dead, you're dead.*

He grasped her wrist. "Help me!"

Blood dripped onto her hair as she half supported and half dragged him through the door. "You've got to help me," she said through gritted teeth. Shirley didn't know if he heard her or not. Then he got his feet under him, barely lightening her load. "Good," she said with a grunt.

For once she was glad of the man's work he'd forced her to do. They stumbled once in the pitch dark of the moonless night but finally made it to the old pickup. Once she had him inside the cab, he leaned against the door, and Shirley drove toward town. They'd just reached the tavern he'd just come from when death rattled in his chest.

A quarter of a mile past the tavern, she pulled over on the shoulder of the road and stopped. The dim light of the dashboard revealed his chest no longer rose and fell as his breathing became shallower. When he took his last breath, she rested her head against the back of the seat. He was beyond hurting her ever again.

This wasn't her fault.

"You shouldn't have made me do it," she said softly.

She couldn't leave him here like this, though.

Shirley angled the pickup toward the deep ravine on the side of the road. Then she pulled his body into the driver's seat.

After wiping the steering wheel clean, she put the truck in neutral. Then she climbed out of the pickup. Slowly, it inched toward the ravine, picking up speed until it shot down the steep grade. Shirley ran like the hound of the Pit was after her.

The explosion happened just as she got past the tavern. She looked over her shoulder as a ball of fire rose from the trees.

For the first time in her life, she drew a free breath.

# 1

Elvis is in the building, and he wants to see you.
:-)

Homicide detective Rachel Sloan stared at the screen on her phone and then glanced at the clock. Four fifty-five on Friday afternoon was no time to joke around about the possibility of staying late.

She frowned and rolled her chair so she could see around the partition that boxed her in. Her heart sank at the sight of an aging Elvis look-alike in a white sequined jumpsuit standing at office manager Donna Dumont's desk, talking to one of the sergeants in Homicide.

The middle of August in Memphis meant Elvis Week and a city full of Elvis wannabes, but why did one of them want to see her? And where was Donna?

She rolled back to the desk she'd just cleared off for the weekend and dialed the number on the text. "What does he want?"

"He won't say, just that he needs to see *you*," the detective said.

"He called me by name?" She slipped off the heels she'd worn for the court appearance earlier in the afternoon. It'd been the DA's idea for her to wear the heels with a knee-length skirt and white blouse under her suit jacket. He'd said it would make her look professional, but the two male jurors ogling her hadn't escaped her attention.

"Yes. He actually asked for Det. Rachel *Winslow* Sloan . . . oh, and his name is Vic Vegas."

"You're kidding." She wiggled her toes. "Tell him to give me five minutes," she muttered and glanced toward the cubicle across the aisle. Her gaze collided with Lt. Boone Callahan's dark brown eyes as he stood in his doorway. The air between them crackled with electricity, and Rachel quickly dropped her gaze.

She thought he'd left for the day. No, she'd hoped he'd left. She and Boone had gone out a few times before she joined the Homicide division, but then she broke it off with him. Since then, they'd mostly avoided each other, him working the shift opposite hers until this week.

"Do you need something?"

His rich baritone sent shivers down her arms. "No. I thought you'd left for the gym."

"Gym?"

"Yeah, getting ready for tomorrow's competition." He was determined to beat her time. But that had never happened and wasn't happening tomorrow, either.

Rachel had inherited her father's competitive gene, a trait that had surfaced before kindergarten. Even as a four-year-old, she had to be the best dancer, then in school she went after the top honors, and athletically, she pushed herself, practicing until she was the top player, no matter the sport. That hadn't changed when she became a cop, and tomorrow would be no different.

"I'm ready for you," he said with a slow smile. "Tomorrow I'm taking that trophy."

"Not happening, Boone." She tried to ignore the way her heart beat against her rib cage like a bird trying to escape.

"Don't count your chickens before they hatch." He nodded. "See you tomorrow."

"You're the one with the bad math," she called after him. Her shoulders slumped as he turned the corner. If her heart kept whacking out every time he spoke to her, it would be impossible to work the same days as Boone, but there was nothing she could do about it. She was on loan from Burglary and had no seniority. And it was clear she still had feelings for him. But he was her supervisor now. As long as she was in Homicide, there could be no relationship. It was against the rules. She'd known that when she transferred in.

She waited until she was certain Boone had left, then walked up to the front entrance where Vic Vegas waited.

"Miss Rachel?" the man asked, a questioning smile on his full lips. Then he nodded and hooked his thumbs in the huge rhinestone belt encircling his ample waist.

"Yes. We can talk at my desk."

Once they were in her cubicle, he said, "The last time I saw you, you reminded me of a colt—all legs and trying to get your feet under you. I understand you married . . . and that your husband died. So much tragedy in your life. I'm sorry."

A chill shivered down her spine. How did he know so much about her? She didn't remember ever seeing this man before in her life. The creepiness factor even overshadowed the usual lead weight of guilt that settled in her stomach when Corey was mentioned. "Do I know you?"

His shoulders drooped. "You don't remember me?"

She studied him. A faint memory tickled her brain. Her mom with an Elvis look-alike on either side of her. One of them had called her Miss Rachel. "Maybe. It was a long time ago."

"Seventeen years," he said.

"A charity event," she replied, still searching her memory bank. "An Elvis tribute affair . . ."

"That's right. For St. Jude. It was a competition at the convention center. I'm on my way now to one being held at Blues & Such tonight."

Rachel sneaked a peek at her watch. "How can I help you?"

He indicated a chair beside her desk. "May I sit?"

She mustered a smile. The day had just gotten longer. "Of course."

He settled in the straight-backed chair and arranged the white cape attached to his jumpsuit so that it didn't wrinkle. Then he took a photo from his shirt pocket and handed it to her. "This was taken the last time I saw you."

Rachel stilled. Her fingers shook as she examined the picture. Four Elvis impersonators stood beside her mother and Rachel, who was presenting a trophy to the winner. She remembered exactly when the photo was taken because later that night, her mother had died. The gala was the last thing they had done together. She swallowed. Her entire life had changed the night her mother was murdered.

She'd been pushing memories of that night away for the past week.

*Focus.* Trying not to look at her mother, Rachel studied the men in the photo. It took a second look to recognize that the man standing next to the winner was the one sitting across from her. He appeared to be in his late thirties in the photo, but the intervening years had not been kind to Vic Vegas. Seventeen years would only put him in his midfifties, but he looked older. Maybe it was the jet-black pompadour and long sideburns . . . or the forty pounds he'd added. She lifted her gaze. "I'm not sure I understand."

"It's the last time we were all together. I've written everyone's name on the back," he said.

She tried again. "I still don't understand."

"A few nights after this was taken, Harrison Foxx was murdered.

14

He's the one you're handing the trophy to. His murder has never been solved."

Memories scratched at the back of her mind. "And you want me to solve it?" Rachel had enough cases without adding another one, particularly one that delved into her past. "This is a cold case, and I don't work cold cases." She started to hand him the photo. "Wait, did you say Harrison Foxx?"

The memory finally surfaced, though it was cloudy. He was her mother's friend. And somehow her father was involved, but it was all jumbled in her mind. "Why are you bringing this to the police now?"

"I brought it to the attention of the police last year, and they didn't do anything about it. This week marks seventeen years since he was murdered. It's time somebody paid for what they did."

Rachel felt there was more. He held himself too rigid, and when she didn't comment right away, he shifted in the chair.

"Is that the only reason?"

Vic swallowed and moistened his lips. "I may be in over my head. I think someone broke into my house last night, and my gut says they were looking for information about Harrison's murder."

"Why would anyone be looking at your house for information on his murder?"

He hesitated. "You'll think I'm crazy. My daughter does. For years, I've been trying to solve Harrison's murder, but this last month I really got into it. I've been calling around and asking questions of people we knew back then, even followed up and went to see a few of them. I think I asked the wrong person the wrong question."

*Joy.* An Elvis impersonator *and* an amateur sleuth. It was her lucky day. "Are you saying that generally or are you talking about a specific person?"

"I don't have enough proof to call any names, just the same gut feeling I had seventeen years ago."

"This break-in. Did you report it?"

He shook his head. "I couldn't find anything missing."

Oh boy. This was sounding stranger and stranger. Maybe his daughter was right. Vic obviously believed what he was saying. She doodled on her desk calendar. "So, why bring it to me? We have an excellent Cold Case Unit."

"They're the ones I took it to last year, and they said there were a lot of cases ahead of this one and they'd contact me. So far, no one has. I thought the case might be personal to you since he was a friend of your mother."

She had no recollection of Foxx being murdered, but if it had happened around the time of her mother's funeral, it was no wonder. Grief and anger had consumed Rachel then. While the grief had lessened over the years, the anger remained hot as ever.

Vic's intense gaze held hers. The cases already on her workload hung in the back of her mind. Maybe a quick look at the cold case file would provide information that would satisfy him that everything had been done to find Foxx's killer. Either way, she had to fill out a report, so she took out a notepad and one of the mechanical pencils she liked to use to write her notes. Made erasing easier. "I don't suppose Vic Vegas is your legal name?"

He grinned and ducked his head, much like she'd seen Elvis do in film clips.

"Actually, it is. I had it legally changed in '95. It was less confusing."

*O-kay.* "Give me your original name for the records." She wrote "Phillip Grant" on the pad as well as the stage name, then asked for his contact information. After he gave it to her, she tilted her head toward him. "I'll talk with someone in the Cold Case Unit Monday." And hope Sgt. Brad Hollister didn't laugh her out of his office.

"Would you like my files on the murder?" Vic asked.

"Files?"

He nodded, raising his eyebrows. "I typed up everything—the people I've talked to in person or on the phone, what I learned, everything—and put the notes into files."

"You have a list of people you've questioned?" That might save time if anything in the cold case files warranted a second look at the case.

He nodded. "I even talked to your dad."

That was bound to have gone over like a ton of chicken feathers with the Judge. "Why would you talk with my father?"

"He represented Harrison in a legal matter a year or two before Harrison died. And he was there the night of the contest."

She caught her breath. Vic was right. An image of her dad in the audience flashed in her mind. She'd been surprised that he had attended the charity event because he and her mother had been separated for about a month then. If Vic hadn't mentioned it, she probably never would have remembered it. To her knowledge, it was the only time he attended anything Elvis. Her dad thought all the hoopla around Elvis Week was ridiculous. Which never sat well with her mom, since she'd been one of Elvis's biggest fans.

"Do you have the files with you?" Rachel doubted Vic had uncovered anything worthwhile, but the Cold Case Unit might be interested.

"Afraid not," he said. "Stopping here was kind of a spur-of-the-moment thing. And I don't have time to go get them before the competition starts."

Surely he wasn't competing in the contest. Her question must have shown on her face because he held up his hand.

"Don't worry, I'm not competing. They're honoring a bunch of us old geezers," he said. "But I can bring the files to you tomorrow."

She handed him her business card. "Monday will be fine. I won't be able to get access to the cold case files before then. And if I'm not here, just leave them with our office manager up front."

Vic's shoulders dipped, and a small sigh escaped his lips. "Sure."

17

He hefted his body from the chair, offering her his hand. "I really appreciate you looking into this. I'd really like to see Harrison's murder solved."

She slipped on her heels and stood, accepting his hand. "Don't thank me just yet—I haven't done anything."

"But you will—I checked up on you, and when you take a case, you don't quit until it's solved."

"I've been told I'm stubborn." His praise pinched her conscience. She saw no way of spending more than a couple of hours on the case. "Why don't I walk out with you?"

At the door, Vic glanced around at the empty room. "It looks like I've kept you past quitting time. Sorry."

"No worries."

At the elevator she pushed the down button before turning to Vic. "So how long have you been an Elvis impersonator?"

"I've been an Elvis *tribute artist* for thirty years," he said. "Ever since I sang 'Peace in the Valley' at a church talent show. Dyed my hair and grew my sideburns." The elevator door slid open, and they stepped inside. "I don't compete anymore, just show up with a few others from back in the day to remind the younger ones we were some of the first to give tribute to the King."

They rode in silence to the first floor.

"Thanks again for agreeing to help me," he said as they stepped out of the elevator.

She tried to think of something to say that would keep him from getting his hopes up. "Cold cases like this are really hard to solve, and I don't have much time to devote to working on it . . ."

She warmed under his intense gaze. He knew she wasn't going to dig very deep.

"What if I told you Harrison's murder is connected to your mother's death?"

Her heart almost stopped. "That's impossible."

"Doesn't it strike you as strange that your mother dies in a burglary that's never been solved, and Harrison is murdered three days later?"

Every word of the crime report was imprinted on her mind. The short version was there had been a rash of burglaries in their neighborhood, and her mother had apparently surprised a burglar in their home and had either fallen or been pushed when she confronted the unknown subject or subjects.

"Believe me," she said, "I've looked at every angle, and even though no one has been caught, the evidence all points to my mother's death being the result of a burglary gone bad. There were other break-ins around the neighborhood. Nothing suggests that her death was anything other than that."

"But what if the evidence was wrong?" he asked. "All the break-ins in your neighborhood were attributed to the cleaning service ring that was arrested not long after Gabby was killed. But they never admitted to the job at your house."

"How do you know that?"

"I reviewed the court case and talked to a couple of the people arrested. They denied your house was ever a target."

"Of course they'd say that. They don't want to serve time for murder." But he'd done his homework. There might actually be something in those files he talked about.

His gaze was unwavering. Vic Vegas was much smarter than she'd given him credit for. He'd known he would hook her by tying her mother's case to Foxx's. But what if he did have something?

She was off tomorrow and had two morning events inked on her calendar. Maybe she could meet him here between them. "Can you bring your files by here tomorrow morning? Say ten thirty?"

❖

Shirley stared at the front of the Criminal Justice Center building as Vegas stepped through the glass doors of the CJC. It'd been nothing but dumb luck when she saw him enter the building.

19

"Okay, Vic. I've about reached my limit with you." She spoke the words aloud even though there was no one to hear them inside the car.

Click. The zoom lens of the camera captured the Elvis wannabe and Det. Rachel Sloan standing beside him.

Not good. Not good at all. Should've done something about Vegas when he called, snooping around again.

Another click captured a close-up of the detective, and further examination brought an unexpected visceral punch in her gut. In the photo, Rachel bore a strong resemblance to her dead mother.

Same color honey-blonde hair framing an oval face, same hazel eyes, and while Rachel's lithe frame and long legs were more athletic, her stance was like her mother's. And like Gabby, she was too beautiful for her own good.

No telling what Vic had been filling the detective's head with.

"Just don't take the bait, Detective Sloan. Unless you want to end up like your mother."

# 2

As Rachel walked across Washington Street to the parking garage, Vic Vegas's question triggered emotions she thought she'd buried. She'd made two decisions that haunted her in life. The first was the night her mother was killed.

Rachel had fuzzy memories of leaving her mom and spending the night at a friend's house. While her mother had gone home and surprised a burglar, Rachel spent the night having fun. Her jaw clenched. It didn't matter that she'd been only fifteen, and it was improbable that she could have done anything to stop what happened. Rachel should have been there.

She knew it and her father knew it. Sometimes she believed he blamed her. Why else would he have been so distant after it happened?

Her father. Judge Lucien Winslow. He could have stopped what happened if he'd been there.

Pain shot from her jaw to her temple. Ancient history. But if she could solve the crime she'd switched careers for, her mother would have justice.

She slid across the front seat of her ancient Honda Civic and turned the key. Two clicks and then nothing except a punch of adrenaline in her veins. She did not need a dead battery today. She

21

tried it again and smiled as the motor came to life. After supper with the Judge, she'd stop in at the parts place she frequented and buy a new battery—something else to add to her schedule.

Fifteen minutes later, Rachel pulled into the gym parking lot, where Donna stood beside her red Mustang. Like Rachel, she hadn't taken the time to change out of her office clothes. At least the Homicide division had the best-dressed office manager in the building. The black cropped jacket looked great over a white silk shell, and the pencil-thin skirt that stopped just below her knees completed her outfit. No, the four-inch red heels and cinnamon-red Dolly Parton–style hair completed it. Rachel felt underdressed even in her court clothes and would love to get inside the office manager's closet.

"Okay, spill the beans," Donna said. "What did Elvis want?"

"How did you know about him? You'd already left."

"No, I was in the storage room and got a glimpse of you talking to him. If I'd been at my desk, I would have told him you had already left."

"Don't let Boone catch you doing that," Rachel said. Donna watched over her detectives like a mother hen. While she always meant well, sometimes she went a little too far.

Donna brushed her off with a laugh. "Now what did Elvis want?"

"Didn't you know that curiosity killed the cat?" Rachel opened her trunk and took out her gym bag. In spite of the difference in their ages, she and the office manager had become friends very quickly when Rachel moved from Burglary to Homicide. Partly because Donna was privy to all the homicide reports and she was a closet sleuth. She'd indicated early on that if she were in her thirties, she would apply to the academy.

Donna fell in beside her as they walked to the door, her high heels clicking on the pavement. "You know you're dying to tell me, so spill it. I'll know Monday, anyway, when I enter your notes into the computer."

"He wants me to investigate an old friend's murder," she said.

"He's been investigating on his own and has some files he's going to drop off in the morning."

"Aren't you off tomorrow?"

"Yeah, but I'll be near the CJC for the physical fitness competition."

"Surely you don't expect to learn anything from an armchair detective dressed in an Elvis suit, do you?"

Rachel shook her head. "I doubt he has anything useful. I'm mostly interested to see who he's talked with about this case he wants me to look at and why. Not even sure the case will go past this initial phase. It really belongs to the Cold Case Unit."

Donna pushed open the door and checked out the treadmills to their right. "Four machines are open—ought to still be two by the time we change. Want to run with me?" she asked.

Rachel glanced at her watch. Her personal trainer had probably arrived. "Don't have time. Terri is probably waiting for me now to start the ballet class. Why don't you join us?"

Donna tucked a strand of red hair behind her ear. "My joints are too old for ballet."

"Really? Too old for ballet, but not those heels. I don't know how you walk in them all day."

"Vanity. As long as I wear these, no one thinks of me as old."

"Believe me, no one thinks of you as old!"

Donna cocked her head. "Besides, I got on the scale this morning, and I've gained two pounds! Running will burn more calories than ballet."

The office manager had obsessed over gaining weight since the day Rachel first met her, and she wasn't sure why, since she couldn't imagine Donna ever being overweight. "I promise, ballet will burn calories."

"Really? For real, you think it helps?"

"It's kept my weight down. And not only that, since I've been doing it, I've shaved several seconds off my time in the depart-

ment's physical fitness competition. Five seconds at the last one."
Her first-place wins in the monthly competitions were one of the
reasons every Monday, Wednesday, and Friday found her at the
gym doing pliés and tendus. "You really need to try it. And you
don't look a day over forty."

Donna blushed. "See, the shoes are working. One day maybe
I'll join you in the class, but not enough time tonight. I have to be
at Blues & Such by seven to help with the Elvis competition," she
said, fanning herself.

Rachel nodded and then turned to go to the locker room. "Have
fun if I miss you after the class. Monday will come soon enough."

"I'll see you tomorrow night at your grandmother's party. And
I'm working Sunday."

Rachel paused. "I didn't realize you were coming."

"Your father invited me. You don't mind, do you?"

"Of course not." It just surprised her. Donna had accompanied
Rachel to one of her father's dinner parties, but she hadn't known
the two of them had hit it off so well. She hoped things wouldn't
get sticky around the office if the Judge—as she'd called her father for years—stayed true to course and dropped Donna after a
couple of dates. But Donna was old enough to know what she was
doing, and Rachel wasn't about to tell her how to run her love life.
Goodness knows she was no expert. Her relationship with Boone
was evidence of that.

"You just make sure you win tomorrow. We women have to
stick together."

Rachel gave her a thumbs-up. Boone was her top competitor. If
she could beat his time, she didn't have to worry about the others.
Not only that, but winning over Boone gave her more satisfaction
than beating anyone else. Payback for the way he micromanaged her.

A few minutes later in the dressing room, she slipped on her
ballet shoes, then glanced up as her coach, Terri Morrow, came
through the door. "I figured you were already here."

"Got held up in traffic." Terri set her bag down and pulled off the oversized top she wore over her leotard and tights. She was only slightly taller than Rachel's five eight, but much thinner—another person who really worked to keep her weight down. "You ready for tomorrow's competition?"

"As ready as I'll ever be." Rachel bent to adjust her shoes. There'd never been a time Terri hadn't been around. First as her mom's best friend, then Rachel's dance teacher, and now her fitness coach.

"Will you be finished in time to take your grandmothers shopping?"

"I should, barring an emergency. But just in case something happens, can you cover for me?"

"Sure. I was going anyway," Terri said. "But how about tonight? Still meeting your dad later?"

"It's Friday night and I don't have a date." As usual. It was her choice, though. Rachel wrapped her hair in a scrunchie and eyed her coach's pixie cut that set off her high cheekbones. More than once she'd considered going for the shorter style, but in the end the convenience of shampooing her longer hair and putting it up in a ponytail won out. "Want to join us? I'd like to see you and Dad . . ." Rachel raised her eyebrows.

"Not tonight," she said with a laugh and pulled on her ballet slippers. "And your father and I will probably always only be good friends. Besides, I'm having dinner with Erin—we're going to Blues & Such for the Elvis tribute contest."

"Rats. You make a good buffer, but enjoy your dinner with Erin." Rachel had always admired how Terri made her younger sister such a big part of her life. But then, everyone adored Erin, who was just two years older than Rachel. Erin had been a late-in-life baby for Terri's parents, and the pregnancy had been high risk. When delivery time came, labor had been long, causing a delay of oxygen to Erin's brain.

Terri laughed. "It won't go as bad as you think."

Dinner with her father was always a strain. But at least he was trying now. Not like after her mom died.

"Erin is really excited about you picking her up in the morning and taking her to Elmwood with you," Terri said.

"She always brightens my day," Rachel said. Erin lived in a group home with other mentally challenged adults, and she loved going to the eighty-acre parklike cemetery filled with angel statues. "Oh, could you pick her up at the McDonald's near Elmwood a little earlier than we planned? I have to meet someone at the CJC before the competition."

Terri grew quiet. "It is almost that date, isn't it?"

"Yeah." Every year on the anniversary of her mother's death, Rachel took flowers to her grave. An atonement for not going home with her that night. For the past few years, she'd taken Erin because . . . Rachel didn't really know why, except Terri's sister had a special place in her heart and Erin's joy over almost anything was contagious. She looked up. "What are you doing for her birthday next month?"

"We're going back to Hershey, Pennsylvania, to the candy factory."

"Is it still there?"

"Not the one she remembers. Her memory is like a computer except it never crashes and she never deletes anything. I'm afraid she'll be disappointed, but she's been asking to visit there again." Terri tilted her head. "Any chance you can drop her off at the group home Sunday? I have a recital for my ballet students Sunday evening and your grandmother has offered to take her, but after Erin spends the night with her following the party and then all day Sunday, I hate to ask her to drive across town that late in the evening."

"Sure, barring—"

"I know, barring an emergency." She grabbed a towel. "Erin's excited about coming to the party."

"I'm glad she'll be there." For the last few years, her dad usually

26

arranged something special around this time of year to lighten everyone's mood. This year it was a surprise birthday party for his mother.

Terri nodded toward the door. "Ready to get started?"

For the next hour, Rachel worked through an intensive routine of ballet moves and finished off the workout with four laps around the track. When they finished, Rachel wiped her face with a towel while Terri had barely broken a sweat. At least her face was red. "How do you do it?"

"Do what?"

"Not sweat. And you're barely even breathing hard." It was difficult to believe Terri was nearing sixty.

She laughed. "Good shape, maybe. And I don't do caffeine."

Had to be the caffeine. "Well, I want to be you when I grow up." Rachel grabbed her bag. She would shower at home before meeting her dad. "Sure you won't reconsider and meet us at Corky's?"

"Barbecue?" Terri tilted her silver head. "Tempting, but I better not, since Erin is really looking forward to the Elvis thing. Tell Lucien hello for me, and I'll see you both tomorrow."

"Will do." She didn't quite understand Terri and her father's relationship. Rachel didn't remember a time that Terri wasn't part of the family, and while she and her dad had always shared an easy friendship, romance didn't appear to be in the picture. Not that Rachel would mind. Maybe if he had a romantic interest, he'd have something to do when he wasn't on the bench other than keep tabs on her. "Did you know Donna Dumont is coming?"

Terri stiffened. "No."

"Is that going to be a problem?"

Her friend's lips thinned. "I don't know what your father sees in her, but if he wants Donna there, so be it."

# 3

As Rachel stepped inside Corky's, speakers blared Elvis music, rekindling the question that Vic had brought up about her mother's death being connected to Foxx's murder. She considered whether to repeat it to her father as she threaded her way through the crowd to his table.

If he hadn't dallied with some law clerk, he would have been home where he belonged. The thought was there before she could block it, and Rachel shrugged it off. She had no proof he'd had an affair, and the past was the past. Let it go.

A waiter passed holding trays loaded with barbecued ribs, and she stopped, giving herself time to regroup. She'd dealt with this issue in her twenties and made a choice to get past it. The Judge was the only parent she had, and blaming him for not being home when her mother was murdered was useless. Not that her father ever admitted anything was his fault. At least he didn't give her the "look" as often—the one that made Rachel think he blamed *her* for what happened.

If she brought Vic's question up, it could ruin their evening together, and Rachel didn't want to do that. For most of her life, her father had been too busy for her, but lately he'd made a point of them getting together on the Friday nights both were free. Surprisingly, they met more often than not.

His effort to be a part of her life touched her, even if almost every week brought a subtle pressure for her to return to her old law firm. The Honorable Lucien Winslow had never fully accepted her decision to leave the law firm he'd handpicked for her and made it plain he didn't understand why she wanted to be a detective instead of an attorney.

She slipped into the oak chair opposite him. The Judge was dressed impeccably, as usual, in a white polo shirt and navy dress pants. Even at sixty, he had no more than a smattering of gray at his temple. She frowned. It was unusual that his dark hair needed a trim.

He crossed his arms. "You're late."

"How are you?" Rachel unfolded the cloth napkin and placed it in her lap. "I'm fine, thank you so much for asking."

The hint of a smile tugged at his gray eyes. "Sorry. But I'm hungry. I've already ordered two rib plates for us. Should be out any minute."

Good thing she was hungry for ribs. A family two tables over caught her eye, and her heart warmed as a little girl offered her crayon to the man Rachel assumed was the father. He gently tucked a curl behind the child's ear before he colored where she pointed. A good man, for sure.

The Judge tapped his fingers on the table, attracting her attention. He looked a little on edge. She hoped that didn't mean he'd grill her about something before the evening was over. He'd gotten better about that lately. "So, how's your week been?" she asked.

His drumming stopped. "Busy with a murder case coming up on the docket. The defense is trying every tactic in the books to delay the trial. And I'm getting ready for tomorrow night's birthday party for you and your grandmother. You'll be able to take her shopping tomorrow afternoon, right? And then bring her to the house at six?"

The competition would end no later than noon, giving her the afternoon free. "Shouldn't be any problem."

Rachel's birthday had always been combined with Gran's. Not that she minded, at least not as an adult. She was so glad her father had decided to throw a surprise party for her grandmother's eighty-third. "And Terri said she'd fill in for me if anything comes up. I understand you invited Donna Dumont to the party."

"Yes. We had dinner together last week, and don't change the subject."

He rubbed his thumb along his jaw, a sure sign he wasn't happy, and she braced herself for whatever criticism he was about to send her way.

"I expect you to do everything in your power to be at the party. I'll be making an announcement I think you will find interesting."

"I'll do my best." Relieved it was no more than that, she searched his face, looking for a clue as to what his announcement was, but she couldn't read him. Not that he would ever tell her before he was ready, and with her luck, it was probably an offer from her old law firm to come back—an offer he'd think she couldn't pass up.

"You know, Silverstone and Webster would love to have you back."

And there it was. "I'm not interested. I like what I'm doing now. You know, protecting people. It's never boring." She refused to look away from the hard stare he pinned her with. "Can we talk about something else? Like how *my* week has been?"

Finally, he broke eye contact. "So, how was your week?"

She fingered the silverware. She'd decided he would want to know if someone was poking around in her mother's case, and he would expect to be told sooner than later. "Interesting, especially this afternoon."

"How so?" The Judge turned his head, scanning the room. "What's taking so long for our food?"

"It's always busy here on Friday night. Besides, it's Elvis Week," she said. If he didn't return to the subject, she would let it drop. Briefly Rachel studied her father as he again drummed his fingers on the wooden table. He wore power well even without his three-piece suit. When his gray eyes bored into her, she believed he could make even the president uncomfortable.

He shook his head. "How did I manage to forget it was Elvis Week? We should have eaten takeout at the house."

Their waitress evidently had noticed her father's agitation and approached. "Judge Winslow, I'm sorry for the delay, but it won't be much longer," she said. "It's just that the kitchen is shorthanded, and we're slammed, to boot."

"No problem. Thank you for keeping us informed."

Rachel was amused that her father could be gracious when he wanted to be. He was used to special treatment and getting his way, and other than her career choice, even she usually placated him.

"So what made today so interesting?" he asked.

A little surprised that he'd returned to the subject, she re-arranged her knife and fork. "I had a visitor just before five. Vic Vegas. I think you've met him."

His trim eyebrows lowered as he frowned. "Vic Vegas? Don't recall meeting him, and the name doesn't sound familiar—it's one I would have remembered."

"He's an Elvis tribute artist, has been for thirty years. Said he talked to you a few years ago about one of your former clients, Harrison Foxx."

His nostrils flared slightly. "That name I remember. Murdered, I believe."

"He was." There had never been anything wrong with the Judge's memory, so she was surprised he didn't remember Vic.

"Exactly what did this Vegas want?"

"He wants me to look into Foxx's murder."

Her father lifted his tea glass to his lips and took a deep drink before setting the glass back on the table. "It's a cold case. Why would he come to you?"

Unease settled in her stomach. It had been slight, but his fingers had shaken as he reached for the glass. Vic's visit to her had rattled him. Why?

"Maybe because he remembered me from seventeen years ago at an Elvis contest. Or because he knew Mom was friends with Harrison Foxx."

The Judge's face darkened. "They weren't all that close."

Rachel flinched at the venom in his voice. "Are you saying they weren't friends?"

He didn't answer right away, and his eyes registered a faraway look. Then he was back. "Okay, they went to school together a couple of years and had some kind of bond. Harrison was a con artist. Not that I ever got your mother to believe me. You know how loyal she always was."

Maybe her mom didn't believe her friend was a con artist because she didn't see everything in black and white like the Judge. And maybe Foxx had been a shoulder to cry on during a difficult time.

He grimaced. "She liked to help people and was using her contacts to help him break into show business."

"Vic said you represented Foxx."

"He was accused of swindling a woman out of five thousand dollars. Don't remember her name now."

"Why did you represent him?"

"Your mother twisted my arm. She thought the woman was crazy. Didn't believe Foxx swindled her, but from what I learned about him, it was probably true." He shook his head. "He got quite a bit from Gabby. Always loans, of course."

Surely her mother hadn't given the man money. "How did you settle the case?"

"I encouraged her attorney to settle for half of it, which she refused. It dragged on in court, and he died, and she didn't get anything."

When the waitress appeared with their order, Rachel was still trying to reconcile her mother being friends with someone like the man her father described. The interruption gave her time to collect her thoughts. She wasn't certain how far she wanted to carry this conversation. At least not until she had a chance to look through the files on Foxx's murder. Besides, given the direction the conversation had taken, anything further would probably ruin both of their appetites, and Corky's had great barbecue and the best fried pickles she'd ever eaten. She picked up a pickle and crunched into it. But why would her mother give money to Foxx? The question nagged at her. "Why—"

"Let's not talk about this anymore," he said.

The Judge had put on his bench face. She'd get no more information from him tonight.

"When was the last time you saw Boone?" he asked her.

"Today," she said. Of all the topics he could have chosen, why did he pick Boone Callahan? "He's working the same days I do now."

"Bring him around sometime."

"We haven't dated in six months."

"I'm sorry he broke it off," the Judge said. "I enjoyed talking with him."

"He didn't," she said tersely. Smoke was bound to be coming from her ears.

Her father stopped with his fork halfway to his mouth. "Didn't what?"

"He didn't end the relationship. I did."

Oh, for a camera to capture the look of astonishment on her father's face.

# 4

THE FLUORESCENT LIGHT from the lamp beside the sofa cast a glare on the journal. The photos in it mocked Shirley as she turned the pages. Every one of them betrayed her one way or the other.

*Why don't you get rid of the journal?*

"Leave me alone!" She couldn't get rid of it. The photos reminded her of who her enemies had been and what they'd done, fueling her anger and helping her to put words on the paper.

*Don't talk to me in that tone, Shirley. Do you remember that leather strap?*

She flinched until she remembered he could no longer hurt her. At least not physically. "My name is not Shirley, and I'll keep these photos as long as I want."

*Little Shirley Baker, didn't no one like her . . .*

"Stop it! That doesn't even rhyme." There had to be a way to get his voice out of her head. She slammed the album shut and pressed her fingers in her ears. *Think about something else.*

But it wasn't long before Shirley rubbed the blood-red cover, unable to keep her thoughts and fingers away from the journal as she opened it again. It was important to keep a record of those who had wronged her. To show the world one day why they had to die, that it hadn't been her fault.

She'd thought Vic was her friend. Thought they all were her friends. Showed how much she knew about people. Always believing the best until they betrayed her. Her gaze slipped to the photo of Gabby and Harrison. She traced a finger over the image of Gabby showing off the diamond guitar-shaped necklace that Harrison had given her just before the picture was taken.

"You don't have to be jealous of her," he'd said. "She's only a friend." What baloney. She'd seen the looks of pity others shot her way when Harrison and Gabby were together. Even Gabby's husband knew they shared more than friendship.

She hadn't intended to kill Gabby. All Gabby had to do was break off the relationship with Harrison and give Shirley the necklace. But Gabby had laughed at her when Shirley told her the necklace was hers, that it was her money that bought it.

Gabby shouldn't have laughed at her, shouldn't have said Shirley ought to know better than to give Harrison money if she couldn't afford to lose it.

It wasn't like Gabby even wanted him or the necklace. But she'd gotten angry, said she'd been friends with Harrison most of her life. They'd argued, and the next thing she knew, Gabby was on the floor, unconscious.

It wasn't her fault.

*Says you. You were always a loser.*

"I'm not listening to you tonight," she said through her teeth.

*Only losers are stupid enough to wear a stolen necklace.*

Oh, why had she worn the pendant tonight? Because it made her feel special. She could pretend Harrison had given it to *her*, not Gabby.

When she saw Vic coming toward her, she'd removed it from around her neck and dropped it in her purse. The room had been so crowded, and someone came along and knocked her purse over, spilling the necklace onto the table while Vic was talking to her.

He'd yanked it off the table and got right in her face, accusing her of killing Gabby. Shirley thought she'd managed to talk her way out of it until he wouldn't give it back.

She clamped her jaw tight. Vic should not have kept it.

But where was it now? The necklace hadn't been in his coat pocket or anywhere in the house. What had he done with it?

She regretted she'd killed him before finding out and before finding the files he'd compiled on Harrison's murder. But he shouldn't have laughed when she demanded the necklace back. He hadn't laughed when he saw the gun. That had been priceless . . .

She paced the bedroom floor, worrying her problem over. If anyone found where he kept his files . . . Wait, she hadn't been able to find Vic's hiding place. And if she couldn't find it, neither would anyone else. Her mind calmed. She was smarter than the cops . . . smarter than anyone. She'd gotten away with five murders. They would never catch her, and if she kept her cool, everything would be okay.

Suddenly an image of Vic showing Randy Culver the necklace flashed through her mind. Her knees turned to water. Why couldn't Vic just let Harrison's murder go? Why did he have to go see Detective Sloan?

What if she was assigned to investigate Vic's murder? Shirley hadn't considered that, but it was a real possibility since he'd gone to see her today. If Sloan got the case, she would interview everyone Vic talked to at Blues & Such tonight. She swallowed hard. If the detective talked to Randy and he described the necklace, she would realize it was the one that Harrison had given to her mother. After all, how common were diamond necklaces shaped like a guitar?

Maybe Sloan wouldn't even remember the jewelry. No, she would remember a unique necklace like that one. And even if she hadn't thought about it since that night, all it would take was Randy mentioning it.

This was spiraling out of control. She could not allow him to talk to the detective.

# 5

AT EIGHT SATURDAY MORNING, Erin beamed at Rachel from the passenger seat as they crossed the narrow bridge leading into Elmwood Cemetery. Both the bridge and the Gothic cottage they passed, along with the eighty acres of gently rolling hills, were on the National Register. An oasis in the middle of the city.

Erin clapped her hands. "This is where the angels are!"

"Yep." A poster proclaiming the 165th anniversary of the cemetery next week caught her eye. They were celebrating with an evening stroll walking tour. At night probably because of the heat.

While touring a cemetery might sound strange to some, Rachel loved the idea, especially at this one. Elmwood was rich with the history of Memphis, dating back to 1852. Beneath the ancient elms and magnolias, some of Memphis's most famous and infamous had been laid to rest among the ordinary people. Since the tour was planned for evening, she quite possibly could do the tour.

"We're going to visit your mother."

Erin forgot nothing and was always direct and to the point. "Her grave," Rachel said. "I have flowers for the vase."

"I liked Gabby. Remember what she used to say?" Without waiting for a reply, Erin spoke in a voice that mimicked Rachel's mother. "Erin, you are the most special person I know. And don't you ever forget it."

"She loved you very much," Rachel said. She was always amazed at Erin's ability to mimic people she'd been around.

"Can we look at some of the angel statues?" Erin asked. "And stop at the butterfly garden?"

Rachel checked her watch. At nine, Terri was meeting them at McDonald's to pick up her sister and take her to get a haircut, so that gave Rachel an hour before the competition started. A portion of that time included a quick meeting with Vic Vegas to get his files. Sometimes she felt like a juggler trying to keep all her balls in the air.

She blew out a long breath, wishing she'd put off the visit to her mother's grave until later, but later was even busier with the grandmother outing. Plus, she'd made the mistake of telling Erin they'd go first thing this morning and hadn't wanted to disappoint her. She'd had enough disappointment in life. "We can take about ten minutes for the angels—that way we'll have time to stop at the butterfly garden on the way out." In this heat, Rachel doubted they'd find any butterflies, but of the three formal gardens in Elmwood, Erin loved the butterfly garden most.

"Good! Can I put the flowers in the vase?"

"How about we do it together? And leave your seat belt buckled until we stop," Rachel said as Erin unsnapped the restraint. In some ways Erin was wise beyond her years, but in others much like a child. Rachel had to be alert always.

"I saw Elvis last night."

"Really? Oh, that's right, you went to see the Elvis contest."

"Mmmhmm. Can I have an Elvis pin?"

"I don't see why not." She took a right after they passed the cottage and wound around to where her mother was buried. If it weren't almost ninety degrees in the shade, they would have walked. There was no place as calm and peaceful as Elmwood.

"I want one with diamonds and—Oh, look, there's an angel."

"I see it," Rachel said, her mind on arranging flowers as she pulled off the lane onto the grass so another car could pass if need be. "Would you carry the flowers?"

"And then can we look at the angels?"

"Sure."

Once they had the flowers in the vase, Rachel stood quietly for a moment, remembering her mother. If only Rachel had gone home with her after the contest, the night might have turned out differently. But she hadn't, and it was something she had to live with.

"What's heaven like?" Erin asked beside her.

"I'm not sure," she replied.

"Terri says it's a beautiful place and it's where God lives. Do you talk to God every day?"

"Not every day." More like hardly ever.

"I do and so should you. Can we go look at the angels now?"

"In just a minute." Rachel stared at the date on the tombstone. It was hard to believe it'd been seventeen years since her mother died. Time had passed so quickly. With a last look at her mother's tombstone, Rachel followed Erin down the narrow road as she searched for her angels.

It wasn't long before Erin turned to her. "I'm thirsty. Can we go to Gallagher's now? You know, where Boone goes? Terri can pick me up there instead of McDonald's."

Sometimes she wished Erin didn't have such a good memory. One time they had run into Boone at Gallagher's, and he had joked around with Erin. Now she often wanted to stop by Gallagher's when they came to the cemetery.

"Please," Erin said when she didn't respond right away.

Boone should be at the police gym getting the competition ready, so the odds of running into him were low. "I'll have to call Terri and tell her to meet us there," she said.

She made the call as they walked to the car, and Terri agreed to the change. The motor was slow to crank when Rachel turned the key, and her heart sank. One of the balls she'd dropped was picking up a new car battery last night. She tried the ignition again and the motor roared to life. She had to get a battery sometime today.

The drive to Gallagher's was short, and a few minutes later, Rachel paused for her eyes to adjust to the dimness as they stepped inside.

"There's Boone!" Erin pointed her finger toward the man standing at the counter, talking to the barista.

Boone? He should be at the gym. But no, here he was in the flesh. When Erin made a beeline for the lieutenant, Rachel sighed and followed, her heart doing that crazy little dance like it did whenever she was around him.

Boone's six-two frame towered over Erin, who gazed up at him with a happy grin on her lips. "Terri's coming to get me, and I'm getting a haircut. What are you doing here, Boone?" she asked. "I bet you knew we would be here."

"I stopped to get some of Gallagher's good coffee, and I didn't know you'd be here, but I'm glad you are," he said, winking at Erin.

Rachel's heart caught at the way he smiled down at the petite, childlike woman then back up at her.

"Hello, Rachel," he said.

She found it hard to breathe. It'd been hard enough running into him at the monthly fitness tests or the occasional times they worked together. Now that they were working the same shift, she had to steel herself against the magnetic pull he had on her. But today . . . she just wasn't expecting to see him this morning. Later, yes, at the gym. After she had time to prepare.

"I'm surprised to see you," she said, trying to keep her voice from sounding breathy.

He turned to get his coffee, and Erin said, "Can we sit with Boone?"

"Oh, Erin, I don't—"

"You're welcome to," Boone said. "Unless you think it might constitute a date." Hurt darkened his eyes.

And behind the hurt were questions. Questions she didn't want to answer. They had gone out a few times until she broke it off when she had the chance to be loaned out to the Homicide department. He was a lieutenant and she wasn't even a sergeant. Against protocol. But even before that, she'd realized she was in over her head. He never mentioned the word marriage, but from their conversations, it was plain he was ready to settle down, start a family. She wasn't marriage material—been there, done that, with disastrous results.

But looking into his dark brown eyes made her wonder if she'd done the right thing. She hadn't run across many men like Boone, and there was no denying he made her heart do funny things. Not to mention oxygen was having a hard time getting to her brain.

"What can I get for you?" the barista asked.

The question cleared Rachel's head, and she turned to the clerk. "A . . . a skinny mocha latte. Make that two." She almost forgot Erin.

"Come on, Boone!" Erin tugged at his hand.

"Are you sure you have time?" Rachel asked, hoping he didn't.

"Oh, I think I can take a few minutes." He winked at Rachel. "If you don't mind."

Her stomach flipped. Why did he have to agree? "Of course I don't mind, but don't you have to get ready for the competition?"

"I'm ready and so is the gym."

She'd run out of excuses. "Then lead the way."

Rachel followed as Erin found a table in the corner she liked.

Boone looked around the room as Erin studied the photos around them. "Every time I come in here, I'm impressed how much Elvis stuff Gallagher's has collected."

Rachel laughed. "This is nothing compared to what Nana and my mother collected. Nana has boxes of it. She's even collected programs from the different concerts she's attended."

41

It wasn't long before the barista brought their drinks, and after Erin finished hers, she said, "I'm going to look at the other pictures."

When she was out of earshot, Boone leaned toward Rachel. "I've missed you."

"Boone—"

"Just saying."

"We only had, what, five dates? And one of them was dinner with my dad and grandmothers." Her father had discovered she and Boone were seeing each other and had pressured her into the dinner. She sighed and glanced toward the door, hoping Terri would suddenly materialize. No such luck. She tilted her head toward him. "Besides, you know we can't work in Homicide together and date."

"You'll only be there six more months, so maybe after—"

"It's not just because we work together. You want more out of the relationship than I do."

"I'm not going to hurt you, Rachel."

She dropped her gaze and worried a hangnail on her thumb. Finally she looked up. "You wouldn't mean to, but eventually what I have to offer wouldn't be enough."

"Why not let me be the judge of that?"

"Don't make this harder than it is," she said. "I just can't do it."

He studied her for a minute, and then nodded. "If you ever change your mind—"

"We went to the cemetery today to visit Gabby," Erin said to Boone when she returned to the table.

He quizzed Rachel with his eyes.

She'd never really talked to Boone about her mother's death. "My mom. She . . . she died seventeen years ago tonight." She swallowed past the lump that had suddenly formed in her throat.

Sympathy filled his eyes. "I'm sorry. Anniversaries are always hard. Cancer?"

"No." She didn't want to discuss her mother's death in front of Erin and gave a slight shake of her head, hoping he'd take the hint.

"Rachel doesn't talk to God every day," Erin said. "But you do, don't you, Boone?"

"All the time." He turned to her, his eyes quizzing her.

Her cheeks flushed and she busied herself with the latte. In the beginning, after her mom died, she had turned to God. She wasn't sure exactly when she'd decided he didn't hear her pleas for justice for her mother and quit praying.

"I heard Elvis came to see you yesterday."

He got the hint. "Yeah," she said. "Too bad you didn't stay—you could've met him."

He offered her a grin. "And rob you of all the pleasure? What'd he want?"

"This is *good*!" Erin said. "Can I have another one?"

Saved by Erin. She did not want him to know she was looking into Harrison Foxx's murder, because then he'd want to know why she was looking into a seventeen-year-old case instead of working on one of their backlogged ones. And she certainly didn't want him to know Foxx's murder might be a lead on her mother's death.

"We can talk about what he wanted later," she said as the door to Gallagher's opened and Terri hurried in.

"Sorry I'm late," she said when she reached the table.

"You're not late, you're right on time," Rachel said with a smile.

# 6

AT TEN, BOONE SURVEYED the participants entering through the doors of the Memphis Police Department gym. Rachel had arrived five minutes ago, looking none too happy. He noted other members from the Homicide division and a few from other departments. It looked as though there would be about twelve officers competing, so they should finish before eleven. The competition wasn't mandatory, but he wished it were since fit officers made good ones.

Boone became the driving force behind the competitions after one of his overweight detectives succumbed to a heart attack while chasing a suspect. Just as in Iraq, his officers were his responsibility, and he pushed them to work out. But it wasn't until he started the monthly competition that they embraced the idea. Had to be the challenge.

His heart did a number on him when he zeroed in on Rachel, who had donned a bullet-resistant vest over her workout clothes and then buckled on a gun before pulling her blonde hair into a ponytail. He'd noticed at the coffee shop that she wore little makeup, but with her flawless skin and thick eyelashes, she didn't need it.

He'd been attracted to her from the day they met. Why couldn't she see they were perfect for each other? Rachel turned his way and caught him staring. Boone gave her a nod, hoping his tan hid the blush burning up his neck to his ears.

Did she even have a clue how difficult it was for him to work in the same office with her? He'd been duty bound to inform his superiors of their former dating relationship, but he went beyond that when he reminded them she had yet to make sergeant in hopes they would not assign her to Homicide. But with her law background and excellent record in Burglary, they'd brushed aside his concerns.

They'd been right—Rachel made a great detective, and until recently he'd been able to avoid her, working nights or the days she was off, but with one of the other officers on medical leave, he was forced to work the same shift as Rachel now.

Not to mention they had a problem, one he would have addressed at the coffee shop if Erin hadn't been with her. She bristled every time he made a suggestion and always questioned his directives. She thought he was micromanaging her cases, and he was. Every homicide he supervised was personal to him, and every case rested on his shoulders. He didn't care if she thought he was a micromanager.

Iraq had taught some hard lessons, and while Memphis wasn't a war zone, sometimes it felt like one. If he was honest with himself, yeah, maybe he was a little harder on Rachel. She, along with every other officer, put her life on the line every time she walked out the door. It didn't help that the department had lost two detectives this year—one to an auto accident and the other to an ambush when a drug deal went bad.

He caught sight of her jogging in place. She was a distraction, for sure, and right now he needed to focus on the competition. Boone couldn't figure out how she managed to beat everyone's time each month, especially his. He worked out, did sprints and pull-ups, stood a good half foot taller, and had the advantage of being male. She shouldn't beat him.

A frown tensed Rachel's full lips, and she walked his way with a certain grace in her stride, almost like a dancer.

"Why do you have me next to last?" she demanded when she reached him.

"Why do you ask?" he said. As usual, she had her guard up. Sometimes it was hard to remember the gentler side he'd seen when they were dating.

"Elvis didn't show, and I'm hoping he's just running late. I want to get back to the CJC in case he shows up."

"Did you try calling him?" He wasn't moving her to a different spot. She was right where he wanted her—just before him.

"Yeah, no answer."

He glanced down at the twelve entries. This wouldn't take an hour. "We'll be done just a little past eleven. Call and leave word at the front desk for him to wait if he comes in."

Her frown deepened.

"Tell you what, if you get a call that's he's there, I'll put you in right away."

Rachel didn't quite mask her annoyance, but she gave a short nod and started to walk away. She turned around and arched her neck, managing to look down her nose at him even though he towered over her. "I'm surprised you didn't put me last. But then, you wouldn't know what time you had to beat, would you?"

She'd always been good at reading his mind. He shifted his gaze from the hazel eyes that glinted a challenge. They both knew she was the one to beat today. He'd have to shave five seconds off his time to even beat her last run. Maybe today she'd be slower. In his dreams. "Today's the day, Detective."

"*Excuse* me, Lieutenant. Didn't know we were being so formal. Or maybe you were trying to intimidate me?"

"Now why would I do that?"

A whistle blew, and she shook her head. "Can we get back to this later?"

"Sure," he said, and they both turned toward the timekeeper as he called for the first competitor, who looked like he might have played linebacker in college. Boone was pleased when she remained close by. "Know him?"

She nodded. "Jones. Worked with him in Burglary. Usually clocks in around two and a half minutes."

So she kept up with everyone's time. Boone pulled up the stopwatch app on his phone. When the whistle blew again, he started the clock, aware of her presence beside him. He shifted his attention back to the runner.

Each contestant ran the same course—two laps around the perimeter of the gym while performing activities that a police officer might engage in during a foot chase. Jones made the first round of obstacles easily, then stumbled after clearing a four-foot-high balance beam on the second round. He dashed to the steps and climbed up then down and rounded the second turn to the four-foot cube.

"He lost a few seconds there," Rachel pointed out, her voice all business as Jones had trouble getting over the cube.

He missed the easy camaraderie they'd once had, but what did he expect? Maybe this was as hard on her as it was him and it was her way of coping. Maybe the brass was right in banning relationships in the office. Except it was too late to turn back the clock. So he better get his act together.

At the end of the course, a 150-pound dummy waited to be dragged to the middle of the gym. Jones struggled with getting a handle on the dummy. As soon as he pulled it across the line, Boone glanced up at the time on the scoreboard. Two minutes, thirty-one seconds.

One after another the officers ran the course. He glanced toward the clock. They would finish well before eleven. Should make Rachel happy. When it was her turn, the time to beat was a minute and forty seconds—the same as Boone's best time. He raised his eyebrows. "I see you didn't get a call."

"But I could have." She tilted her head, her eyes warming to a soft almost-brown. "Wouldn't care to make a wager on whether you'll beat my time, would you?"

Rachel appeared to have had an attitude adjustment, but why? Possibly an apology for her annoyance a few minutes ago? Boone gulped down the catch in his throat. He'd take it regardless. "Gambling, Detective Sloan? That's illegal."

"Only if money is involved."

"What do you have in mind?"

"That old car of mine you think I should get rid of? It needs a wash job. How about if I beat your time again, you'll detail it?"

She knew he hated detailing cars. But the way she smiled at him made turning her wager down impossible. He'd just have to win. "You're on. But you have to do the same for my four-wheel-drive pickup if I win."

"Deal. But I won't lose."

She cleared the first round without breaking a sweat. He didn't know how she made it look so easy as she left the steps and hopped on top of the cube and then dropped to the floor and sprinted across to the dummy. When she pulled it across the line, he stopped the clock. One minute thirty-four seconds. The best time for the day and six seconds faster than he'd ever completed the course.

She didn't say anything when he passed her on the way to the starting line. She didn't have to—canary feathers were practically caught in her teeth.

He bounced on his feet, loosening up as he waited for the whistle to blow. The first round went quickly, and as he started the second round, he felt good about his time and was barely winded. He cleared the bar and made quick work of the steps, then rounded to the cube and went up and over it with no problem. When he reached the dummy, he dragged it to the middle of the gym.

Without looking, Boone knew it was the best he'd ever competed. He checked the scoreboard.

# 7

RACHEL HELD HER BREATH as she waited for Boone's time to appear. She had him down two seconds from her time on her stopwatch, but she could have started her timer too soon.

One minute, thirty-five seconds. *Yes!* She'd beat him by one second!

She wanted to do a happy dance, but catching the flash of disappointment on Boone's chiseled features, she dialed back her excitement. Then dimples appeared in his cheeks as he acknowledged her win with a smile. Now she wished he'd tied her.

"Good job," she called as he trudged toward her. She didn't blame him for not wanting to hurry over.

"Not good enough. Congratulations."

A lock of brown hair dangled over his forehead, and she clasped her hands together to keep from reaching out and brushing it back.

"Thanks."

"How do you do it?" he asked.

"Terri says it's the ballet." She chuckled when he gaped at her. "It prepares me mentally and . . ." She struggled for the right words. "My body feels lighter when I put myself in that mind-set. Helps me to run faster and do the obstacles more efficiently—which I need since the cube slows me down."

He considered her words. "I guess that makes sense. When do you want me to detail that heap you call a car?"

She palmed her hands. "You don't have to. I couldn't resist baiting you."

"No, a deal is a deal. How about now? You can pull it around to the car wash."

Why had she made that stupid wager? Because he'd riled her by not moving her race time up. The Judge always said her temper would get her into trouble. Her phone rang and she glanced at the screen. Langley, one of the uniformed officers. "Give me a minute." She turned away from him. "Sloan."

"We have a murder victim, and he had your card in his wallet."

A shiver ran over her arms, leaving goose bumps. Over the seven years she'd been a police officer, she'd handed out her card to hundreds of people, but as far as she knew, none of them had ended up dead. Until now. "Do you have a name?"

"Vic Vegas."

The sickening thud Rachel felt was her stomach hitting the floor. "What's the cause of death? And the circumstances?"

"Bullet to the chest. He was at home, and the house has been trashed. Doesn't look like anyone broke in, so he may have known his attacker. Can't tell what's missing and what's not. His daughter is too distraught to be of any help."

The skin on the back of Rachel's neck prickled. If it turned out he was murdered because of the files he'd mentioned or something he'd uncovered about the Harrison Foxx murder . . . She should have taken him more seriously. "I'll be there ASAP."

She hung up and turned to Boone. "Afraid the detailing will have to wait. I have a murder to investigate."

"It's your weekend off."

"I know, but I have history with the victim." He listened intently while she gave him the details from the uniformed officer's report.

"I'll go with you."

Rachel bristled. Ever since Boone showed up on her shift, he'd hovered over her. "Why?"

"Why not? I'm your lieutenant, and besides, anyone else would welcome my input."

"That's just it. *I'm* the only one you micromanage." She didn't see him hovering over the other investigators. He must think her really incompetent.

"I'm not riding herd on you because I question your tactics or ability. I can see you being assigned to Homicide after you make sergeant, and you'll be a good investigator, one the department will be proud of. But for now—you've been here barely six months."

*Oh.* Not because he was trying to get rid of her. She rocked back on her heels. Boone thought she was a good detective? Even so, the last few days of him picking her cases apart rankled, partly because he came into those cases late and didn't have all the background information. And partly because she wasn't accustomed to it. The lieutenant in Burglary had never criticized her work.

"Look," he said, resting his hand on the gun at his waist. "For the record, I've micromanaged, as you call it, every investigator in my department. I'm treating you no different. So, if you're ready, we'll check out this homicide."

"I'm sorry," she said, swallowing the defense that threatened to spill from her lips—even though she wanted to say she'd never seen him question any of the other investigators. But it'd do no good. She'd never noticed before Boone became her superior how much he was like the Judge. Always right. Always in command. But he was her superior. Time for her to remember that and forget what they'd had in the past. Even so, it'd be a while before she embraced his constant assessment of her work.

"You're welcome to ride along with me," he said, his tone softer.

It was going to be hard enough working with him without being thrown together in the close quarters of a pickup. "Thanks, but then you'd have to bring me all the way back downtown."

"No problem."

"I'd still prefer to drive my own car."

"Suit yourself."

In the gym locker room, Rachel quickly changed into jeans and a sleeveless pullover and hurried to her Civic. The faint *tick, tick, tick* when she turned the key drew a groan from her lips. She'd put off buying a battery one time too many. She tried again, but no amount of coaxing would put life in the battery. So much for her independence. It took all the self-control she possessed to refrain from slamming her fist against the steering wheel.

Two options stretched before her. Call Boone to return to the parking lot and pick her up, or . . . She didn't have time for the second option. It'd take too long for AAA to get here and replace her battery.

Rachel clenched her jaw and yanked out her cell phone as she exited the car. Before she could dial Boone's number, he pulled in behind her and lowered his window.

"Car trouble?" he asked sweetly.

"Yes. Dead battery, so if the offer's still open, I'll ride with you."

"Sure. Once we're done at the crime scene, I'll stop at a parts store so you can pick up a new one. I'll even put it in for you."

She opened her mouth to tell him she knew how to install a battery but instead grabbed her shoulder bag that contained notepads and pens along with the photo Vegas had left with her. "Appreciate that."

Boone's red Ford pickup had a running board, and she used it to climb in the seat. After buckling up, she focused on the road.

"That wasn't so hard, was it?" he asked.

Her mouth twitched. "I'm not used to asking for help."

"Or accepting it. I've always wondered, why is that?"

This was the very reason she didn't want to ride with him. She didn't want him psychoanalyzing her. "You know the Judge. Independent is the only way I know how to be."

"How is your dad, by the way?"

"Fine. He asked about you just last night." She still smarted from her father's assumption that Boone had broken off their relationship.

"The Friday night dinners," he said. "Is he still trying to get you to return to the law firm?"

"Did the sun come up this morning?" She'd quit courting her father's approval a long time ago. "When he raised me to be independent, I don't think he considered I might not follow in his footsteps."

"You've made a good cop." He took the Mt. Moriah exit off the interstate. "Tell me what you know about Vegas."

"There's not much to tell." She quickly filled him in on the details of Vic's visit, and it wasn't long before they turned onto the street where Vic Vegas had lived. She surveyed the ranch-style brick homes. The well-tended flower gardens and trimmed yards gave the neighborhood the feel of permanency, like the residents had lived here most of their lives.

Boone pulled behind a white van with a medical examiner logo on the side door and killed the motor. "The murder he wanted you to investigate. Was it recent?"

"No, seventeen years ago." She pulled the photo from her bag and handed it to him. "He gave me this yesterday. His friend, Harrison Foxx, is the one accepting the trophy from me. He was murdered a few days after the photo was taken."

"You knew the victim prior to yesterday?"

"Not really. I was helping my mom the night the photo was taken."

He studied the photo. "You think the two deaths are related?"

"I don't know. The officer who called said there were no signs of forced entry and that the house had been trashed." She chewed her bottom lip. "The thing is, Vic told me he'd been trying to solve his friend's death. That he'd been asking questions and had compiled files on the case—files I was waiting for him to bring this morning. What if someone killed him for those files?"

Once again, guilt reared its ugly head. Vic might still be alive if she'd followed up on the files instead of waiting until today. "I should have taken him more seriously when he said he'd been investigating the murder."

"So why didn't you?"

She stiffened.

"I'm not being critical," he said. "You have to quit taking offense every time I ask you a question."

Rachel forced her body to relax. "I know, and I'm sorry. It's just that you sounded like the Judge."

He laughed. "Do you still call him the Judge to his face?"

"Yep. Have since he was appointed to the bench. Before that, only under my breath." She thought of her distant, somber-faced father. "The robe suited him long before he became a judge. But back to your question about Vic Vegas. It's kind of hard to take seriously a person in a white jumpsuit with their dyed black hair combed in a pompadour."

"I see your point."

Her shoulders slumped as she remembered it'd only been after Vic had mentioned the connection to her mother that she'd even been interested in the case. "That doesn't change the probability that the files are gone now. I should have insisted on getting them yesterday."

"Maybe they're in the house," Boone said and opened his car door.

She had a gut feeling they wouldn't be.

An incoming text chimed on her phone. It was Gran asking what time Rachel would arrive for their outing. She sucked in a breath. Vic's death had blown away all thoughts of the shopping trip.

Another of the balls she was trying to keep in the air just hit the ground.

# 8

BOONE FOLLOWED RACHEL into the small brick house. She was a little prickly when it came to her father. But if Judge Lucien Winslow were *his* father, he might be prickly too. Not that he didn't admire the Judge and enjoy talking with him. His fairness in the courtroom was legendary. But so was his total control. Boone had been in the courtroom once when a defense attorney tried to slip in evidence that had already been disallowed. When the Judge finished with the attorney, he'd practically slithered out of the courtroom.

From the doorway, Boone surveyed the living room, glad he wasn't a tech working the crime scene. Someone had been in a hurry. Books had been dumped from their shelves, table drawers emptied, papers scattered and wall hangings stripped from their frames. Making sense of this mess, let alone photographing it, was better suited to someone other than him.

"I don't think the murderer found what he was looking for," Rachel said.

"What makes you say that?"

"There's nothing left untouched. If the files had been found, *something* would be intact."

"Good point." He turned to one of the techs. "Where's the body?"

"In the kitchen."

They found the medical examiner, Laurence Caldwell, finishing up his investigation.

Boone's gaze went around the room. Either the killer didn't believe the kitchen held anything of importance, or he'd found what he was looking for. Or she. Other than a few open drawers, nothing was out of place. He steeled his emotions and turned his attention to the body on the floor. Death was never easy to view, even though he'd seen it often enough. The man on the floor had lived and loved and now he was dead, taken before his time. He deserved justice, and Boone hoped they found it for him.

Since Vegas was still wearing an Elvis jumpsuit, Boone assumed the murder took place not long after Vegas returned home. "Can you give us an idea how long the victim has been dead?"

"Judging from rigor mortis and body temperature, I'd say at least eight hours. Probably happened at 12:48 a.m.," Caldwell said.

The ME had never expressed a definite time at a crime scene before. "How can you be so precise?"

Using his pen, Caldwell touched the dead man's watch on his left arm. "First bullet went through here, stopping the watch at 12:48, then it traveled through his wrist, severing the ulnar artery. My hypothesis is he realized the person was going to shoot him and he threw up his arm. But that's not what killed him." The ME pointed out a bloodstained hole in the jumpsuit. "The fatal bullet was the one to the heart."

"You're sure of the sequence?" Rachel asked.

He nodded. "Too much bleeding from the wrist for it to have been after the heart wound."

Boone made notes on his iPad. "Anything else you can tell us?"

"Since he hadn't changed out of *that*"—he indicated the jumpsuit—"I assume he'd just gotten home."

Sounded like the ME thought no one in their right mind would wear the Elvis costume any longer than they had to.

Caldwell looked over his glasses at them. "I'm assuming he was an Elvis impersonator."

"Tribute artist," Rachel said, swallowing hard.

She looked a little green around the gills as she turned away. Probably hadn't seen that many murder victims, and he felt for her, remembering his first cases. Her phone dinged, and she took it out.

Rachel glanced at the screen and then looked up. "The uniformed officer who was first on the scene is next door with the daughter. Want me to interview her?"

What was up with that? It was primarily her case, and not like her to ask who should do the interviewing. Did him being here bother her enough to make her insecure? He'd never intimidated her before, and he didn't know what to do about it other than to step back and let her take over. Which meant dialing himself back. Not an easy task for someone as take-charge as he was. "It's your case, and she'd respond better to you. I'll stay here and see what I can find out. When you finish, I'd like to compare notes about the case."

◆

Rachel tried not to let her surprise show. Ever since they'd stepped inside the house, Boone had been in charge and she'd been relegated to second fiddle. Happened every time he was with her on a case. Not that it was particularly his fault or he even noticed—it was just the way it was. She stopped at the door. "See you in a bit."

A text chimed again. More than likely her grandmother again. A quick check confirmed it was the other grandmother. Nana had been invited to go along on the three o'clock shopping trip, and she wanted to know when to be ready. Sometimes Rachel wished her grandmothers had not learned to text.

> I'm tied up on a case. Terri will pick you up at three fifteen.

Ooh! Can't wait to hear about it.

Wrong message to text. Her family was divided into two camps on her career, and Nana championed the law enforcement side, much to the Judge's chagrin. She was the one person he couldn't intimidate. Correction. The one person other than his mother. Gran and Nana. Having two strong-willed grandmothers could be a headache, especially when they were usually on opposite sides.

Rachel pocketed her phone and climbed the steps. Officer Langley answered the doorbell, relief showing in his eyes.

"How's the daughter holding up?" she asked.

"Not good. She hasn't stopped with the crying, and I'm not sure how much help she'll be. Name's Dianne Colson, and she's in the den." He handed her his pad. "Here's what I have so far."

She scanned his notes into her phone. "Thanks. You want to interview a few of the neighbors? I'll check with you when I finish here and grab the ones you haven't talked to."

"Gladly." Like most men, Langley probably wasn't comfortable around crying women.

The house was laid out similarly to the one next door, and she had no trouble finding the den. Two women looked up as she entered the room. One held a tray with a teapot and two cups, which she set on the coffee table. The woman was older and heavy in the hips, and Rachel guessed her age to be close to Vic's.

The younger woman huddled on the hearth, shock registering on her splotchy face. Rachel knew how she felt, and while time helped, the memory of finding her mother always hovered in the back of her mind.

"Ms. Colson? I'm Det. Rachel Sloan, and I'm sorry about what happened to your father."

"Thank you." She put a fist to her mouth.

"I'd like to ask you a few questions if you're up to it."

The young woman untucked the thin legs she'd been hugging to her chest and sucked in a breath. "I . . . I'll try."

"May I call you Dianne?"

Nodding, Dianne fished a crumpled tissue from her pocket. The other woman in the room handed her a fresh tissue, then turned to Rachel.

"I'm Laverne Crenshaw. Vic and I have been neighbors for close to thirty years," she said. Laverne poured a cup of tea and handed it to Dianne before offering one to Rachel.

"Thanks, but no," Rachel said. "Did you see anyone coming or going last night?" She directed her questions to the older woman so Dianne would have time to regroup.

Laverne poured another cup of tea and picked it up, cupping it in her hands. "No, but I went to bed early."

"How long have you known Vic Vegas?"

"Ever since he and his wife moved in. Dianne was just a kid. And when Josie died a few years later, I kind of looked after Dianne up until she married."

"So you knew him pretty well?" Laverne might possess more information than the daughter.

"I did. He was a fine man and a good daddy. I just don't understand why anyone would want to kill him."

Dianne moaned. Rachel froze as Laverne's words set the daughter off again and she buried her face in her hands, sobbing. The neighbor wrapped her arms around the younger woman, and Rachel breathed again. Like the uniformed officer, she did not do emotional outbursts well. In the Judge's world, one simply did not cry. Even when a parent died.

Once Dianne had herself under fragile control, Rachel took her time, searching for words that wouldn't trigger more crying. "I know this is hard."

Dianne nodded, twirling a strand of dishwater-blonde hair around her finger.

Rachel held up her phone. "Do you mind if I record our conversation?" When they both agreed, she set the phone to record. "Again, I'm sorry, but I need to ask if anything is missing from his house."

Dianne blew out a shaky breath. "The only valuable thing he owned was his TV, and it's still there. He didn't have much jewelry, and he never kept over fifty dollars on him."

"How about a laptop?"

"I-I don't remember seeing it."

Rachel made a note to look for it, but it looked like burglary could be ruled out. "Do you know if he had any enemies?"

Laverne stood up and stepped forward. She brushed a strand of gray hair away from her face. "I can answer that. Vic Vegas wouldn't hurt a soul. He was one of the kindest, most gentle men I've ever known."

Dianne nodded. "She's right. Everybody liked him."

That had been the feeling Rachel got yesterday. "Did he ever talk about his friend Harrison Foxx?"

A swift intake of breath came from Laverne. "Harrison? I told Vic to let his murder go, that he had no business digging into that case. That if he accidentally stumbled onto something, it would be nothing but trouble. Do you think that's why he was killed?"

So much for subtleness. Rachel braced for more tears from his daughter, but they didn't come. "We're looking for motive. He came to see me yesterday about Foxx's murder and indicated he had compiled files on his investigation. Do either of you know anything about them?"

Dianne set her untouched tea on the hearth, rattling the delicate china. "Those stupid files. He was always talking about how he'd put together a case to whoever would listen, but no one took him seriously. Last night on the phone when he said he'd found some really important evidence, I told him that nobody cared about it."

"He talked to you about Foxx's murder last night?" Was it possible he had actually uncovered evidence? "What time did you speak with him?"

She knit her brows together. "It was after the ten o'clock news, but I hadn't gone to bed yet. Maybe eleven." Her eyes widened. "You don't suppose he really discovered something, do you?"

Rachel would think it unlikely except Vic Vegas was dead. "Did he say what he'd found? Or where he'd found this evidence?"

"No. He was always afraid his phone was tapped. He was so paranoid . . ." A hollow laugh escaped the daughter's lips. "I thought he was losing his mind, but now . . ."

"Do you know where he kept the files?"

"He wouldn't tell me, said it was better if I didn't know."

"I asked him about the files once," Laverne said. "But he would only say they were in a safe place."

Rachel could kick herself for not getting them yesterday. She bit her bottom lip. He hadn't found this evidence yet when he'd spoken with her or he would have mentioned it. Sometime between 5:00 p.m. and 12:48 a.m., Vic Vegas had encountered someone or something that led to his death. "Does he have a safe or a lockbox?"

"No safe, for sure, at least not in the house," Dianne said. "And he never mentioned a lockbox. I'm on his checking account, and I think if he had a box, I would have been on it as well."

So where would Vic Vegas have hidden the files? Good thing she'd gotten Terri to take over with the grandmothers. Tracking the last hours of Vic Vegas's life would consume the rest of her day.

# 9

SHIRLEY FORCED HERSELF not to go stiff as her aunt wrapped her arms around her. "It's good to see you too, Aunt Treva." She wiggled past her in the doorway, breaking her aunt's firm grasp on her waist, and stepped into the hall. Immediately, the sweet gardenia scent from her aunt's garden assailed her nose. Aunt Treva had her windows open again. Didn't she know how dangerous that was? Someone off the street could easily break into the house.

"What brings you to see me?"

"Nothing. You were on my mind and I realized I hadn't been by in a while."

"Almost a month." The accusation hung in the air.

After Shirley's husband died, she'd moved in with Treva for a few months—until her aunt's clinginess and wanting to know Shirley's every move had about driven her crazy.

"That long? Well, you know how busy life is. How have you been?"

"My knee has been acting up. Other than that, can't complain."

She followed her aunt as she limped down the hallway through a narrow path of stacked newspapers and magazines into the small but bright sitting room with yarn and knitting needles scattered in various chairs. Here, too, stacks and stacks of yarn gave evidence to her aunt's hoarding. Not as bad as she'd seen on TV, but bad enough, and so much worse than when Shirley had lived in the house.

"Move that stuff and sit awhile," Treva said.

She did as she was told. "What's wrong with your knee?"

"It's wore out. Doc wants to operate, but I just don't know."

Shirley half listened as her mother's sister rattled on about her aches and pains, saying, "Too bad" or "I hate that" at the appropriate time. She had to get into the kitchen. "Have you had breakfast?" she asked when her aunt stopped long enough to take a breath.

"Not yet. Haven't felt like making it."

"Then I'll make you some eggs and toast, and a cup of tea as well."

"No, you're my guest. I'll fix it." Treva struggled to get her footing.

"I am absolutely not a guest, and I know where everything is. I'll make your breakfast while you just sit right there and rest your knee."

"You're a sweet girl. Thank you," she said. "I haven't changed anything since you left."

"Or thrown very much away," Shirley muttered under her breath as she surveyed the kitchen off the sitting room. Knickknacks from the fifties lined every counter and shelf. Several insulin bottles filled with different colored beads rested on the windowsill over the sink. A cardboard box with only a few empty vials sat on the kitchen table.

Last year her aunt had given her ornaments made from the small bottles, like Shirley even had a Christmas tree. She sorted through the box, looking for one with a Lantus label.

Panic set in when one by one, she found only fast-acting labels. With only two vials left, her hand shook as she picked up one. *Lantus.* Shirley breathed again. Half her mission accomplished.

"Did you find the tea?" her aunt called from the sitting room.

Shirley opened the cabinet and took down the tea canister. "Yes, ma'am. Green tea or Lady Grey?"

"Lady Grey."

"Do you still take cream with your tea?" she asked, rummaging in the refrigerator. Where were her insulin bottles? She picked up what looked like a blue pen and examined it. Humulin R U-500. Her breath stilled in her chest. She had come across the stronger insulin in her research. At the time, she had thought it'd be the perfect drug but had no idea how to obtain it. And now here it was, a gift.

"And honey—it's in the cabinet. And those cinnamon rolls on the table—bring them instead of making toast."

"Yes, ma'am." The teakettle shrieked, and she bumped her head when she jerked out of the refrigerator. She always hated that kettle and the way it screamed like a Tasmanian devil.

*Breathe in, breathe out.* Once her nerves settled, Shirley grabbed a couple of eggs and scrambled them, then arranged the cinnamon rolls on a plate and took them to the sitting room. "If you haven't taken your insulin this morning, I can draw it for you."

"I might get used to being waited on," her aunt said with a smile. "There's no need to draw it, though. I'm using a pen now, but I better check my sugar first."

Shirley waited while her aunt pricked her finger and stuck the strip in a meter and frowned. "It's a little high, but I think my regular dose will be fine. The pen is on the counter beside my pill organizer, and would you chart it on the fridge for me?"

"Yes, ma'am." Shirley returned to the kitchen, took one of the blue Humulin pens from the refrigerator, and slipped it in her pocket with the empty vial. Next she located the pen on the counter. "Where's the needle?"

"It's in the bottom of that white container that should be beside the pill box."

Shirley fitted a needle on the pen, then smiled as she examined it, noting the dosage marked on the dial. She'd been worrying that just switching the fast-acting insulin with the regular might not be enough to kill Randy, but five times the strength should be more than enough . . . Shirley glanced toward the den. If she doubled the amount her aunt was taking, that would give her a clue about how it would affect Randy.

Her fingers lingered on the dial, then she shook her head and left the dosage where it was. Better not experiment today. She didn't have time to fool with going to the hospital with Treva. . . or possibly arranging a funeral. Shirley had way too much to do for that.

Two hours later, she paced in front of the drawn curtains over her patio door. The darkened room soothed her like a comforting blanket. It was so good to be home, away from the over-sweet scent of her aunt's flowers and the bright sunlight streaming through the windows.

But she'd accomplished what she needed to. It'd been no problem filling the Lantus vial with the U-500 insulin. Then she'd wiped it clean and wrapped it in a tissue before placing it in her purse. Now, the problem was getting the vial switched out with the one in Randy's medical kit.

She had no doubt she'd be successful. Everything had fallen into place too easily for it to turn out badly—it was as though it was meant to be.

That was the only explanation of why she'd sat at the table next to Randy's last night. She'd never sat close to him before. And Fate explained why she'd overheard him tell one of the other performers how important it was to take his insulin every night at the same time, even when he wasn't home. Evidently the other guy was a diabetic too, because he asked what insulin Randy used. Lantus 100, along with a fast-acting insulin. Just like Shirley's aunt. Or at least what she used before her doctor changed her to the pen.

All Shirley had to do was switch the bottles before he filled his syringe for his nightly dose. She didn't anticipate a problem.

Randy kept his blue medical kit on whatever table he claimed, and she just had to catch a time when no one was watching. With everyone's eyes glued to the stage during the performances, that shouldn't be a problem. The key was to act as though opening his kit was an everyday occurrence. No looking furtively around to see if anyone was watching.

Shirley shook her head. Cleaning up the mess Vic had caused was so inconvenient.

*It wasn't Vic who caused the problem. You shouldn't have worn the necklace last night.*

It wasn't her fault! Besides, what was the use in having the necklace if she couldn't wear it sometimes?

*You should never have stolen it in the first place.*

"Why not? Gabby was never going to wear it again." She pressed her fingers in her ears. She had more problems than the necklace. Shirley rubbed her hands up and down her arms. Just as she'd feared, Detective Sloan was investigating Vic's murder. She was the only person who would recognize the significance of the necklace and know that the only person who could have stolen it was her mother's killer.

*That's just the beginning. It'll be a chain reaction. Like dominoes falling.*

"No," she spoke into the empty room. "Rachel Sloan getting the case is a piece of bad luck. That's all." It was nothing she couldn't handle. She was much smarter than the detective and was already a step ahead of her.

*They'll find the necklace and Rachel will recognize it. And then Gabby Winslow's case will be reopened, and once the police start poking around in it, they'll look at everyone she knew. Then they'll discover all the other people you've killed.*

"No one cares about them, and if I can't find the necklace, neither will she."

*She doesn't have to.* His voice snaked through her mind. *Once*

*Randy Culver describes that diamond guitar pendant Vic showed him, Rachel will make the connection. She'll bring in a sketch artist for him to work with and they'll have your ugly likeness.*

She was not ugly, not since she'd lost weight. Besides, there were so many women there last night that Randy wouldn't remember her.

*What if you get caught switching the vials?*

"I'm not going to get caught." Everyone said she had nerves of steel. "I'll take care of Randy Culver tonight."

*But Sloan won't give up. She'll find the connection to the necklace. You have to get rid of her.*

He was right. Hidden things had a way of coming to light, but shooting Sloan and getting away with it was so risky—she always had other cops around. The odds of getting caught were high. Maybe Shirley would send her a warning.

Yes. She would give her an opportunity to back off, just like she had Gabby. And if the detective didn't, then whatever happened would not be Shirley's fault. It would be Sloan's.

*Are you crazy? All you're doing is giving her the opportunity to discover the truth. You have to get rid of her.*

"It's foolhardy to shoot a cop," she said.

*Who said you had to shoot her? Do I have to tell you every move to make? You still have that ricin. And tonight is the perfect opportunity to take care of her.*

The ricin. Stealing a tiny vial from the lab where ricin was being used in experiments to treat cancer had been like stealing insulin from little old ladies. That was before it was touted as a terrorist's tool. She'd used it only once, then resealed the small bottle.

Was that the answer to her problems? She chewed on her thumbnail, her heart beating hard against her chest. It had worked once before . . . It would work again. *Yes!* She pumped her clenched fist.

Unlike the necklace, the ricin couldn't be traced. The idea was brilliant. She knew exactly how she would deliver it if Detective Sloan didn't give up the case.

# 10

By two, Rachel had interviewed the neighbors surrounding the Vegas house. No one had seen anything. Everyone agreed Vic was a nice guy. The crime scene techs were clearing out as she walked back to the house.

That left her with no leads and a list of Elvis impersonators to interview since that was who Vic had spent the last hours of his life with. And a feeling she'd missed something. Perhaps if she gave the house one last look. It would also give her a chance to take her own photos, and might help her figure out what she'd overlooked.

Boone met her at the door. Since she couldn't be in two places at once, she grudgingly admitted to herself it was good he'd come since he'd stayed with the techs, going over each room with them. He made a few notes on an iPad as she filled him in on the information she'd gotten from the daughter and neighbor next door.

"Techs said they found nothing, but did you see anything that might be considered evidence in the Foxx murder?" she asked.

"No. There was no sign of forced entry, either. I tried a credit card on the door and slipped the lock, so if he didn't lock the dead bolt when he returned home, whoever killed him could have entered that way. Or Vegas let them in," he said. "We found bank statements in his office. Every month he balanced his account on the back of one of the sheets. And there was a monthly planner in his car with his schedule neatly written in the squares. That should help you track his movements this past week."

Boone transfered the notes on his iPad to her phone.

"Are you ready to head back downtown?" he asked.

"Thought I'd walk through one more time."

He nodded, and she stepped past him. Using her phone camera, she snapped photos of each room. "Was the attic checked?"

"Yep. There were only a few boxes of Christmas ornaments up there. Vegas was definitely not a pack rat." He followed her to the kitchen. "You know, copies of the crime scene photos will be available later this afternoon."

Rachel pressed her lips together. She framed the kitchen table in her lens. "You do things your way, I'll do them mine," she said and took another shot. "But for the record, I like having my own pictures."

His eye twitched. "Just trying to be helpful."

"I know." She aimed her camera at the beige wall phone beside the refrigerator. According to the daughter's phone, he'd used his landline to call her at 10:53 last night. Could it have been this phone?

She tried to visualize his last hours, but it was hard with the contents of the cabinets littering the countertops and floor. If only she'd gotten shots earlier, before the techs pulled everything out. She'd have to rely on the crime scene photos that were taken before anything was touched.

"Do you remember what this room looked like when we got here?"

Boone scratched his jaw. "Neat. There wasn't any food or dishes on the countertops or the table."

"That's what I remember." Poking in the garbage can under the sink revealed nothing but paper towels and bits of lettuce. If there'd been any food, the crime scene techs would have taken it. From the looks of everything, Vic had tidied up after himself. She checked the canned goods on the table, assuming they'd been placed much like they'd been in the cabinet. Everything was grouped together. The man was definitely neat. And organized. And thorough.

So where would a well-ordered person like Vic Vegas hide his valuables?

◆

On the way back to Rachel's car, Boone stopped and picked up a battery. Knowing her the way he did, there would be an argument over him installing it for her. He didn't know anyone as prickly or independent as she was.

He hated to admit it, but the more he was around her, the more he realized what a good detective she was. His superiors had been right about her. And when her year in Homicide was up, they'd probably arrange it so she could stay. He glanced toward the passenger seat as another text dinged on her phone, the third since they'd left Vegas's house.

"Problems?"

"Sort of. Gran's eighty-third birthday is Tuesday, and I was supposed to take her shopping and then get her to the Judge's in time for the surprise party he's arranged tonight. I had Terri take over for me, but both grandmothers keep texting to see if I'm joining them."

"And this investigation messed you up."

"Something like that."

He laughed. "I'm still amazed that your grandmothers text."

"Sometimes I wonder if one of my biggest mistakes was teaching Nana to text. Gran wasn't to be outdone. Those two still compete over everything." Her fingers flew as she focused on her phone, then she looked up. "They both have Facebook pages now, by the way."

Texting and Facebooking grandmothers. Probably where she

got her independence. But if he thought about it, if his own grand-mothers were still living, they'd probably be doing the same thing. It was a different world from ten years ago. "You know, it won't hurt for you to take time to have a cup of coffee with them and at least make an appearance at the party."

"I know, and I am. I talked with the manager at Blues & Such, and the semi-final Elvis tribute competitions are tonight and tomor-row night. He indicated most of the performers who were there last night would be back tonight. I can catch them all at one place, and since most won't start arriving until after seven, I'll have time to pop into the party for a few minutes."

"Good."

A traffic light caught them, and while they waited, Rachel flipped through the pages of her notebook.

"Looking for something?"

"My notes from the interview with Vic. I feel like I'm missing something. Here they are." She was quiet for a minute, and then she groaned. "I can't believe I forgot that."

"What?" He glanced her way. She was hunched over her notes.

"He told me he thought someone had broken into his house Thursday night. But he wasn't completely sure about it, and he'd just told me his daughter thought he was crazy . . ." She pressed her fingertips to her forehead. "At that time, I actually agreed with his daughter, but how could I have forgotten it? I even jotted the information down."

"Come on, Rachel, it happens to the best of us, so quit beating yourself up. You're not perfect."

"You don't understand. What if one of the neighbors saw some-thing? If I'd questioned them last night about the break-in, maybe Vic Vegas wouldn't be dead now."

"You're not working Burglary, and that's all it was at that point. Besides, you just indicated he wasn't even sure someone had at-tempted to break in." When she still looked uncertain, he said,

"When you canvassed the neighborhood, did anyone mention suspicious activity around his house this past week?"

"No, but I only asked about last night and today."

"You know as well as I do that after a murder if anything suspicious had happened in the past month, someone would have mentioned it." He liked his detectives to be conscientious, but . . . "Okay, what's the deal? Why does this bother you so much?"

"I've never forgotten anything this important." Rachel stared at her notes as if an answer might appear.

"It only shows you're human. File it under lessons learned."

While she nodded that she would, her eyes said she wasn't letting it go.

"That's an order, by the way."

Red crept into her cheeks. "All right . . . but maybe the break-in slipped my mind because his visit was so weird—the Elvis costume, and then he was investigating Foxx's murder, someone my mother had known."

"Foxx and Vegas knew your mother?"

"I thought I mentioned that when we discussed the photo earlier."

"No, only that the two of you were there when the photo was taken. Not that you actually knew any of the people in it. How well did you know them? Well enough that I might need to assign this case to someone else?"

"No! You can't remove me from this case!"

Why was Rachel so concerned? "If this case is too personal, you won't be able to look at it objectively."

"I didn't know them personally. I don't even know if Mom knew Vic. She and Foxx went to high school together, so they must have been pretty good friends."

He eyed her. "Why do you want this case so badly?"

She tapped the side of her leg. "I let Vic Vegas down. If I'd followed him home, gotten his files, he might still be alive."

He knew guilt when he saw it. Solving the case would soften her *if onlys*. But it was hard to shake the feeling in his gut that said to assign the case to someone else. It was the same gut feeling he'd had in Iraq before everything went south.

Boone shook off his apprehension. They weren't in Iraq, and there was no good reason to assign the case to anyone else. If he did, World War III would probably break out, and he wouldn't blame her.

# 11

Rachel's fingers itched to take over as Boone meticulously cleaned the battery posts. She could have had it installed five minutes ago and been on her way to the CJC.

"Try it now," he said, pulling his head out from under the hood.

She hopped in the front seat and turned the key. The engine cranked smoothly, and she lowered her window. "Thanks."

"Not a problem." He let the hood down. "What's your plan for the rest of the afternoon?"

"I want to look at those bank records you found. Vic kept those files on Harrison's murder somewhere. Possibly in one of those mailbox places, and maybe he wrote a check for the rental." Rachel really wanted a look at those files. "It's three now. If I have time, I may return to Vic's neighborhood and see if I can catch a couple of the neighbors who weren't home."

"Sounds good."

She enjoyed being around this side of Boone. Maybe they could work together, after all. "What about you?"

"Not sure yet. I have some paperwork to catch up on."

"Want to come to Gran's birthday party?" The words shot out of her mouth before she thought it through. The startled look on Boone's face was almost worth the invitation.

"You're asking me to the party? Why?"

She bit her bottom lip, wondering if she could rescind the invitation. *No.* "Gran liked you."

*"You really shouldn't let that man get away, Rachel."* Gran's words echoed in her brain.

"Well, thanks for the offer, but I think I'll pass tonight."

"Okay," she said, hoping her relief didn't show. She quickly pulled out of the gym parking area. What had she been thinking, inviting him to the party? Rachel couldn't understand why she kept sending Boone mixed messages, but it had to stop.

Unfortunately, she didn't know how, not when he kept her emotions in turmoil. Working with him today—bouncing ideas off each other in an easy camaraderie—that was how it'd been when they dated, and she missed that. Not to mention that the way he looked at her sometimes with those brown eyes set her heart in high gear.

The captain had hinted when he approved her loan from Burglary that because of her law background, they might find a way to keep her permanently. If only there was a way to stay in Homicide *and* date Boone. But unless Boone moved out of the department, there was no hope for them. She didn't see that happening. Still thinking about him, she found a parking space in front of the CJC and pulled parallel to the curb. Just as she pressed the lock button on her key, her phone dinged with an incoming text. She glanced at the screen.

Drop this case or you'll live to regret it.

Her heart slammed against her ribs. She jerked her head up and scanned the area. Normal traffic. Heat shimmered from the tops of parked cars. A few people walked along the sidewalk in the August heat. But what if someone had a gun trained on her back? She swallowed hard and hurried to the front door of the tan building.

Inside the CJC, cool air chilled her body. Why did someone want her off the case? And why send a warning? That didn't make sense. And what was she going to do about the text? Certainly not tell Boone. He was looking for a reason to take her off the case. Her stomach churned as she rode the elevator to the eleventh floor, but when the door opened, her mind was made up.

This was her case, not Boone's. And he wasn't her partner. Her superior, yes, but before she showed the text to him, she needed to check it out, see if she could discover who sent it. It could be a prank for all she knew.

"Are you okay?"

Boone's voice sent her heart racing again. She turned toward his cubicle. "What?"

"You look troubled. Is it because you thought I might take you off the case?"

Was he reading her mind?

"That did bother me." She still had the feeling he was looking for a reason to hand it off to another detective. *Tell him about the text.*

No. This was something she had to take care of herself. But if Boone discovered she'd withheld the information, he'd be so angry, he might get her kicked out of Homicide. Duty warred with her hunger to solve her mother's murder. If he took her off the case, she would lose access to the files that might point to the killer.

"Earth to Rachel," Boone said.

"I'm sorry, I—"

"It's okay, I was just saying that I was sorry, but department policy says if you personally know a victim, you can't work the case. I'm sure you can see how it might adversely affect an investigation."

"I suppose. Thanks for clarifying the policy for me." Rachel would just have to solve Vic's case before Boone found out about the text.

She settled in her cubicle and booted up her computer. There must be something about Vic's case the person who sent the text did not want her to discover, but what? Rachel massaged her temples and let her mind roam while she waited for Google to come up. What if the person who killed Vic was the one who killed her mother and Harrison Foxx? But what was the connection between the three murders?

She typed her query into the search engine. It didn't take long to realize she didn't have the computer know-how to track the text, but she knew someone who did. She'd met Kelsey Allen earlier this year on another case she'd worked with Brad Hollister. Rachel had been impressed with her computer skills. She dialed Kelsey's number and laid out her problem without disclosing the actual text.

"Your text probably came from a burner phone," Kelsey said. "Give me the number, and I'll see if I can trace it."

Rachel had figured it was a burner. She skimmed through Vic's bank records while she waited.

"Yep," Kelsey said a few minutes later. "Looks like it was purchased at a discount store in East Memphis."

"Probably with cash," Rachel said and wrote down the address Kelsey gave her. It wasn't that far from Vic's neighborhood.

"You can count on it. And they probably used a fake account when they activated it. How hard is it to get your cell number?"

"It's on my business card."

"So it's probably someone you know or have interacted with."

Goose bumps raised on her arms again. She hadn't considered how the person who sent the text had gotten her number. If her mother's case was related to the other two, it was very possible she knew the murderer. The thought sobered her.

"Thanks for the help," Rachel said and hung up. The disturbing thought hung on as she finished going over the bank records. Nothing indicated Vic had paid for any type of storage place by check. No credit card statements had been found in his office, and she put in a request at the credit companies he'd written checks to for his records. It'd be Monday morning before anything came back—if the companies didn't require a subpoena.

Her thoughts returned to the text. Not telling Boone gnawed at her. Used to be when she had a problem she couldn't solve, she had turned to prayer. But it'd been so long, she wasn't sure God would know who she was. Besides, she was pretty sure God would side with telling Boone about the text. And she really didn't want to hear that. She glanced toward Boone's desk. Good. He was gone, and it was time for her to talk to the neighbors she'd missed in Vic's neighborhood.

◆

Before Rachel fastened her seat belt, her phone alerted her to another text, making her heart race until she saw it was Nana.

Where are you? We're at Starbucks on Kirby.
Can you join us?

She checked her watch and chuckled. After an hour with the grandmothers, Terri was probably going nuts about now. Rachel should have known if Nana was with them, they would be making a Starbucks run. The one on Kirby wasn't a mile out of her way, and she could use a shot of caffeine before she questioned the neighbors again.

See you in fifteen.

The two grandmothers were sitting at a round table when Rachel entered the coffee shop. Oil and vinegar. Or salt and red pepper if one were describing their hair. Color had never touched her grandmother Winslow's white curls, whereas Nana's monthly touch-ups were written in ink on her calendar.

Terri sat between the two grandmothers, probably refereeing since it looked as though they were arguing. As usual. Sometimes they wore her out.

Nana spotted her first. "Rachel, dear," she called out. "Would you please explain to Adele why it's important for her friend's granddaughter to take part in the debutante season."

She stopped at the table, telegraphing Terri a plea for help, and all she received was a laugh.

"Not touching that one with lead gloves," Terri said. "I lived through this argument your debutante year."

A groan welled up inside Rachel. The Debutante Wars, as she dubbed them, had been going on ever since Rachel turned four and Nana insisted her granddaughter should start dance and etiquette classes with Terri. Nana believed every girl should be a debutante, and it was essential for training to begin at a young age since most debutantes made their grand entrance into society between the ages of sixteen and twenty-one.

Practical Gran had survived World War II in bunkers in England and thought being presented to society was frivolous and a huge waste of money and time. Each was a staunch believer in her own cause.

"Happy early birthday." Rachel leaned down and hugged Gran, then did the same for Nana.

"It's not until Tuesday. Surely I'll see you again before that," she replied. "Now sit down and answer our question."

"Let me order a dark roast." Rachel should have said no to Starbucks, but since she hadn't, she'd have to make the best of it.

After getting her coffee, she returned to the table and sat across from the grandmothers. "Where's Erin?"

"Oh, she'd forgotten a favorite pin she wanted to wear tonight, so I brought her back to the home. I'm picking her up at five-thirty for dinner—right after I drop off a couple of baskets at Blues & Such."

Terri worked part-time at a gift shop, and Rachel nodded as she turned to her grandmothers. "So, are you finished shopping?"

"We are through." Gran smoothed the blue linen blouse that

complemented her porcelain skin and blue eyes. "And you will not dodge the question. I know for a fact that you hated being a debutante, and this child feels the same way. Explain to Rose that the girl's mother and grandmothers should not coerce her into it."

"She did not hate it." Nana placed a manicured hand on Rachel's arm. "Did you, sweetheart?"

She hated being in the middle of one of their arguments and looked from one to the other, trying to gauge how far this squabble would escalate. "Hate's a strong word, but I wouldn't want to repeat the debutante season."

"See there, Rose." Victory laced Gran's voice.

Nana's stricken face made Rachel wince. And now she was going to hurt the other grandmother, but they shouldn't have asked her opinion.

"However, being a debutante did have its benefits—I wouldn't have learned ballet and dance, or which fork to use, until I was much older if Mom and Nana hadn't groomed me for it."

The memory of the orchestra playing "The Blue Danube" as her father waltzed her around the ballroom when she was nineteen hit her unexpectedly. The joy of his undivided attention was exquisite, if for only one night. She'd thought that finally things were going to be different. Then came the disappointment when nothing changed . . .

She brushed the memory aside and continued, "It wasn't all about the fun. There was the community service aspect. Feeding the homeless taught me about real poverty. As for your friend's granddaughter, unless the whole thing makes the girl physically ill, it will be good for her."

"I still say it's a silly, outdated practice." Gran lifted an eyebrow at Rachel. "And why didn't you pick us up? Instead of forcing poor Terri to cart us around. Are you taking over our shopping trip now?"

"No, she's not taking over," Nana said. "She has a murder case to solve."

Her other grandmother narrowed her eyes at Rachel. "Is that true? Do you have a case?"

"I'm afraid so."

"Can you tell us who the victim is?" Terri asked.

Rachel hesitated. It would be on the nightly news, so there really was no reason not to. Besides, Nana might remember Vic or Harrison Foxx. "It was an Elvis impersonator, Vic Vegas."

"Why is that name familiar?" Nana tapped her finger against her lips. "Oh, wait. He was at Blues & Such last night. An old guy."

Everyone at the table turned to look at Nana, and color rose in her face. "Not old-old—he was younger than me, but old for a performer."

"You actually saw him?" Rachel said, taking out her notepad.

"You went to Blues & Such by yourself last night? Beale Street? Really, Rose!" Gran frowned at Nana.

"I didn't go by myself. Gerald accompanied me. Terri and Erin were there as well."

"That's right. You were there." Rachel turned to Terri. "Did you happen to talk with him?"

"Briefly. He talked with several people in the crowd." Terri smiled. "He was really sweet to Erin."

"Anyway," Nana said, her voice rising, "this new crop of tribute artists is really good. One of them sang 'Don't Be Cruel,' and if I shut my eyes, I could almost imagine Elvis singing it. I went to school with him, you know."

Gran snorted. "If we don't, it's not because you've haven't told us often enough. And I don't know why you took Gerald. He couldn't fend off a feather and would have been no protection at all. You could have been mugged or even killed down there."

From the look in Nana's eyes, she was searching for a snappy comeback, and before she could find it, Rachel said, "How about you, Nana. Did you happen to talk to Vic Vegas?"

Nana's perfect eyebrows lowered. "Why no. Why would I do that?"

Rachel took the photo Vic had given her and showed it to Nana. Her grandmother had a phenomenal memory for people and dates. "He came to see me yesterday. Do you recognize the man I'm giving the trophy to in the photo?"

Nana fished her glasses from her purse and slipped them on. After studying the photo, she tapped Foxx's likeness. "I don't recall his name, but he and your mother attended Humes High together for a couple of years—ninth and tenth grade, I believe. After your grandpa died, I transferred Gabby to Miss Hutchinson's School for Girls."

The same finishing school Rachel had attended. "His name was Harrison Foxx."

"Why, of course," Nana said. "Don't know how I forgot it."

"Why did Vic Vegas come to see you?" Terri asked.

"He wanted me to take a look at an old case."

Nana sucked in a breath. "I just remembered. Harrison Foxx was murdered the same week Gabby died. I always thought it was strange the way that happened."

Silence fell over the table and was finally broken when Terri cleared her throat. "Is that the case he wanted you to look at?"

"If it is," Gran said, "you need to let someone else take over."

Rachel took the photo from Nana. "I can't do that. It's my case. And if it happens to be connected to Mom's death, don't we want to know who was responsible?"

"Of course," Terri said. "But it's been so long and the police said it was a burglary."

"Vic Vegas thought otherwise." She'd almost said he'd had proof but caught herself. She'd probably said too much already.

"If you remain on this Vegas's case and you have to dig into the other man's murder, just remember that Gabby was in his circle of friends," Gran said. "You might stir up some painful memories."

PATRICIA BRADLEY

That thought had occurred to Rachel. "Handing the case off isn't an option."

Besides, it was possible Vic's death had nothing to do with Foxx's murder. She stared at the photo again. "Nana, you were there the night this was taken. Do you recognize anyone else in the photo? Or any of the names on the back?"

Nana looked at the photo again and then examined the names Vic had written down.

"I didn't stay for the whole program, so I didn't meet everyone . . . I knew him, of course," she said, tapping Foxx. "And the name Randy Culver sounds familiar. I think that's him there."

Nana pointed at the third man to Foxx's right. "Of course he'd look different now. Look at how Vic Vegas changed—Oh! Hold on a minute." She dug through her purse and pulled out a program and flipped through it. "Yes! I knew I'd seen that name somewhere. It says Randy Culver right here. He hasn't changed as much as Vegas. Still a handsome devil." She pointed to a photo at the bottom of the page.

Rachel compared the two photos. In the one Vic had given her, Culver appeared to be about eighteen, which would put him in his midthirties now. And it definitely was the same person.

"He'll be at Blues & Such tonight for the second round of competition, but I think I heard something about a rehearsal this afternoon," Nana said.

Gran took the program and stared at the photos. "At least the Culver guy isn't an old geezer," she said, handing it on to Rachel.

"Hardly. He's the one who was so good," Nana retorted.

"Can I have this?" Rachel asked. If they were having a rehearsal this afternoon, she could get the interviews over with. Alone.

"Sure, I'll get another one tonight."

"You're not coming to my party?" Gran asked.

Everyone turned to stare at her.

"Oh, come on. Do you think I'm getting senile? I know this

83

shopping trip is just a ruse to get me out and then to the party Lucien has pulled together." Gran checked her watch and stood. "Speaking of which, if Terri's going to deliver those baskets and get to Lucien's by party time, we better get moving. And don't worry, I'll act surprised."

"Gran, you're a mess," Rachel said and hugged her.

"Will you be there?"

"I may be a little late, but I'll try."

# 12

IT WAS TOO LATE after Rachel left Starbucks to interview the families she'd missed in Vic's neighborhood or to drive to the discount store where the burner phone had been purchased. Not if she wanted to check out Blues & Such. So she phoned the store, and the clerk laughed when she asked if there were sales records for the phone. "How about an ID?" Rachel asked.

"You'll have to talk with the manager on Monday, but as far as I know, somebody pays cash, we don't ask for ID. Least I never have."

Rachel asked for the manager's name, then thanked the clerk before ending the call. Dead end, just like she figured, and she was glad she hadn't wasted time driving there. Next, Rachel dialed the number on the program for Blues & Such and was told that a rehearsal was in progress. She drove downtown and showed her badge to the attendant at the parking garage across the street from the restaurant. He directed her to a space near the entrance.

It crossed her mind to call Boone, but then she'd have to wait for him to arrive and that would take time she didn't have. Of course, she could have called him on the drive in, but she didn't see the need to involve him. If he had a problem with it, he just had a problem. A hot wind off the river did little to dispel the heat, and she welcomed the cool air when she stepped into Blues & Such.

A hostess offered her a menu. "No, thank you," she said. "I'm Det. Rachel Sloan with the MPD. Can I speak to whoever is in charge of the Supreme Elvis rehearsal?"

The hostess frowned. "Is something wrong, Detective?"

"No. I'm working a case, and he may be able to help me."

"The rehearsal is over, but Ms. Carpenter hasn't left yet. Wait right here. I'll get her."

So the person in charge was a woman. While she waited, Rachel surveyed the almost empty tables. A few people were at the bar and a couple sat by the windows. She'd figured the place would be hopping, then remembered hearing on the radio earlier there was an event from five until six at Graceland. Muted footsteps on the carpeting drew her attention, and she turned as a woman in tight-fitting black pants and a white linen tunic approached.

"I'm Monica Carpenter, event coordinator with the Supreme Elvis contest."

Rachel had been expecting someone much younger, not this rail-thin person with her brown hair slicked back in a bun.

"How may I help you, Detective . . . ? I'm afraid the hostess didn't catch your name."

"Rachel Sloan." She took out her notepad to keep from focusing on the oversized rose-tinted glasses that magnified Ms. Carpenter's brown eyes. The glasses would have looked ridiculous on most people but somehow they fit the fiftysomething coordinator. "I'm investigating Vic Vegas's death."

"Vic Vegas?" She pursed her lips.

Rachel took out the program and pointed out his photo. "Do you know him?"

Ms. Carpenter tapped her chin with her fingers. "Oh yeah, Vegas. I do remember him. He was quieter than the others. What about him?"

"He was murdered sometime after he returned home."

She paled. "Murdered?" Carpenter swallowed hard. "You don't

think anyone here is responsible, do you? That would be horrible publicity."

"This was the last place he was seen alive."

"Oh, dear." She worried a diamond pendant on a chain around her neck. "You need to talk to Jerome."

"Jerome?"

"He's the emcee and works directly with the contestants of the Supreme Elvis contest."

"So what do you do?"

"I coordinate everything else. The contest is huge. This week culminates months of preliminary contests held all over the country, and the finale is next Saturday night at the end of Elvis Week. It's a big job."

"So you were here last night."

"Of course. It was the first round. There will be two more rounds, and then those winners will compete next Friday and Saturday night."

"Did you see Vegas talk with anyone last night? Or remember anything unusual about him?"

"No." Carpenter adjusted her glasses. "Wait a minute. I remember seeing him talk to Randy Culver. He's one of this year's finalists."

He was also in Vic's photograph. "Is Culver here?"

"No, everyone has gone." She crossed her arms.

Rachel looked up from her notes and waited.

"He'll be back later."

Carpenter radiated tension like a wound spring. "How long have you been in this business?" Rachel asked.

She uncrossed her arms and rubbed the bridge of her nose. "I've worked with the Supreme Elvis contest since its inception in 2006. As far as my company is concerned, this is the only official contest."

Rachel put her notebook away. "So what about all the other Elvis impersonator contests?"

Carpenter's lips formed a thin line. "These men are not impersonators, they're tribute artists, and this contest is a tribute to Elvis. As for the other events, they do not have the endorsement of our company. The Supreme Elvis contest is just what it says. It is the best. Now, if you will excuse me . . ." She turned to leave.

"Wait. Do you recall Harrison Foxx?"

"Name's familiar. Let me think about it."

Did she detect a quiver in her voice? Rachel would ask about Foxx again when she returned later tonight. "This Jerome you mentioned. Is he with your company?"

"No, we hire him each year to serve as the master of ceremonies. And really, I have a lot to do to get ready for tonight. Can you come back later when there will be people here who can answer your questions better than I can?"

"Is Jerome here?"

"No," she said over her shoulder. "But he'll be—"

"Back later tonight, I know. Thank you for your time."

Rachel paused outside. One thing for certain, her questions had made Ms. Carpenter nervous. Hard to tell if it was from fear of bad publicity or something else. At least she'd given Rachel a contact for tonight. Jerome. Should have gotten the last name. She turned to go back in, and movement from the corner window caught her eye.

Someone had been watching her.

◆

Shirley pulled off the latex gloves and mask she'd used while she loaded the ricin, and using a pen she printed Detective Sloan's first name in caps on the beautifully wrapped box. Shirley had decided that even if the detective dropped Vic's case, she was still a cop and the odds of her learning about the necklace were too high.

She probably wouldn't heed the warning anyway. Just like Vic.

She'd warned him to leave Harrison's case alone . . . and Harrison, if he hadn't threatened to go to the police . . . Why couldn't they see that when they crossed her, she had to punish them?

*"You're lying to me."*

The leather belt stung her back.

*"No, Daddy, I didn't eat the cookies. Please don't hit me again . . ."*

The pen in her hands snapped, splintering the plastic. No. She would not think about that.

*Harrison.* She didn't want to think about him either. But shooting Vic had brought back memories of the night she killed Harrison. Memories that played over and over in her head like a video gone crazy.

Harrison had been restless after Gabby's funeral and suggested that they drive around. When dark came, they'd parked on a lonely road out in the country where he was more than ready to fall into her arms. But that was Harrison. Not loyal to anyone. That made it hard to understand why he got so upset when he'd been looking for a cigarette in her purse and found the necklace he'd given Gabby. She'd done it for them, so they could be together.

But he'd laughed at her. Said she was the last person he'd ever marry. And then suddenly he accused her of killing Gabby. Didn't believe it was an accident. Threatened to go to the police. White-hot rage ripped through her soul at his rejection. He was just like every other man she'd ever loved. But he'd paid for his betrayal.

Shirley closed her eyes, reliving the moment she'd pulled the .22 from her purse. She'd never shot anyone before, and thought it would feel different. But no. It was like the time she put ricin in her husband's soup. Twelve hours later, she took him to the hospital and calmly reported he had a stomach virus and she believed he was dehydrated. She felt nothing when he died of cardiac arrest. Somehow it should have been different with Harrison.

After she'd wiped the car clean with a towel she'd found in the trunk, she had walked the dark road until she came to the city lights and a bus line. By the time she reached home, she'd put the whole ugly incident behind her.

She shook the memories off. *Focus on the problems here and now.* Like how to get the present to Rachel . . .

# 13

RACHEL'S CELL RANG as she drove toward the Judge's house. Boone. Probably checking up on her to see if she'd been back to question the neighbors again. "Sloan," she answered.

"Are you still planning to check out the performers at Blues & Such tonight?"

"I am."

"How about if I tag along. With two it'll take half the time."

Her double-crossing heart stuttered in her chest. "Why?"

"I'm not micromanaging. Just offering my help."

She'd let him think he read her mind rather than admit how the thought of spending Saturday evening in his presence upended her emotions. If only she could say no, but it wouldn't make sense that she'd want to work twice as long. "No need in taking two cars. Want me to pick you up?" She could explain on the way that she'd already been downtown and talked with the event coordinator.

"Sure. What time?"

She checked her watch. It was six forty-five. By now Gran had been "surprised" and the party was in full swing. "How about around seven thirty?"

That would give her time to make an appearance at the party

and give Gran the present in the passenger seat, a sweater she'd taken great pains to wrap.

"See you then."

She didn't understand why he was so interested in this case. She didn't know any of the other officers well enough to ask if this was standard operating procedure. Except maybe Brad Hollister. She'd ask him Monday.

Part of her believed Boone just wanted to make sure she didn't mess up, and she didn't understand why that bothered her. In Burglary she'd always appreciated her supervisor's input. But her supervisor hadn't constantly looked over her shoulder. He trusted her. So why didn't Boone? An answer played around the edge of her mind.

Maybe Boone didn't trust anyone. But why? For that she had no answer.

Fifteen minutes later, Rachel pulled into the long drive to the Judge's house, the house where she'd grown up. Even from the street, the Federal style two-story brick home reminded her of the Judge. Cold. Imposing. She liked houses with lots of painted wood and wraparound porches.

Rachel had begged him to move after her mother's death, but he'd refused. "Winslows don't run" had been her father's stock reply. She'd spent most of her time either at Gran's or Nana's.

Terri was coming out the door when Rachel parked and climbed out of her car. She couldn't help comparing her to the event coordinator she'd met earlier. Her ballet teacher's face was so much smoother than the other woman's. One of these days Rachel was going to ask Terri if she'd had a few nips and tucks on her face.

Terri had changed from the jeans and sweater she'd worn shopping to a slinky black outfit, confirming that Rachel's decision to change from her street clothes into a pale blue sheath that skimmed her knees had been a good one. "You look great," she said.

"Thank you. So do you. And your father and grandmother will be so glad you could make it," Terri said.

"I wouldn't miss Gran's party for the world. Where are you going?"

"I'm making a grocery run. The Judge thought I was picking up ice cream, and I thought he was getting it. I'll be right back. Erin was asking where you were a few minutes ago."

"You haven't said anything about us running into Boone at Gallagher's, have you?"

"No. Almost mentioned it at Starbucks, but thought better of it. Gotta run."

"Thank you for not saying anything," she called after Terri. Both grandmothers had liked Boone, and she didn't want them to get started on what a nice young man he was again.

Rachel's heels clicked on the marble entryway as she walked toward the music playing in the back of the house. In the family room, Gran held court, opening presents in front of her friends. She looked up as Rachel handed her the present she'd brought.

"Oh, you made it! And you shouldn't have gotten me anything."

"I couldn't not." She hoped Gran would like the pink summer sweater she'd found. Her grandmother complained of being cold winter and summer. Rachel scanned the room, and Erin motioned her over.

"My, you look nice," Rachel said.

As usual, a shy smile graced Erin's face. She dropped her gaze to Rachel's feet. "I like your shoes. They don't look like Gran's."

"Thank you." Erin always noticed what kind of shoes people wore. "I like your turquoise shoes better."

"Do you like my necklace? It's my favorite, but I like yours better. Can I wear it?"

Rachel touched the small cross dangling from a thin chain. Jewelry was something else Erin always noticed. "Maybe later. Right now I need it for the party." She brushed a strand of Erin's dark hair back. "I like your haircut."

"Me too. It's like Terri's. When are we going to have ice cream?"

"As soon as your sister gets back." Rachel turned as her father approached.

"I'm glad you could make it," he said.

"Me too." She checked to see if Donna had arrived and spotted her coming into the room from the kitchen area. She'd certainly made herself right at home. Rachel noted Donna had gone all out in flowing black pants and a white sparkly top and had piled her red hair up in a messy bun. Rachel turned back to her dad. "I see you got a haircut today too."

"Too?" He frowned, and she pointed to Erin's hair.

"Oh. Yes, you look very nice, Erin." Then he smoothed a hand over his full head of dark hair and turned to Rachel. "I saw the look on your face last night that indicated it was too shaggy."

"I never said anything, but it does look nice tonight." His pale blue polo shirt showed off his tan. "I see you've been hitting the tennis courts too."

He laughed. "You don't miss much, do you?" He nodded toward his mother. "She seems to be enjoying herself. She was really surprised."

Rachel swallowed a smile, glad he was in a good mood, but sometimes she wished they could talk about real issues instead of superficial ones. "Yes, she does appear to be having fun." Rachel's gaze followed Erin as she drifted toward the punch bowl where her other grandmother ladled the pink drink into cups. "Thanks for inviting Nana."

"Rose would have been highly insulted if I hadn't. And Mother would have been disappointed. Those two might love to argue, but I think they really care about one another." He frowned. "You don't suppose Rose is spiking the punch, do you?"

"I'll check and see."

"No, wait until I make my announcement. I was waiting for you to get here." He cleared his throat. "Can I have everyone's attention?"

Everyone turned toward the Judge. "I have some news that I want to share."

He glanced at Rachel, and her stomach clenched. *Don't let this be about an opportunity for me with a law firm.*

The Judge scanned the room and then smiled broadly. "It hasn't been released to the media outlets yet, but I've been chosen by the president of the United States to sit on the Sixth Court of Appeals."

Stunned silence filled the room, and then everyone started talking at once. Erin clapped, even though Rachel wasn't certain she understood what was going on, and Gran hurried to his side and hugged him. "You didn't breathe a word! Congratulations!"

"Why didn't you tell me?" Rachel said. She couldn't help but notice how Donna hung on the Judge's arm. "How did you keep this a secret?"

"I couldn't say anything until it was official," he said, still beaming. "Of course, I have to be confirmed by the Senate."

"You know that won't be a problem," Gran said. "You don't have one skeleton in your closet."

# 14

GRAN WAS RIGHT. If anyone was squeaky clean business-wise, it was her father. He had a solid reputation in the judicial field. The only blip on his personal life was the separation from her mother over a fling. Not that Rachel ever knew the woman's identity, and as far as she knew, no one other than herself knew about the affair, not even Nana. In this day and age, it probably wouldn't matter, and he would sail through the confirmation hearings.

Rachel hugged him as others gathered in to congratulate him, and then she spied her other grandmother still by the punch. She wanted to see Nana before she had to leave.

Donna intercepted her. "Isn't that the greatest news?" she said.

Rachel studied her friend, looking for . . . she wasn't sure what. Maybe a sign that said "I won't get hurt when your dad dumps me." "I'm happy for him. How long have you two been seeing each other?"

"Oh, not long. And I have you to thank for bringing me to the dinner party that time."

In her peripheral vision, Terri set down a pretty package to congratulate her father, and Rachel finally put her finger on why Donna and the Judge seeing each other bothered her. She'd hoped he and Terri would get together. But if they hadn't in seventeen years, they probably wouldn't. Tamping down her disappointment, she extended a warm smile to Donna. "Just be careful. He's not known for long relationships."

"He may make an exception this time."

Rachel suppressed a groan. She hadn't figured Donna as one of those women who thought "this time would be different." That she would accomplish what no other woman had in seventeen years. "I need to see my grandmother before I leave. I'll see you later."

Donna gave her a hug. "I'm leaving as soon as I tell your dad bye. I promised to hand out flyers at Blues & Such advertising the candlelight service Tuesday."

"Then I'll probably see you there," Rachel said. She walked toward Nana, still savoring her father's good news. He'd worked hard for this and he deserved the seat. "Spiking the punch?" she said.

Nana jumped, almost spilling her drink. "You scared me to death. And no, I'm not spiking it. Although it needs it."

"You look terrific." And she did in a melon-colored tunic over white pants. "Great news, huh?"

"Excellent. But it doesn't surprise me. Your father is a good man and a fair and honest judge."

Rachel's heart warmed at the high praise coming from her grandmother. The Judge was a lot like his mother, and while Nana didn't always agree with the two of them, she respected and loved them both. Sometimes it was like a Steel Magnolia butting heads with Downton Abbey. "Did Gran act surprised?"

"Academy-Award performance." Nana set her cup down. "Are you still going to Blues & Such?"

"As soon as I leave here."

"I wouldn't mind tagging along. Gerald can't go."

"Hmm . . . Afraid not. My visit will be official, and I don't know how long I'll be there. And you definitely don't need to drive downtown by yourself at night."

"I was afraid you'd say that." She took a sip of her punch. "I've been thinking about that night the photo was taken. Wasn't your father there?"

"He was." A memory niggled at the back of her mind. "I think it's the only time he ever came to an Elvis function." If only he'd gone home with Mom. But her mother hadn't been ready for him to move back in. And that had left Rachel to fill in the gap, only she hadn't.

"Stop what you're thinking."

Rachel jerked her head up. "I wasn't—"

"Thinking you let your mother down? You were a fifteen-year-old kid. You couldn't have changed the outcome. We could have lost you too."

Rachel couldn't convince herself of that truth. She ladled punch into a cup.

"If anyone could have changed the outcome, it was your father. He should have been home with her, not living in some hotel."

She stopped with the punch halfway to her lips. She'd never heard Nana blame her father for not being there the night her mother died.

Nana shook her head. "Forget I said that. This is a happy night. I guess it was the photo this afternoon that's brought that horrible night back."

"I wish I hadn't discussed the case with you or asked you about Vic Vegas now." Out of the corner of her eye, Rachel saw Terri hand the pretty package she'd had earlier to Gran. Which reminded her that she hadn't seen her grandmother open the gift she'd brought.

"Let's join Erin and watch Gran open her presents." Rachel hooked her arm into Nana's and they walked to where Erin sat beside Gran.

"This is for you," Terri said, handing her the gift as Rachel sat in one of the chairs that had been brought in.

"For me?" All of the guests were here for Gran, and she hadn't expected a present from any of them. "Where did it come from?"

Terri shook her head. "It was on the front doorstep when I came back. Maybe one of the neighbors who couldn't come to the party?"

Erin clapped her hands. "Can I open it?"

Rachel searched the package to see who it was from, but the only name on it was hers. It was wrapped in expensive, creamy white paper, but under the paper, the box felt rigid, like it was wooden.

Goose bumps raised on her arms.

Something was off. No card, no mention of who the gift was from. She glanced up, and her grandmothers were watching. Even her father looked interested.

*Drop this case or you'll live to regret it.*

Rachel had almost been able to put the text out of her mind. Her mouth dried. What if she was holding a bomb? Everyone in the room could be killed.

Blood rushed from her head to her thumping heart, leaving her face icy cold. *Get a grip.* What if it was nothing? She'd feel like a fool.

"Are you going to open it?" the Judge asked.

She pulled off a smile. "My birthday isn't until Tuesday. I think I'll wait."

Rachel stood, taking care not to jostle the package. Just in case. But the way her legs trembled, she wasn't certain she could move. "I better get back to work."

In a blur, she managed to get out the door, but instead of going to her car, she searched for a place to lay the package. If it was a bomb, it was probably a plastic explosive, and she had no idea how far the explosion might reach.

The house sat on a two-acre lot with most of it between the house and street. The best place looked to be the middle of the yard near the hundred-year-old pin oak. She'd hate to lose the tree she'd climbed to the very top of as a kid, but she set the package ten yards from it and double-timed it to the front steps, dialing Boone on the way.

"Tell me you're almost to my house."

"I may have a problem," she said and tried to get her breath. What if she was wrong? She'd never live it down.

"What is it?"

"I'm at the Judge's and someone left a birthday present on the doorstep for me. No name on it but mine. I have this feeling . . . it's probably nothing . . ."

"But it may not be nothing. I'm on my way."

"The package is under the big tree in the front yard." Just knowing he was coming eased the tension in her chest. *The text.* She hadn't told him about it. There would be consequences to pay.

Then she had a worse thought. What if she'd let Erin open the package? And there had been a bomb inside it?

# 15

THERE WAS JUST ENOUGH ROOM for Boone's truck to get by the cars parked in the driveway. His lights caught Rachel with her arms hugged close to her body as she stood on the stoop of the huge two-story brick structure that was the Judge's house. She looked quite different from when he last saw her. Heels and a sleeveless, formfitting dress were not normal detective attire—in spite of what was shown on TV.

He hadn't expected to see her standing alone. Where was her father? It had occurred to him if the package did contain a bomb, it could be meant for Judge Winslow. He was certain to have made a few enemies during his career.

Boone parked and climbed out of his truck, glancing toward the tree where a white package lay on the ground. He dialed the head of the bomb squad and filled him in on exactly where the package was, and then walked toward the house where Rachel waited at the steps. "The bomb squad is on the way," he said.

She closed her eyes as if gathering strength. "There's something I should have told you earlier."

Sentences that started out with those words never ended well. "Go on."

"I . . ." Rachel swallowed and opened her eyes, leveling her gaze at him. "I received a text this afternoon telling me to drop the case or I'd live to regret it."

"What?"

Rachel flinched. "I'm sorry."

"You're sorry? What if"—he turned and pointed toward the package—"that is a bomb? And you had opened it in the house?"

"You can't say anything I haven't already thought. I made a stupid mistake."

"Yes, you did. Why didn't you tell me?"

"I didn't want to give you a reason to take me off the case." She folded her arms across her chest. "You want to anyway."

"Why is this case that important to you?"

Her mouth twitched. "I told you already. A man is dead because I didn't act fast enough."

"That's no excuse for not telling me about the text. I could have already traced the number."

"I'm not exactly stupid. I traced the message back to the phone it came from. A burner from a discount store. No ID required when paying with cash."

Boone rocked back on his heels. Rachel's tenacity was a plus but . . . He eyed her grimly. "No more withholding information. Got that?"

Her nostrils flared slightly. "Got it."

He glanced toward the house. "Have you told your father what's going on?"

She shook her head. "In spite of the text, I couldn't wrap my head around someone wanting to harm me. I figured you'd take one look at the package and say it was nothing."

"Do you want me to fill him in?"

He thought she was going to say yes, but then she shook her head. "No, I'll do it."

Before Rachel had a chance to head inside, her father opened the front door and stepped onto the porch.

"Rachel, what's going on? And Boone, what are you doing here?"

Rachel glanced at Boone. "There was a little problem," she said.

Boone offered his hand. "Good to see you again, sir. Sorry it's under these circumstances."

"What circumstances do you mean? What's going on?"

Rachel lifted her chin. "The present, the one Terri found on the front porch. It may have a bomb in it."

"What?" The judge rubbed his forehead and shifted his gaze to Boone. "But . . . why would anyone . . ."

"I don't know, sir," he said. "Just wanted to let you know what was going on before you heard the sirens."

Right on cue, the not-too-distant wail of sirens could be heard. "That should be the bomb squad. We'll need you and your guests to stay inside until it's clear."

"I understand." He shot Rachel a look Boone couldn't read. "I suppose bomb threats are to be expected in your current line of work."

Boone flinched as what little color had been in Rachel's face disappeared.

"I—"

Winslow silenced her with his upraised hand. "Don't tell me we would be standing here discussing a bomb if you had remained with the law firm."

"That's enough, Lucien." A soft but firm voice came from the doorway.

Boone turned as Rachel's grandmother stepped outside the house and onto the porch. Tall, and like the Judge, her regal bearing commanded respect.

"Gran, you shouldn't—"

"I shouldn't what, Rachel? If something is going on, I want to know what it is."

"That package she wouldn't open is possibly a bomb," her father said.

"Excuse me, sir," Boone said. He felt the need to defend Rachel against her father's anger. "If it is a bomb, there is a possibility your daughter isn't the target. You could be."

Rachel's eyes widened. Evidently a threat toward her father had not crossed her mind. "You may want to let your guests know what's going on," he said. "Just don't let any of them leave the house until we give the okay."

Winslow gave a terse nod. When he'd gone, the older woman came closer.

"Boone," she said, "it is so good to see you again."

"Thank you, Mrs. Winslow," he said, taking the hand she held out, wincing as she raised her eyebrows. "Adele," he corrected.

She smiled and then turned somber. "Is my granddaughter in danger?"

"That's what we're trying to find out." He wished Rachel had told him about the threatening text earlier. The sirens grew louder, and Boone turned as blue lights flashed at the end of the drive. "Please stay inside until we know what we're dealing with."

"Gran?"

Everyone turned as Erin stood in the doorway. She'd had a haircut since this morning, and the shorter cut made her look even younger. Or maybe it was the way she looked up at Rachel's grandmother with childlike innocence.

"Erin," Adele said. "Please go back to the party."

"But something is wrong. Everyone is acting funny."

Rachel hurried to Erin's side. "It's going to be okay, but you need to go back to the den."

It touched him the way Rachel was never impatient with Erin. In fact, it was obvious the whole family cherished her.

Erin turned and caught sight of him. "Boone! You came to the party. You'll tell me what's wrong."

"It's nothing that concerns you. Just police work, and after it's

104

over, someone will explain, but right now you need to do what Rachel said."

"Okay." Erin looked down at his feet. "Cowboy boots. They're my favorite." She lifted her gaze and smiled at him. "I like you. You're cute." Then she turned to Rachel. "If you don't marry him, I am."

"Erin!" Rachel looked over her shoulder toward the door. "Where's Terri?"

"Talking to Nana." The pint-sized woman put her hands over her ears as another emergency vehicle wailed to a stop. "I don't like that noise."

"Me, either," Adele said. "Let's go back to the party." She started to leave, then turned to Boone. "Please take care of my granddaughter."

"Yes, ma'am."

"Sorry about that," Rachel said when the two had left.

He shot her a quizzical glance. "For . . . ?"

"I can take care of myself, and as for Erin, you've been around her enough to know she pretty much says what's on her mind."

He grinned at her. "I kind of like what both of them said."

Rachel drew in a shaky breath. "Well . . . thanks for taking up for me in front of my father . . . I don't usually let him get to me like that."

"He's probably just worried."

"No, he really hates me being a cop." She tilted her head toward the driveway. "Do we stay here or—"

"We definitely stay here until the all clear."

◆

Sweat trickled down Rachel's back as the humidity wrapped around her. She and Boone and the other officers had congregated on the lawn far enough away from the package that if it blew, no one would be injured. The robot was in place and inching its way past the live oak tree to the spot where she'd laid the box.

"All this trouble . . . what if it's nothing?" she said to no one in particular.

"Then we'll try to figure out why someone gave you a present and didn't put their name on it." He nudged her. "You never said the party was for you too. Is the gift from a special guy? Maybe there's jewelry in there."

"I can guarantee there's no jewelry, and I don't do birthdays."

"Everybody does birthdays. But I didn't think today was yours."

"It's not." She knew what he was doing. Trying to distract her. But she wasn't about to tell him what day her birthday was if he didn't remember.

"It's Tuesday, same day as your grandmother's."

So he hadn't forgotten. Rachel glanced up at him, her heart hitching as he winked at her. If he meant to distract her, he certainly had. She swallowed down her panic, remembering the way she'd cut and run before. After her husband died, she'd been gun-shy of men for more than one reason. With her thoughts a tangled mess, she shifted her attention back to the yard.

The robot picked up the package with its long arms and moved to the X-ray machine that had been set up. "All clear. No bomb," the tech said.

Her knees wobbled, and she caught herself before anyone noticed. She probably would never hear the end of the jokes, but at least no one wanted to kill her. Stepping off the portico, she said, "Let's see what's in it."

"Wait," Boone said. "Let the experts handle it."

Rachel halted as another K-9 dog approached the package, but he showed no interest. "No drugs, at least. Now can I open it?" Her answer came in the form of a man in a hazmat suit. "Why is—"

"You get the whole enchilada."

"What?"

"They're making sure there's nothing hazardous in it."

"As in poison?" That thought had not even entered her mind. "Who's in the hazmat suit?"

"Rodney Cortez."

She didn't blink as Cortez unwrapped the package. White powder sprayed the air, and he pushed the box away from him without dropping it. Within minutes, he had sealed the box in a plastic bag.

Another officer in a hazmat suit vacuumed up the powder on the ground. Cortez peeled the white suit off and rolled it inside out before sealing it in another plastic bag. He walked the evidence to his van before joining them.

"What do you think it is?" Boone asked.

"Won't know until it's analyzed," he said, glancing toward Rachel. "I'm sorry, but I guarantee it's not good. It was spring-loaded to release when the top of the box was lifted. If it's something like anthrax, everyone in the room could have been affected."

Rachel hugged her waist. She didn't trust her voice to answer, not the way her insides were shaking. Seeing the white powder fly into the air had stunned her, but wrapping her mind around someone actually trying to kill her stretched beyond her grasp. And even though she faced danger every day she strapped on a gun, this was different.

This was personal.

But who and why? She had no past cases that warranted this type of response. And the only homicides on her present caseload were normal gang-related or domestic violence homicides. Except for the Vegas case. But what made it so dangerous?

*What if I told you Harrison's murder is connected to your mother's death.* Vic's words. She couldn't get away from them. And if the three murders were connected, why would that make someone try to kill *her*? The text warned her off the case . . . What if they weren't trying to kill her but trying to get her removed from Vic's case? What did she know that someone was afraid of?

Since she had no proof the deaths were related, she would hold on to her suspicion until there was something tangible to take to Boone. Until that happened, this was her case. Period. She looked up into Boone's dark brown eyes studying her and squashed the guilt that flooded her mind.

"Do you want me to tell your father?" Boone asked.

That was twice he'd offered to be a buffer for her. Rachel shifted her gaze to the white van where Cortez had stored the evidence. She'd forgotten all about her dad and the people inside. She straightened her shoulders.

"No. He'll expect a report from me," she said, hating the quiver in her voice. Rachel turned and marched up the steps, her high heels clicking on the concrete.

"Wait, I'm going with you."

He wasn't asking. And she was glad.

Her father waited in the chair by the front window, had probably returned after they left. Terri sat on the sofa, and both of them looked shell-shocked.

"I gather it's not a bomb," he said.

"No." Boone spoke before she had a chance to. "It's some type of white powder. And since it was delivered here rather than her home, I'm not certain it was meant for Rachel. Who found the package?"

"I did." Terri leaned forward and placed her hand on her knees. "I had no idea it might be anything like this—I just can't comprehend this is real." She shifted her gaze from Rachel to Boone. "Who would do something like this?"

"That's what we're going to find out," Boone said.

"I assume my daughter has been put on administrative leave."

"Why would you expect me to be put on leave?" Rachel asked. "If officers were put on leave every time someone threatened their life, there wouldn't be any left to work. Besides, we don't even know if I'm the target."

"But you don't have to worry about her investigating this," Boone said. "If it turns out to be some sort of poison, Tennessee Poison Control will take over the case. And if it's something like anthrax, the feds, as well as the US Marshals' office, will step in since a federal judge is involved. Probably will anyway."

*Tennessee Poison Control. Feds. US Marshals.* She must be more rattled than she thought not to realize how big a deal this was.

The Judge unfolded from the chair, towering over her. "Take a few days off, Rachel."

She held his gaze, not wavering. "I'm sorry, but I can't. Investigating homicides is my job. And what if the package *was* for you? You have more enemies than I do."

"Then it would have had my name on it, not yours. Who are these enemies you might have?"

He would latch on to that. "I misspoke. I don't have any enemies that I know of."

"I believe you have at least one," he said quietly.

# 16

RACHEL BIT BACK THE RETORT on the tip of her tongue. She and her father were like sandpaper, but she relaxed a little as Boone shook the Judge's hand.

"We're finished here," he said and turned to Rachel. "What time did you say the performers would be at Blues & Such?"

She checked her watch. "Now. Are you ready to leave?"

"Give me five minutes to talk to Cortez."

She nodded. That would give her time to see the grandmothers and Erin to let them know she was all right.

Boone was ready to go by the time Rachel came out the front door, and since her house was only a mile away, she agreed to drop her car off there and ride downtown with Boone.

"Thanks for helping me out with the Judge," she said, fastening her seat belt. "You probably saved me from saying something I would have regretted."

"I don't remember such . . . intensity between the two of you. What happened?"

"I don't know." They had been snapping at one another more than usual. Rachel stared straight ahead as twilight slipped away and overhead lights blinked on. "The middle of August is always a hard time, but this year is worse. We've both been edgy for a couple of weeks now."

"Understandable. But tonight was the first time I realized he doesn't like you being a cop. I mean, he's a judge. He ought to be proud of you."

"Oh, he has nothing against the police. You just don't understand our family dynamics. Since I was a child, there were expectations. On both sides." She'd often felt like she was in the middle of a tug-of-war game. "My mom and Nana on one side of the fence and Gran and Dad on the other."

"What do you mean?"

"One side was planning my debutante season from the time I was born and the other my career as an attorney. I'll let you guess which was which. In spite of my mother's death, I did have a debutante season, and then went on to get a law degree, and passed the bar on the first try. But when Corey died, everything unraveled." She sighed. "I thought Dad would have a stroke when I resigned from Silverstone and Webster and entered the police academy."

He turned onto Poplar. "I always wanted to ask what made you do that."

She didn't answer right away, trying to decide how much she wanted to share. "I was bored to death at the law firm. One day I woke up and realized I could stay in a job I hated or I could leave. So I left." She turned to him. "And I love being a cop. Especially a homicide cop."

"You're good, I'll say that. But that was quite a change just because you were bored."

Rachel should have known he wouldn't be satisfied with her answer. As she searched for something that might be acceptable, she realized she hadn't filled him in on her visit to Blues & Such earlier. "Um, there's something I should have already told you. I drove downtown earlier to interview some of the tribute artists that were there last night, but they had left. I interviewed the event's coordinator for the contest instead."

"You're doing it again," Boone said as he stopped at a traffic light.

She turned toward him. The muscle in his jaw pulsed. "Doing what?"

He checked the light and then glanced at her, wistfulness plain in his eyes. "Changing the subject."

"I guess I am." Even if she wanted to open her heart up to Boone, she couldn't. She'd learned that with Corey. Her heart lay in the center of a frozen wasteland, and she couldn't do anything to change it. That Boone was still even interested surprised her.

"If you gave me any encouragement, I'd be willing to transfer out of the department."

"You can't do that. Homicide is your life! I won't be responsible for taking you out of a job you love."

"I'm tired of work being all there is. Don't you ever think about settling down? Getting married and having children?"

Since Corey's death, she'd avoided dating relationships until Boone talked her into getting a cup of coffee one day. "This is getting us nowhere."

A sigh escaped Boone's lips. "Yes, ma'am. Did you learn anything when you went downtown?"

She relaxed a little. "Ms. Monica Carpenter is one uptight lady. I think she's afraid Vic's murder might bring bad publicity to the Supreme Elvis contest."

"Supreme Elvis? Oh, wait, I remember seeing that advertised on TV."

"At first she acted as though she didn't remember Vic Vegas, but I think she knows him better than she indicated." Rachel pulled two folders from the bag she'd retrieved from her car. "I googled her and it looks like Monica Carpenter has been involved in Elvis events for a long time, so it doesn't make sense she wouldn't know Vic."

"Good work," Boone said. He pulled his truck into the same parking garage she'd used earlier.

Thank goodness he'd shifted into detective mode. "After I showed her his photo, she admitted to seeing Vic talk to Randy Culver, one of the contestants. I pulled some information off the internet on him as well." She handed him copies of what she'd printed out.

He scanned the paper, then folded and pocketed it. "Ready?"

She nodded and climbed out of the truck. It had dropped maybe five degrees since the sun went down, but ninety-three was still ninety-three and humid. Even so, Beale Street hummed with tourists and music poured out of the open doors of establishments up and down the street.

Cool air and a voice that sounded remarkably like Elvis singing "All Shook Up" met them at the door of Blues & Such as Rachel followed Boone inside. Energy crackled in the crowd of mostly women whistling and clapping to the beat of the music. Donna waved at her from a corner table. She'd wasted no time in getting here.

"Are you crazy?" Rachel mouthed. She couldn't imagine willingly getting in the middle of this crowd.

Donna laughed and shook her head, then pointed toward Boone: But it was too late. Rachel hadn't seen him stop and bumped into him. He steadied her with his hand on her elbow, and she felt his touch all the way to her shoulder.

"Who would've thought there'd be this many people here," she said over the noise.

"Heard on the news this morning there are people from all over the world in Memphis for Elvis Week," he said and nodded toward the stage. "That guy is pretty good."

Rachel glanced at the performer. Time froze, throwing her back to seventeen years ago. A stage like this one. Her mother mesmerized by the performer. Only it wasn't this Elvis impersonator strumming a guitar. It was Harrison Foxx, and her mother was looking at him in a way she had no right to.

Was that really why her parents were separated? Her mouth dried up. Where had that come from? A hazy memory played just out of reach. Her mother told her to keep her plans and go with her friends. Because she had other plans? Plans she didn't want her daughter to know about? No. Rachel shook off the ridiculous thought. Her mother loved her father and they were working on getting back together.

Rachel jerked as she realized Boone had said something.

"This way," he repeated, pointing toward the steps to the side of the stage.

A Mr. Clean look-alike stopped them, and Boone flashed his badge as Rachel stepped forward.

"We're looking for either Jerome or Ms. Carpenter," she said.

Muscle-bound pointed toward a side door. "Go through there. You'll find them in the staging area."

"Can you tell me what Jerome's last name is?" Rachel said.

"Winters."

The staging area held more white jumpsuits and black pompadours than Rachel had ever seen in one place, even seventeen years ago. She spied the event coordinator talking to one of the artists and called her name.

Monica Carpenter turned and palmed her hands when she saw Rachel. "Not now, Detective."

"If you don't have time, could you direct me to Jerome Winters?"

She jerked her thumb toward the stage. "He's introducing the next contestant. Can't this wait until we're finished?"

Without answering, Rachel turned toward the stage. Jerome must be the one not wearing satin and sequins and holding a microphone. Midforties. And possibly wearing something to hold his stomach in. That or he worked out.

"Ladies, and the one or two gentlemen I see out there," he said, his mellow baritone flowing from the speakers, "our next contestant is Randy Culver, coming to us from right here in Memphis where he was runner-up Supreme Elvis Tribute Artist of the Year last year. Let's see if he has what it takes to win the whole thing this year. Please give Randy a warm welcome."

He clapped his hands, encouraging the audience to do the same before he stepped to the other side of the stage and Culver stepped into the spotlight with his guitar.

Randy Culver. One of the names Monica had mentioned earlier. His name was on the back of the photo, and Rachel pulled it out and compared the singer to the men in the photo. Third man from Foxx on the right. Unlike Vic, Culver had aged well, but then he'd been much younger seventeen years ago. She turned and handed the photo to Boone as Culver sang to the crowd.

Shivers ran over her body as the dulcet tones of "Can't Help Falling in Love" flowed from his lips. She glanced at the audience. They were on the edge of their seats, spellbound. Rachel wouldn't be surprised if Randy Culver won this year's Supreme Elvis contest—if she could vote, he'd have hers.

But what if he turned out to be a viable suspect in Vic's murder? Not to mention, he was around when Harrison Foxx was murdered. It was quite a coincidence that he was now connected to two murders—three if she counted her mother's death.

She could see jealousy or ambition as a motive for Culver killing Foxx, and even if Culver thought Vic had evidence pointing toward him. But what motive would Culver have for killing her mother?

Motive. Once she knew that, she could find her mother's killer.

# 17

BOONE SCANNED THE INFORMATION Rachel had pulled off the internet about Randy Culver. Thirty-seven, truck driver, singer. She'd also added a handwritten note that Culver had competed against Vegas and Foxx seventeen years ago.

After the last guitar chord, Jerome Winters popped back on stage and again asked for a big round of applause. Boone was waiting for Culver when he walked off.

"Culver," he said, catching the singer's attention.

He turned, and his gaze slid to Rachel as she joined Boone. "Yes?" he said, not taking his eyes off her.

Was he checking out the detective? Couldn't say Boone blamed him. The way the dress hugged Rachel's curves almost made *him* forget he was her superior. Something he needed to keep in mind, even if he believed she cared for him.

Six months ago he'd thought they'd been on the way to something special. They had connected and the chemistry was good between them. She'd been loosening up, and then suddenly *wham*! She turned into an ice statue and the next thing he knew she was breaking off the relationship. No explanation, other than the transfer into Homicide. Boone didn't believe that was the whole story.

He focused his attention on the job at hand as Rachel flashed her badge with a little more attitude than was necessary.

"We'd like to ask you a few questions," she said, her voice all business.

Culver narrowed his eyes, his interest abruptly waning. "What about?"

"A murder investigation," Boone replied.

His eyes widened. "Why don't we go down to the green room," he said. "No, there'll be too many listening ears there. If you can ignore the noise, how about my table on the floor?"

They followed the singer to a table with an elaborately decorated gift basket sitting on it. "Randy Culver" was spelled out in glitter on the purple ribbon, and beside the basket was a blue bag with a medical cross on it.

While not exactly quiet, it would do. Culver moved the gift basket to a chair and sat where he could see the stage. With Rachel to his right, Boone took the chair against the wall. Since Iraq, he liked to sit where he didn't have to worry about his back.

"What's this all about?" Culver asked.

"Vic Vegas," Boone said.

"What about him?" Culver looked around. "He should be around here somewhere."

It was hard to believe he hadn't heard about the murder. It should have been on the evening news and had definitely played on the radio. And Ms. Carpenter knew. Evidently she hadn't mentioned it, either.

"He's dead," Boone said.

"What?" Culver rocked back in the chair. "How?"

"Someone shot him."

"Jealous husband?"

Was he serious? From the look on the singer's face, he was. Or Culver was trying to divert attention away from himself.

Culver blinked his eyes like he was trying to clear them, then he grabbed a water. "I don't know why I'm so thirsty. Let me check my glucose level first. Be right back."

"Glucose level? Are you a diabetic?"

"Yeah." He checked his watch. "Oh, wait, it's past time for my shot."

Culver grabbed a water bottle from the basket, then picked up the blue bag and took out a vial of clear liquid. He filled a syringe almost halfway and capped it. "Be right back."

While they waited, Boone eyed the designer bottles of water with gold labels in the basket. He'd seen the brand at the gym but had never felt the need to spend almost five dollars on water. Then he noticed the sugar-free candies.

When the singer returned, Boone nodded at the basket. "Is that from a fan?"

Culver uncapped the bottle and took a long draw. "Yeah. Not sure who. Monica said it was sitting on one of the tables when she got here tonight. But I would have known it was for me even without my name on it since it has sugar-free candy and drinks in it."

"So your fans know you're diabetic?" Rachel said.

"Yeah. I've never made a secret of it, in fact, just the opposite," he said. "You know, educating the public."

"I had a friend that way. He made sure I knew what insulin he was taking so that if anything happened when we were together, I could inform whoever responded to the emergency," Boone said. He made a note about Culver being diabetic and then looked up. "You said earlier that a jealous husband might have killed Vegas. Why?"

Culver lifted his shoulder in a half shrug. "Vic was really friendly with everyone, especially the women. Sometimes husbands took exception. Not that he ever meant anything by his attention, but even at his age, he still got some fancy gifts from female fans—there's just something about being on that stage that gets to women. And he enjoyed it," he said, sliding his gaze to Rachel again. "Like me, he wasn't married, so why not?"

Color rose in her cheeks. "Do you know if he had any girl-friends?"

"Didn't know him that well. It's not like we hung out together or anything. Only saw him at these contests, and the past few years he wasn't around as much. Heard he was doing parties and that kind of thing." Culver looked past them to the stage. "Parties are about all you do when you reach his age."

Boone pulled the photo from his shirt and handed it to him. "Is that you on the right?"

He took the photo and stared at it. "Oh, wow. That's from way back when." He looked closer and then lifted his gaze to Rachel. "That's you, handing Foxx the trophy. You're still quite the looker."

It amused Boone the way her lips twitched. He could have told the singer Rachel wasn't impressed or comfortable receiving compliments.

Rachel focused on her notebook. "Did you see him with anyone last night?"

"He was all over the place, working the crowd like a politician. You would've thought he was in the competition—part of the vote is based on the crowd's applause. But just one person . . . ?" The singer started to shake his head. "Wait . . . yeah, I did. Saw him sitting at the back." He pointed across the room to a dark corner. "He was with some woman. Don't remember what she looked like, just that I thought they were having a deep discussion the way their heads were together."

Rachel scribbled in her notepad. "Are you sure you can't de-scribe her?"

He laughed. "Look at this place. It's packed with women. Hon-estly, there's always women hanging around. You get to where you don't pay any attention to them. Sorry."

"Did you talk to him last night?" Boone asked.

He took a sip of water. "I was really busy all night, but we spoke a couple of times."

"About . . . ?" Boone asked. Getting information from Culver was like pulling teeth.

"He wanted to talk about old times. Vegas was at the top of his game when I first got into this Elvis tribute business. He and a friend of his gave me a few tips." He tipped the bottle of water up and finished it off.

"Harrison Foxx?" Rachel asked.

He almost choked on the water. "How did you know?"

"Last night, did he say anything about Foxx's murder?"

Culver turned to answer Boone. "Yeah. Vic brought up Harrison and his murder every time we ran into each other. It was getting to where I tried to avoid him, and when I couldn't I'd just nod my head like I was listening." He rubbed the side of his jaw. "You know, now that I think about it, he was upset that last time I saw him."

"What was he upset about?" Boone noticed Culver bouncing his knees.

"He was going on about some woman he just talked to." The singer fanned himself with his shirt. "Are you two warm?"

"Not really," Boone said. While it was a little stuffy, it wasn't hot enough to cause the kind of sweating Culver was doing. "What about the woman?"

The singer pulled a handkerchief from his pocket and mopped his face. "He had this necklace . . . asked if I'd ever seen it before."

"Culver!" Jerome walked toward them and jerked his head toward the stage. "Time for your second song."

He nodded toward the emcee. "Coming." With a shrug, he stood. "Sorry. Can we finish this when I'm done?"

"Sure," Boone said. Sweat still beaded the singer's face. "You okay?"

"Yeah. Once I'm on the stage, I'll be fine."

Culver started toward the stage and stopped to grab another bottle of water, downing it while he waited for the cue to go on.

"What do you think?" Rachel asked.

"I don't know," he said as Culver tossed the empty water bottle in the trash and stepped onstage. "He was nervous and that might have been why he was so hot. I definitely want to know more about that necklace."

They both turned toward the stage as Jerome announced Culver's name. When the first chords of "Jailhouse Rock" started, screams from the audience almost drowned out Culver's raspy imitation of Presley's voice.

"I liked the first song better," Boone said.

"I don't know. This one has a sound all its own," Rachel said. "I'd like to know what woman Vic talked to last night."

Suddenly, the only sound coming from the stage was the recorded music. Then a woman screamed, and Boone jerked his gaze to the stage. Culver's knees buckled and he collapsed on the floor.

Boone jumped up, and Rachel grabbed the blue medical bag, and they both raced to the side of the platform. The singer lay facedown on the floor.

# 18

Rachel reached Culver first. She placed the blue medical bag on the floor and turned him over, noting his gray face as Monica Carpenter crowded in. "Call 911."

"Already have," she said. "They said to keep him still, that paramedics were stationed on Beale Street. They should be here soon."

Boone knelt beside Culver's body. "He's breathing," he said. "Have you checked his heart rate?"

Rachel felt his neck for the carotid artery. "It's really slow." She looked up at Boone. "He said he was a diabetic. Do you think his blood sugar dropped?"

"Does he have a glucose monitor?"

Rachel felt Culver's pockets. No monitor. "Maybe he has one in the bag." She unzipped the small tote. All of Culver's medical supplies were neatly arranged inside. The capped needle he'd used was secured with an elastic band, as was a small vial of insulin that looked like the one he'd drawn from earlier.

"Here's the vial he used." She peered closer. "Says it's Lantus." She searched the side pockets. "That's crazy—there's a place for a meter, but it's not here."

"He had it earlier. Check the table."

She stood and almost bumped into the event planner.

"Have you given him candy?" Carpenter said. "Once before he almost passed out, and he popped a piece of candy in his mouth."

"I don't think we need to do that." She didn't know much about diabetics, but she knew enough to not give an unconscious person anything.

Donna intercepted Rachel as she hurried to the table where they'd been sitting.

"Is he going to be okay?" she asked as she set her oversized purse in a chair.

"I don't know." Rachel didn't see a monitor on the table. She looked around the basket in the chair and then under the table. No monitor.

"What are you looking for?"

"A glucose monitor. There wasn't one in his tote."

Donna helped her look. "It's not in the chairs," she said.

They searched the area thoroughly for the meter. Where were the paramedics? Almost fifteen minutes passed before they burst into the restaurant.

"He's on the stage," Rachel said and followed them out to where Culver had collapsed. She stayed out of their way but chewed her nails as the medics put him under oxygen and started an IV.

"He injected insulin about fifteen minutes before he collapsed," Boone said. "And he indicated it was his nighttime dose. The bottle he drew the insulin from is in that blue bag."

"Thanks, we'll take it from here," the medic said.

"Do you think he could've injected the wrong insulin?" Boone persisted. "I had a friend with diabetes and he worried about that."

"We'll check it." He kept working on Culver.

Rachel nudged her partner. "We're in the way."

Boone nodded, and they moved off the stage.

"The monitor wasn't at the table," she said. Her feet were killing her, and she wished she could take her heels off.

"It has to be somewhere around here," Boone said.

She agreed. "What do you think happened? He was acting kind of funny after he injected himself."

"What if there was something other than insulin in the vial?" Boone glanced toward the basket. "Or someone put something in his water?"

Their gazes locked. Rachel moved first, limping toward the table where they'd been sitting. The remaining water bottle was gone.

She scanned the area. With everyone huddled near the stage entrance, it would be easy enough for someone to whisk the water away unnoticed. *He was drinking water before he went on stage.* She jerked her head toward the trash basket where Culver had tossed his last bottle. Boone must have had the same idea, and she let him take the lead.

Yes. An empty water bottle with a gold label lay on top of the trash.

Boone produced a handkerchief and retrieved it. "Find a to-go bag to put this in. We'll send it for testing—just in case this is more than him being diabetic," he said.

Rachel asked a waitress for a couple of bags and was given several. She held one of them open, and Boone dropped the bottle inside. Suddenly, a cramp attacked her calf, and she bent down to massage her leg. It would be heaven to get out of the heels. She should have changed shoes when they dropped her car off.

"Maybe we're making too much of this," she said and looked up, catching concern in his brown eyes.

"I don't think so." He frowned. "Are you okay?"

She straightened. "Yeah, just tired."

"Come on, let's sit down."

She slowly followed him to the table where they'd sat earlier, sinking down on the padded chair and propped her feet on the one beside it. "Yeah, that's better."

"Good." His lips curved up.

His smile teased her already upside-down emotions. What was wrong with her? She glanced at her watch. Almost ten thirty. And suddenly it hit her. Seventeen years ago her mom would have been preparing to leave the convention center to go home. She swallowed down the lump in her throat and banished the thoughts of what happened next.

Another thought blindsided her. What if she'd opened the package earlier tonight? More than likely she would have died on the seventeenth anniversary of her mother's death. The thought chilled her through and through, and Rachel rubbed her hands up and down her arms.

She looked up at Boone. "What happened earlier at the birthday party may be making us overly suspicious. Maybe the missing water is no more than someone just coming along and grabbing it. And it's possible Culver just took too much insulin."

Boone glanced toward the stage. "But what if the killer thought Vic told Culver something incriminating? I'd like to get that vial and have the contents analyzed."

Rachel followed his gaze and winced as one of the paramedics pulled the insulin vial from the bag. So much for checking for fingerprints. "I wonder if we can get a sample of the insulin? And from the syringe?"

Boone nodded approvingly. "Good thinking." He grabbed two of the to-go bags and walked back to the stage.

She watched as he and the lead paramedic talked, then Boone allowed the medic to draw insulin from the vial and inject it into a tube. When he finished, Boone placed the needle and vial in separate bags and returned to the table.

"Why did the paramedic want insulin from the vial?" Rachel asked. From the corner of her eye, she saw Donna approaching.

"So the hospital can analyze it and make sure it isn't contaminated." He frowned as Donna joined them. "What in the world are you doing here?"

"I don't suppose you found the glucose monitor?" Rachel's question was lost as Boone's voice overrode hers.

Color crept into Donna's face. "Ah . . . watching the show?" she said, answering Boone's question.

"She's a big Elvis fan," Rachel said. "I saw her when we first arrived."

"Elvis? Really?" Boone said.

"Why not?" Donna said. "If you look a little closer at the audience, you'll see a lot of older women," she said, lifting her chin. "Like Lucinda Vetch over there. She's been here every night too."

Rachel glanced at the platinum blonde Donna indicated. She looked familiar.

"I found this. Is it what you were looking for?" Donna held up a tissue-wrapped object. "It doesn't say it's a meter, but it looks like it might be one."

Rachel gasped. "You did find it. Where?"

"In the men's restroom." Red crept into Donna's face again. "But I made sure no one was in there first."

Culver must have left it there. Being careful not to disturb the paper, she took the meter and placed it in the last bag, then looked up as Monica Carpenter joined them.

"Is he going to make it?" she asked.

"I don't know. Did either of you see anyone take any of his water from the basket?" Rachel asked.

"What water?" The event planner's oversized glasses had slipped down her nose, and she used her thumb to push them back.

Rachel pointed toward the basket. "There were four bottles of water with a gold label tucked in it when we sat down. He drank three of them and the other one is missing."

"Maybe someone was just thirsty," Donna said.

"I'm sure they're here somewhere or at least the empty containers should be," Carpenter said, twisting a green emerald on her finger. "Why would anyone steal water from his basket, anyway?

126

The fridge over there is stocked with all kinds of things for the performers, including water."

"Do you mind helping us search for the missing bottle?" Boone asked.

"Right now?" She frowned. "Maybe for a few minutes, but as soon as the paramedics leave with Randy, I've got to get the show back on track before we lose all of the audience."

"You're not canceling the rest of the contest tonight?" Rachel glanced at the crowd, surprised that most of them hadn't left, but sat somber, waiting for something to happen. Somehow, she thought that the rest of the show would be put off until tomorrow.

"Of course not. Randy wouldn't want us to cancel." Then Monica gave both of them an odd glance. "This isn't a crime scene, is it? I mean, he just let his sugar get too low, right?"

Boone exchanged glances with Rachel. They really didn't have a crime scene. Just because Culver collapsed didn't mean someone had tried to kill him.

"No," Boone said. "At least not yet."

Rachel glanced toward the stage. The medics had Culver on a gurney now, and he didn't look good. He was so pale. Like a corpse. And still unconscious.

◆

Boone found a uniformed officer and handed him the to-go bags. "Have the lab check for fingerprints, and I want the contents of the items analyzed. And I need it yesterday."

There was at least one lab tech on night duty, so he should get the results within a couple of hours. Then he made a sweep of the upstairs, looking for more bottles with the gold designer label. Finding none, he returned to the main floor, where Rachel joined him. "I meant to ask earlier, how did Donna find the monitor?" he asked. "And why was she looking for it?"

"She was at the table when I went to look for it, and when the paramedics came, I guess she kept looking." Rachel smiled. "I can't see her barging into the men's restroom, though."

It was hard to imagine the fastidious office manager being an Elvis fan, much less going into the men's restroom. "Where did she go?"

"Home. She's working tomorrow, so I told her to leave, that if we had questions, we'd get them then," she said.

"Don't suppose you found any more gold label bottles."

"No. And no one else received the designer water. Do you think Monica could be right and we're chasing a phantom clue?" she asked.

He glanced toward the stage, where Jerome was introducing another performer. Monica had disappeared right after the paramedics transported Culver to Regional One, which was the nearest hospital, and the show had started a few minutes later. "Possible, but my gut says otherwise."

"Uh-oh." Rachel nodded toward the stage.

Monica was marching toward him with her oversized glasses on top of her head, and she did not look happy.

"I hope you're done here," she said. "You're making the customers nervous."

"We're almost finished," Boone said. "Just a couple more questions. Did you happen to see who delivered Culver's gift basket?"

She shook her head. "All the baskets were here when I returned around five thirty. I'm sure one of the waitstaff will know something." She frowned. "But what's the big deal? Randy's sugar has gotten out of whack before. It's not like someone tried to kill him."

"But what if they did? We have one Elvis impersonator murdered—"

"Tribute artist, please!" Monica pursed her lips. "And Randy isn't dead."

"Does everyone know he has diabetes?" Rachel asked.

"Yes. He never tried to hide it, had actually made a public service video promoting the Diabetes Foundation." She settled the glasses on her nose. "And if that's all . . ."

"One more small thing," he said. "If you don't mind, would you round up all the performers who were backstage earlier? I'd like to get a statement from each of them."

"Statement?" Monica stared at Boone as though he'd lost his mind.

"Just in case this turns out to be more than it looks like." They would know more when the insulin analysis came back, and if there was anything suspicious, they'd at least have statements from the performers.

"Have you heard how Randy is?" she asked.

"I checked with the hospital. He's on a ventilator." Boone rubbed the back of his neck.

Monica paled. "Poor thing. I hope he pulls through. I'll see what I can do about getting the performers together."

By the time he and Rachel had finished interviewing anyone who had contact with Culver backstage, it was nearing midnight. "Are you up for talking about this before we leave?"

"Sure."

He led the way back to the table and took the same chair he'd sat in before.

"Do you always sit with your back to the wall?" she asked as she kicked off her shoes.

"Yep. Are your feet hurting?" A strand of her blonde hair had come loose from the ponytail, and he resisted tucking it back in place.

"A little." She pumped her feet. "Why do you sit against the wall?"

"Seems the thing to do." A memory from the past darkened his thoughts. A memory he didn't want to talk about. "What did you learn from the employees?"

Rachel studied him for a minute and then took out her notes.

"A few of the waitstaff saw the baskets arrive, but they didn't pay attention to the person delivering them. They couldn't be sure they saw the one Randy had gotten since at least five other performers received similar gifts." She looked up from her notes. "By the way, Terri delivered two of the baskets from a shop on Union, and I checked the tags—she didn't deliver Randy's, but she spoke to him."

"How do you know?"

"One of the hostesses saw her at his table talking to him a little after five."

"And the water bottles?"

"No one remembered seeing anyone take the water—everyone's attention was on the stage after he collapsed."

"Not surprising." His cell phone dinged a message, and Boone paused to read it. He'd expected something like this. He looked up, and Rachel questioned him with her eyebrows. "Lab report."

"The bottle tested positive for something?"

"Yes, Humulin R U-500. But it's worse than that. You remember the bottle he drew his insulin from?"

"Lantus-something."

"Lantus 100." Frowning, he looked back at his phone.

"So?"

"This report says the insulin in the needle was the Humulin as well—it's five times stronger than Lantus 100. If he took his usual dosage, that's what caused his sugar to drop. It's a wonder it hadn't killed him outright."

"You think he put the wrong insulin in the syringe? I'm sure it happens sometimes."

"No. The wrong insulin had to be in the vial."

"What?" Her eyes widened.

"I remember when he took the vial out, it was half full, so it wasn't a pharmaceutical error."

"But that would mean someone loaded a Lantus bottle with the stronger insulin . . ."

He leaned back in the chair. "Yes. They meant to kill him."

Rachel hooked the loose strand of hair behind her ear. "I've been thinking about something since his collapse. If Vic's and Foxx's murders are connected to this attempt on Culver, we could be dealing with a serial—"

"Don't even go there." He did not want there to be a serial murderer running around killing Elvis impersonators.

"If Culver dies, that will make three victims . . ."

"He's not going to die," Boone said grimly. "And three murders do not always mean there's a serial killer on the loose. Besides, the cooling-off period doesn't work. They don't go cold for seventeen years and then commit two murders in twenty-four hours."

"We could be dealing with a plain old sociopath then. And if we are, all bets are off."

"A sociopath?" he repeated. "You're just full of fun suggestions."

"Just trying to be helpful. But if that's what our killer is, there's no way to anticipate what he or she might do."

"I know." He'd read once that 4 percent of Americans were sociopaths with no conscience and could do whatever they pleased without feelings of guilt. Sometimes he thought that was a low percentage.

She tilted her head. "You ever do the test to see if you could think like a sociopath?"

"What?" He frowned. His studies about the criminally insane didn't include a test on thinking like one.

"You know the one. A sociopath is at her mother's funeral and meets a man, gives him her phone number. He promises to call, but doesn't. After a week, she kills her sister. Why did she kill her sister?"

Boone stared at Rachel. Maybe he was just tired, but the question didn't make sense. He shook his head to clear it, and then said, "Okay, I'll bite. Why did she kill her sister?"

"So she could see him again. If he came to her mother's funeral, he would come to the sister's." She gave him a crooked smile. "Glad to know you don't think like a sociopath."

In a crazy sort of way, it made sense and fit what he knew about their behavior. "Heaven help us if we're dealing with someone who thinks like that."

"I know. If we do and he's fixated on Elvis impersonators, we could have a real problem on our hands."

"But why would he threaten you?" Thinking aloud, he answered his own question. "Because you're investigating the crime. But why not me as well?"

She shook her head. "If we're dealing with a psychopath, there's no way to justify anything he does. There's one other thing—Culver could have purposely used the wrong medicine. It wouldn't be the first time someone used insulin to commit suicide."

Boone rocked back in the chair. He hadn't even thought about suicide. "Culver doesn't come across as the type to kill himself. And if he did, he went to a lot of trouble to make it not look like suicide. Are you up for stopping by the Med to check on him?"

"You bet."

He waited while Rachel slipped her shoes on, and then they walked to where he'd parked his truck. The drive to Regional One took less than five minutes since it was only a few blocks away.

They caught the doctor coming out of Randy Culver's room.

"Doc," Boone said, showing his badge, "could you give us a few minutes?"

"I don't know how much I can help you, but sure."

"How is he?" Rachel asked.

"It's touch and go. The lab reports indicated the insulin he used was Humulin R U-500 rather than the lower dose of insulin he was supposed to take. He's lucky to be alive."

"Do you know how that could have happened?" Boone asked.

"His doctor could have changed his medication, and he mixed up the bottles."

"The vial was labeled Lantus 100."

The doctor frowned. "But that would mean—"

"Afraid so. How hard is it to get insulin?"

"Not hard at all if you have a prescription."

"And if you don't?" Rachel asked.

"I'm sure you can get it on the black market, but if I were going to do something like this, I'd steal it from a friend who is diabetic."

That scenario had already crossed Boone's mind. "Do you think the friend would report the theft?"

The doctor shook his head. "Might not realize it's gone for a couple months. A lot of diabetics buy three-month supplies."

"Do you think he's going to make it?" Boone asked, nodding toward the room. "And if he does, will there be brain damage?"

"Hard to say. He's in a coma right now. If he pulls out of this, he may not remember anything surrounding the incident."

Boone handed him a card. "Give me a call if there's any change."

As they descended the outside stairs, Boone eyed Rachel's heels. "How have you walked in those all night?"

She leaned against the wall and took one shoe off, massaging her foot. "Not well. I don't know why I didn't grab a pair of sandals earlier."

"Stay right here and I'll get my truck."

After pulling to the curb, he got out and opened the passenger door and she limped to it. Once she climbed in and fastened her seat belt, he returned to the driver side. "We've done about all we can do tonight," he said, starting the motor. "But first thing after you get a couple hours of sleep, will you get your father to sign a search warrant for Culver's house and meet me there at nine?"

"Do we have anyone else who will sign one?"

He hesitated with his hand on the gearshift. "Why don't you want to ask your father?"

"You saw how he acted tonight. I'm not exactly his favorite cop and don't know if he'd even give me one."

"He will. Or I can ask, if you'd rather."

She didn't say anything, and then she sighed. "No. I'll ask him. And nine isn't a problem. I'll catch him before he goes to church."

A text chimed on Boone's phone and he glanced down, wincing at the message.

"What is it?" Rachel asked. "Has Culver died?"

"No. It's about the package at your father's." He gripped the steering wheel. "The white powder was ricin."

# 19

AT SEVEN THIRTY, Rachel parked in front of her father's house and picked up the Sunday paper in the drive. Her father was an early riser, so she was surprised it was still there.

She'd texted him half an hour ago that she was stopping by. The sooner this was behind her, the better. In spite of her resolve, her gaze shifted to the yellow crime scene tape that cordoned off the area where Cortez had opened the box.

Had it been only twelve hours ago that someone had tried to kill her with ricin, of all things? And then tried to kill Randy Culver? It was no accident that the vial had been filled with insulin five times the strength labeled on the bottle.

As for the ricin, Boone had received a partial analysis on the white powder. The substance had been mostly flour, laced with traces of the poison. But even a trace of ricin was more than enough to kill.

Questions filled her mind. Who hated her that much? Or wanted her out of the way? Or was it meant for her father? And how had they gotten their hands on ricin in the first place? It wasn't a substance that was readily available to just anyone, not the quality this tested. If she'd opened the box inside the house . . . When she'd googled ricin and saw what a horrible death it caused and that there was no antidote, she'd almost thrown up.

Rachel slipped the newspaper out of the plastic sleeve and glanced at the front page. August thirteenth. A band tightened around her chest, cutting off her breath. Seventeen years ago at this precise time, she'd been walking up the drive just as she was now. She closed her eyes, trying to block the memory of finding her mother in the library, dead from a blow to her head.

Was it possible the burglary scene had been staged? The police thought the thief panicked after her mother died and fled, leaving a pillowcase with a computer, silver tea set, and sterling silverware at the back door.

Rachel faltered. She couldn't do this. Why hadn't she told Boone to find another judge to sign the warrant? She slipped her phone from her pocket and fumbled for the buttons.

*"Buck up, Rachel. Winslows don't cry."* Her father's voice from all those years ago stopped her. *"Your mother is dead and crying will not bring her back. We have to do the next thing."* She didn't understand him then, and she still didn't. But she hadn't cried for anyone since, not even when Corey died. She might as well put on her big girl shoes and deal with it.

With a fortifying breath, she walked to the back of the house and entered through the back door. "Anybody home?" she called, wincing at the tremor in her voice.

"In the breakfast nook," her father replied. "Grab a cup of coffee in the kitchen and bring it in here. I'm curious to know what you want."

He knew she wasn't coming just to visit—a sad commentary on the state of their relationship. She grabbed a napkin and then found her favorite mug in the cupboard and filled it with the dark roast the Judge favored. She didn't have to worry about weak coffee here.

"How are you this morning?" she asked.

"Fine. And you, after what happened last night?"

Did he know about Culver? *No.* He was talking about the package. "I'm fine as well." Winslows were never anything but fine. She sat at the end of the table where she could watch the birds outside the bay window. Her mother had decorated the breakfast nook in pale yellows and had left the window untreated, allowing the morning sun full rein. It was her favorite room in the house. Surprisingly, the Judge hadn't changed anything. "I hope what happened didn't ruin Gran's party completely."

"She's stoic." He tented his fingers and studied her. "Worried about you, though."

"I wish she wouldn't." Rachel held his gaze, waiting.

He tilted his head. "Why didn't you want to be a lawyer?"

Her hands jerked, sloshing coffee on the linen tablecloth.

"I'm sorry." Rachel dabbed at the beaded drops of brown liquid with her napkin. The Judge had never asked that question outright.

"Why would that upset you so?"

Buzzing in her ears drowned out his words as she stared at the coffee stain spreading over the linen cloth. When had the Judge started using her mother's favorite tablecloth? The one she'd just ruined. She could not do this today. Rachel stood. "I'm sorry. I have to leave."

She made it as far as the door before he spoke.

"Don't leave."

Something in his voice turned her around.

"I know what today is, and I'm sure you're reliving finding her in the library."

Great. He'd remembered while she'd tried to forget.

"Besides, you haven't told me what you want."

Always practical. Well, she could be too. "I need you to sign a search warrant." Did she detect disappointment in his eyes?

"Do you have it with you?"

"Of course." She pulled it from her bag and handed it to him. "You trained me well."

"Get another cup of coffee while I look it over."

She grabbed her mug and took it to the kitchen. "Would you like your cup topped off?" she called.

When he declined, she returned to the table and sat down.

He pushed the signed affidavit toward her. "You had a full day yesterday. Any word on the mysterious powder?"

"You haven't been told yet?" She figured the US Marshal had already informed him. "It was ricin."

His cup rattled in the saucer when he set it down hard. "What? Homemade?"

"I don't know." She knew he was thinking of the case in Mississippi where a senator had received a letter containing a low-grade ricin that the sender had home-brewed.

"Who have you angered enough to try and kill you in such a horrible way?"

"Hey, it's not my fault."

"I'm just stating the obvious, not blaming you."

She folded her arms across her chest. He had a way of making it sound as though he was.

Footsteps rustled behind Rachel and she turned. "Erin?"

"Rachel! When did you come? Have you seen Terri? Can I wear your cross necklace now?"

Behind Erin was Gran, and Rachel stood to give them both a hug. If only she could have her grandmother's porcelain skin and unruffled spirit when she was in her eighties. "I didn't know you were staying over," she said to her grandmother.

"It was your father's idea after Erin nodded off to sleep on the daybed, and we decided not to awaken her," she said. "Terri said you were taking her back to the group home around five. We should be at my place by then."

Gran had been friends with Erin and Terri's mother, and she had often helped out with Erin before their mother's death, so it'd been natural for her to continue to help Terri with the girl. Rachel corrected herself. Erin was a woman even though her simple ways made it hard to think of her as anything other than a girl.

"I should be able to wrap up everything in time to pick her up." She unfastened the cross around her neck and slipped it around Erin's. "Just until I see you tonight, so don't lose it."

"I won't. Gran said you might go to church with us today," Erin said.

"Ah, not today," she said. It'd been a while since she'd gone to church. Not that she had anything against it, she was just so busy. "I have to work."

"You're not supposed to work on Sunday."

"I know, honey. But sometimes I have to."

Erin shook her head. "You always say that."

"Erin's right. We miss you at church." Gran's smile was gentle, but her words were pointed. "How *are* you today?"

"I'm fine. Don't worry about me. You and the Judge raised me to come back like Rocky Balboa."

Gran patted her arm. "Sometimes I think we did too good a job."

"Never. I want to be you when I grow up." Rachel kissed her grandmother's soft cheek. "Gotta go, work is calling."

She picked up the warrant and nodded to her father. "Thanks. I owe you one."

The amused glint in his eyes told her he'd be calling in her debt. Knowing him, it would be when she least wanted to repay it.

She checked her watch on the way back to her car. There was time to swing by Elmwood Cemetery before she met Boone. Sunday morning traffic was light, and her mind shifted into automatic as she traveled the familiar route. It wasn't long before she exited I-240 and drove over the narrow bridge leading into the cemetery.

She parked beside her mother's grave and got out of the car, immediately noticing that even the shade of the old oak tree had not kept the flowers from wilting in the heat. Rachel reached back in the car for a bottle of water and then took her time walking past the two rows of headstones to the grave. The daisies valiantly tried to stand, but their curled petals wouldn't last much longer. *Should have brought fresh ones.* She poured the water into the copper vase. That should hold them today.

For a minute she bowed her head and tried to say a brief prayer. After a couple of attempts, she gave up. Sometimes she just wished she could cry, but the tears wouldn't come either.

Voices carried on the faint breeze, and Rachel shaded her eyes, looking across the rolling hills filled with headstones to see where they were coming from. There, beside a backhoe she hadn't noticed, were two men, one walking to some nearby shade. The machine sat near the edge of a newly dug grave.

The dry grass crunched under her feet as she walked down the hill to the graveside.

An older black gentleman leaned on his shovel near the hole. "Mornin', ma'am."

"Good morning." The earthy scent from the mound of red clay hung in the air. "I didn't think they dug graves on Sunday."

"This here's not an ordinary grave. Coroner will be here directly. And the other police. That one over there," he said, pointing to the man leaning against an elm tree, "he's watching to make sure nobody comes here and steals the body away."

She glanced toward the tree, then back at the man. "You're exhuming someone?"

"Yes, ma'am," he said again. "Seems the remains have to be examined again since they found evidence he'd been poisoned."

"That's terrible." She glanced at the headstone. The man had died ten years ago. That was a long time for the truth to be buried.

"Yes, ma'am, it is. But God has a way of bringing truth to light and giving peace to those who need it."

She took a step back. Had he read her mind? Then she realized he was responding to her comment about it being terrible.

"Well . . ." She didn't quite know what to say. "Have a nice day" seemed a little much. "Don't get too hot."

"You too, ma'am. And don't forget, the truth will set you free."

Rachel turned and walked back up the hill, his words echoing in her mind. She stood for one last minute, staring at the fading bouquet before she knelt in front of the headstone and brushed her fingers across her mother's name. Why didn't God exhume the darkness in her past? Give her peace?

The jackhammer sound of a woodpecker drumming on metal intruded on her thoughts. She sat back on her heels and looked up. The crazy bird was attacking the overhead light fixture. When he continued, she stood and dusted the grass from her knees. As she walked to her car, she glanced at the exhumation down the hill. Maybe she didn't have peace because she wouldn't let God in.

# 20

AFTER REVIEWING RACHEL'S CASES, Boone had driven to Randy Culver's middle-class neighborhood. While he waited for Rachel to bring the search warrant, he interviewed a few people who weren't on their way out the door to church. All said the singer was a quiet neighbor who was rarely home. No one knew of any family he had, and they said he never entertained.

"How is Culver?" Rachel asked when she arrived.

"Still in a coma," he said, using the key he'd gotten from the singer's personal effects at the hospital to enter the house.

"I hope he makes it." She followed him inside. "Do you think we'll find anything here?"

"You never know."

Rachel appeared unduly reserved. He pushed open the door and entered the small living room with a formal dining area on one end that reminded him of the house he grew up in. "Anything bothering you?"

She didn't answer immediately. Then she sighed and said, "I googled ricin. When do you think we'll get a full report?"

"Should be later today. US Marshals have been called in on the case because your father's a federal judge."

"Do you think my dad was the target?"

"If it weren't for the text you received warning you off the case, I would believe he's a more likely target than you. I pulled all your cases this morning and didn't see anything that warrants someone wanting to kill you. I've been trying to see how it fits in with Vegas's murder and the attempt on Culver." He shot her a questioning gaze. "I'm wondering if the killer thinks Vegas told you something."

"How would he know Vic came to see me, unless . . ."

"The killer could have been following Vegas."

"Vic did mention he thought he knew who killed Harrison Foxx, but he wouldn't say who. And thinking that Dad might be the target doesn't make me feel any better." Rachel looked around. "Where do you want me to start?"

"Here in the living room." He understood her fear. "I want to check the refrigerator for his insulin."

The galley kitchen revealed Culver was no neat freak. Dishes sat unwashed in the sink and he'd left a box of Cheerios open on the counter. When Boone opened the refrigerator, he found three bottles of insulin, two still unopened. And none of them were Humulin R U-500.

He picked up the box containing Lantus. He'd researched the drug, and normally it was administered once a day. Boone figured the singer had last used it Friday night. And since he hadn't gone into a coma then, it'd been okay. Someone either came to the house and switched the bottles, or switched it last night at Blues & Such. Either way, it took a person with nerves of steel, especially if it happened at the club.

He joined Rachel in the search of the house. An hour later, they'd found nothing that indicated a motive for someone trying to kill the singer. Rachel had discovered his bank statements in a bedroom that had been turned into an office, and when they finished going over them, Boone said, "A Christmas club account, savings, and checking. Did you find any other accounts?"

"No. And all the deposits are from reputable companies," Rachel said. "So it doesn't look like he was running drugs or blackmailing anyone."

"How about family? Any mention of anyone we can contact?"

"Not here."

Boone stared at the balance on the savings account. He wished his balance looked as healthy. "I'm surprised that impersonating Elvis pays so well."

"He also drove a truck, but from what I gathered on the internet, he's done pretty well as an entertainer. And don't forget he's been in it for over seventeen years. I want to check something right quick." She opened the browser on her phone and typed, then blinked and looked closer at the screen. "Did you know the grand prize for the Supreme Elvis contest is twenty thousand dollars?"

"You're kidding. So, it's possible someone could have been jealous."

"A couple of the people I talked to last night indicated he was the top pick. Maybe this attempt isn't connected to Vic's murder."

It was something to think about. "I'd like to go over everything that's happened in the last forty-eight hours, starting with Vic Vegas's visit to you." Boone's stomach growled and he checked his watch. Only eleven? Didn't matter. He was hungry. "Do you want to grab a sandwich and take it back to the CJC?"

"Sure." She took out her phone again. "Panera or McAlister's? I'll order ahead."

Forty-five minutes later, Rachel laid out their sandwiches and chips on the table in the conference room while Boone found a whiteboard and rolled it in.

After he finished his sandwich, he grabbed a bag of chips and walked to the board. "Tell me everything Vic Vegas said to you Friday."

Rachel laid her half-eaten panini on a napkin and flipped through her notebook. "He asked me to investigate Harrison Foxx's case."

He wrote *Harrison Foxx* on the whiteboard. "Why you?"

"Said it would be personal to me since my mother knew Harrison." She looked up. "Mom attended Humes High with him during her freshman and sophomore year."

"Humes? Didn't you say that was where Elvis went?"

"Yeah, many years earlier. Gramps—my grandfather—went there as well. It's where he met my grandmother, and he wanted his daughter to attend there. He and Nana fought about it. Humes wasn't in the best part of town, and they were living in a ritzier section of Memphis by then. She thought Mom should attend Miss Hutchinson's School for Girls, and she did after he died."

He added Gabby Winslow's name to the board and turned around. The blood drained from Rachel's face. "You okay?"

She took a breath. "Yeah. Just seeing her name up there . . . I don't know. I stopped by her grave today. It's so hard to believe it's been seventeen years."

The pain in her eyes pierced his heart. If only there was some way he could make today easier—instead he'd made it worse. "I would have met you there if you'd let me know."

"I know." She shifted her gaze to the half sandwich on the table. She pushed it back where she could have room to work. Then she picked up the photo Vegas had given her. "It's just the timing of Vic's murder and the attempt on Randy's life . . . Why this close to the anniversary of her death?"

She raised her gaze, and this time her hazel eyes had the shiny look of unshed tears behind them. He searched for something to say. "I—"

"I'm sorry." Rachel laid the photo on the table. "This isn't your problem, and you don't have time to babysit me." She squared her shoulders. "Let's get back to work."

Unsure of what to say, Boone studied the photo. He hadn't really noticed Gabby Winslow before, since he'd been paying more attention to the Elvis impersonators. Dressed in a flowing silver gown, she posed on the other side of Harrison Foxx as her daughter handed him the trophy. A beautiful woman, Gabby appeared to be in her midthirties. He didn't have to look up and compare their features to know Rachel bore a striking resemblance to her mother. High cheekbones, the same square jawline, the full lips with a Cupid's bow . . . "I'm sorry you haven't had closure on her death."

"Thanks." She avoided his eyes. "One day I will find her killer. It's why I became a cop over my father's objections—and that should have been my answer last night when you asked."

"I still don't understand why he isn't proud of you being a police officer."

"It's not that he isn't proud of me. He just always expected me to become a lawyer like him, and I did for a while. When I couldn't stand being one any longer . . . you can see that he didn't take it well when I resigned. By then Corey had died, and I didn't care."

Boone had known Rachel's husband. Corey Sloan had been a ruthless defense attorney that Boone had tangled with in court on more than one occasion. Knowing Rachel now, it was hard to see the two as a couple.

Boone examined the photo again. Gabby Winslow had died the night it was taken. Harrison Foxx, a few days later. And now Vic Vegas was dead, Randy Culver lay near death, and an attempt had been made on Rachel's life.

He pointed to the fourth man, Daryl Cook. "I interviewed him last night. Lives in Las Vegas. Has his own Elvis show at one of the casinos."

Rachel nodded. "According to some of the other performers, he runs a close second to Randy Culver in popularity."

Boone tapped the photo. What was the common denominator? "What if your mother's case wasn't a burglary? What if someone used the other burglaries in the area to cover a motive to kill her? And Foxx's murder is connected to hers?"

She stiffened and shifted her gaze toward the board again.

"That's reaching," she said with a shake of her head. "The detectives who investigated her case couldn't find a motive for murder other than the burglary, and so far, I can't either. They even checked out my dad because my parents were separated. The detectives ruled him out after he had an ironclad alibi—he was in a bar with at least twenty-five witnesses who swore he never left after he arrived at ten thirty that night. And he volunteered to take a lie detector test and passed it."

"Why were they separated?"

She hesitated. "The Judge was, still is, a workaholic, and Mom got tired of being by herself. About a month before she . . ." Rachel looked toward the window, then back at him. "Anyway, they were seeing a counselor. One other thing in his favor was Mom didn't have a big insurance policy listing him as beneficiary. It was the other way around—he had a million-dollar policy on his life, payable to her."

"No enemies? No women jealous of her?"

Rachel shook her head. "She wasn't the type to attract enemies."

He finished off his bag of chips. "I'm going to leave her name up there, if for no other reason than her case has never been solved, and Foxx died only a few days later. Have you uncovered a motive for his death?"

"I don't have his case file yet. I meant to call Brad Hollister yesterday when we finished with the competition at the gym, but we got the call on Vic Vegas."

Had it just been twenty-four hours since the competition? The look on her face mirrored his thoughts. He'd worked with Brad in Homicide before his friend transferred to the Cold Case Unit. "I'll give him a call right now."

Fifteen minutes later they were in the cold case storage room, sorting through files that were grouped together according to years.

"Here it is," Rachel said. She held up a manila envelope.

"Doesn't look like there's much in it."

147

Back in the conference room, they dumped the contents on the table. A few photographs, investigation reports, and that was it.

"Do you know the investigating officers?" Rachel asked.

Boone glanced to see who the detectives were. Les Fields and Joe Takenaka. "Both were working Homicide when I joined the force. Don't remember much about Fields, except he died a few years ago. Worked with Takenaka before he retired. A good man. Usually thorough. Unfortunately, he recently passed away as well, so no help there."

He spread the crime scene photos on the conference room table. It was sad when photos like these were the last ones taken of a person. He picked up one that showed the entry wound. Rachel looked over his shoulder at the photo, and he felt her shiver.

"Looks like a small caliber gun was used," she said.

He nodded, very aware of her nearness. "Close range too."

"Like, maybe something a woman would use," she said.

"Good point." He opened the folder and started reading the first page of Takenaka's report. "Says here that Foxx was killed in his car on a remote road in Shelby County. Shot once in the head."

"What was he doing out in the boondocks in the first place?" she asked and picked up another folder. "It looks like Fields asked that same question. And came up with either a girlfriend or a drug deal gone bad. I'd go with drug dealer since someone wiped the car clean."

He tried to visualize a girlfriend shooting him. "If it were in the heat of passion, we'd more than likely be looking at a bullet to the chest. This is more of an execution-type killing."

"Except drug dealers like big guns. Too bad we don't have the files that Vic Vegas put together." Rachel finished reading Fields's report and laid it on the table. "It doesn't look like they had much to go on."

Boone looked over the top of his file. "This is interesting. According to this, Foxx gambled quite a bit out in Vegas. Borrowed money from some shady characters."

"In addition to the women he hit up?" Rachel asked.

"Looks like it. Takenaka had two theories. One, he'd run afoul of a loan shark, or two, it was a lovers' rendezvous gone bad. The detective favored the loan shark angle." Boone tended to agree. Not many women had the nerves to shoot a man in the head.

He looked over the list of people interviewed. Mostly family or people associated with his career in the entertainment business. He stopped at Judge Lucien Winslow's name and scanned the interview.

The Judge was noncommittal about Foxx, and according to the report, he'd represented the entertainer at one time. It had been a matter involving a woman who claimed the Elvis impersonator had swindled her. Lucinda Vetch.

The name sounded familiar, and he wrote it down. Maybe she got even with him. No, the detective indicated she had an airtight alibi. Still, she could have hired a hit man. He grabbed a phone book and scanned the Vs. There weren't too many people in Memphis with the last name Vetch, and none named Lucinda. Maybe she'd married. It was definitely a lead he wanted to check out.

# 21

COLD AIR BLEW into the conference room, chilling Rachel. She figured she should at least try to finish her sandwich, so she picked up the other half and took a bite. Sawdust would go down easier. It was her taste buds and not the turkey melt.

She slid her gaze toward Boone. It was a little late to figure out that if ever there was a man she would risk her heart with, it was him. Sometimes she wished she hadn't pushed her way into Homicide and had given their relationship a chance to develop. But from their first date, she'd gotten the feeling Boone was looking to settle down, and that's what frightened her. She wasn't ready to get married again.

She hadn't been ready when she married Corey. Rachel had just let Corey sweep her along with his plans until it was too late to back out. It didn't help that her father approved of the marriage. It was only afterward that she realized she didn't love her husband the way she should. Sometimes Rachel wondered if she was capable of loving that way at all.

Brushing the thoughts away, Rachel picked up Takenaka's report, and dread squeezed her chest. She should have told Boone that Vic thought Harrison's and her mother's cases were connected. That *she* thought they were.

Maybe she should have told him the real reason her parents separated. She'd never told anyone that the Judge had been having an affair . . . But had he actually been involved with someone? All she really had to go on was what she'd overheard her mother say. What if Rachel had heard wrong? She rested her forehead against her hand. It was all so muddied in her memory now.

They'd argued about him working all the time. And her mother had accused him of having a mistress. Rachel automatically assumed it was true when he moved out. She'd been a teenager, not really mature enough to understand their relationship.

Why not ask her father about it? She might be a grown woman, but the idea of asking her father a question like that turned her insides to Jell-O. And since she didn't know for sure, she'd been right to hold that information back.

But she had to watch it when she was around Boone. He had a way of making her want to confide in him, when he wasn't driving her crazy with his micromanaging. Wait a minute—that wasn't fair. If he micromanaged, it was because he only wanted the best from his detectives. When his questions made her second-guess herself, maybe she needed to step back and reevaluate the situation.

Was that so different from the Judge, and even Corey? Maybe not so different from her father—she figured he'd always had her interests at heart. But once she and Corey had married, Corey had undermined every thought Rachel had if it disagreed with his. She massaged her temple. *Enough. Eat and get back to work.*

With dogged determination, Rachel finished the sandwich. She'd get a headache if she didn't eat, and she couldn't afford that. She sorted through the other items and picked up a spreadsheet Sergeant Takenaka had created. It was a timeline, starting with the first incident report. A farmer taking a load of steers to market stopped to investigate when he saw Foxx slumped over the steering wheel of his parked car. Finding him dead would have been a horrible shock.

She scanned the timeline. The detective had interviewed Randy Culver as well as Vic and other Elvis impersonators. Where was that program Nana gave her? Her bag. She pulled it out and compared the names of some of the older performers. Takenaka had interviewed three of them. Hair on her arms raised when another name caught her eye. Monica Carpenter. "Boone—"

"It says here Sergeant Takenaka interviewed your father," he said, sliding a folder toward her. "And that he represented Foxx in a lawsuit."

The sandwich soured in her stomach. She should have realized that information would be in the detectives' report. "After Vic mentioned the Judge had represented Foxx in a lawsuit, I asked Dad about it," she said. "He indicated he represented him one time and that Foxx was a con artist."

"That's pretty much what this report says."

He handed her the file, and she looked over it. Lucinda Vetch—that must be the name the Judge couldn't remember Friday night.

"What do you remember about Foxx?"

"I barely remember him. He was Mom's friend, and at fifteen, I thought her friends were old." She laughed. "They weren't much older than I am now."

"Anyone else in her circle of friends acquainted with Foxx?"

She searched her memory, then said, "Nana remembered him. Oh, and Terri would have known him. She choreographed the routines and would have been involved with all the performers. But look at this."

She showed him the timeline. "Sergeant Takenaka interviewed several of the people involved in the Elvis contest, including Monica Carpenter."

"So Ms. Carpenter lied to you about knowing Vic Vegas." He flipped through his notes. "I have her address. What do you say we pay her a visit?"

"How about the others he interviewed?"

He flipped through the report. His eyes widened. "Did you see this? Why would Takenaka interview Donna Dumont?"

"Donna?" Rachel shook her head to clear it. "She's a big Elvis fan, but I didn't realize she went back that far. I certainly don't remember her."

"Let's see what she can tell us," Boone said.

Rachel dialed Donna's extension and asked her to come to the conference room.

A few minutes later Donna appeared at the door. As usual, she was impeccably dressed in a yellow linen jacket that came to her knees over skinny white pants. And as usual her red hair was fluffed high. Rachel wondered how much gray was under the red dye.

"Sorry to be so long, but I couldn't find anyone to cover the desk. What's going on? And have you had an update on Randy?"

The office manager had already waylaid Rachel when she walked through the door with questions about Randy and if she'd learned any more about the present with Rachel's name on it.

"No." She waved toward the papers. "We're going over another case, and your name came up. Got a minute?"

"Sure. What case?" She sat at the end of the table.

"Man's name is Harrison Foxx."

Her face clouded. "I remember him. Tragic what happened. He was a really good Elvis tribute artist, and one of the first I met when I first started going to the Elvis Week events."

Rachel noticed she didn't say *impersonator*. "Do you remember seeing me there?"

Donna's eyes widened. "You were there?"

She nodded. "I was with my mom, Gabby Winslow. She was in charge of the gala."

"Oh, I wouldn't have known any of the important people," the office manager said, waving her hand dismissively. "I'm kind of embarrassed to say I was starstruck. I loved Elvis growing up, and some of those guys were really good."

"What do you remember about Harrison Foxx's murder?" Boone asked and handed Rachel the file.

The tiniest of shrugs accompanied the older woman's lifted brows. "How awful I felt. It crushed me, just knowing someone who'd been murdered. He was only thirty-five."

Rachel scanned the file. "It says here you went out to dinner with him once."

Her lips spread in a wide smile. "Yes. It was like being with a celebrity. People stopped by our table and asked for his autograph. I think that's what made his death so hard. I never got to really know him. Who knows where our relationship might have gone."

And now she had her cap set for the Judge, and if Rachel weren't rooting for Terri, she wouldn't mind seeing Donna and the Judge get together. But knowing her father, that wasn't going to happen—he was too much like Rachel. "Do you know of anyone who had it in for him?"

Donna thought a minute. "Not really. Like I said, I didn't get a chance to know him that well."

"How about the other performers? Was anyone jealous of him?" Boone asked. "Or maybe girlfriends?"

A frown creased her brow. "There was this one incident . . ."

"Go on," he said.

"Harrison had invited me backstage at another event, downtown, I think. A woman jumped all over him, claimed he owed her some money. Embarrassed him. He told me later she was crazy, but I didn't believe her, anyway."

The man was dead, and Rachel refrained from telling her she should have believed it. "Do you remember her name?"

"It was Monica. Monica Carpenter from the contest."

Boone leaned forward. "How about Vic Vegas. Did you know him?"

"The man that was here Friday? I saw him at Blues & Such Friday night, and those were the only times I can remember ever

154

seeing him, although I probably have. I can't believe he's dead too." She gasped and turned to Rachel. "That case he wanted you to investigate—was it Harrison's?"

Rachel had forgotten she mentioned at the gym why Vic came to see her. "Yes," she said.

"You were there last night. Did you see anyone around Culver's table?" Boone asked.

Donna's eyes widened, and she shook her head. "No, I was watching the performers. I hope he's going to be all right."

"It's still too soon to tell," he said.

"That's the impression I got from the news reports. Someone said he used the wrong insulin."

"Where did you hear that?"

"I overheard one of the waitresses talking when I left. They think someone tried to kill him. Is that true?"

"We don't have all the lab reports back yet," Boone said. "But if you hear anything else, let us know."

# 22

RACHEL PICKED UP THE TAKENAKA REPORT again and scanned it, stopping when she came to Lucinda Vetch's name. "Did you get an address for Ms. Vetch?"

"Not a home address, but I did find a Lucinda Vetch with a modeling agency. But it being Sunday, I only got her answering machine. Maybe Monica Carpenter knows her. She seems to know everyone else, so I think it's time to go talk to her again."

Boone drove them the short distance to Monica Carpenter's condo in Midtown and parked beside a black BMW in front of the event planner's house number. Rachel was surprised to see the front blinds were closed and a Sunday paper on the stoop. "Do you think she's home?"

"Only one way to find out."

They walked to the condo, and after Rachel rang the doorbell twice, Monica Carpenter answered the door in a robe, her brown hair hanging in a single plait over her left shoulder. The oversized glasses were missing. While Rachel hadn't been sure of her age, the harsh August sun exposed the fine lines her makeup had covered yesterday. Definitely a contemporary of Foxx and Vegas.

"What do you want?" Carpenter used her hand to shield her eyes from the overhead sun.

"We'd like to ask you a few more questions," Rachel said, taking the lead. "May we come in?"

"You could have called."

"I'm sorry," Boone said. "We were in the neighborhood and thought you'd probably be home. We really do need a few more answers. Can we come in or would you prefer we ask them here while your neighbors look on?"

Her gaze darted past them, and she reluctantly stepped back. "Might as well. I doubt you'll leave until I talk to you. The living room is on the right."

"Thank you," Rachel murmured as she stepped past her. Vaulted ceilings gave the sense of the room being larger than it was. She scanned the area. Monica Carpenter's taste in decorating ran to vintage fifties.

A gallery of Elvis's 78-rpm covers hung on one wall, serving as a backdrop for a black piano. A jukebox claimed a corner, and a boxy red sofa and chair rounded out the mid-fifties theme. Stale cigarette smoke permeated the room. Rachel sat on the firm sofa while Boone took the chair.

Monica picked up a pack of Marlboros from the top of the piano and tapped out a cigarette. "You don't mind if I smoke, do you?"

"Your house." *Your death*, Rachel wanted to add. Instead, she took out her notepad and a pencil. Maybe the smoke wouldn't trigger an allergy attack.

After Monica lit the cigarette, she pulled out the piano bench and picked up a small black ashtray. How long had it been since Rachel had seen one of those? She waited while the other woman took a long draw and then blew smoke out the side of her mouth.

"What questions do you have that you didn't ask last night?"

"Just a few we missed." Rachel put the date at the top of the pad. "Is it okay to call you Monica?"

"Sure."

Interrogation 101, make friends with the suspect—although

she didn't think it would work in this instance. "How long have you been in the entertainment business?"

"Since I was eighteen. Started out as a singer, but I recognized right away I wasn't good enough. Started working backstage, learned the business inside and out." She took another drag. "It didn't take me long to figure out I could earn more money planning events, so I made it a practice to talk to the agents I ran into, and I met some big names along the way. When I decided to go out on my own, everything was in place."

"When I asked about Vic Vegas, you indicated you didn't know him. But—"

"I never said I didn't know him."

"But you let me believe you didn't. Why?"

Monica's shoulder came up in a dismissive shrug. "I had the Supreme Elvis contest to think about, and when a police detective asks questions about someone, it's never good." She studied the red tip of the cigarette. "There's a lot of advertising dollars riding on the contest, and when you said Vegas was dead, I could see money flying out the window if the show was shut down. Sorry if you think I was misleading you, but I don't want to lose this client. Not at my age—it's too hard to get new ones."

Boone leaned forward. "So you did know him?"

She shifted toward him. "Not well. Over the years, we crossed paths. Seems like he was always around. Never made it big, though."

"How about Harrison Foxx? How well did you know him?"

Her face flushed and a struggle appeared in her eyes. Then she pulled another cigarette out and lit it off the one she was smoking. "He owed me money when he died." She stubbed the short butt in the ashtray. "But I'm sure you already know that."

"Why did you loan him money?"

"Harrison was a good-looking man. He borrowed money from a lot of women." She gave Rachel a sly look. "But your mother could have told you that if she weren't dead."

Rachel's pencil lead snapped. "How did you know who my mother was?"

"Are you saying Gabby Winslow loaned Foxx money?"

Rachel and Boone spoke at the same time.

Monica shot her a "gotcha" grin. "Which question do you want answered?"

Rachel clamped her mouth shut, clenching her jaw until it ached.

"How about both of them, one at a time," Boone said.

"Harrison told me of at least one occasion when Gabby had loaned him money. Pretty sure he never paid it back. As for how I knew Gabby was your mother, you look just like her when she was your age, and I googled you after you left yesterday."

"Did you kill Harrison?" Rachel asked.

"Goodness no. Why would I want to kill him? He owed me money."

Rachel made a note about the loan. "If he was such a loser, why did he have so many women after him?"

"He was some kind of good-looking, for one thing." Monica's features softened and her eyes became unfocused, then she snapped out of it. "When you were with Harrison, even in a crowd, he made you feel like you were the only person in the room."

Rachel knew exactly what Monica was talking about. Her husband had that gift. It was one reason he won so many court cases. And probably why she married him against her better judgment. People just didn't tell Corey no.

The fumes from Monica's cigarette made it difficult for Rachel to breathe. "Any chance you can put that out?" she asked. "Or open a window?"

"A little hot to open a window. How about finishing your questions and leaving?"

"How about we take this downtown?" she said evenly, not bothering to take the hard edge off her voice.

Monica shot a glare toward her, but she knocked the glowing end off the cigarette. "Cost too much to throw away," she said, putting it in the ashtray. "What else do you want to know?"

"Do you know a woman named Lucinda Vetch?"

"Lucy? She was a groupie then, and she still is." Monica shook her head. "If I had her money, I'd be on the French Riviera with a good-looking man instead of running after these fake Elvises."

"Do you have an address for her?"

"No, but you can probably catch her at Blues & Such tonight—she never misses a show during Elvis Week." She rolled her shoulders. "Are you done? I didn't get into bed until almost three."

"One more question. Where were you the night Foxx was murdered?" Boone asked.

"At home asleep, just like I was when Vic Vegas died. And I had no motive to kill either of them." She cocked her head. "I heard Randy used the wrong insulin, and that's something he would not do. If I were the police, I'd look at who had the most to gain from getting rid of their competition."

"What do you mean?"

"Randy was the odds-on favorite to win the Supreme Elvis this year. Twenty thousand dollars is a good incentive. Not to mention Harrison was really hot the year he was murdered."

"That doesn't explain Vic Vegas's death," Rachel pointed out. "He certainly wasn't in the running."

"Maybe he knew too much. He said he'd solve Harrison's death one day. Maybe he discovered who killed him."

"We'll check that out." Boone stood, and Rachel followed suit. "Will you be at Blues & Such tonight? In case we have more questions."

"Sure."

Rachel inhaled a breath of clean air as they walked back to the truck.

"What do you think?" Boone asked.

"She's still not telling us something." It might be a good idea to come back and interview the event planner without Boone.

The sense that Monica was watching them followed Rachel as she climbed into Boone's truck. Only after she fastened her seat belt did she allow herself to glance toward the condo. Yep. One of the slats in the blinds was raised just enough for someone to peek through them. Then it abruptly slid back in place.

Boone started the motor and turned to her. "You know it would help if we had a list of the performers from that event seventeen years ago. Do you think your grandmother might have a program from that night in one of those boxes she has?"

Adrenaline stabbed her heart. Somewhere in the back of her mind, she'd known he was going to ask this. Her throat tightened, choking off the words she needed to say.

# 23

IF BOONE COULD SNATCH BACK the request he'd just made, he would. How could he be so stupid? He might as well have asked her to jump off the Mississippi River Bridge. From the looks of her pale face, she'd probably rather do the jump than go through her mother's effects, today of all days.

He wanted to bang his head on the steering wheel. Not only that, he'd sent her to the house where she'd found her mother dead on the anniversary of that morning, when he could have asked another judge to sign a search warrant. No wonder she'd been so quiet earlier.

And what if he ended up having to take her off the case? If the Culver and Vegas cases linked to her mother's, he would have to remove her, and that'd be like bathing a cat. On second thought, Boone believed he'd rather bathe the cat.

He let the truck idle. "Can you handle dealing with your mother's death in this case? Because, like it or not, we'll be rooting around in her life and around events she was involved in."

She gripped the seat belt strap and pulled it away from her chest. "I can handle it."

The grim expression on her face and white knuckles on the strap told a different story. He'd seen shell-shocked soldiers, and she had the same look. "Look, it's Sunday afternoon. Why don't you take the rest of the day off and regroup? We can get the list tomorrow, and tonight I'll question the performers at Blues & Such."

Rachel jutted her jaw and stared straight ahead, not blinking. Slowly a calm came over her face and color returned to her cheeks. She took out her phone and dialed a number. "Nana," she said, her voice steady. "Do you still have Mom's Elvis stuff?"

She listened for a few seconds. "Good. Can I come over and look through it?" A minute later she ended the call. "I'm pretty sure Mom saved the programs from the tribute events she was involved in, and after she died, Nana took charge of the mementos. There are several boxes, and I imagine that program is in one of them. If you'll drop me off at the parking garage, I'll grab my car and drive to Nana's and find it."

The strain in her voice pierced him. He was asking a lot of her to go through those things today. "Why don't I go with you and help?"

"Nana will be there."

He doubted Rose Lee wanted to go through her daughter's things any more than Rachel did. "There may be other items pertaining to the case, items your grandmother wouldn't recognize as evidence. And two of us can get through the boxes twice as fast." If he were with her, he'd know if the memories were too much.

"Uh . . . are you sure you want to do that? I mean, it's a *lot* of Elvis stuff."

Maybe she needed space and didn't want him to go. He glanced toward her. Rachel's knees bounced and she still had that shell-shocked look. Boone put the car in gear and backed out of the space. "I like Elvis."

"O-kay. Just don't pay any attention to Nana."

"What do you mean?"

"You'll see." The knee bouncing resumed.

"Does she still live at Trinity Meadows?" The gated, condo-style complex was in East Memphis.

"Yes. I keep trying to get Gran to move there too."

Rachel had two very interesting grandmothers that she talked quite a bit about. One from England, the other a Southern belle with Irish roots. "Did I ever tell you that before I met Rose, I half expected to meet Miss Daisy?"

"Nana . . . a Jessica Tandy clone? That is hilarious."

It *was* after he met her. The first time he'd met Rachel's maternal grandmother had been on his and Rachel's third date and she'd asked him to stop by Trinity Meadows so she could drop off something. Rose had been dressed for tennis with a sweatband keeping her red hair away from her face. While she still held to her Southern heritage, she also fit very well in today's world. As her texting and Facebook page attested to. And like Rachel's other grandmother, she'd quickly told him she didn't want to hear any of that Mrs. Lee stuff, to call her by her given name.

"If she'd been Miss Daisy, Gramps would have been her Hoke. He kept her grounded," Rachel said with a laugh. "And since he died, Gran thinks she inherited the responsibility."

He pictured Adele with her chin-length silver hair. "It's hard to believe either of them are in their eighties."

"Tell me about it."

"It'll be good to see Rose again. Was she at the party last night?"

"Yes, and I was surprised she didn't come outside and join us like the others. She did call early this morning to get the details on what happened."

Boone wished he had memories of his grandmothers. His dad had been orphaned in his teens, and he barely remembered his maternal grandparents, missionaries who had died in South Africa in a car wreck. "You have an interesting family."

He was glad to see a tiny smile cross her lips.

"You might say that."

He showed his ID to the guard, then drove through the gates

and turned to the right. Rose's condo was on the backside of the complex, near the tennis courts.

A wide smile spread across Rose's face the minute she opened the door. "You didn't tell me you were bringing Boone. Come on in." She practically dragged him through the doorway and gave him a hug. "I don't know what my granddaughter meant, breaking it off with you. Being a Callahan, you'd make a fine grandson-in-law."

"Now you know what I meant," Rachel muttered.

"What can you tell me about that present you received last night?" Rose asked as she led them to a sunny room that looked out on a lake.

"Not much," Rachel said.

Rose turned expectantly to Boone.

"She's right," he said. "There's not a lot we can tell you other than it's being investigated."

"Well, you watch after her, Boone Callahan."

"Yes, ma'am." He shifted his gaze from Rachel to the room as a grandfather clock chimed the two o'clock hour. He noted ten boxes on the floor against the wall paneling. Ten? That was a lot of memorabilia.

"You should have waited and let us get these out for you," he said.

Rose dismissed him with her hand. "Why would I do that? The weights I lift every day are heavier than those boxes. Now, if you two don't mind, I have a tennis date."

"In this heat?" Alarm flared in Rachel's face.

"Of course not. I'm not an idiot, in spite of what Adele thinks. Did you forget we have an indoor court with air-conditioning?"

Rachel grinned. "My bad. Go have fun. Do you want us to lock up when we leave?"

"If I'm not back. We only have the court for an hour."

"Who are you playing with?"

Blue eyes glinted mischievously. "Gerald." She walked toward the front door and stopped. "Do be sure to tell Adele that since he's met me, he's working out and playing tennis."

"Do you think *I'm* an idiot?"

When the door closed behind her, Boone said, "What was that all about?"

"My grandmothers are like water and fire. Gerald is a man they met at church, and Gran thinks Nana is throwing herself at him, says that Gerald is only interested in Nana's money."

"What do you think?"

Rachel laughed. "As flighty as Nana appears, she's an excellent businesswoman. She had Gerald checked out after their second coffee date. He is very well set and has a great reputation. Of course she's told Gran none of this, instead lets her believe what she wants to."

"Why don't you tell her?"

"And ruin Nana's fun? You met Gran. Nothing ruffles her. Besides, if it wasn't Gerald they were fighting over, it'd be me." She picked up one of the boxes. "And believe me, I'd much rather it be him."

"Well, I like your grandmothers." Boone scanned the boxes. Some of the boxes had "Elvis" written on them, and the first box he sorted through had photo albums and high school yearbooks. He set it aside to return to later. By the time he opened the third box, he feared the program hadn't been saved.

He checked to see how Rachel fared. It was hard to tell. She sat cross-legged on the floor, chewing on her bottom lip as she pored over what looked like a journal. "You okay?"

She looked up, her face flushed. "Yeah. This is my mother's diary from her year as a deb."

"A deb?"

"Debutante. I was one too."

Rachel had mentioned being a debutante before. A term not unfamiliar to Boone, but it'd been a while since he'd heard it. Mostly he remembered it from when the Cotton Carnival had been more of a high-society event than a party to raise money for children's causes. And as a kid growing up in the part of town he had, he certainly had never been part of the Carnival set. "So exactly what does a debutante do, other than attend parties?"

Amusement lit her face. "Well, first of all, it's almost a way of life. I knew from the time I was four and Mom got me started in dance lessons that I would have a debutante season."

"Four? You're kidding."

"Serious as a mortician. Terri was my dance teacher, by the way. I don't know that it starts that early now since I'm not in those circles, but Nana could tell you. She still champions the cause."

"Why would you do that? Spend all your life preparing for one year?"

"It never occurred to me to question it. It's just what one did if you had a grandmother like Rose Lee." A strand of blonde hair had slipped loose from the band that held it in a ponytail, and she hooked it behind her ear.

"In my mother's family, it was a tradition. Nana was presented to Atlanta society at the Piedmont Driving Club because her grandparents lived there, and she saw to it that my mother was presented as well. They had the honor of being double debs by also being presented to Memphis society during Carnival week. When it was my turn, Nana and Terri took over after . . ."

He hoped she didn't stop her story, because he was seeing a side that Rachel kept hidden. She stood and walked to a bookcase, returning with two framed eight-by-ten photos.

"This is me, the night I was presented." She handed him one of the photos. "With the Judge."

The photographer had captured Rachel and her father waltzing. Dressed in a flowing white gown, she appeared to be nineteen or twenty and was the picture of understated elegance. "He looks very proud of you here."

"I think he was. Said I looked like Mom."

She leaned in and touched the photo, and a light fragrance enveloped him.

"It's the only night I ever remember having his undivided attention."

The wistfulness in her voice startled him. When he glanced up, longing reflected in her face as she stared at the photo. An urge to take her in his arms, to make her world right, caught him off guard.

Rachel turned and caught him staring at her. Their gazes locked and her pupils dilated as electricity arced between them. The pounding of his heart silenced all other sounds, even the seconds ticked off by the grandfather clock. Abruptly, she stepped back, breaking the spell.

"This is my official portrait," she said, her voice husky as she handed him the other photo.

He almost dropped the picture. What was wrong with him? She had made it plain she wasn't interested in him. But that wasn't what her eyes had just said. *Get a grip.* She hadn't exactly fallen into his arms. Besides, he was Rachel's supervisor, and as long as she was in Homicide, he had to remember she was hands-off. Period.

Time to refocus his attention elsewhere, maybe get interested in someone else. Not that he hadn't dated and had relationships before Rachel came along, but those had always been casual, usually ending for lack of commitment on both sides. His feelings for Rachel had been new territory for him, and he hadn't been sure how to handle it. Evidently that hadn't changed.

Rachel's voice broke past his thoughts. "The original is hanging in the library at Dad's."

The lightness in her voice sounded forced. Everything was awkward. He muscled his attention to the picture. She wore the same gown as in the other photo, but in this one, her golden hair had been swept back in a loose bun. The elegance he'd noticed earlier emanated from the photograph. "Wow. You are . . ." He caught himself before he said *beautiful*. That would have really made things worse. "Looking really good there."

She propped her hand on her hip. "And I'm what, chopped meat now?"

And just like that, everything was back to normal. "Maybe chopped sirloin."

Rachel ducked her head, but he could see the grin on her face.

"The pearl necklace and earrings I'm wearing were my mom's. Dad had just given them to me before the photo shoot, just like Gramps had given them to Mom before her debut, and my great-grandfather to Nana."

It suddenly dawned on him that she was way out of his league.

# 24

RACHEL DIDN'T KNOW how it happened, but a few minutes ago, Boone almost kissed her. And she would have welcomed it.

Thank goodness neither of them acted on the impulse. And that's all it was. An impulse that would not happen again. She had too much to lose and so did Boone. Besides, as much as she wished she could fall in love with him, something held her back. It wasn't that he didn't make her heart pound—he did. But until she could give him her whole heart, there was no need to encourage him. It would only end up making it difficult for them both. Like it wasn't already.

"I can see why your dad wanted you to stay with the law firm," Boone said.

"What are you talking about?"

He glanced at the portrait again. "If I had a daughter like this, I wouldn't want her putting her life on the line every day."

"You have to be kidding." She stared at him. "You're not, are you?" When he didn't answer, she shook her head. "But I love being a cop. Maybe I joined the department to find who was responsible for my mother's death, but it didn't take me long to find out some crimes just aren't solvable—not enough leads or the leads are dead ends. By then I'd discovered I loved investigating, figuring things out and bringing closure to victims and their families."

"If you couldn't do it for yourself, you would do it for others," he said.

The image of her mother, lying on the floor, her body cold, whipped through Rachel's mind. If she knew what had happened that night, she might be able to put that image to rest. "Nothing is more important than closure. The not knowing drives families crazy. I can't bring the murdered victims back, but if I can get justice for them, the family can sleep easier. It's why I want to work in Homicide. If I make sergeant next year, I'll be eligible to be here permanently."

And one day she would discover her mother's killer. Rachel palmed her hands up. "I'll get off my soapbox now."

"You'll make it," he said. "You have a cop's heart."

"Why did you become a cop?"

He focused on opening the last box. "It was the thing to do when I returned from Iraq."

A wall slid between them, just like it had the one other time she'd asked him about his past. Rachel had suspected before that Boone had secrets, and judging by the set of his mouth, he intended to keep them. She understood that and sat down beside him. "If the program isn't here, I don't know where else to look."

"Then we go to plan B." He handed her a stack of papers and several packets of photos developed at Walgreens.

"Which is?"

"Don't ask. You won't like it."

The first packet of photos was of her tenth birthday, and she laid them aside. She opened another and caught her breath. "Pay dirt."

"What?"

He leaned toward her, and a whiff of his aftershave reminded her of the ocean. *Focus.* She handed him the first picture. "This was taken the night of the Elvis contest. That's Mom with Harrison Foxx."

171

Rachel sorted through the pictures that were of her mother and the performers from that night. "Here's one of Mom and Terri. They were the best of friends." She pulled another one out. "Oh, look. Here's one of Foxx and Monica Carpenter."

He glanced at the photo. "She hasn't changed much. Just older."

"She doesn't have the owl glasses yet." So Monica was there that night. She flipped through the pictures, finding another one of Monica and Vic Vegas and Randy Culver. She handed it to Boone and examined the next photo. Foxx had his arm around a woman she didn't recognize, even though she looked familiar.

"Culver was really young then," he said.

"Yeah." She frowned at the next photo. Someone, Nana maybe, had caught Foxx and her mother in an embrace. She chewed her bottom lip, caught between wanting to tear the photo in half and defending her mother.

Guilt flooded her heart. *No.* She knew her mother, and she would not betray her marriage—that's what her dad did. If this photo were anything other than innocent, Nana would not have saved it. Still, it was with reluctance that she handed it to Boone. "I'm sure this isn't what it looks like."

He studied the photo. "Who do you suppose took it?"

"Terri or Nana. One of them was always taking pictures."

Boone waved his hand toward the boxes. "How did your mother get involved in this Elvis stuff, anyway?"

"That can be blamed on Nana. I told you she went to Humes High with Elvis, but I don't think I told you she graduated with him." She sorted through the photos, looking for . . . exactly what, she wasn't sure. "They were in the class of '53," she said, looking up.

He frowned in concentration a moment and then winced. "That means Elvis would be eighty-two? That's hard to picture."

"Yeah. And I don't think he would have aged as well as Nana." Not many people aged as well as her grandmother. "Nana stayed in touch with Elvis off and on, even after he became famous. He invited them to Graceland when Mom was thirteen. Gave them the million-dollar tour, and Mom was hooked. She never got over being a fan."

He turned the photo over. "Harrison's name is on the back. How about the others?"

She hadn't checked the backs. The names were written in a distinctive slant. "Yeah, they all have names on the back. This looks like Terri's handwriting." Rachel looked up. "So even if we don't find the program, we have the names of several of the performers."

"Let's keep looking, though. I'd like to have the name of every performer who was there that night. Any of them could have been jealous of Foxx."

"And if Vic was on to something and told the wrong person . . . that's motive for his death."

"As for Randy, maybe the killer saw Vic talking to Randy Culver and was afraid he'd told Randy what he discovered."

"I wish we could have talked to him longer. Have you heard how he is?"

Boone took out his phone. "Not lately. I think I'll check."

He dialed the Med and asked for ICU. When he hung up, he said, "He's in and out of consciousness. They said we could go in to see him, though. That he might wake up any time."

"Great." As she began putting the papers back in the boxes, the front door opened, and Nana came in, looking almost as fresh as when she left. "Have a good game?"

"Yes. I let him win the last set, and he asked me out for coffee after church tonight. Are you coming? I missed you this morning."

"I doubt it. I'm picking Erin up at Gran's and taking her to the home."

Boone stacked the boxes. "Where would you like me to put these?"

"In the garage," Rose said. "Go through the kitchen. I'll show you."

"I think I can find it."

Once he left, her grandmother beamed at her. "I'm so glad you and Boone are back together."

"Nana! We are not together. He's my boss."

"Oh, posh! Why don't you bring him to dinner some night? You're not getting any younger, you know. And I'd like a great-grandchild."

She could never bring Boone around Nana again. "Please, don't say anything like that around him. Okay?"

"Well, he's a hunk, if you ask me," Nana said with a twinkle in her blue eyes. "But you know I wouldn't embarrass you."

Sure, she wouldn't. Rachel picked up the photos on the table. "Do you know who took these?"

Nana took the photos and gave a small gasp. She closed her eyes as tears formed on her lashes.

She'd wanted to get her grandmother off her case, but not like this. "I'm sorry, Nana. I shouldn't—"

"No. It's all right. I was looking at her wedding pictures earlier today." She straightened her shoulders and examined the top picture again. "Terri took these the night Gabby died, using her camera. Terri had them developed and gave them to me later, but I never got around to looking at all of them." She sorted through the others. "I don't believe I ever saw this picture. He was in love with your mother, you know. Had been since high school."

She looked to see that Nana held the photo of her mom and Harrison embracing. "How did she feel about him?"

"She wasn't in love with him, and she would never betray your father. But with Lucien so caught up in his work, sometimes I think she enjoyed the attention Harrison showered on her."

What if her mother and Harrison . . . No, they did not have an affair. A memory flickered in her mind. Her parents arguing that night . . . about Harrison? And then it was gone. "How did the Judge feel about Harrison's attention?"

"He didn't like it, and I didn't blame him. I told Gabby she didn't need to encourage Harrison. He was a ne'er-do-well, even hit me up for a loan, and he liked the women too well. Your mother wasn't the only one he paid special attention to."

"You didn't loan—"

"Of course not. His history of repaying loans was not good."

"Do you have anything else that needs to go into the storage room?" Boone asked as he came back into the room.

"No, that's it."

He shifted his gaze to Nana. "Do you know any of the people in those photos?"

She glanced down at the pictures in her hands. "I haven't looked at them all."

Nana went through the stack, occasionally pulling out a photo. When she finished, she spread the ones she'd chosen on the table and tapped the one nearest her. "Monica Carpenter. I saw her the other night at Blues & Such. She always was a funny little thing. I didn't like her, but Gabby was kind to her. Besides hanging around Harrison, she and this stagehand were tight."

She pointed to another photo. "He was there Friday night too. Emceeing."

"Jerome Winters?" Rachel looked at the chubby teenage boy in the picture. She supposed a skinnier version could be Winters. "He worked the stage? Are you sure?"

"Oh yes. Looks different now. The way I remember him, he had a lot of ambition, and he thought Monica could help him." Nana snorted. "Poor thing couldn't help anyone. She had too many of her own problems, starting with Jack Daniels."

"She has a drinking problem?"

"She did back then—heard Gabby and Harrison talking about it once."

Interesting. If she still hit the bottle, it might account for the way she'd looked this morning and the dark circles under her eyes. Maybe her drinking came from hiding something. Like a murder. The event planner definitely deserved a second look.

"Did you see her talking to anyone?" Boone asked.

"She talked to everyone, especially the Elvises. She even talked to me, asked if I was coming back Saturday night. I said probably not, that I was attending a party at Judge Winslow's." Nana nodded with a wink. "Impressed her, I did."

"Did she know who you were?"

The older woman frowned. "You know, she did. She called me by name."

Rachel exchanged glances with Boone. Maybe Monica didn't have to look Rachel up on Google yesterday. Maybe she already knew who she was.

"Could she have remembered you from when Mom was involved with all those Elvis shows?"

"Why, that's probably it. I was always there with Gabby, helping out." She glanced at the other photos. "It's funny how many of the people in these photos are still hanging around the Elvis events. Like Randy Culver. He's really done well. I heard on the news this morning he'd collapsed. I hope he's going to be all right."

"I do too," Rachel said. "Who are the other people in the photos?"

Nana shuffled the photos again, stopping at a shot that looked as though it was taken backstage. She pointed out a brunette who looked to be in her thirties. "Can't remember her name, but she was moonstruck on Harrison. Followed him around like a puppy."

Rachel looked closer at the photo. She'd seen her in another photo. The woman's round face looked vaguely familiar. Even though probably a hundred pounds overweight, she was dressed stylishly in a gray-and-silver metallic top and black satin pants.

Nana tapped a photo of Harrison Foxx with his arm wrapped

around a shapely blonde. "Lucinda Vetch. She had a thing for Harrison. She came into Blues & Such Friday night with someone half her age."

Ah, the elusive Ms. Vetch. "Do you know her well?"

"So-so. She's high up in the deb scene."

"Do you have an address for her?" Boone asked.

"Not offhand, but I can get it for you."

"Thanks." She hugged her grandmother. "Call me when you get it."

Nana saluted like she had her marching orders. "Yes, ma'am."

After they bid her grandmother goodbye, they stepped out into the afternoon heat. "Are these temperatures supposed to break anytime soon?" Rachel asked.

"I think a cool front is supposed to come through by Monday or Tuesday. Probably bring some storms."

Anything would be a relief compared to the heat, and they sure needed the rain.

Boone used his remote to unlock his truck door. "I think the next thing we need to do is talk to Culver. He mentioned that Vegas argued with someone Friday night. Maybe it was Monica."

It was sweltering inside the car, and she fanned herself until cool air flowed from the air conditioner. "Randy also mentioned a necklace. I wish we could find out more about it."

Something about the necklace Culver mentioned intrigued her. Why would Vic make a big deal out of a necklace? Maybe Monica saw the argument. It was clear she hadn't told all she knew. Rachel definitely wanted to follow up alone with the event planner.

Boone nodded toward the photos still in Rachel's hand. "Maybe whoever killed Foxx thought he had a thing for your mother . . . or your mother had a thing for him."

He was referring to the embrace between her mother and Harrison.

Rachel refused to believe there was anything between them.

But hadn't she seen the covert glances they exchanged? *No.* She'd misread their body language.

"Anyone who knew my mother would know better. My parents may have been separated, but it wasn't because of anything Mom did."

She slipped the photos into her bag. She was so tired of hiding her father's affair, but to bring it up now could cost him the Appeals Court nomination. "I've gone over her file so much I can almost quote it. When the detectives discovered my parents were separated, they dissected the marriage and concluded it was exactly like the Judge said. He was to blame for never being home. Mom and Harrison were friends. Period. Nothing else."

She'd often wondered why his affair hadn't been discovered.

"But what if someone *believed* they had a thing going?"

"How could they think that? If anyone knew her, they knew she and Dad were working out their problems." Except . . . she tried to push the memory away. Her mother and father yelling. No—her mother yelling, the Judge infuriatingly calm as always. She couldn't recall exactly what they argued about, but somehow Harrison Foxx was involved. As soon as they realized she'd heard them, they dropped the argument . . . But was Rachel making more of it than it had been?

"Tell me more about your mother's case and the burglaries going on in the neighborhood."

"We've already been over this."

"Humor me."

She knew the cases by heart. "The MO was the same for all the break-ins. No forced entry, the homeowners were all out of the house, and only jewelry and electronics—things that were easily fenced—were stolen. A housecleaning service was the common denominator."

"And no one was charged with your mother's death."

"No." That had bothered her from the first time she looked into the case. "Six people were involved in the ring, and the night our house was broken into, all but one of them had an alibi. They were in jail, rounded up in a drug bust. That's how they were caught—when they were printed, one of their fingerprints matched prints left at one of the burglary sites. They pleaded down and pinned the burglary at our house and Mom's death on their absent buddy."

"So they arrested him?"

"No. He died of an overdose. And then they recanted what they said."

"Convenient."

She'd thought so too. But she hadn't been able to find evidence that pointed to anyone else. Until Vic said Foxx's murder was connected to her mother's. If only she'd believed him and gotten his files. For more reasons than one.

# 25

RACHEL WAS SILENT BESIDE BOONE as he drove downtown, allowing him to make a mental list. Pull Gabby Winslow's case once he reached the CJC. Maybe the other detectives had missed something. Call the US Marshals for late-developing information on the ricin. Check out—

"It won't take both of us to interview Culver," Rachel said suddenly. "Why don't you drop me off at the parking garage and go see him by yourself?"

"And you?"

"I think I'll catch Monica Carpenter before she leaves. Nana brought up some interesting things that Monica might feel freer talking about without you along."

"What sort of things?" He didn't like the idea, especially if Monica turned out to be the one Vegas was arguing with.

"Her relationship with Harrison and possibly even Winters. And you don't need me to talk to Culver."

"Just watch your back. Someone tried to kill you or the Judge last night. And for all we know, that person could be Monica Carpenter." He sensed her stiffening.

"Even if she's the killer, she's not going to kill me in her condo," she said evenly. "I face danger every day I put on a gun, just like everyone else in the department. You don't have to hover over me."

"I'm not hovering." Okay, so he was. But his kind of hovering had brought the soldiers under him home from Iraq. All alive. Except one. "It's one thing to face down a criminal holding a gun—that's not personal and you're well trained for it. Whoever sent the ricin is a different breed and doesn't care who they hurt to get to you."

"But—"

"No buts. I'm coming with you to interview Carpenter."

"Really, it'll be better if you don't—the questions I plan to ask aren't the kind she'll want to answer in front of you. You need to do your thing and let me do mine," she said. "I'll be okay. Criminals who do things in secret aren't apt to attack in broad daylight. Besides, Monica Carpenter didn't send me the ricin. She wouldn't have known I would be at the Judge's. Or where he lives."

"His address would be easy enough to find out. And Rose told her about the party he was having—Monica could have assumed you would be there." He made a left turn and then pulled into the parking garage. "But you're right. You're a cop and you can handle the situation. Just watch your back."

"Ten-four."

He grinned. "Where are you parked?"

"Second level."

Once she got in her car and drove away, he took her parking space. The Med was a block from the Criminal Justice Center, and the short walk would give him time to sort out his thoughts on the case.

He'd just left the relative coolness of the parking garage when his phone rang. "Callahan."

"This is US Marshal Steve Lock. I'm handling the ricin case involving one of your officers, Rachel Sloan, but she's not answering her home phone, and I don't have her cell number. Can you get me in touch with her?"

"She's on her way to interview a person of interest. Let me text you her number."

"Great. I'd like you to be present when I go over the events of last night. Say in half an hour?"

"Not a problem." He'd still have time to check on Culver. "Why don't we meet at the CJC?"

"See you then."

Rachel would not be happy about having her plans interrupted, and sure enough two minutes after he sent the marshal her number, a text dinged on his phone from Rachel.

Did you call the US MARSHAL?

He texted back.

Nope. See you at the CJC.

Her reply was a frustrated emoji.

Boone laughed. He resumed his trek to the Med and decided walking may have been a mistake. The pungent odor of hot concrete and asphalt burned his nose. It was hard to concentrate on anything except the heat that had hovered near the hundred-degree mark for five straight days. That and the humidity wrapping around him like a hot towel until his white shirt stuck to his back. By the time he walked into the hospital, his body begged for the cool relief.

In ICU, a nurse was checking the ventilator breathing for Culver. The heart rate monitor had been silenced, but it showed a steady, albeit high, rhythm. "I'm Lt. Boone Callahan. How is he?" he asked, showing his badge.

She gave a cautionary glance at Boone and then waved her hand back and forth. "He's better than he was. Slowly coming out of the coma, and we're trying to let his lungs take over from the ventilator. He still needs it, though."

Which meant Boone couldn't have a conversation with him. Culver's eyes fluttered open, and the overhead monitor indicated his heart rate jumped. He focused on Boone, pinning him with a hard stare.

"Just stopped by to check on you," Boone said. He thought he detected a slight nod but couldn't be sure as Culver closed his eyes and slipped back to sleep.

Boone followed the nurse outside the room where she entered data into a computer. "When I called, I was told he was awake."

She looked up. "I know, and I'm sorry about that. When the doctors tried to wean him off the medication to raise his blood sugar, he reverted. Maybe if you come back in a couple of hours, he'll be more alert and possibly even off the vent."

Boone nodded. "Do you know when the doctor will be around?"

"He's on the floor if you'd like to talk to him." When he said yes, she called a number on her cell phone and spoke to someone, then looked up. "He'll be here in a few minutes."

Boone stepped back inside the room but remembered a question he wanted to ask and stepped back out. "Has the patient had any visitors?"

"One lady with big glasses. I thought it was his mother or an older sister, but I asked him when he was more alert, and he shook his head."

Monica. Boone heard soft-soled shoes behind him and turned around. The same doctor he'd talked to earlier approached. "How much longer do you think he'll be on the vent?" Boone asked.

The doctor rubbed his chin. "Hard to tell. I thought he'd be off by now. And awake."

"So you can't tell me when?"

"Afraid not," he said. "I understand you picked up the bottle the paramedics brought in. Were there any fingerprints on it?"

"The paramedics' and a partial of Culver's thumb and index finger."

"So you think it was wiped clean before it was switched."

"Yeah. And the water bottle had traces of Humulin R U-500 in it as well. No prints other than Culver's on it, either. Is there any possibility that Culver tried to kill himself?"

The doctor shook his head. "People have used insulin to commit suicide, but I don't know of any cases where they went to the trouble to put it in the wrong bottle. I don't believe this is an attempted suicide case. Randy Culver has been fighting too hard to live."

That was what Boone wanted to know. "Thank you for your time."

Before he left, he handed the nurse a card. "Would you give me a call if he becomes alert again before your shift ends?"

She assured him she would, and he walked back to the CJC, where Rachel waited in the conference room at the end of the table.

"Did you learn anything at the hospital?"

He shook his head. "Culver isn't awake yet."

Rachel was quiet for a minute, and then she looked up. "What do you think the marshal has come up with?"

He shrugged. "No idea."

Her phone rang and she grabbed it.

Boone laughed. "Is that 'God Save the Queen'?"

"Yes." She slid her finger across the screen. "Hello, Gran. Is something wrong?"

He turned and walked to the window, but Rachel's voice followed him.

"Hold on a second."

He turned as she called his name.

"Do you think we'll be finished here by five?"

He checked his watch. It was barely three. "I don't see the meeting lasting two hours."

"Thanks." She spoke back into the phone. "I should be there by five thirty. Is that all right?" After a slight pause, she said, "Good. See you then."

"Anything wrong?" he asked.

"Not at all. It was about Erin."

"She's all right, isn't she?" He'd hate for anything to happen to the petite brunette.

"Yeah. I'm picking her up from my grandmother's, and she wants me to stay for dinner before I take Erin to the group home."

"We should be through in plenty of time." It was clear Rachel really connected with Erin. Not everyone did when someone was different.

"Good. After I drop her off, I plan to go back to Beale Street and interview a few of the Elvis impersonators."

"I'll meet you there. Seven thirty again?"

Rachel nodded. "I should have Erin home by then."

"How long have you known her?"

She walked back to the table and sat down. "Off and on all my life, but I've been around her more since Terri became her guardian."

He'd wondered more than once what was wrong with Erin. She didn't appear to have Down syndrome and no particular problem that he could see, other than something didn't seem quite right.

"What happened with her?"

Rachel hesitated. "Something to do with lack of oxygen during delivery. Her mom was in her late forties when she was born and died when Erin was seventeen. Her father died a couple of years later, and Terri has been her caregiver ever since."

He liked Terri and admired that she'd taken on the care of her sister. "That's a big responsibility."

"Terri has never acted like she minds. She's devoted to Erin."

A shadow darkened the door, and he turned as Steve Lock came into the room.

"Sorry I'm late," he said.

Boone checked his watch. "Only five minutes." He introduced the US Marshal to Rachel. "What have you learned?"

"Not much." Steve placed his briefcase on the table and took the chair opposite Boone. "No prints on the box or wrapping paper. And while the paper is expensive, it can be bought at any party store. The most important thing we learned is that no one was ever in danger from the ricin."

"What?" Boone and Rachel spoke at the same time.

He unsnapped the briefcase and took out a sheet of paper. "Take a look. The latest analysis shows the poison is inactive."

Rachel scanned it first, then handed it to Boone.

"But it is ricin?" he asked.

"Yes. Definitely ricin. And laboratory quality."

"What do you mean?" Rachel asked.

"Our analyst thinks it came from someone experimenting with ricin at a research facility."

"Who experiments with a poison?" Boone asked.

"Scientists looking for an antibody to target cancer cells."

"Okay," Rachel said. "Then it shouldn't be hard to trace."

"Unfortunately, researchers using less than a hundred milligrams are exempt from reporting it," Steve said. "And no one has reported a theft of ricin in the past five years."

"Then how would someone get ahold of it?" she asked. "And why send it to me if it isn't going to kill me?"

"Could be the person or whoever they bought it from didn't know it'd lost its toxicity. Or they may have wanted to just intimidate or scare you." Steve took out his tablet and booted it up. "Any idea who might fit this profile? Or can you think of any enemies you might have made?"

She shook her head. "The only thing that makes me think I might be the target is the text I received Saturday afternoon, warning me off the case we're currently working on."

"Have you received any other texts?"

"No."

Steve typed notes on his tablet, then looked up. "How about your father? Does he have any enemies?"

"He's a judge and has the potential to make enemies in every case he decides."

"He's next on my list to interview. Do you know if he's received any demands or if he's involved in an important case?" Steve said.

"He'd tell you all his cases are important, but nothing high profile that I know of. Although he did mention he was frustrated with the defense in a murder case he's trying. Something about trying to delay the trial," she said. "And I think he would have mentioned if he'd received any kind of demand, or at least reported it to someone. Particularly since this happened last night."

Rachel stared down at her clasped hands. "There is something I should mention, even though I don't think it has anything to do with the ricin."

When she hesitated, Boone said, "It might be important."

"I know. It's an announcement that I'm supposed to keep under wraps, and no one around here knows about it, so I don't see how it can be important."

Steve leaned forward. "We won't know until you tell us."

"He's being nominated for the Sixth District Court of Appeals."

Boone had not expected that and evidently neither had Steve since her announcement silenced them both.

"That's not usually something a person would be killed over," Steve said.

"My thoughts too. Please keep it quiet until it's announced."

They both nodded and Steve asked, "How about other cases you've handled?"

She thought a minute. "Nothing stands out. I was in Burglary before I transferred to Homicide. Nothing I can think of there. Except for one, my homicide cases have been routine, if murder can be routine."

"What was that one?"

"The one involving the Pink Palace earlier this year. But it was resolved and no threats were made."

"I remember the museum case," Steve said. "What's the current case you're working?"

"We think it's tied to a cold case," Boone said. He explained the details to Steve.

Steve shook his head. "This ricin attack bothers me. There's no apparent motive, no leads, and I can't even be sure if it's a viable threat. The agency can't do anything unless the person responsible makes another move, and even if it's a scare tactic, it could escalate to a real attack. We don't know what we're dealing with or why. If they tried it once, they'll be apt to try it again."

Steve had just articulated every thought that had crossed Boone's mind.

# 26

THE SUN WAS STILL HIGH when Rachel checked her watch as she crossed Washington to the parking garage. Five o'clock. The meeting that had just ended with Boone and the US Marshal troubled her. Why would someone send her ricin that was ineffective? Did they just not know? She certainly didn't know the poison could go stale.

She couldn't shake the feeling that the ricin was connected to Vic Vegas's death, which would connect it to Harrison Foxx's murder. Was it possible someone wanted her off the case bad enough to try to kill her? Or maybe think an attempt on her life would put her on administrative leave? It was a reach . . .

Rachel drove to her grandmother's house, making the turns and stops automatically. One thought after another chased through her head, landing on a memory that played around her subconscious. Her parents arguing. The memory was so close, like a word on the tip of her tongue that she couldn't get out. Frustrated, she shook her head. She needed time to process all she'd learned. A luxury she didn't have.

Maybe her father could shed light on the argument. The thought of asking him dropped rocks in her stomach. Two more turns brought her to Gran's street. Being around Gran and Erin would help shake the dread from her mind. When she pulled into the drive, for a second she stared at the ranch-style house, glad that Gran was still in the home Rachel had spent so many nights in growing up. But she feared the upkeep was getting to be too much for her grandmother.

Of course, Gran could move in with the Judge. He certainly had enough room. Rachel snorted. That was so not happening for the same reason she would never move back home. Gran would hold on to her independence as long as she could. Rachel parked in the drive and rang the doorbell. The door opened almost immediately.

Erin's concerned face greeted her. "I thought you forgot me."

"How could I do that?" she asked and hugged her friend. "Did you look before you opened the door?"

She stared down at the floor. "I forgot. I'm sorry." Suddenly she raised her head and made a stern face. "Erin, you know better than to open the door without checking to see who is there."

"You sounded just like Terri."

"That's what she says, every time—to look before I open it."

"You need to listen to her. Where's Gran?"

"Making pizza. When I told her I wanted her to eat with us, she said she'd make pizza. I'm making the salad."

When it came to her grandmother, what Erin wanted, Erin got. Which was fine with Rachel. She was just glad she didn't have to go to a noisy restaurant. Blues & Such later would be loud enough. "I'm sure you're doing a great job."

"Can I still wear your necklace?" she asked, touching the cross. Rachel had forgotten the silver cross. "Sure. Just don't lose it."

"I won't. Will you take me to light the candles at Elvis's house this week? Terri is supposed to, but sometimes she doesn't feel like doing what she promised."

"Ah . . . if I'm not busy."

Her grandmother smiled when Rachel entered the kitchen. "I

hope you like the pizza," she said. "It's vegetarian, and I've tried a new cauliflower crust."

"I love your pizza." But cauliflower? What would her grandmother think of next? She hugged her and looked around. "Can I help?"

"No. We have it under control, don't we, Erin?"

Sometimes Rachel feared watching after Erin was too much for Gran. But for several years now, she'd been letting Rachel know she wasn't dead yet and to mind her own business. Both her grandmothers were so independent. Exactly like Rachel wanted to be when she was their age.

Dinner was fun, and Erin kept them laughing with imitations of Terri and some of the women she shared a home with. It warmed Rachel's heart to know Erin was in a good place, both physically and emotionally. Terri called to let them know the recital went well and that she would see Erin on Tuesday. After they cleaned up the kitchen, Gran sent her to gather her things.

"Okay, the pizza wasn't that bad," Gran said when Erin left the room. "But you picked at your food and barely talked."

"No, it actually tastes pretty good."

"Then what's eating at you?"

All evening, the elusive memory of her parents' argument had played around the edge of Rachel's mind. "It's this case. I really need to talk to Dad about it, and you know how he feels about my job."

"I wish you were still at the law office myself, especially since someone tried to kill you. I heard on the *news* that the package contained ricin," Gran said.

Rachel winced. "Sorry. I should have called, but I just haven't had time."

"Hmph." Gran eyed her with a you-better-make-time look. "Have you learned anything about who sent the package?"

Rachel draped the drying towel over a rack. "Only that I never was in danger. The ricin was too old to be dangerous."

"So whoever sent it wasn't trying to kill you?"

"Who knows? They may not have realized it'd lost its power."

"How would they have gotten their hands on it in the first place?"

"That's the million-dollar question. The US Marshal thinks it may have come from a laboratory where scientists conduct cancer research."

Erin set her overnight case on the floor. "Bobby did cancer research."

Rachel turned to stare at Erin. Terri's husband had died when Erin was three, so like Rachel, she didn't remember him. Rachel hadn't known he'd been a scientist. "How do you know that?"

"Terri told Martha."

Martha was the housemother at the group home. "Why did Terri tell her that?"

"Don't know." She switched into Terri mode. "'I wish you could have met Bobby. He was working on a cure for liver cancer when he died.' That's what Terri told her."

Rachel couldn't keep from smiling. Erin had captured her sister's mannerisms to a T.

"I'm ready to go home." She grabbed Rachel's hand and tugged.

"Well then, I guess I'm ready to take you." She hugged Gran. "I'll try to get by for supper one night this week."

"I'll hold you to that."

"How about I take us both out for our birthday Tuesday night?"

"No," Erin said, "you promised to go to light the candles Tuesday."

That was right. "Maybe lunch," Rachel said. "And don't worry about me."

Gran's long fingers cupped Rachel's chin. "I won't. You're a Winslow and Winslows are tough, but they also watch their backs."

# 27

THIRTY MINUTES LATER, Rachel dropped Erin off with a promise to go to the candlelight service at Graceland Tuesday night if she possibly could, and then she dialed Boone's number. He'd said something about checking on Culver before meeting her. "I'm on my way to Blues & Such. Where are you?"

"Parking," he said. "Did your dinner go well?"

"Yes. Gran had a pizza ready when I got there so I didn't have to go out. How about you?"

"Hot dog."

"Eww. Do you know what's in those things?"

He laughed. "Don't lecture me. You had a pizza."

"A vegetarian pizza made with a cauliflower crust."

"Don't tell me you're a health food nut."

"No. Gran is." She turned into the parking garage and saw him standing by his car. Rachel pocketed her phone and pulled in beside his car. "How is Culver?"

"It's still touch and go. His blood sugar isn't dropping as drastically when they try to wean him off the medicine, and he's off the vent. The nurse thought he should be alert enough tomorrow for me to ask him questions."

"Maybe we'll get some answers then," she said as they crossed Beale Street. "Busy here tonight."

He nodded toward the entrance to Blues & Such where tourists were streaming in. "Yeah. Everyone looks like they're going to the same place we are."

Inside the café, strains of "That's All Right, Mama" rocked the building as they worked their way to the door they'd gone through just last night. She scanned the crowd to see if Donna was there but didn't find her. The fans went crazy when the song ended, clapping and whistling. It was a little quieter as they stepped into the backstage area.

"Well, if it isn't the Bobbsey Twins."

She turned. Monica Carpenter leaned against the wall with a coffee cup in her hands. For some reason, her body language was more relaxed, and she definitely had a better attitude than earlier in the day. "You're dating yourself," Rachel replied.

"What can I say? They were a part of my generation." She took a sip from the cup. "This generation doesn't know what they're missing. What are you looking for this time?"

"Just answers to questions," Boone said.

"What? You're not finished with me?"

Her voice had lost its usual sarcasm, and Rachel wondered if there was anything other than coffee in the cup, because she was definitely warmer.

"Actually, no." He pointed to a camera. "I'd like to view the video from Friday and Saturday."

"Sorry. No clue about that. You'll have to talk to the manager."

While Boone went to find the manager, Rachel said, "Is Lucinda Vetch here yet?"

Monica walked to the door and scanned the audience. "Third table, the blonde in the black strapless top."

Lucinda Vetch looked nothing like Rachel had expected. She'd pictured a lonely older woman, maybe overweight. Not this blonde bombshell with her arms raised and moving to the beat of the music. Since she didn't look like she was leaving anytime soon, Rachel pulled out a list of performers she'd made from the photos at her grandmother's house and handed it to Monica. "Do you recognize any of these names?"

She looked over the list. "A few of them. They used to perform at some of the events I put together. Where did you get these names?"

"On the back of photos that were taken when Harrison Foxx won the contest seventeen years ago. Are any of them here tonight?" Last night they had not questioned any of the performers about Foxx's case.

Monica looked at the list again. "Daryl Cook. I saw him a few minutes ago."

Boone had interviewed him last night. "Where?"

Monica nodded toward the stage.

Rachel turned. She'd noticed Cook was one of the better-looking singers and was about her age, maybe a little older. He was about to take the stage. She would catch him when he finished. "Are you sure you don't remember seeing Vic Vegas talking to someone Friday night?"

Hesitation crossed her face before she set the coffee cup on a nearby table. "I'm sorry, but I was busy, and my coffee break is over. I have work to do."

Monica Carpenter definitely knew more than she was saying.

"Get anything more from her?" Boone asked when he returned.

"Not tonight." Tomorrow, at her condo, would be a different story. "Lucinda Vetch is here." Rachel pointed her out to Boone. "She's next on my list to interview. How about you? Did you get the video?"

"I'm going to tap into their feed as soon as we finish here."

She nodded. "I'll catch Jerome and then talk to Ms. Vetch."

"Why don't I talk to her?"

"Sounds good." Boone would probably get more out of the

lady than Rachel. While he threaded his way through the crowd, she walked over to where the emcee stood in the wings waiting for Cook to finish. "Do you have a minute?" she asked.

"That's about all I have. Daryl should be finished soon."

"Did you see the basket Randy Culver received last night?"

He frowned. "Not really. Flowers, baskets, so many of them arrived Friday and Saturday that I stopped noticing who got what."

"Did you notice anyone around Culver's basket?"

"No. Did someone take something from his basket?"

"Someone stole his bottled water."

He turned his head toward the stage to watch Cook. "So, someone grabbed a water."

"Someone also switched out the insulin in his travel bag."

Jerome snapped his attention back to Rachel. "What? Are you sure? How do you know?"

"Because the vial he had in his bag had insulin five times stronger than what was on the label."

"That doesn't make sense. Why would anyone do that?"

"I was hoping you could tell me."

He shook his head. "Everyone likes Randy. Unless . . ."

"Unless what?"

"He *is* the favorite to win the Supreme Elvis next Saturday. Daryl's the odds-on second." He glanced toward the stage. "Look, I gotta get on stage in less than a minute."

"One more quick question. Did you see Vic Vegas talking to anyone Friday night?"

He rubbed the back of his perfectly coiffed blond hair, being careful not to disturb the style. "He talked to everyone."

"Did he talk to you?"

"Yeah. He pigeonholed me just before stage time. Asking questions about Harrison Foxx. Like I would remember *anything* about that time."

"You don't?"

"That's when I was doing a little weed." He held his thumb and forefinger together like he was holding a joint. "Well, not a little. A *lot*. Pretty well stoned, so those days are kind of hazy."

Daryl Cook ended his song and Jerome said, "Gotta go."

She caught the singer as he bounded off stage. "That was good," she said. "Can I have a minute of your time?"

"I told that other detective all I know last night."

"It never hurts to tell it again." She asked him the same question about Culver's basket, and he scratched his ear.

"Maybe."

Her heart caught. "Could you elaborate?"

"The basket was here when I arrived. Sitting right beside one for me, only it was bigger than mine. We usually leave them on the table, but I noticed later someone had moved them both. By the way, I much prefer a goody basket to flowers," he said with a grin. "In case you're wondering."

She ignored his comment. "Did you see anyone fooling around with the baskets?"

He winced. "Oh, man! I forgot all about seeing a brunette grab the water out of it after Randy collapsed. Just figured she was thirsty."

"Can you describe her?"

He scratched his jaw. "Not really, other than she wore something big and flowing. It reached the floor."

"Would you recognize her if you saw her again?"

"I didn't really get a good look at her face, just that she was a brunette. I couldn't even tell you how old she was."

"How about Vic Vegas? How well did you know him?"

"I've hung out with him over the years. Nice guy. But he'd bug the daylights out of you about Harrison Foxx's murder."

"What do you remember about that?"

"Not much. Never particularly liked Foxx. He was always stringing at least two or three women along. Wouldn't surprise me if one of them didn't kill him."

"You don't happen to remember some of their names, do you?"

He scratched the side of his cheek. "Naw. There are always women hanging around a stage. And his women were a little too old for me."

"Did you see Vic talking to anyone Friday night?"

"Didn't pay much attention to Vic, either. Probably anyone who'd talk to him."

Monica called Daryl's name, and he shrugged. "If you'll excuse me, I have to get my picture taken."

For the next hour, Rachel interviewed the other contestants one after another to the backdrop of ballads, hymns, and rock and roll. If anyone remembered seeing Randy Culver's basket arrive, they didn't remember anything else about it. Everyone was focused on the singers until Randy Culver's collapse.

When she questioned them about Vic Vegas, a couple of the performers remembered seeing him talking to different people, but no single description. A blonde, a redhead, a brunette. He evidently talked to men and women. But no one mentioned an argument or even a deep discussion. Hopefully, Randy Culver would be able to give them more information on the person he saw with Vic.

# 28

"DEPUTY LOCK"—ANDI HOLLISTER, the reporter for WLTZ, pointed the microphone at the US Deputy Marshal—"are you saying the police detective who received the ricin was *not* in danger?"

"I didn't say that. I said the ricin the officer received was inactive."

"Why would someone do that? Do you think it was a warning?"

"Possibly. Or perhaps the sender didn't know that ricin loses its toxicity rather quickly." He looked into the camera. "But we will apprehend the person responsible. Not that many companies use ricin in their research. It's just a matter of tracing the chemical to its point of origin. This person will be caught and put in prison."

Prison was not an option. And the marshal would never trace this ricin. With a click, the TV screen went black. But the ricin wasn't active? She'd gone to all that trouble for nothing? At the very least, Shirley had been counting on the ricin to put Rachel in the hospital.

But Rachel hadn't opened the package, had called Boone Callahan instead. She was proving to be a smarter opponent than Shirley expected. "I'm smarter than you, Detective Sloan," she muttered. "You were just luckier this time."

She paced her den. It'd been bad luck the detective was at Blues

& Such when Culver collapsed. And grabbed the blue travel bag, making it impossible to switch the bottles again. Otherwise, no one would have questioned the coma or known the bottle contained the wrong insulin. She ground her teeth.

Her father's maniacal laugh filled her head. *You can't do anything right, can you, girl? Now the police will be looking for you.*

Shirley rubbed her temple. "The police will not be looking for me. No one saw me make the switch."

She'd hidden the small medical bag in the fold of her caftan and taken it to the ladies' room, where she made the switch and changed into her regular clothes. Getting the medical bag back to Randy's table had been easy—she'd hidden it under her shirt and made sure she never faced the cameras in the room.

But she couldn't let Randy Culver tell Rachel about the necklace, and since he was out of her reach now, she'd have to get rid of Rachel. And that would silence Shirley's father's voice once and for all.

But a new plan would have to be put into place. In the corner of the room, a .22 caliber Browning rifle braced against the wall. This was a riskier plan and would require a disguise just in case someone saw her in the area.

Thirty minutes later, a quick look in the mirror confirmed the disguise was perfect. A short red wig and the scruffy red beard was a nice touch. Now to see where Rachel was. Putting the tracker in the wheel of her car had been a good idea.

Still downtown. Good. There was time to get in place before she drove home.

# 29

As Boone approached Lucinda Vetch's table, she eyed him like he was a T-bone steak. "Mind if I sit?" he asked. The musicians had taken a break, so at least he didn't have to shout.

Her gaze rested on the gun he wore, and a slow smile spread across her tanned face. "Big guy, you surely can. What's your name?"

Oh, great. A badge bunny. "Lt. Boone Callahan, ma'am."

"Well, Boone, have a seat. You don't mind if I call you Boone, do you? What can I do for you?"

As he'd walked toward her, he'd found it hard to tell how old she was, but when he sat down he could see the crow's feet around her eyes along with tiny lines framing her lips. Late forties, he figured, maybe even midfifties. "I'm investigating the murder of a man I believe you were once acquainted with. Harrison Foxx."

The transformation was instant. Her eyes hardened, and she clenched her jaw. "Let me know when you find out who killed the dirty, two-timing sleazeball. I'd like to pay for their lawyer."

"I take it you weren't fond of Foxx."

"Nope." A waitress set a glass of red wine in front of Lucinda, and she signed her name on the tab. "But since you know who I am, you're already aware of that. For the record, I didn't kill him."

"Do you have any ideas on who might have?"

She raised the drink to her lips and took a long sip. After she set the glass down, she tilted her head. "That happened a long time ago. Why are you investigating it now?"

"Does it matter? A man is dead and I want to find his killer. Tell me about your relationship with him."

"It wasn't much of a relationship. I was one of many on his string of wealthy girlfriends. He took *my* money and bought gifts for them."

"Do you remember any of their names?"

"Do you want the names of those who wanted to do him in, or just generally?"

"Let's start with the first."

"Other than me, Monica Carpenter would be next on my list of those who wanted to kill him."

"Why Monica?"

Lucinda took another sip of wine. "She really thought he was going to marry her. And then there was one of the women working backstage at the contests that year. A dancer." She flipped a strand of the platinum hair back. "Terri was a mousy little thing. I was more worried about her killing herself than killing him."

"Anyone else?"

She lifted her gaze upward. After a few seconds, she shifted her focus back to Boone. "There was another woman who hung around him, overweight, not really his type. Don't remember her name. And there was no love lost between him and a few of the other tribute artists. About the only friend he had in the business was Vic Vegas."

"Do you know all the tribute artists?"

"Only the best ones." She waved her glass toward the stage. "I have a stressful career, and this is my downtime."

"What do you do?"

"I run a modeling agency." She shuddered. "You haven't lived until you manage a group of prima donnas."

He jotted the information on his notepad. "Do you remember where you were the night Foxx was murdered?"

She considered his question and then shook her head. "Afraid not. One forgets a lot in seventeen years."

"How about Vic Vegas and Randy Culver? Any idea of who would want them dead?"

"Do you think what happened to them is connected to Harrison Foxx's death?"

"It's possible. Were you here Friday night?" When she nodded, he asked, "Did you see Vegas talking to anyone Friday night?"

She turned and scanned the room. "The way he was out here working the crowd, you would've thought he was competing, but no one stands out in my memory. Have you checked the security video?"

From the corner of his eye, he saw Rachel approaching. "Not yet, but I will." He took out one of his cards and handed it to her. "If you remember anything related to Vegas's or Foxx's deaths, give me a call."

Lucinda glanced at the card, then lifted her gaze and winked at him. "I will, Lieutenant."

"Did you learn anything?" Rachel asked when he joined her.

He told her what little he'd discovered and then said, "You want to go back to the CJC and watch the video?"

"What I want to do is take a run and clear my head, but I'm good with looking at the security videos." She put away her notepad. "Of course, if you're up to it, we can always stop by the gym on the way home and get in a couple of miles on the treadmill."

"Won't the place be closed?"

"I have twenty-four-hour access," she said, giving him a smug grin.

Which probably explained why she always beat his time in the personal fitness tests.

# 30

BOONE SET HIS LAPTOP on the conference table and booted it up. It'd been a long day, but the first forty-eight hours were crucial in an investigation. They'd gathered a lot of information, and maybe the video feed would give them more.

Rachel sat beside him with her laptop so they could view more than one feed at a time. The light fragrance he'd noticed earlier still lingered, reminding him of honeysuckle. He refocused and typed in the information the security company gave him. The live feed popped up on the screen, divided up into five frames. Two outside cameras, three inside.

"The tech said to go to file, then archives, and find the time frame we want," he said. "And we can speed the film up so we're not here all night."

Once they had the files opened, he clicked on Saturday and started the film rolling at 5:00 p.m., thirty minutes before the first basket arrived.

"I'll take camera one," she said, tapping on her mouse pad.

It showed the entrance and front tables. Anyone coming or going would show up. "I'll take camera three—backstage," Boone said.

Half an hour later, Rachel nudged him. "I think we have something here."

Boone shifted toward her. "What is it?"

"Someone is delivering a basket." She backed the film up.

The front door opened, and a delivery person carried in a basket. The images were dark, like there was too much sunlight in the background. He couldn't tell if it was the basket Culver grabbed a bottle from. "Pause the feed right there where you can see the ribbon. Can you read what's on it?"

She leaned forward, squinting at the computer screen. "Is that an R on it?"

He leaned forward as well. "Maybe. We'll let the techs see what they can do with this tomorrow." Boone stared at the delivery person. Looked like some type of uniform, and whoever it was wore a ball cap pulled low over wild blond hair. "I can't see the face. Can you?"

She shook her head. "I can't even tell if it's a man or a woman—the hair could belong to either. Let's see if the lighting gets any better."

They watched in silence as the person set the basket on a table and turned. Rachel froze the feed. "There. Is that a beard?"

He looked closer. This frame was blurred, and he could barely make out the jaw. "Maybe. Could be a shadow."

"Whoever it is, they never looked toward the camera," Rachel said. "It's like they knew where it was."

"We know we're not dealing with your run-of-the-mill killer. Let's see the rest of the video."

Boone fast-forwarded the video, stopping when Terri came into view carrying two baskets. They watched as she set the baskets on a table, then talked to Randy Culver. The video went to snow briefly, then picked up with Terri still standing near his table, but Randy was not there. Boone fast-forwarded again.

"Look at the video here—this is where the baskets were moved," Rachel said. She paused her feed then backed it up. "Here."

He looked over at her computer. Monica Carpenter picked up

two baskets and walked out of camera range. "One of those must have been Daryl Cook's basket that he mentioned," she said.

Boone nodded and returned to his video as it showed a brunette in a flowing caftan walking toward the table where Culver's basket sat. Her back was to the camera, and he couldn't see what she did at the table.

"Look at this," Rachel said a minute later. "It's the woman in the caftan. She's going to the ladies' room."

He stared at her screen. The video was grainy, and the woman kept her head ducked, keeping him from making out her features. "Let's see how long she's in there."

A few minutes later a brunette came out, but she kept her head down as she walked toward Culver's table and he couldn't be certain it was the same person. "Have you seen this brunette in any of your feeds?"

Rachel paused her feed and shifted her attention to his screen. "No."

Soon, the video showed Rachel and Boone talking to Culver, then the singer leaving.

"I think Randy's collapse is coming up. Watch for someone avoiding the cameras," Boone said.

A few minutes later chaos broke out on the tape as people focused their attention toward the stage, except for one person. She no longer wore the caftan, but the hair was the same style and color.

Boone kept his eyes on her, and beside him Rachel stiffened as the brunette barely glanced toward the stage. Instead, she calmly sidled around the table until her back was to the camera. Then it appeared she reached for something. "I think we have our person," he said. "Could you tell anything about her features?"

She shook her head. "It's so dark in that corner and then she turned around."

"Maybe our video techs can pull something out that we can't."

206

He rubbed his eyes. "I think I'm done. You okay with quitting for the night?"

"I won't argue with you."

When they reached their cars in the parking garage, he waited until she had her door unlocked. "I'll follow you home."

"My house is in the opposite direction from where you live, Boone." She looked at her watch. "It's almost midnight. No one is sitting on my street waiting to jump me when I get home. You're tired. I'm a cop. Go home."

He was too tired to argue with her. "Okay, Miss Independent. Have it your way."

Boone waited until she pulled out of the space before he climbed into his truck. But when she took a right out of the garage, he took one as well. He wasn't too tired to follow her home, just too tired to argue about it.

He knew a shortcut to her house and took it, so he was waiting when she pulled into her drive. When Boone climbed out of his truck, humidity was thick enough to swim in. He approached her Civic as she lowered her window.

"I can't believe you," she said, shaking her head.

"Believe it." A dog barked to his right. Suddenly the skin on the back of his neck prickled. His ears picked up a faint creak, like a door scraping against concrete. With his heart thrumming in his ears, Boone scanned the area.

Tall oaks cast eerie shadows from the full moon overhead. The darkened cars could conceal someone just waiting for Rachel to get out of her car alone. In the park across the street, swings hung empty. He pinned his gaze on the pavilion. Perfect vantage point for a sniper.

*Sniper?*

He wasn't in Iraq. And Rachel wasn't Corporal West.

"What's wrong?"

With his eyes still on the pavilion, he said, "I don't know, but you're a sitting duck out here. Pull into your garage."

Her body stiffened as she, too, scanned the area. "I don't see anyone," she whispered.

"I feel someone out there. Come on. Raise the garage door and get inside."

After she pulled into the garage, Boone ducked inside. He couldn't put his finger on why he thought someone was there, but he'd learned in Iraq not to ignore his internal alarms.

When the door was half closed, a car motor turned over. "Raise the door again," he said and dashed back into the drive, trying to find the vehicle. Halfway down the street, a small dark car shot away from the curb, but he couldn't make out the model.

"What happened out there?" she asked as soon as they were inside her house.

"I don't know."

"Well, you scared me to death."

"Sorry, but someone was out there."

She swayed and reached for the doorframe. "I didn't see anyone."

"Trust me, someone was waiting on you."

Rachel shivered and ran her hands up and down her arms. "Are you sure you aren't seeing things that aren't there?"

No, he couldn't be 100 percent sure. But the one time he hadn't listened to his gut, someone had died. "I don't know how to explain it, but when I was in Iraq, somehow I just knew when the enemy was near. It still happens sometimes."

She glanced toward the door. "Do you think they're still out there?"

"I don't think so now. I saw a car pull away from down the street. I couldn't see what kind, other than it was small. Do you know—"

"Only about twenty people I know drive small cars."

Her voice held irritation, and she probably thought he was manufacturing the whole thing. He didn't care. "Sorry I can't be more precise." At least she was safely inside now. "It's getting late, and I better go."

"Look, I'm wound tight, and didn't mean to take your head off." Rachel rubbed her arms again. "I'm going to have a cup of chamomile tea. Would you like to join me? Maybe a cup of decaf for you?"

"Sure." It surprised him that she wanted him to stay . . . and how much he wanted to stay. Only to make sure she was okay, though. He followed Rachel to her kitchen, noticing that, just like her desk, her house was neat.

He'd never been inside her home since she'd never asked him in when he picked her up for their dates. In fact, he would not have met her family if not for the dinner at her father's, a dinner he was certain the Judge had insisted on.

The house was open concept, with a fireplace that warmed both the living room and kitchen in the winter. The living area was filled with comfortable chairs and a leather sofa. "I've been looking for furniture. Where'd you get yours?"

"My grandmother." She glanced around. "Nana wanted all new furniture a year or so ago, so I got her old stuff. This was from her den."

"Then she has good taste."

"Oh yeah." Rachel laughed as she placed tea bags in a pot and turned on her water kettle along with the coffeemaker. She waved her hand toward a carousel of coffee pods. "Take your pick."

Coffee didn't keep him awake at night, so he chose a hazelnut blend instead of decaf. He knew he'd surprised her when she raised her eyebrows.

"I wouldn't have figured you for flavored coffee."

"Not all the time, but that's what sounds good to me tonight."

She started his coffee and rummaged through her cabinets. "Mug or china?"

"Mug, please. Then I won't have to worry about breaking it." He sat on one of the bar stools at the kitchen counter. "I like your house."

"Corey picked it out. It's the right neighborhood, the house is stately enough but not too showy, and he liked that there was a park across the street for our 2.5 kids."

"Kids?" Rachel didn't have children. "Wait a minute. Two-point-five?"

"Haven't you heard? That's the perfect family, and Corey wanted everything perfect."

"And he died before any children came along." It sounded as though the steamrolling attorney Boone knew in court wasn't any different at home. He'd observed there were no photos of him sitting around.

"He thought the ideal time to start a family was after three years of marriage. We were closing in on the second-year mark when he died . . ." She gave a slight shake of her head. "I don't know how we got on the topic of Corey when we were talking about the house."

"It's really a nice place."

"You should have seen it before I changed it." Rachel glanced toward the living area. "He had an interior decorator come in and furnish it before we moved in. Her tastes were more modern than mine, and after . . ." She bit her bottom lip. "Well, it just wasn't me, so when Nana downsized, I changed everything out."

"I'm sure his death had to have been hard." Boone took the steaming mug she handed him. She never talked about her husband. "It was some kind of accident, wasn't it?"

# 31

THE KETTLE WHISTLED, allowing Rachel time to collect herself while she filled the teapot with hot water. Talking about Corey's accident was never easy, but for some reason, she found herself wanting to share the story with Boone.

"It was a boating accident. One that wouldn't have happened if I'd gone on the trip with him." Sometimes Rachel surprised even herself. She'd never said those words to anyone except Nana. Once she'd poured the steaming water in the teapot, she moved it to the counter and sat across from Boone.

"You don't know that it would have made any difference if you'd gone."

"Yes, I do. If I'd gone, he wouldn't have been fishing at the dam when they started up the turbines. I wouldn't have let him," she said.

"He was a grown man. Not much you could have done if he was determined to fish there."

"Now we'll never know." Guilt hung over her like a storm cloud. If only she'd gone on the trip. "That swirling mass of water . . . the way it rushes through the gates. Just thinking about it terrifies me. I can't imagine what it was like in his small boat. A log came through the gates and caught the boat and flipped it. No one is sure which hit him on the head, but he drowned before anyone could get to him."

Rachel raised her gaze, and his brown eyes sympathized with her. "You know why I didn't go? Because I was mad at him. So mad I didn't want to be in the same room with him."

"What did he do?"

At least Boone didn't automatically believe it was her fault. Even so, she wasn't certain she wanted to tell him the real reason she hadn't gone. That she had proof Corey was seeing someone, a client of all people, and he'd told Rachel he wasn't going to stop seeing her. He expected Rachel to accept it. "We'd spent the last month arguing because I wanted to have a baby. I didn't want to wait another year."

"Could you have worked out your problems if you'd gone?" Boone asked. "You had a good marriage, right?"

A good marriage? No. Maybe things would have been different if she'd gone into it with the right attitude, but she would never forget Corey standing at the front of the church with her father's arm locked in hers like she might run away. And she might have, given the doubt that plagued her at that moment. Doubt that proved true.

"The Judge thought Corey was perfect for me, but I think I knew from the beginning, something was missing. Even before we married, he set out to mold me into what he thought a governor's wife should be. That's what he wanted, you know." Lead settled in her stomach as she remembered the day she realized their marriage had been nothing but a stepping-stone for him. That he'd married her for the Judge's connections and because she would be an asset in his career.

"Is that why he didn't want children yet? He wanted to concentrate on running for office?"

*The truth will set you free.* The words from the man at the cemetery. She stared at the tiny periwinkles on the teapot that had been a wedding gift from Nana. Nana, who had told her not to marry Corey. She couldn't do it. Rachel was tired of perpetrating the lie.

"The argument wasn't about having a baby." Rachel lifted her gaze, ignoring the tightness in her throat and her burning eyes. "Corey was seeing another woman. He accidentally sent me a text intended for her. I needed those five days alone to cool off. I do regret not getting the chance to tell him I was sorry for the things I said before he left." And not just for her angry words, but for letting him down . . . for not being enough.

"Wasn't he afraid news of the affair might leak out and ruin his political career?"

"Corey was one of those people who believed rules didn't apply to him and that if they did, people wouldn't hold it against him. If you think about it, affairs haven't appeared to hurt other politicians."

Rachel took a deep breath and released it, then picked up the teapot and poured herself a cup of chamomile tea. She didn't exactly feel freer, but she did feel better. "And that's my sad story," she said, putting a bright spin in her voice. "At least one of them."

"I didn't know." He gave her a gentle smile. "You deserved better."

Bless Boone's heart. He was trying to make her feel better. "Thanks, but I think I'm just not good marriage material."

"That's probably true of half the people who are married. But they make it work," he said.

"I thought our marriage was working up until I received the text." Corey would not have it otherwise. "Maybe not as good as it could have been, but I had made a commitment to be the best wife I could be."

Why was she babbling like this? It wasn't like her, and she took a sip of tea to calm her mind.

"And I'm sure you were."

When she looked up, Boone was staring at her with a question in his eyes she knew he'd never ask. "You're wondering why I married him, aren't you?"

A flush crept into his face. "It crossed my mind."

"How well did you know him?"

"Not well, but enough to know you deserved much better."

Boone was tactful if nothing else.

"When he wanted to be, Corey was the most charming man in the world. He had a way of making me feel special. Told me what I wanted to hear. That I was pretty, that I was smart, that he loved me. I didn't hear those kinds of words from my father."

The compassion in Boone's eyes almost undid her, and she dropped her gaze. "You see it happen all the time. Girls seeking love because their fathers were absent. And a father doesn't have to be missing to be absent."

"I agree," Boone said. "It's probably why I haven't married yet and had kids—right now I'm too focused on my job. If I ever have a family, I want to devote time to them."

She'd always pegged him for one of the good guys. And right this minute, she didn't understand why she'd thought working in Homicide was more important than seeing if something could develop between them.

Rachel rubbed at a water spot on the granite counter. It bothered her that she'd made it sound like her failed marriage was all her husband's fault. "Corey wasn't all to blame for our problems. If I'd been the person he wanted me to be, he wouldn't have gone looking elsewhere."

"That's baloney. If you have problems, you work them out. Go see a counselor. You don't go looking somewhere else. I hate that he hurt you."

"Did you have many dealings with him?"

"Just in court." He cocked his head. "And I have a hard time seeing you two together."

"Looking back, I feel the same way, sometimes." She tried to swallow a yawn.

He checked his watch. "It's getting late. I better leave since five comes pretty early."

"Sorry I bent your ear. Someday you'll have to tell me your sad story."

"You don't want to hear mine," he said softly. He looked around. "I don't suppose you'll let me camp out on your sofa?"

"Boone Callahan, I'm armed and trained to use my weapon. I appreciate your concern, but—"

"Okay." Then he stood. "You do have an alarm system?"

"The best. Corey made sure of that."

"Make sure you arm it after I leave. And wait for me to come by in the morning to pick you up."

"Why?" She folded her arms across her chest. Rachel really did appreciate his concern, but she was a cop. "I'm not riding with you. I need my car because I want to talk to Monica Carpenter again. Among other things."

"So? I'll go with you."

Rachel shook her head. "We've been over this already. I'll get more out of her if you're not along."

"What? You're going to waterboard her?"

"No. But I think if it's just the two of us at her condo, she might open up."

He considered what she'd said. "Okay, but come and go through your garage from now on. That way you won't be an open target. And make sure there's plenty of traffic on your street when you leave. Even though it doesn't seem to make any difference whether you're in a crowd or not, I'd feel better."

"Thank you. What's on your agenda for tomorrow?"

"I haven't dismissed the possibility that your father may have been the target, instead of you. So, I plan on meeting with him to get a list of cases where someone may have felt he made an unfair ruling."

As much as she hated to think someone had sent her ricin, she'd hate even more to think it was meant for the Judge. She walked with Boone to the front door. "Thanks for looking out for me."

"No problem. I don't want your grandmothers after me."

If nothing else, she always had Nana and Gran in her corner. "Don't know if you can tell, but I'm not used to someone helping me."

"No kidding."

Her face flushed, heating her cheeks. "And while I'm confessing, I want to apologize to you."

"About . . ."

"Thinking the last six months that you were a male chauvinist."

"You actually thought that?"

"Some of the time. Other times I thought you were a micromanager, but these last couple of days have made me realize that you just want the best from your officers."

He opened the door. "I thank you for that apology, and I'm sorry you thought otherwise. Maybe I need to make myself clearer, but Iraq wired me to act first and apologize later."

"You'll have to tell me what happened over there someday."

For a second, it looked like he quit breathing and his brown eyes darkened to almost black, sending a shiver down her back.

Then Boone tipped his head slightly. "We'll see. Make sure you set your alarm."

After he closed the door, she listened for his truck to start, hoping he wouldn't decide to spend the night in her drive. A minute later the motor turned over. He must not think anyone was lurking about now. Relief surprised her. Not that she was certain anyone was out there earlier.

Even with a dull crime scene textbook from her reading pile, sleep came slowly, bringing dreams of storms and being lost. Rachel didn't know what woke her, but she jerked upright, sending the book in her hands crashing to the floor.

Too late for stealth now. She grabbed her pistol from the nightstand and jumped out of bed with her heart jackhammering in her chest. Why wasn't her alarm screaming? She had set it, hadn't she?

She stood at her door, her mouth so dry she couldn't swallow. Her ears strained for footsteps, movement, anything. Silence enveloped her like a fog. She felt a presence in the house. Rachel grabbed her phone, and her thumb hovered over Boone's number.

What if she'd just been dreaming? But something had awakened her. When she heard no other sound, she flung open her bedroom door and fumbled for the light switch in the hall.

Empty. She crept toward the front door, flipping on lights in each room. She found nothing disturbed. Then she remembered the first months after Corey died, how she would wake up, thinking she'd heard him cough or rattle around in the kitchen.

Thankful she hadn't called Boone, she settled on one of the stools at the bar and rubbed her temples. Stress. It did funny things to the body. She needed a good workout. And tomorrow evening she would get it. With a sigh, she stood and checked the alarm. It was on. No one had been in the house. She retraced her steps to the bedroom, checking every door and window to make sure everything was locked down.

In her spare bedroom, her breath caught. The window was not locked. *Call Boone.* No. She shook her head. Locked or unlocked, there was no evidence anyone had tried to break in other than her wild imagination.

She had a fingerprint kit. Why not check the window for prints? Rachel retrieved the kit from her office and dusted the windowsill, feeling more than a little foolish when the sill only had her prints on it. And relieved, she'd have to admit. Still, first thing tomorrow morning she would check outside the window for footprints or other signs someone had been there.

# 32

I⊤ HAD ALMOST BEEN A DONE DEAL. There would never be another opportunity like this one with the unlocked window. But
abandoning the plan had been the only option when the light came
on in the hallway.

*You are so stupid, you can't do anything right. You should have
waited for her to come into the bedroom and shot her.*

Her father's voice filled her head.

"Yeah—like she was coming into the bedroom without her gun.
I know what I'm doing. Tomorrow. I'll take care of her tomorrow."

*If you don't and she finds that necklace, prison waits for you.*

Prison. The thought took her breath.

"I'm not going to prison. Now go away. Don't bother me." Of
course the voice wouldn't go away. It'd been a haunting companion
for so long.

He was right, though. So much rode on the necklace that Gabby
had worn the night she was murdered. Where could Vic have hidden it after he left Blues & Such Friday night?

Vic Vegas. This trouble was all because of him. Should have
gotten rid of him years ago.

*You should never have let Vic get his hands on the necklace.*

"What was I supposed to do? Cause a scene at the place?" And then he showed it to Randy Culver, who probably was going to die if he hadn't already. Again, Vic's fault.

*Your fault. Your fault.*

She pressed her hands over her ears to block the voice. But her father's voice echoed in her head, mocking her.

It was not her fault. She closed her eyes. If they had only done what she told them to do. All Gabby had to do was back off from Harrison. And Harrison. She couldn't let him go to the police. And Vic. If he had left Harrison's murder alone . . . but after he figured out what happened, he had to die. Should she go see Randy tomorrow? Or take a chance he wouldn't tell about the necklace? Maybe he wouldn't remember it.

She bit her lip. He was still in a coma. But it would look suspicious if she showed up and he died right after she left.

Gabby's daughter was the only one who could connect the necklace to her mother's murder. Which would connect to Harrison. If Rachel thought the two cases were connected, she would not stop until she found every woman who'd ever had contact with Harrison.

Why couldn't Rachel just drop the case, like Shirley had asked? She'd done everything in her power to get her taken off the case. Now she had to kill her. But that was certainly preferable to going to prison.

Boone Callahan made getting close to the detective difficult, but Shirley had a plan to fix it. She'd figured out all she had to do was make the police think the ricin was for the Judge all along. His letter should arrive tomorrow, pulling police attention away from Rachel. The note she'd put in it with the ricin should do the trick.

Then she'd have the opportunity to get to the detective.

*Won't do you any good. You're still going to prison. You forgot about Erin.*

"What about Erin?" she whispered. She'd bumped into the girl in the restroom on Friday night, and Erin had noticed the guitar

219

pendant and asked to see it. "I'm sorry, it's too hard to get off and on," Shirley had explained.

*"I saw you kissing Elvis."*

Her heart had almost stopped when Erin said those words. No way she remembered her from years ago, not after she lost weight and changed her hair. But what Erin said next made Shirley realize the woman did remember her.

*"Oh, Harrison. Do you love me?"*

Shirley's own voice came from Erin's mouth. Somehow she'd recognized her voice. Thank goodness no one else had been around, and afterward she'd been so focused on getting rid of Rachel that the incident had slipped her mind. "No one will pay attention to anything Erin says."

*What if they do?*

"Shut up." Shirley felt like a juggler with too many plates in the air. One slip and everything could come crashing down. *Think.* There could be no more mistakes. She licked her lips. Maybe she could get Rachel and Erin together. Take care of both of them at the same time.

# 33

AFTER THE MORNING BRIEFING, Boone went back to his office to set up a meeting with Judge Winslow. The Judge was on his way to court but agreed to meet on his lunch break at noon. Boone typed it on his phone calendar and set a reminder for eleven thirty. Then he checked with the computer tech who was combing through Vegas's computer for any files related to Foxx's death. Nothing there either. He looked up as Rachel stopped outside his door. She looked pale. "You okay?" he asked, glancing at the clock on the wall. It was eight thirty.

She held up her hand. "Sorry I'm late, but I didn't get much sleep last night."

Rachel didn't have to tell him that. The dark circles under her eyes spoke volumes. "Anything in particular?"

She blew out a breath. "I don't know if it was bad dreams or a noise that woke me. I thought someone had broken in."

"What?" He should have parked outside her house.

"It turned out to be nothing." She wrinkled her nose. "When I checked, I discovered I'd left a window unlocked, but I got my fingerprint kit out and dusted the sill for prints. And checked this morning to make sure no one had been outside the window."

"Make sure you don't leave a window unlocked again."

"Don't worry. When I found I hadn't locked it, that almost scared me as much as whatever woke me."

He remembered the sense that someone had been watching them last night. "You're sure no one had been outside the window?"

"As much as I could tell. It hasn't rained, so the ground was hard. I think after everything that's happened, I'm just on high alert."

So was he. "What do you have planned for today?"

"I want to touch base with Brad Hollister about Harrison Foxx's murder—see if he's looked into it as a cold case—then visit Monica Carpenter. Other than that, maybe interview Jerome Winters again. He was evasive last night, said something about being stoned all the time seventeen years ago."

"Let's start with Brad." He grabbed the box of files to take with them.

They found Sgt. Brad Hollister in his office. "Did you have any trouble finding the case on Harrison Foxx?" he asked.

"No." Boone handed him the original files that had been photocopied. "Have you looked at it at all?"

"That's one we haven't gotten to yet."

"Did you know the investigating officers, Takenaka and Fields?"

"Afraid not. That was before my time here." He flipped through the papers and then leaned back in his chair. "You might talk to Harvey Warren. He was working Homicide seventeen years ago, and he's pretty sharp. Might remember something that will help you." He scrolled through his cell phone. "Here's his phone number and address."

Brad's cell phone rang. "Excuse me a minute. I need to take this."

When Brad stepped out of the room, Boone texted Warren's phone number to Rachel. He wanted to talk to Brad without her present. "Why don't you set up an appointment with Warren? We can interview him this afternoon."

"I have a better idea. Why don't we split up? You have Randy Culver to check on, and didn't you say you wanted to talk to the

Judge? I really don't want to be in on that one, so while you're talking to my father, I'll go see Monica. Then swing by and talk to Sergeant Warren. That way we'll cover more territory."

His chest tightened, then he consciously loosened up. He had to trust her instincts. "Think you'll be finished by three? We could compare notes over a cup of coffee at the shop around the corner."

"I should be," she said and stood. At the door she turned back. "If I were a male detective, would you have hesitated?"

Would he? He stared out the small window behind Brad's desk; the smog was making everything hazy. A frontal system had stagnated over the city, resulting in an orange ozone alert.

"That's what I thought. You think I can't handle the job."

"No! It's not that at all. You're more than capable."

"Then what is it?"

Boone would have to search inside himself for that answer. He'd worked with female officers before and hadn't felt this need to protect them. Footsteps neared the door. Brad was returning. "Can we discuss it later?"

She leveled her hazel eyes at him. "I think we need to."

He hated it when life got complicated.

"I'll catch you later," Rachel said to Brad as he came in from the side door.

After she left, Brad asked, "How's Rachel handling the ricin incident?"

"Better than I am. It's like she's pushed it on a back burner and is getting on with this case."

"You think she can handle it?"

"Sure. She's a good detective."

Brad raised his eyebrows. "So then are you hovering because she's a woman?"

Boone tapped down his irritation. First Rachel, now Brad? "I hover over everyone. You know that. It's a by-product of Iraq."

"You sure it's not more than that?" The cold-case sergeant

leaned back in his chair. "I noticed that you two had a connection when we worked on the case at the Pink Palace together."

"Yeah. Like crossing two hot wires and seeing the sparks shoot."

"Not what I meant."

"I know, but not much way to get around the fact that we're in the same department, and she's a detective and I'm a lieutenant. The brass wouldn't be too happy about that." Not to mention that boat had left the dock. "You know she beats me in the personal fitness test every time."

"Yeah, I heard," Brad said with a laugh. "So what else can I do for you?"

"There was a burglary/murder seventeen years ago just a few days before Foxx's murder. The victim was Gabrielle Winslow. I want to take a look at the file before I go see Judge Winslow."

"Winslow?" Brad said. "Was she his wife?"

"Yeah. Also Rachel's mother."

"You're kidding. I didn't know that."

"Mrs. Winslow knew Harrison Foxx, and her death during what looks like a burglary occurred just days before his. She also knew Vic Vegas, the victim in Saturday's case. Those are coincidences I'm not comfortable with."

"So you think her death may be tied into Foxx's?"

"Maybe. And not just Foxx's but Vegas's and possibly the attempt on Randy Culver's life."

Brad rose from behind the desk. "I'll help you find it."

It didn't take long to locate the box with the file, and they returned to Brad's office to go through it.

"I see Jason Lancaster was the investigating officer," Brad said. "And he retired a couple of years ago."

"Do you know if he's still around?"

"Let me check with personnel, but if he's deceased, Warren would be a good one to ask about this case too."

While Brad checked on Lancaster, Boone scanned the sergeant's notes on the case. Unfortunately they were scanty. He'd run into two types of detectives. Those who wrote lengthy reports with their own opinion of a case and those who did not. Lancaster fell into the latter category.

Brad returned the phone to its cradle. "He's around and works as a security officer at the Med." He pushed a piece of paper toward Boone. "Here's his phone number."

"Perfect." He punched in the number, and Lancaster answered on the second ring. Boone explained who he was and what he wanted. "You wouldn't happen to be at the Med now, would you? I'd like to discuss the Winslow case with you."

"Sure am, but I'm not due for a break for another hour. Why don't I meet you out front then?"

"Great." Boone hooked his phone on his belt and grabbed the files. "I need to go over this before I meet with him. Thanks for your help."

"Sure thing. Let me know if I can do anything else."

Boone assured him he would and took the files back to his office. When it was time to leave for the Med, he hadn't found a connection between the two murders. So why did his intuition say otherwise? Maybe Lancaster could give him some answers.

His cell phone rang as he walked to the elevator. "Hello?"

"This is Randy Culver's nurse at the Med. I told you I'd call when he was awake, and while he's still drowsy, I think he can talk to you."

"I'll be there in about thirty minutes." Finally, maybe he would get a few answers.

# 34

IN THE PARKING GARAGE, Rachel dialed Sergeant Warren's number, explained what she wanted, and asked if she could drop by later in the morning. The retired detective acted eager to help. Then she backed her car out of the slot and exited the garage.

Once Rachel turned on Poplar, she glanced in her rearview mirror, half expecting to see Boone tailing her. She appreciated his concern. To a point. She tried to think if the roles were reversed if she'd hover over him. No. She trusted him to be competent and aware of his surroundings. A shot of anger burned her. That meant he didn't trust her even though he denied it.

Or . . . something had happened in his past that made him overly cautious. He'd mentioned Iraq, and once, when Rachel complained to Brad Hollister that Boone was micromanaging her, Brad told her that Boone had lost someone under his command.

Rachel would like to know a little more about that, but he always evaded any discussion about his time in Iraq. It must have been really hard for him. The memory of the heated gaze he'd given her yesterday at Nana's tripped her heart. On second thought, maybe she didn't need to know more about him.

At the condo complex, she parked in the space beside Monica's car. It was after nine, but once again the curtains were drawn. Surely she wasn't sleeping. Rachel rang the doorbell and was poised to ring it again when Monica opened the door. No, not sleeping, as she was dressed in a coral shell and white pants. And the oversized glasses were in place, magnifying the fine lines around her eyes. She looked every bit her fifty-plus years.

"What do you want now?"

"I'd like to ask you a few more questions."

"I have an appointment."

"This won't take long. Can I come in?"

"I don't suppose it'd do any good to say no," she said and stepped away from the door. "You know where the living room is. I'm going to get me a cup of coffee."

Rachel detected a faint odor of alcohol on Monica's breath as she walked past her. Nana may have been right about Monica having a drinking problem. Rachel chose to sit on the red sofa again. With the curtains drawn and the blinds shut, the room had a dungeon effect. She took out a pencil and pad and then flicked on a lamp.

A low rumble from the kitchen startled her, and she touched the pistol on her belt. The noise turned to gurgling, and heat crawled up her face. A pod coffeemaker. She heard the same sound every morning in her own kitchen. She would have been mortified if Boone had been there to read her body language.

Coffee sounded pretty good right now. Probably too much to hope that Monica would offer her a cup. She hadn't guessed wrong when Monica returned with a single cup and sat on the piano bench like before.

"I don't know what you expect me to tell you that I haven't told you already." She picked up the almost empty pack of cigarettes, but she didn't take one out.

"I'd like you to take a look at photos taken the night Harrison won the Elvis contest at the Cook Convention Center," Rachel said, taking the package from her bag. "You are in quite a few of them."

"I never said I wasn't there." She drank from the mug and then pulled a cigarette from the pack. "Look, I didn't kill Harrison."

"Did you love him?"

The question rocked Monica back. She set the cup down hard and fumbled for a lighter. Without looking up, she raised the cigarette to her lips and flicked the wheel of the lighter. Flicked it again when it failed to ignite.

"Did he return your love?" Rachel pressed.

"I didn't say—"

"You didn't have to." She waited.

Monica stared at the end of the cigarette as though it would magically light up. Finally she returned it to the package. "Yes, he did. Unfortunately, there weren't many women he didn't love."

"Did that make you angry?"

"I was thirty-five and had spent the last five years waiting on Harrison to propose. Time was running out if I wanted children. And then I realized he was in love with someone else. Wouldn't that make you angry?"

She did not want to think about just how angry it would make her. Angry enough to stay home when her husband wanted her to go fishing with him. Angry enough to feel nothing when she learned he'd drowned on the trip. She attributed her lack of emotion to shock, and later she did feel something. But instead of grief, what she felt was guilt.

"You're thinking about someone who hurt you right now, so you know how I felt."

"We aren't talking about me." She focused on the pencil in her hand. "How did it make you feel?"

Monica snorted, drawing Rachel's gaze. She wished she'd kept looking at her pencil. The oversized glasses magnified the glint in the older woman's eye. Rachel hadn't fooled her.

"Whatever." She pushed the glasses up on her nose. "Made me angrier than a wet cat, but I didn't kill him. You know why?

He swore it was just business. And like a fool I forgave him." Her eyes turned misty. After a few seconds, she shook her head, as if to clear it. "And then someone killed him."

"Did you catch him with someone?"

"More or less."

"What do you mean?"

"I heard him talking to someone on the phone. Pledging his undying love. I confronted him. That's when he said it was only business on his part." Her lip curled like she'd tasted something rotten. "I demanded the five thousand dollars he owed me. 'Aw, baby, don't be like that,' he said. 'There's a lot more than five grand involved. This pigeon is loaded.'"

"Are you saying you have no idea who the woman was?" She would not let herself even think Monica was talking about her mother.

"It could've been an older woman. I hate to say it, but Harrison was bad to play up to those old biddies." She played with the pack of cigarettes in her hands, turning it from top to bottom. "He was a sorry piece of trash . . . but there was just something about him that I couldn't get out from under my skin."

It hadn't been that way with Corey. As soon as he left on his fishing trip, Rachel had contacted a divorce attorney she knew. "Randy Culver said Vic Vegas was in a deep discussion with someone Friday night. Was it you?"

"We talked, but I wouldn't call it anything deep."

"Did you see him talking to anyone else?"

"I was too busy to follow him around."

"Randy also commented that a jealous husband could have killed Vic. Was he like Harrison? With the women, I mean. Could he have been killed over a woman?"

An amused smile quirked Monica's lips. "No, he was nothing like Harrison. Yeah, he flirted with the women—it was part of who he was—but Vic Vegas was a straight arrow. Always kind of surprised me that he was so intent on finding Harrison's murderer with all the lousy things Harrison was involved in."

It made Rachel feel better to know that about Vic. That had been the sense she'd gotten about him until Culver made that remark. She put her pencil and paper away and stood. "Thanks for talking to me. I have a better picture of Harrison than I did."

The event planner nodded. "Look, I didn't mean anything yesterday about your mother loaning Harrison money. To be truthful, I was always kind of jealous of her and Harrison, even though he always said they were just friends."

"They'd known each other a long time."

Monica dropped her gaze. Indecision played out on her face. Rachel waited, letting the silence grow. Most people couldn't stand dead air and usually rushed to fill it. Especially if they had something they wanted to get off their chest.

"You seem like a nice person. Like your mom . . ." She hugged her arms to her waist.

"Thank you."

Again Rachel let the silence lengthen.

Monica lifted her chin and removed the glasses. "I've never told anyone this, and it's always bothered me that I didn't. But something else happened you should know about."

She stood and walked to the window, where she moved the curtain and opened the blinds to look out. It took every ounce of Rachel's self-control to not push her. Monica's shoulder straightened and she turned around.

"Like I said, I liked your mom, went to her funeral. After the service, I went back to get a rose from one of the arrangements." Monica ducked her head. "It sounds silly now, but I wanted a memento of Gabby because she was so kind to me when others weren't. Anyway, Harrison was at the graveside, arguing with someone, accusing them of killing Gabby . . . threatening to go to the police with what he knew unless this person made it worth his while to keep quiet. The other person told Harrison he should have gotten rid of him years ago. That night Harrison was killed."

The hair on the back of her neck raised. "Who was the person he argued with?"

Monica licked her lips and swallowed. "Your father."

Cold seeped into Rachel's face as the room tilted. "Th-that's impossible." Her voice sounded hollow to her own ears. "I don't believe it."

"That's one reason I've never told anyone. Who would believe me over Lucien Winslow? I'd had a couple of drinks, and there was no proof, other than what I'd heard. The police probably would have laughed at me. And if he did kill Harrison, I didn't want to end up dead too."

Rachel couldn't imagine the Judge that angry. He just didn't lose control like that. She shook her head to clear it. "Getting rid of someone doesn't necessarily mean killing them."

"I just know what I heard and who I saw saying it. You'd believe your father could have done it if you'd seen the look on his face—he could've killed Harrison right then."

The dark room closed in on her. She had to get out of here. Rachel stood. "If I have more questions, I'll call."

"Sure." Monica slid a cigarette from the pack and lit it. After a long drag, she blew smoke out the side of her mouth. "You don't believe me, but I'm telling you the truth."

Rachel planted her feet, as if that would ground her in the spinning room. Monica Carpenter actually believed her father had killed Harrison. "He may have threatened Foxx, but he would never act on it. He's spent his life upholding the law."

"Given the right circumstances, we're all capable of committing murder. Even Judge Lucien Winslow."

"No. You're wrong about my father." What if Monica spilled this to reporters? "I wouldn't repeat this crazy story to anyone else. They might think you made it up to divert suspicion away from yourself."

"Is that a threat?"

"Of course not. But if you think about it, you had motive to kill Harrison—he threw you over for someone else. Maybe Vic figured it out."

"You're crazy. I thought you wanted to know the truth, but you don't. You're not even going to investigate this. You only care about what happened to Harrison as long as it doesn't inconvenience your father."

"That's not—"

"Don't lie. Besides, I'm not going to tell anyone, at least not right now, but not for the reason you think. I don't have time to deal with the publicity if this hit the news. Now if you don't mind, I have an appointment."

The weight of the accusation about her father followed Rachel to her car. She should report what Monica said to Boone. But if she did . . . No. She had to keep this to herself until she knew more. The Judge could not be a murder suspect. The senate would soon vote on his nomination to the Sixth District Court of Appeals.

Rachel rubbed the back of her neck. Her father would never forgive her if she derailed his nomination.

# 35

"JASON LANCASTER?" BOONE ASKED. Unlike a lot of the guards around the hospital, Lancaster had kept himself in shape since his retirement.

"That'd be me."

The two men shook hands, and Lancaster said, "You want to go inside or stay out here?"

"Inside." The way sweat was running down Boone's back, he was pretty sure the temperature was already in the midnineties. In the lobby they found a spot away from the main foot traffic.

"Been thinking about the case since you called. I don't like leaving things undone, and that case is one of the reasons I hated to retire. So, I'm hoping you can finish what I couldn't."

"The report indicates that Mrs. Winslow surprised a burglar."

"Yeah. The thing is, at first I thought the break-in looked staged . . ." He scratched his chin. "Not exactly staged, more like an afterthought. But then I couldn't find a motive for anyone killing her. There was no huge insurance policy on her or anything that pointed to something other than a break-in.

"I did think I had something when I learned the Winslows were separated, but that turned out to be a dead end. Judge Winslow had an ironclad alibi, and from what everyone said, they were working on getting back together. He freely admitted the separation was his fault for working all the time. I couldn't find any signs of someone else being in the picture, even though she had a few male friends. But everywhere I asked, turned out that's all they were—friends. Winslow volunteered to take a lie detector test and passed it with flying colors, and I marked him off my list. The woman apparently didn't have an enemy in the world."

"None of the neighbors saw anything?"

Lancaster shook his head. "Their house is on a wooded lot, back off the road. They hadn't lived in the neighborhood that long, and they entertained quite a bit so there were a lot of cars coming and going."

He'd described the Winslow property to a T. It'd be easy enough for someone to pull in unnoticed. "I noticed prior to her death there'd been a burglary ring operating in the area. I understand those cases were solved, that it was a cleaning service."

"Yeah." The security guard frowned. "Never did like it that the person who supposedly broke into the Winslow house died of an overdose before I could question him. You might pick up a little more information about the ring if you talk to the guys in Burglary—could be someone is still around from seventeen years ago."

He made a note to check. "So it is possible she encountered a burglar."

"It's possible. There were several expensive items in a pillowcase at the back door, like maybe the thief got scared and ran off and left it," he said. "But you know how sometimes you have these hunches?"

Boone knew exactly what he was talking about.

"I don't have a clue of who or why, but my hunch says it wasn't a break-in and my first instinct was correct—the mess in the house was created as a diversion. I believe someone went there with the intention of killing Mrs. Winslow." Lancaster tilted his head. "And

I'm not the only one who thinks that way. Have you talked with her daughter? Rachel Sloan? We've discussed the case numerous times. She's determined to get to the bottom of it."

It didn't surprise him that Rachel and Lancaster had discussed her mother's case, but why hadn't she mentioned talking to him? Was she withholding any other information? That was the problem with a detective working on a personal case—too much secrecy.

Boone thanked him for his time. He turned the case over in his mind as he took the stairs down to Culver's room in ICU. The nurse he'd talked to yesterday was working at her computer, and he stopped before going into the room. "How is he today?"

"Ask him yourself," she said with a smile. "He's awake."

She followed him inside the room. The head of Culver's bed was raised, and he looked alert. Culver eyed Boone curiously. "Do I know you?" he asked in a raspy voice.

"Lt. Boone Callahan," he said. "We talked before your collapse."

The blank look on Culver's face indicated he had no memory of their talk. "I'm sorry. I don't remember a lot of what's happened lately."

"Do you know what happened to you?"

"Nobody tells me anything around here. Just that I overdosed on my diabetes medicine, and I don't see how that's possible. I'm real careful about that." He tried to pull himself up in the bed but couldn't make any headway.

"Here, let me help you," his nurse said, and Boone jumped to help her.

"Why am I so weak?" Culver asked as they pulled him higher in the bed.

"You've been very sick," she said. "I'll leave so you and Lieutenant Callahan here can talk, but if you need me, I'll be outside the door."

"Do you know what happened to me?" Culver asked when she left.

"I'm afraid someone tried to kill you."

"What?"

Boone hadn't thought the singer could get any paler, but he managed it.

"Why would anyone do that?" His eyes narrowed. "How?"

Boone pulled a chair up to the bed and sat in it. "Do you remember anything about Saturday night?"

Culver rubbed his hand over his face. "Singing. I remember being on the stage—who won?"

"I don't know, and I'm not sure who won last night, either."

The singer tried to sit up again. "I've got to get out of here. This contest is my big break."

"Whoa," Boone said. "You're not able to leave just yet."

The words didn't deter Culver. He swung his legs over the side of the bed. An alarm went off, and his nurse was back in the room almost immediately.

"What are you doing?" she demanded.

"Getting out of here . . ."

Culver's eyes rolled back in his head, and Boone grabbed him as he slumped forward.

"Help me lay him back," she said. Once he was stretched out on the bed, she took his blood pressure. "Way too low. He needs quiet. You'll have to go."

Boone hung around until the nurse came back to her station. "Is there any chance his memory will come back?" he asked.

"Anything is possible," she said. "But from my experience with critically ill patients, he's remembered about all he's going to."

# 36

RACHEL'S FIRST IMPULSE was to drive straight to the courthouse and question her father about Monica's accusation. But he was in court. She probably needed to think this through, anyway. According to Monica, Foxx had evidence that the Judge killed her mother. So far Rachel hadn't found it. And Vic never alluded to her father being his friend's killer.

Monica said she'd been drinking. What if she had hallucinated? Or made the whole thing up? What if she killed Foxx? She was angry enough. But if she killed him, why didn't she report what she'd overheard to throw suspicion in a different direction? Maybe because she never was a suspect and wouldn't want to draw attention to herself. Perhaps Sergeant Warren could shed some light on the case.

The retired officer lived in East Memphis on a cul-de-sac. As Rachel parked on the street, her cell phone dinged with a text. Terri.

I'm teaching a class at the police department gym. Want to join us? Thought we might have dinner afterwards to celebrate your birthday tomorrow.

Her birthday. Rachel had been so busy it slipped her mind. She could definitely use the workout, and over dinner would be a good time to unofficially question Terri about Harrison and her mother. Terri had been at her mother's funeral. If anyone knew anything about her father threatening Foxx, she would.

Sure. See you at six? Will Erin be joining us?

They sometimes picked up Erin when they went out to eat. A text dinged back.

Not tonight. Be prepared to sweat. ;-)

Exactly what Rachel needed. She locked her car and walked to the bungalow that had a riot of color across the front. Marigolds. The pungent, half-pleasant scent brought back memories of working with her mother in their yard as she climbed the steps to a porch that stretched across the front of the house. The man who answered her knock fit the comfortable-looking house. "Sergeant Warren?"

"Been a while. Just call me Harvey, and you must be Detective Sloan. Come on in."

He limped ahead of her, and she remembered he'd had a broken leg when Brad talked to him back in May. She followed him inside to a neat living room with crocheted doilies on the tables and framed photos of children and grandchildren. Rachel sat on the sofa. "How's your leg?"

He rubbed his thigh. "Doc says I'll probably always have a limp. But it's better. What can I do for you?"

"I hope you might remember a case I'm working on."

"Be glad to help, if I can." He cocked his head to the side. "Weren't you on that case with Brad Hollister earlier this year? The one that involved the Pink Palace?"

She nodded as she took out a notepad and pencil. "That's how

I knew you'd broken your leg. I didn't meet you then, but I heard from Brad you were a lot of help."

"Don't know so much about that. But it was good to feel useful again." He studied her with clear blue eyes. "Been thinking about the Harrison Foxx case since you called."

"What do you remember?"

"He was an Elvis impersonator. Takenaka was the lead and Fields assisted. I interviewed some of his neighbors, but none of them knew anything." He scratched his head. "But there was a guy who was really interested in the case. He called me a couple times when I was still at the CJC to ask questions."

"Vic Vegas?"

"Yeah. That's the guy. Heard he was murdered. I think he fancied himself some sort of investigator. Came over here earlier this year and we talked about the case and investigative procedures. He was pretty sharp, even had a few gadgets. He showed me his shoes where he'd hidden some kind of key in the heel."

She jerked her head up. "What did you say?"

Warren pointed to his shoes. "He was really into spy stuff, and the last time he came, he took off his loafer and showed me a secret compartment in the heel. He had a key in it, like for a lockbox . . . or maybe one of them mailboxes you can rent."

Hope sent her heart rate soaring. Was it possible that Vic had hidden a key to some sort of lockbox that contained his files on Foxx's murder? She would check as soon as she left here. "Did you have any impressions on Foxx's murder?"

"I believe Takenaka thought that Foxx had gotten into debt with the wrong people. Loan shark, which sounds like he could have gotten mixed up in organized crime. I personally leaned toward an ex-girlfriend . . . or maybe a husband. I remember the next-door neighbor saying he had a different woman every month. Said he called 'em his Flavor of the Month girls. But none of his women friends floated to the top of the list of suspects."

Foxx was a real piece of work. "Did you interview any of the people he worked with?"

"You mean the other Elvis impersonators? No. Fields and Takenaka did that."

Rachel tapped her pencil on the pad as she debated asking the question that was topmost in her mind. "Were there any rumors of Foxx blackmailing anyone?"

"Blackmail?" Warren shook his head. "Not that I remember. But like I said, I wasn't the lead detective so I wasn't privy to all the information. If there were, it should be in the report."

Rachel stood. She was anxious to check Vic's shoes. "Thanks for seeing me," she said and handed him her business card. "If you think of anything about the case, give me a call."

Back in her car, she called Boone. "Where are you?"

"I'm just leaving Culver's room at the Med."

"How is he?"

"Very weak. He can't remember anything about that night. Don't figure he'll be much help. What do you have?" he asked.

She told him about the possible false heel in Vegas's shoes.

"It's worth checking out," he said. "The crime scene investigators should still have a key to his house. I'll get it and meet you there in half an hour."

"See you there."

How in the world was she going to keep what Monica told her from him?

# 37

When Rachel arrived at Vic's house, it occurred to her that his neighbor, Laverne, might have a key, and she walked next door.

"Detective Sloan," Laverne said when she answered Rachel's knock. "Won't you come in?"

"Thank you, but I don't have time. Do you have a key to Vic's house? My lieutenant is on his way with one, but it may take him a little while to get here."

"Actually, I do. Wait and I'll get it."

When she returned, Rachel asked if she would accompany her to the house to unlock it. That way she wouldn't have to return the key. "How is Vic's daughter?"

"Better. It was just such a shock for her. Do you know who killed him?"

"Afraid not. Did you see any suspicious activity here in the days before his murder?"

"I've been thinking about that. Friday night sometime before midnight, the dog on the other side of him started barking up a storm. I didn't think anything about it until after you left, but that dog hardly ever barks." Laverne unlocked the door. "I got up and looked out the window toward Vic's house, but I didn't see anything. You may want to ask the dog's owner if they saw anything. I don't think you've talked with them yet—they were out of town Saturday."

Rachel flipped through her notepad and didn't find anything for the neighbors on the other side of Vic. "I'll catch them when I finish here if they're home. Thanks for letting me in."

"No problem."

Laverne craned her neck to see inside the house, and Rachel swallowed a smile. Car wrecks and crime scenes drew a lot of curiosity. She shut the door behind her and texted Boone that she was already in the house. Then she walked to the bedroom where she'd seen several shoe boxes. By the time he arrived, she was sitting on the floor surrounded by loafers—none with a false bottom in the heel. "Nothing so far," she said in response to the question in his eyes. She returned the shoes to their boxes.

"Did you learn anything new when you talked to Sergeant Warren?" he asked.

"Only that Foxx definitely had a lot of girlfriends—Warren thought one of them might have done him in. And he remembered that Takenaka thought Foxx had gotten involved with a loan shark. How about you? Did you learn anything?"

"Talked to the detective who investigated your mother's death."

She forced herself to breathe and busied herself with stacking the shoe boxes. "Sergeant Lancaster? Why?"

"Your mother knew Foxx and Vegas. Lancaster isn't convinced about the burglary aspect."

"I've looked at her case from every angle. So far all I've hit are dead ends." Until today.

"You never mentioned talking to Lancaster."

She looked up from the boxes, and their gazes collided. Boone's face was guarded. "It's something I do on my own time."

"I see." He folded his arms across his chest. "If you discover a connection to Foxx's murder, you'll tell me, right?"

She made sure the tension that gripped her stomach didn't show in her face as she held his gaze. "Why wouldn't I?"

She was dancing around the truth, but Rachel couldn't bring herself to tell Boone about her father's connection to Foxx. Not until her father had a chance to explain. If she told Boone, he'd have to question her father and put it in his report. Records available to anyone in the department. What a headline that would make if the wrong person saw it. It would ruin her father. The relationship between the two of them was already troubled. This might kill it.

Finally he nodded. "Just don't let it interfere with the case you're working on. Did you stop off at Monica Carpenter's yet?"

Another minefield. "Yes. She was in love with Foxx, had loaned him money, and caught him with another woman."

"Do you think she could've killed him?"

"It's not impossible. Scorned woman and all." Rachel held her hand out for him to help her up, not expecting the sizzle that his touch brought to her heart. Flustered, she quickly released his hand. "There may be something in Vic's files if we ever find them."

"I gave the uniformed officers a list of storage units to check. And I'm waiting on a report from the guy looking through his computer for any files he might have stored pertaining to Foxx's murder," Boone said. "Have you checked the other rooms?"

"Not yet." Still reeling from the way his touch had made her feel, she avoided looking at him. What was wrong with her? She'd worked with other men and not felt this attraction. But the other men weren't Boone, and she didn't have history with them. *Get a grip.* Rachel couldn't throw away the seven hard years she'd worked to get into Homicide. She took a deep breath. "I'll take the bedroom across the hall."

Their search yielded more shoes in another bedroom, but none with a key hidden in them. Rachel tapped the side of her leg. "I never saw a man with so many shoes."

"Maybe he was wearing the shoes we're looking for when he

was killed," Boone said. "Check with the medical examiner to see if they still have his clothes."

"They may already be in the evidence room."

Boone's phone chimed, and he checked it. "I have an appointment with your father in thirty minutes. Why don't you check on the shoes, and at three we'll meet back at the CJC instead of the coffee shop."

"If I find them, I'll text."

When Rachel checked with the medical examiner, she discovered Vic's clothes had been sent downtown to the crime scene lab. As she drove to the CJC, she reasoned with herself about Boone, mentally listing the pros and cons of her non-relationship with him. They'd had a few coffee dates, dinner with her family, and dinner and a movie before she was offered the opportunity to move into Homicide. Sunday at Nana's was the closest he'd come to kissing her.

*He listens.* The thought stopped her cold. Last night, when she'd talked about Corey, he'd really listened to her. It was almost like he shared her pain. Like maybe he'd let someone down, or someone had let him down. Rachel bit her bottom lip.

Boone wasn't like Corey, questioning her every move in order to make himself look better. No, Boone had her back, and sometimes that meant he looked over her shoulder. He didn't want a clone of himself. He respected her abilities and opinions. Boone was all in or nothing.

That's what scared her.

Rachel had been hurt when Corey cheated on her, but it'd been more a blow to her pride than her heart. Not that she didn't love Corey, but if she were honest, she had never given him her whole heart. They'd married too quickly for that, and he'd proven she'd been right not to give it. But any relationship with Boone would require all of her, heart and all.

She shook her head and turned into the parking garage. Life

was complicated. After parking, she walked across the street to the CJC. Complicated or not, she had a job to do. And mooning over Boone Callahan wouldn't get it done. First on her list was examining the shoes, then investigating whether her father had threatened Foxx.

She ran into Donna as she stepped out of the elevator on the eleventh floor.

"Been missing our workouts," the office manager said.

"This case has taken all my time."

"How's Randy Culver? I heard at Blues & Such last night he wasn't doing too good."

Rachel frowned. "I didn't see you at the club."

"I was there late. Randy—is he going to be okay?"

"I think so, but Boone would know more. The problem is, he doesn't remember anything that happened Saturday night."

"Really? Well, I hope he gets well enough to finish the competition," Donna said. "He's my favorite. Do you think it'd be okay to drop by and see him?"

"Sure," she said, and remembered Culver's smooth voice. "I think he's a favorite with a lot of people."

"Have you had lunch?" Donna asked. "I'm on my way to get something if you want to come."

"Thanks, but I don't have time." Rachel nodded and continued down the hall to the evidence room, where the CSI team had processed and stored Vic's clothes. After signing for the box, she slipped on latex gloves and opened it in the presence of the officer in charge. Her heart caught. A pair of black loafers. She examined the heels, and after not seeing anything unusual, she held one shoe upside down and twisted on the heel. Nothing.

"What are you doing?" the officer asked.

"Looking for something." She pressed against it while twisting at the same time. The heel moved. She repeated the process, and the heel slid to the side and a small key fell onto the table. *Yes!*

"You gotta be kidding," the officer said. "Was the guy who owned the shoes CIA?"

Rachel stared at the small brass key. "No. Just a little eccentric. I'd like to sign this key out after you log it in."

The key was a little bigger than the one she used to open her post office box, and she pulled her key ring out to compare the two. Much bigger. Vic's had a number engraved on it. But no company name. If they didn't find some sort of record of where Vic had paid for a place to store his files, all they had was a key. Without a lock to open, they had nothing.

# 38

BOONE ARRIVED AT THE COURTHOUSE at five minutes to noon and collected his thoughts as he walked up the steps to the Federal Building. He didn't know what to expect from Judge Winslow. Saturday night he hadn't been exactly unfriendly, but then neither had Boone been friendly.

The Judge's secretary ushered him into a spacious room filled with law books, and he took a seat in the wingback chair that faced the Judge's massive oak desk. A side door opened and Judge Winslow hurried in, shrugging out of his black robe. "I can give you fifteen minutes," he said tersely.

"Thank you, sir."

Winslow sat behind his desk. "Before you begin, what can you tell me about the attempt on my daughter's life?"

"Not much, I'm afraid. Other than the ricin had lost its effectiveness."

"I heard that from Marshal Lock. So was someone sending her a message?"

"Or possibly you. Lock is looking into it along with Tennessee Poison Control." He took out a notepad and flipped it open. "It's possible whoever sent it didn't know ricin loses its toxicity pretty quickly."

"How would they even obtain it? I understand it's well regulated."

"It is, although small amounts used in research don't have to be reported."

"Research? What type of research could it be used in?"

"Cancer research hospitals have experimented with it. Evidently there's been some success with it reducing tumors."

"Like Crockett Cancer Institute?"

"Why do you ask about that company?"

"Gabby worked there early in our marriage in PR." He frowned. "Along with Terri Morrow and her husband, Robert."

Boone made a note to interview Terri Morrow. "Do you know what their jobs were?"

"Terri was Gabby's assistant. She was trying to start her dance school, but she didn't have the capital and wouldn't accept a loan, not even from her husband. Every penny she made at Crockett went into savings. Her husband worked in research and development, and he was a good ten years older than Terri."

Was it possible Robert had access to ricin? Boone would have to check that out. "Her husband. Where would I find him?"

"Cemetery. He died years ago." The Judge checked his watch.

Time for Boone to get to what he came for. "I understand you represented Harrison Foxx when you were practicing law. I'd like to ask you a few questions about him."

Judging by the sour expression on Lucien Winslow's face, he might get kicked out before his time was up.

"I hadn't thought about the man in years until all this happened. If you want my impressions of him, find the interview that was conducted by your own detectives when he was murdered."

Boone didn't recall seeing that interview. "I gather you didn't like Foxx much."

He shrugged. "I never made any secret of it and didn't approve of the way he used women. Always conning them out of money and calling it a loan. A loan he never repaid, that I could see."

"How about your wife? Did he borrow money from her?"

"Excuse me?" Winslow's steely eyes bored into Boone.

He was probably ruining any chance of a future friendship with the Judge. "I don't like asking these questions any more than you like hearing them. But I have two men dead and another at the Med that I'm not sure will make it."

"I get it's not personal."

"Thank you. It's my understanding that your wife loaned him money."

"Occasionally."

"Did they spend a lot of time together?"

The Judge drummed his fingers on the desk. "Only during August."

"What was their relationship?"

The drumming stopped. "My wife went to school with him, and they were thrown together every August in that stupid Elvis event. He had a thing for her, I don't doubt that. But she didn't return the favor. My wife and I had our problems, but we were seeing a counselor and were working them out. Why are you asking questions about her?"

"I believe your wife's murder and Foxx's could be connected."

"What are you talking about? Gabby was killed by a burglar—that was the final call by the detective who investigated."

"He's rethinking the case now and believes it could have been staged to look that way. I understand that you have an alibi for the night your wife was murdered. How about the night Foxx died?"

The Judge's face flamed. "I did not kill him. And why would you question whether there was a burglary at my house the night my wife died? What about the items left at the back door?"

"That's one of the things that I'm having trouble with. Why would a burglar leave his haul behind?" he said. Boone hadn't pulled everything together yet, but his gut instinct told him Gabby Winslow's death was connected in some way to Harrison Foxx's and was not from a burglary. "Do you know of anyone who had a grudge against your wife or who might want your wife out of the way?"

He shook his head. "If it'd been me who'd been killed, you would've had plenty of suspects, but everyone liked Gabby. She didn't have an unkind bone in her body."

"Did you ever talk to Foxx about his attention to your wife? Is it possible one of his girlfriends could have been jealous of her and Foxx? Jealous enough to kill her?"

The judge's eyes narrowed. "I don't like what—"

His office manager burst into the room. "Excuse me, Judge Winslow, but the DA wants a word with you."

He turned to her. "Thank you."

"And here's your mail," she said, plopping a stack of letters on his desk. "The envelope on top says 'personal' so I didn't open it."

Judge Winslow turned to Boone. "I'm sorry, but we'll have to continue this discussion at a later time."

"Could you at least answer that last question?"

"Not adequately with no more time than we have."

"Maybe later then." Boone stood and extended his hand. The Judge accepted and Boone said, "Thanks for seeing me. I do have a few more questions. When would be a good time for me to come back?"

The Judge's mouth twitched. "You're wasting your time. I don't know anything about Harrison Foxx's murder, but I'll answer whatever questions you have after court recesses at five—unless the defense is successful in delaying the case again. If they do, it could be earlier." Then he leveled his gaze at Boone. "You just make sure you find who sent my daughter that box before another attempt is made."

"Don't worry, I will," he said as his gaze rested on the stack of mail the secretary placed on the Judge's desk.

"Personal" was written in bold print on the top letter. And there were three Forever stamps in the right corner. Way too much postage for a simple letter. "Do you often get mail like that?"

Judge Winslow looked down and frowned. "No."

"I think you need to move away from the desk," Boone said, dialing the bomb squad. Maybe the ricin Saturday night really was meant for the Judge and not Rachel.

"You don't think it's—"

"I don't know, but it looks suspicious. We need to evacuate the building."

"What if it's nothing?"

"I'm not willing to take that risk. Where's your fire alarm?"

Once the building was evacuated and the bomb squad was inside, Boone called Dep. Steve Lock and filled him in on what was going on. Then he called Rachel. "Your father received a suspicious letter and we're outside the Federal Building."

"A bomb?"

"Not sure. Could be something else, like ricin."

"I'll be right there."

Lock arrived first. "What do you think is in the envelope?"

It had been thin. "It wasn't bulky enough to be explosives. Ricin comes to mind."

"Are you saying the package the other night was meant for me?" the Judge asked.

"I considered that then, but I didn't have proof." He caught sight of Rachel in his peripheral vision.

"Proof of what?" Rachel asked as she joined them.

"That the package Saturday night was meant for your father."

"I had hoped that wouldn't be the case."

"Definitely not ruling you out, but it's making more sense that your father could have been the target. He's the one with the high-profile cases."

Deputy Lock nodded, turning to the Judge. "And you're now

under the protective services of the US Marshals' office. Either one of my men or I will be with you at all times."

The Judge gave a curt acknowledgment and then turned toward Rachel. "I'm glad it's not you they're after."

Boone noticed that even though his words were warm, he didn't make an effort to embrace Rachel. Nor did she try to reach out to him, just a perfunctory nod. Boone turned as Rodney Cortez exited the building and walked toward them. "What do you have?"

"A note and white powder," Cortez said. "It looks like the same stuff we found Saturday night, but won't know if it's ricin until it's tested. Figure it's not active since the note that was in the envelope said the next time it'd be the real deal. My people are checking the mail delivered to the other offices in the building now."

While Boone hated that the Judge was in someone's crosshairs, he was glad Rachel might be off the hook. They had enough to contend with as it was. If she weren't the target, it would be easier to focus on the case.

"Do you know when we can reenter the building?" the Judge asked.

"Not today," Cortez said. "Should be clear by tomorrow morning."

"Since we can't go to your office, do you mind coming to mine, Judge Winslow?" Steve asked. "Your secretary was kind enough to go through your files yesterday and pull any cases where there'd been threats either implied or said outright, and I'd like to go over them with you."

The Judge ran his hand through his dark hair. "I still have trouble believing this has happened."

Rachel stepped toward her father, and for a second, Boone thought she was going to give him a hug. Instead, she simply touched his arm. "I'd like to stop by the house later."

Surprise crossed his face. "That would be nice. Any particular time?"

"Around eight?"

"Sounds good."

"Until then, be careful and watch your back."

A tiny smile formed on his lips. "A Winslow always watches his back."

"Oh no!" Rachel raised her hand to her lips. "Gran! One of us needs to call her before reporters get hold of this."

"I'll call on the way to the deputy's office," he said.

So the grandmother brought out concern in both of them. Boone turned to the Judge. "Once you finish there, I'd like to go over those things we talked about. Can you join us, Steve?"

"Sure thing," the deputy said.

"I think you're on the wrong track, Boone," Winslow said before he turned and followed the US Marshal to his car.

"What was he talking about?" Rachel rubbed her arms as they drove away.

"I was questioning him about Foxx's murder. Your mother's too." He raised his eyebrows. "Ready to walk back to the CJC?"

"Sure."

"Did you find a key in Vegas's shoes?" Heat shimmered up from the sidewalk as they walked toward the Criminal Justice Center. He felt sorry for all the tourists in town for the Elvis doings and hoped it cooled off before tomorrow night's candlelight vigil. If it didn't, there'd be a few people passing out from the heat and humidity.

"Yep, but it won't do us any good if we don't find what it fits. How about you, did . . . ?" Her voice faltered. "Did you learn anything from my father?"

"Not as much as I'd hoped. His secretary had already ended our meeting when I saw the envelope. I have a few more questions for him. Did you know your friend Terri Morrow worked at the Cancer Institute along with her husband before he died?"

Rachel shook her head. "I didn't until Erin said something last night. She indicated he worked in cancer research."

"Do you know if he was working with ricin?"

"I didn't know him at all, and Terri never talks about him."

*If* Robert Morrow had been conducting experiments with ricin, that meant he had access to the poison. Boone needed to check with the Crockett Cancer Institute. But even if Morrow had handled ricin in his research, he was dead.

But Terri Morrow wasn't. She'd worked there as well. What if she'd somehow gotten her hands on even a minute amount? But why would she want to kill the Judge . . . or Rachel? Was it possible she'd been in love with Harrison Foxx? And wanted Gabby out of the way?

Boone pictured Erin's sister and had a hard time believing she was a cold-blooded killer, but he'd been fooled before.

"How about that cup of coffee we talked about earlier?" he said, nodding toward the coffee shop at the end of the block.

Rachel fanned her shirt. "An iced coffee, maybe."

They entered the shop and found a table. Boone pulled a chair out for her. "What do you want? My treat."

"No—"

"Not taking no for an answer. You've had a bad afternoon."

She eyed him, then shrugged. "Mocha frappe . . . with whipped cream."

He lifted his eyebrows. He'd never known her to drink something with that many calories.

"I skipped lunch."

Evidently she'd read his mind. Boone approached the barista and ordered the frappe and a glass of iced tea, and when he noticed they had sandwiches, he ordered them each a club. While he waited, a quick check on the internet gave him the phone number for the cancer center, and he called only to find out that the head of the human resources department was in a meeting. Maybe he'd just drive out to the facility.

# 39

RACHEL HADN'T BEEN TOO KEEN on stopping at the coffee shop with Boone. What she wanted to do was talk to her father, ask whether he had threatened Foxx. But she'd followed Boone inside to a table and almost laughed when he said she'd had a hard day.

If he only knew. Boone called someone while he waited, and when he returned to the table, he brought not only the frappe and his iced tea but two sandwiches as well. "I skipped lunch too."

"If I'd known, I wouldn't have added the whipped cream," she said as her stomach growled. Rachel hadn't realized how hungry she was. "Thanks."

"You're skinny enough a few extra calories won't hurt you. I thought we'd eat and then drive out to Crockett Cancer Institute to talk with the head of the human resources department. She was in a meeting when I called. That is, if you want to go with me."

Her appetite suddenly deserted Rachel. "You don't think Terri had anything to do with this ricin attack, do you?"

"I know she's your friend, but I googled *ricin* and the cancer center while I was waiting, and found they've conducted experiments with ricin to reduce tumors since the early eighties."

It was impossible that Terri was involved in the attacks. "It doesn't mean that she or her husband had access to it. Besides, this isn't your case. It's the US Marshal's."

A low flush crept up his neck. "But I'm involved in it. Now eat."

Rachel forced the sandwich down and finished her frappe about the same time Boone finished his tea.

He set the glass down. "Let's play a little what-if. Off the record, though. Are we both on the same page that the person who killed Vic Vegas likely also killed Harrison Foxx?"

She nodded.

"What if he or she also killed your mother?"

"What's the motive?"

"I thought you might have some ideas on that since I figure you've already made that jump."

Busted. "If you determine the cases are connected, are you going to take me off the case?"

"I should, but like I said, this is off the record."

She didn't know whether to feel relief or to wait for the other shoe to drop.

"Look, I know how important this case is to you. You're close to finding out who killed your mom. But what if it's someone you know? Like Terri? Can you conduct the investigation impartially?"

"Terri did not kill my mother."

"That's what I'm talking about. You can't be sure of that at this point. And don't forget, she had a conversation with Culver when she delivered the baskets to Blues & Such. She could have easily put the insulin-laced water bottles in his basket."

Doubt muddled her mind. Was it possible? "I want the truth to come out," she said, her voice cracking. She held his gaze as his eyes never left her face. Eyes that flickered with warmth she felt to her toes.

Finally he nodded. "We'll keep this part of the investigation off the record for now. Just don't make me regret it."

She finally breathed again. "If I get something concrete, I'll bring it to you."

"Good. Are you ready to drive to the cancer center?"

She didn't want to argue with him, not after he'd just bent the rules for her, but she couldn't help herself. "I can't see Terri trying to kill me or Dad. I still think it makes more sense to look at my dad's cases—there's plenty of people he's riled with his rulings."

"The marshal is looking into those cases. If there's anything there, he'll let us know," he said. "It's not just Terri I'm looking at, either. Could be someone else who worked there with access to ricin who also has a connection to your family."

That made sense and made her feel a bit better.

The Crockett Cancer Institute was located in the heart of the medical district in Midtown. Once inside, they were directed to the human resources department, where an assistant escorted them to the director's office. As they entered the room, a tall African-American woman who appeared to be in her early sixties greeted them. The nameplate on the desk read Corrine Patterson. Boone showed his badge and then introduced Rachel.

"Have a seat," Ms. Patterson said. They settled in the two office chairs while she sat behind a desk with neatly stacked folders. She leaned forward. "How can I help you?"

"We're working on a case that involves ricin and understand this institution has used the substance in research since the early eighties. We need a list of all the people who have worked with it, and any reports of theft."

"That will take some time to pull together. When do you need it?"

"Yesterday," he said, softening the request with a smile.

"Of course. I'll see if I can get it together by this time tomorrow."

"Thank you," Rachel said. Ms. Patterson was very efficient. "Could we also get a roster of all the employees going back to 1980?"

"And the personnel files on Robert and Terri Morrow," Boone added. "Those I'd like today, if at all possible."

Her eyes widened. "Goodness. Personnel records . . . I'll have to check with our legal department before I hand that information over."

"I can get a warrant if necessary," Boone said. "But I'd hoped I wouldn't have to."

"Since it's so long ago, I'm sure it'll be all right, but give me a few minutes to check."

Fifteen minutes later, she returned with several sheets of paper. "The legal department said to cooperate." She handed Boone the papers. "Personnel records for the Morrows, and the names of all of our employees from 1980 on. There's a column showing their first day of work and one for their last day if they are no longer employed. The other records should be available tomorrow."

"Thank you," he said and handed her his card. "I'd appreciate it if you'd scan them and email them to me."

She nodded and sat behind her desk. "Why are you interested in Bobby? He's been dead for over thirty years."

"Did you know him?" Rachel asked. She knew so little about Terri's husband and didn't want to quiz her friend.

"Yes. A fine man. I worked in research and development with him as a lab assistant."

Rachel leaned forward. "How did he die?"

"A tragic accident. He and his wife were on a second honeymoon." She stared pensively at her folded hands as if she was trying to make up her mind about something.

"Was it an auto accident?" Boone asked.

She lifted her gaze. "No. He fell off a cliff at Big Sur. The authorities who investigated said he'd gone off the trail to get photos of McWay Falls, I believe. I felt so sorry for his wife. She took it very hard. Had some sort of breakdown, I believe."

Rachel didn't like the look Boone shot her. *Another coincidental death?*

Boone took out a notepad. "Did anyone see the accident happen?"

"No. Terri had stopped to rest with a couple of other hikers.

It was believed someone else was on the trail, but that turned out to be a false report."

"Why did they go to Big Sur?" he asked.

"If you'd known Bobby, you would understand. He loved to get away from it all, and after what had happened in their marriage, they both were looking for a quiet place to focus on each other and rebuild what they'd had. That's what the trip was supposed to be about."

"What was wrong with their marriage?"

Ms. Patterson waved her hand dismissively. "One of the research assistants set her cap for him. Poor man didn't have a chance. Although I never knew what he saw in her. Pretty face, all right, but a bit on the portly side. She was furious when he chose to stay with his wife and broke it off."

"Do you recall her name?"

She pressed her fingers to her mouth and looked toward the ceiling. Then she shook her head. "I can't remember her name. Let me see that list."

Boone handed her the papers, and she ran her finger down the names. "Nothing jumps out at me. A couple of employees who worked in R&D back then are still here, but they left at three. I'll ask them tomorrow and include their comments in my report to you."

"Do you remember any thefts of ricin?" Rachel asked.

"Heavens, no. That stuff is lethal. None of the lab assistants would even handle the vials," she said. "Bobby was the only researcher who worked with it at that time. That's one reason his death was so tragic. He'd made a breakthrough in using it to reduce tumors in mice. But I'll check and let you know if there are any reports of theft."

"Thank you," Boone said.

Rachel cleared her throat. "Do you remember Gabby Winslow?"

A slow smile spread across the director's face. "I thought you looked familiar. You must be Gabby's daughter."

"Yes. But it's been so long ago, I'm surprised you remember her."

"Your mother helped me with funding on a project. She was very good at what she did as well as being kind. I hated when she quit." Ms. Patterson's eyes twinkled as she studied Rachel. "But she wanted to be a stay-at-home mom." Then she sobered. "I was so upset when I read she'd died. Did they ever find the person responsible?"

"No."

Ms. Patterson's phone rang and Boone stood. "Thank you so much for seeing us," he said. "We'll find our way out."

"That was very informative," Rachel said as they walked to the car. "I wonder who Terri's husband was having the affair with?"

"Good question. You can look over the list of employees as we drive back to the CJC. See if you recognize anyone."

As they pulled out of the parking lot, she scanned the employee records, pausing when she came to Robert's name, then Terri's, and then again at her mother's. Those were the only three she knew. It was going to be a long night, checking out the people on the list. She'd better text Terri and cancel the workout and dinner.

"What's the rest of your day looking like?" Boone asked as he pulled into the parking garage.

"Same as yours," she said, holding up the papers. "I'd planned on meeting Terri at the gym at six and then going to dinner with her. And afterward stopping by to see my dad."

"That's actually a pretty good idea. I'd planned to question her, but you might learn more unofficially than I could officially."

"But I don't want to leave you with all this paperwork."

He checked his watch. "You have an hour. We'll divvy up the names and you can start on yours and finish up later or in the morning."

She looked askance at him. "You sure?"

He grinned. "I'm sure. A couple of hours away from the case will do you good."

# 40

TERRI WAS WAITING for Rachel when she arrived at the gym. Questions loomed in her mind. Questions about Robert and the woman he'd had an affair with, questions about what Monica had said, but she tamped down the impulse to jump in. That would only shut Terri down.

"Ready for some Pilates?" Terri asked as they walked into the private exercise room.

"Definitely. My core needs working."

Halfway through the hour, Rachel wondered what she was doing here as she did yet another set of crunches. She was supposed to be concentrating on the exercises but the subject she wanted to discuss with her father kept chasing through her mind.

Her father had threatened Foxx the same day he was murdered. Why hadn't he ever mentioned that? Maybe it wasn't true. If those thoughts weren't looping through her mind, questions for Terri about her husband were. She was beginning to dread dinner.

Finally the hour ended and she rolled up her mat.

"Where were you tonight?" Terri asked.

Rachel knew what she meant. "Have a lot on my mind."

"That's why I texted you—so you could forget this case for an hour."

"Thanks, but it's hard to do. Where would you like to eat?"

They decided on a small family-style restaurant around the corner from the gym. Terri ordered a salad, and after an argument with herself, Rachel ordered the same instead of the country fried steak. "Do you ever splurge on something with lots of calories?" she asked, handing the waitress the menu.

"Sometimes, but I didn't see anything worth the calories."

"Why do you count calories? You've never had a weight problem."

"But I have. Years ago, and I don't want it to happen again. I have to stay healthy for Erin. If anything happened to me . . ."

"Nothing's going to happen to you," Rachel said. "You do all the right things."

"I'll do whatever it takes—I'm all she has." Terri squeezed lemon into her water. "Do you have to go back to work?"

She nodded. "After I go see Dad. Have a couple of questions to ask him."

"About the case?" she asked as her cell phone rang. "Hold on a sec. It's Erin calling me on her new cell phone."

"She has a cell phone?"

"Yes. She's taking the bus to her workplace now, and I have an app that lets me keep up with her. Makes me feel better." Terri slid the answer button. "Hey there."

Rachel traced her finger through the condensation on her tea glass as Terri talked with her sister. "Tell her I said hi," she mouthed.

"Rachel said hi." After a pause, she said, "I don't know, I'll ask her." She moved the phone away from her mouth. "Erin wants to know if you're still going with us to the candlelight vigil tomorrow night."

"I don't know. Depends on the case, but I will if I can."

Terri relayed the message, then she said, "Be sure and keep your phone charged and on," she said, then disconnected. "She's bad to leave her phone turned off. And I do hope you can go with us—she's really excited that you might."

"Remind her tomorrow I could have to work," Rachel said. "I noticed on the security tapes that you spoke with Randy Culver Saturday afternoon when you delivered the baskets to Blues & Such."

Terri nodded. "I complimented him on his singing, and we chatted a little, mostly on how hot it's been."

No surprise there. "How about Monica Carpenter? How well do you know her?"

"Monica?" Surprise lit her face. "Not well. The last few years she's usually around during Elvis Week when I take Erin to the tribute artist thing at Blues & Such. I knew her better before your mom died. Why?"

She hesitated, wavering about whether to mention the subject of the threat. "Her name has come up in the investigation into Vic Vegas's death. How about Vic and Harrison Foxx? How well did you know them?"

"So-so. I choreographed the St. Jude Elvis contest back then because your mom asked me to. And in case you haven't noticed, I'm not exactly the social butterfly she was," she said with a chuckle.

Terri was a classic introvert, preferring to sit back and observe people rather than join the crowd, and Rachel laughed along with her. "Did you ever date either of them?"

Her friend sat back in the chair and crossed her arms. "Am I a suspect in Vic's death?"

"No! I'm just trying to get a feel for the two men because I believe their murders are connected."

Terri's eyes widened. "You're kidding! Why? Is it because Vic kept sticking his nose into Harrison's death?"

"So you know about that."

"Yeah, he came to see me not long ago." She sipped her tea. "And I told you already that I talked to him Friday night when he stopped by the table to speak to Erin. For some reason, he always remembered her from year to year and treated her like she was a princess. She called him Elvis."

Terri devoted a lot of time and love toward Erin, always putting her sister's needs above her own. "I admire how you've taken care of Erin."

She shrugged. "Nothing to admire—it's what you do." A pensive look crossed her face. "I haven't told her about Vic's death yet. Friday night she asked to wear his shoestring cowboy tie because it had silver tips and a turquoise slide, and he actually gave it to her."

"Vic seemed like a good guy. What did he want to know when he came to see you?"

"He asked about Harrison and your mom. I assured him there was absolutely nothing between them."

"Did anyone else think something was going on with them . . . like Dad?" She'd committed now and couldn't back up.

A frown tightened Terri's lips. "Harrison is not why they separated. I don't think your father liked him or understood their relationship, but he wasn't jealous of him."

"What was Mom's relationship with him?"

Before she could answer, the waitress appeared with their salads, and they both fell silent until she left. Rachel poured raspberry vinaigrette over hers. When it was obvious Terri wasn't going to pick up where they'd left off, Rachel said, "You didn't say what their relationship was."

"She thought of Harrison as a wayward brother. The two of them had bonded when we were at Humes High for different reasons. Your mom always took up for the underdog, and back then Harrison was definitely that." She laid her fork on the table and leveled her gaze at Rachel. "I may not be the right person to talk about him—I was like your dad and didn't care for him. I thought he used Gabby."

That sounded like the consensus. "How about other women—I understand he had a lot of women fans."

"There were a few who showed up regularly," Terri said. "As well as the ones who worked backstage. Monica was one of those." She tilted her head. "Why did you ask earlier if your dad was jealous of Harrison?"

Rachel picked at her salad. Now that she had the perfect opening, it was hard to get the words out. She laid her fork down and leaned forward. "Monica said Dad threatened Harrison a few hours before he was killed. That Harrison tried to blackmail him."

"Over what?"

Monica's words echoed in her head. "At the graveyard, she overheard Harrison claim he had proof that Dad killed Mom, and he wanted money to keep quiet."

Terri gasped. "That's not true, at least the part about your dad. He would never harm your mother."

"I . . . don't want to believe he did, either. But Monica sounded so sure Dad was capable of killing Harrison."

"Are you still angry with your father because he wasn't there when your mother died?"

"What? No. I got over that a long time ago." Or so she'd thought. Lately Rachel wasn't so sure. Her relationship with the Judge was complicated. For many years she had been angry that he hadn't been there. It had driven them apart. And sometimes when he was distant and aloof, she feared it was because he blamed her for not going home with her mom that night.

Gran's words when she'd voiced her fear once popped into her mind.

*"He's hurting too, Rachel. He not only lost Gabby that night, but he believes he lost you as well."*

It hadn't been long afterwards that their pastor had preached on unforgiveness, and his words shot straight into her heart. While she couldn't tell her father she'd forgiven him—he would never think he'd done anything that warranted forgiveness—she did soften her attitude toward him. Slowly they'd built a new relationship.

"Are you sure you're not still angry? Lately you've seemed different. You haven't been to church in a while, and if you'd truly forgiven him, I don't believe you'd have any question about his innocence."

Rachel stared at the table. "But what if he went home with her and they argued? It could've been an accident."

"No, Rachel. Your father had an alibi. But you have to know he could never, ever harm Gabby. He loved her. Still does."

Pain filled Terri's voice and Rachel looked up. Tears rimmed the older woman's eyes. Rachel knew in that moment that Terri was in love with the Judge. "What's going on with you and Dad?"

"Nothing. Like I said, he's still in love with your mom." She took another sip of tea.

"You don't think Donna will hook him?"

Terri almost choked on the tea. "If he lets Miss Priss turn his head, Lucien will deserve what he gets. But I figure it'll play out like all the other women he's been involved with. A couple of dates and he'll get bored or they'll mention the M-word." She narrowed her eyes. "You haven't told anyone what Monica said, have you? If this gets out, it'll ruin his nomination."

"I know. That's why I haven't told Boone or anyone else yet. I want to talk to Dad first."

"You better do it tonight. *If* Monica has bottled up this information all these years, now that she's told you, she'll tell others. And if she made it up, then she's crazy, and you can't predict what crazy people will do. You have to get it cleared up now."

"I know." Rachel pulled her bottom lip between her teeth. "I have one more question."

"Shoot."

Terri might when Rachel voiced her question. "I understand your husband, Robert, worked at Crockett Cancer Institute in their research and development department. Did he ever mention any ricin being stolen or misplaced?"

into her dad's drive. The front of the house was dark, and Rachel pulled around to the back, where a strange car was parked. The light was on in the kitchen, and she knocked lightly.

"Door's unlocked," her dad called out.

When she entered, he was standing at the coffeemaker, pouring coffee into a carafe. "Whose car?" she asked.

"The US Marshal assigned to guard me." He held up his cup. "Want some?"

"Sure." Might help keep her alert later. And questions were always easier to ask over a cup of coffee. She looked around the kitchen. "Where is he?"

"In the living room setting up his equipment. I informed him you were coming."

That explained why he hadn't met her at the door.

"How's the rest of your day been?" he asked.

"It's been better."

"The report said the ricin I received today wasn't active. That should make you feel somewhat reassured."

"So it was ricin and you've gotten the report back?" How did he . . . ? The US Marshal, of course. "Someone still sent it to you—twice now—and is threatening to send the real stuff."

"Unless the package Saturday night was meant for you. Could be someone wants to get rid of us both."

That was not a reassuring thought. She took the coffee he offered. "Has Boone seen the report?"

"It just came in and that's probably first on the marshal's to-do list. You want to go into the breakfast room?"

"Sure." She sat in the same chair as yesterday morning, noting the tablecloth had been changed. Her father's need for order was as strong as Rachel's.

"So to what do I owe the pleasure of two visits in two days?" he asked as he set the carafe on the counter.

Was it still just Monday? It felt much later in the week. Rachel quickly sipped the hot coffee, wincing as it burned its way down her throat.

"That's hot," the Judge said.

"Yeah. Is there anywhere we can talk without being interrupted? Or overheard?"

"This is about as good a place as any, but let me advise the marshal not to interrupt us."

He set his coffee on the table and walked to the living room. A minute later he was back. "We won't be disturbed."

She hoped his request didn't pique the marshal's curiosity. Rachel fortified herself with a deep breath. "I interviewed Monica Carpenter today, and she indicated that Harrison Foxx threatened you with blackmail the day he was murdered, and you told him you should have gotten rid of him a long time ago."

There. It was out. Silence followed.

"I see." He wrapped his hands around the cup.

Why wasn't he denying it? "Is it true?"

"It's true that he did try to blackmail me. And I may have said the other. I thought it often enough before your mother died."

Her heart sank.

"But I didn't mean murder." His jaw slackened, and then he frowned. "You think I may have killed him?"

"No. But why haven't you told me this before? That you argued with Foxx the day he died?"

"It wasn't one of my finer moments. That man could exasperate me like no one else. We'd just buried your mother, and he accused me of murdering her, then he threatened to tell the police something he'd fabricated unless I gave him money." His eyes hardened. "A *loan*, he called it, but we both knew better. Over the years, Gabby had *loaned* him in excess of ten thousand dollars, and with her death, Foxx's source of easy cash was gone. He was desperate."

A flash of memory. "You and Mom argued about Foxx that night at the convention center."

"Yes. I hope I don't have to tell you that I didn't kill her." Her father leaned back in the chair and crossed his arms. "And as for Foxx's accusation, there wasn't a word of truth in it, but if it had come out, people would have believed it. Just like now, even you have doubts. So no, I didn't mention it to anyone. I've spent my life upholding the law. I didn't kill the man, Rachel."

She wanted to believe him, but he'd never let anything stand in the way of his career. She tried to think back to the night her mother had been buried. Was her father home all night? She couldn't remember.

He leaned forward. "Are you going to the DA with this?"

Indecision must have shown on her face.

"If you do, it'll ruin my nomination. Is that what you want to do? Ruin me?"

Did she? She stood and refilled her coffee cup.

"I thought we'd gotten past whatever problems we had after your mother died."

She stared at him. "How could we? You never acknowledged that we had a problem. It was always, 'Buck up, Rachel. Winslows don't cry.'"

His shoulders sagged. "I was trying to make you stronger, but I realize now that was the wrong way to do it."

The fragment of a memory broke free from the dark corners of her mind. *"I need my dad! Let him move back home!"* Mom, *shaking her head. "I can't, honey."* Then it was gone. "You should have been there that night! Were you with your girlfriend?"

She clapped her hand over her mouth. But it was too late. The words, trapped inside her for seventeen years, had spewed from her mouth like a volcano.

Her father jerked back as though she'd slapped him.

"I'm sorry. I didn't mean that."

"Why would you think I had a girlfriend? I never, ever cheated on your mother. Yes, I worked long hours, and she once accused me of my career being my mistress, but there was never another woman."

She faltered in her certainty. Was it possible she'd gotten it wrong? Her father wasn't faking the shock that registered on his face. Or the sincerity in his voice. Her knees threatened to buckle. All these years, she'd believed a lie about him. There'd been no girlfriend. What else had she gotten wrong? "I . . . I'm really so sorry. I thought you were hiding something and that was the reason you avoided me."

"It's all right." He exhaled a long breath. "I wasn't there for you, and yeah, sometimes I even avoided you . . . but I felt so guilty for not being there."

"I thought you blamed *me* for not being there."

"Oh no, Rachel, I never blamed you. You were just a teenager— you couldn't have done anything. I was glad you weren't there. If I'd lost you too . . ." He shook his head. "Adults can be so stupid sometimes."

He'd never blamed her? All these years she'd believed he had. Her heart pounded against her ribs.

"I should have come home anyway, even though Gabby said no."

His words penetrated her thoughts.

She rubbed her forehead, remembering Mom and Dad talking backstage . . .

*"I've changed, Gabby. No more long hours. We'll take a trip, just the three of us, a month if you want it."*

*"Lucien, I'm just not ready."*

*"You know there's no one else."*

*Her mom nodded. "Just your work."*

And then her dad had left.

He had tried. Why had she not remembered that? Another memory hung on the edge of her consciousness, but she couldn't pull it out. "I'm sorry for the way I've acted all these years," she said.

"It wasn't your fault. We should have had counseling. It's not too late, you know."

If she could find her mother's killer, she wouldn't need counseling. She stood. "We'll see. In the meantime, I have a couple of murders to solve."

"Of course."

Their gazes collided, the unspoken question hanging between them.

The Judge straightened his shoulders. "If you want, I'll tell Boone what happened that night with Harrison. Should've done it seventeen years ago and trusted God to make it turn out right."

"That would have taken a lot of faith," Rachel said. More than she possessed.

"More than I had at the time. When you don't do the right thing, it always comes back to bite you." His lips quirked in a rueful smile. "But the timing couldn't have been worse then, or so I thought."

He had a lot more to lose now. "Let me think about it."

Her father stood and started to put his arm around her. Instead, he let his hand fall to his side. "I . . . I don't tell you often enough, but I'm proud of you."

Tears sprang to her eyes, and she blinked them back. "Thanks."

They stood in awkward silence. Impulsively, she slipped her arm around his waist and hugged him, and was surprised when he leaned into the hug.

"We don't do that often enough, either," he said, his voice husky.

"Must be the British in us."

"Don't blame a whole country for our incompetence. How about we go to dinner tomorrow night and celebrate your birthday?"

A smile curved her lips. "I'd love that—oh! Wait. I'm going to the candlelight vigil with Erin. Maybe Wednesday night?"

It would be a new start for them. Rachel hugged him again. She'd waited a long time for his approval. So why did a dark cloud still hang over her?

# 42

Boone looked up as Rachel came into the conference room. He was concerned that she hadn't gotten more information from Terri. Yeah, he'd said the chat was unofficial, but how hard had Rachel tried? Asking difficult questions could be a problem when a case involved friends and family. He was already second-guessing his decision to let her stay on the case. "How was your dad?"

An expression he couldn't read crossed Rachel's face as she pulled out a chair and sat down. "Better. Getting used to a bodyguard."

He nodded his understanding and tried Terri Morrow's number for the third time. This time it went straight to voicemail, and he hung up. He'd left one message already. "Your friend Terri doesn't answer."

"Probably turned her phone off."

"At eight thirty?"

"I told you she had a migraine."

"And she didn't tell you anything about her husband?"

"Not really. She didn't know the ricin was inactive . . . but she did know that if it came from the cancer institute, it would have lost its potency." Rachel massaged the back of her neck. "You don't really think she had anything to do with sending the poison, do you?"

"She was there Saturday night and found the package. Maybe she didn't 'find' it, but was the one who brought it." Terri Morrow had means and opportunity to obtain the ricin. But why would she wait all these years to use it? "I've been thinking about motive for the ricin. I talked to Steve Lock earlier. If your dad is the target, it possibly could stem from the case he's presiding over now . . . other than it, nothing else jumped out at him. I'm focusing on you being the target."

"But why me?"

"That's the million-dollar question. Been sitting here for the last hour, trying to put myself in this person's head, and I keep coming back to one thing."

"What's that?"

"What if there's something about this case that links all three murders? And what if it's something only you would know? Maybe the person didn't know ricin lost its potency or maybe they only wanted you off the case and thought a threat on your life would be enough."

"Has that ever happened? Putting someone on leave because of a death threat?"

"Depends on how the threat affects an officer. If it compromises their ability to function, yeah, he or she would go on leave."

She grinned at him. "So you thought I was stable enough to stay on the job."

"I figured World War III would break out if I tried to take you off," he shot back. "Maybe the killer thought it'd shake you up and you'd take yourself off. So what do you know that the killer is afraid of?"

Rachel shook her head. "I wish I knew."

Boone's cell phone rang, and he answered. It was Culver's nurse at the Med.

"I told you I'd call if he improved enough for you to ask him questions," she said. "And he said he was willing to talk to you."

"Thanks. I'll be right there." He pocketed his phone. "Culver can talk to us."

Randy Culver was sitting in a chair when they walked into his room.

"You're looking better than you were earlier," Boone said.

"I feel like I've been hit by a Mack truck. At least my head is a little clearer, but I still don't remember much about the night I collapsed." His gaze shifted to Rachel and he smiled. "I certainly remember you."

Her mouth twitched, and Boone figured she was struggling not to say anything snarky as she took out a notepad.

"Do you know who sent the basket?" she asked.

"What basket?"

It was clear Culver would be no help in the case. "Someone brought you a basket with fancy bottled water in it contaminated with Humulin R U-500," Boone said.

Culver swallowed hard. "That insulin is five times stronger than my normal medicine. Why . . . ?"

"That's what I'm hoping you can tell me. And also how insulin five times stronger than your normal insulin got in your Lantus bottle."

He shook his head. "I don't have a clue, and since I've been using the vial I drew out of Saturday night, it didn't come that way from the pharmaceutical company." He bit his bottom lip, and then his shoulders slumped. "Someone really tried to kill me, didn't they?"

"I'm afraid so. Do you know of any enemies you might have?"

"No, not unless it's one of the other performers, and I just don't see that happening. None of those guys would try to kill me. I really wish I could help you," he said. His gaze slid past Boone. "I hope that coffee is for me."

Boone turned. Monica Carpenter stood in the doorway.

"Goodness, I run up to the cafeteria for a cup of coffee, and you get all kinds of company," she said brightly from the doorway.

Tonight the oversized glasses dangled around her neck, but her hair was pulled back in the customary bun. "What do you wish you could help them with?"

Monica entered the room, nodding to him, and then shot an odd look at Rachel, who quickly looked away.

"I can't remember anything about Saturday night and I don't know anyone who wants me dead. Is that my coffee?" Culver asked, glancing toward the nurse's station.

"No. I had you a cup, but"—she nodded toward the RN outside the room—"she confiscated it."

Culver groaned.

"Sorry. It's not that good, anyway." Then she smiled. "But I have some good news for you. While I was downstairs, the head of the Supreme Elvis contest called. The committee approved for you to compete this weekend, if you're able. Do you think you'll be released by then?"

Culver's face lit up. "You're kidding. Doc said I ought to be out of here in a couple of days if I keep improving."

While Monica and Culver discussed the contest, Boone noticed Rachel had grown quieter. Probably thinking they were wasting their time here and wanted to get back to the CJC. Well, so did he.

"We're going to clear out of here," Boone said. "If you start remembering anything, would you give us a call?"

Culver looked away from Monica. "Sure, but I asked the doc, and he didn't think I'd remember anything more."

"Thanks for trying," Boone said and shook the singer's hand. "I'll check back with you tomorrow."

"I'll be here," he said. "And I wish I could've helped. Vic was a nice guy."

"Yeah, me too." He turned to Rachel. "If you're ready?"

"Sure."

Rachel was wound tight as a drum. He could feel the tension radiating from her as she followed him out of the room.

"What do you think she wants from him?" she said when they were out of earshot.

"Why do you think she wants something?"

"That woman doesn't do anything without a payback."

"What happened when you went to visit her today?" he asked as they walked out the hospital doors.

Rachel stiffened. "Nothing."

"You sure? Your attitude toward her has changed."

Her shoulders drooped. "I'm just tired. And I'd hoped Culver would remember something. As soon as we get to the office, I want to check the video feed again. Maybe I'll see something new."

When they walked out of the hospital, a halo circled the full moon that rose over the city. The air was thick with humidity, making the ninety-degree temperature even stickier. He wished the cool front that had been promised would blast through, breaking the heat wave that gripped the area. Even more, he wished they'd get a break in this case.

"Ever regret becoming a cop?" he asked.

"Oh no. Never. How about you?"

"Nope. Even now, when nothing falls into place." Boone took her arm to guide her around a raised crack in the sidewalk and looked down at her, expecting an I've-got-this expression but encountering an amused smile instead.

"You never did tell me why you left the army for the police department," she said.

His heart skipped a beat. She had a way of catching him off guard. A car backfired, and for a second he was in Iraq again, pinned down by enemy gunfire as he cradled Cpl. Stacie Bragg in his arms.

*Had to get her out of there. Another round of gunfire pinpointed the enemy's location thirty yards ahead behind a brick fence. They'd walked right into their trap. Only one way out.*

*He handed the corporal off to the medic. "Give me cover," he*

*shouted to the three other soldiers behind him. When their guns
burst to life, he ran forward as he pulled the pin on his grenade
and tossed it over the fence. Then he dived for cover . . .*

"Boone, are you okay?"

Rachel's voice jerked him back to the present. He was standing
on a sidewalk in Memphis, not in Mosul. Boone took in a ragged
breath. "Uh, yeah."

"I didn't mean to—"

"It's okay," he said gruffly. "For a second I was back in Iraq."

"Do you do that often?"

"Not so much anymore. What did you ask me?"

"I wanted to know why you became a policeman, but if it bothers you, forget it."

"Thanks." They walked another block in silence before he decided he owed her an explanation. "The war was awful, especially
that last year. So many soldiers were lost to IEDs or snipers. I'd
managed to keep my group together until . . ." He paused to take
a breath. "One night we were in Mosul, evacuating a building
under fire, and I didn't listen to that inner voice. You get so used
to danger that you question your judgment. I didn't see the attack
coming that killed one of my soldiers. It was at the end of my tour
and I couldn't take any more losses."

"So you came home."

He nodded. "But I was restless. I had all this training and a degree in criminal justice. I thought if I could catch the bad guys . . ."

"You could redeem your losses in Iraq," she said.

The haunted look in her eyes stopped him. "Yeah. Like you're
trying to do with your mom."

# 43

PAIN SHOT FROM RACHEL'S NECK to her shoulders. She paused the surveillance video from Friday night and looked away from the screen while she blinked moisture back into her eyes. There just had to be a frame that would give them a lead on Vic's case.

She'd struck a nerve with Boone tonight, but at least now she knew what drove him. The same thing that drove her. Rachel hadn't realized it until she saw it in him. They'd both survived when others hadn't. And they both felt they could have done more.

She pushed the thought away as a dull throb started in the back of her head. Rachel checked her watch and massaged the knotted muscles in her neck. It was no wonder she was tense—she'd been hunched over her computer for over an hour.

"You okay?" Boone asked.

"Yeah. Just taking a break." She stood and paced in front of the table. "There has to be something on these videos that will break this case."

Boone's cell rang, and while he talked, she stretched her back.

"That was Monica Carpenter," he said when he disconnected. "She was at the desk asking to see us. I told them to send her on up, that I'd meet her at the elevator."

Rachel's stomach flipped. "Monica?"

She could be here for only one reason. Rachel willed Monica to walk out the front door instead of taking the elevator to the eleventh floor. But that didn't happen. In less than two minutes, Monica Carpenter walked through the conference room door with Boone.

"Have a seat," Boone said as he leaned against the edge of the table.

"Is Randy Culver okay?" Rachel asked.

Monica took the seat Boone indicated. "He's fine. I'm not here about him—I wanted to discuss what we talked about earlier today."

No. Not now. Not in front of Boone.

"Go ahead," he said with a sharp glance toward Rachel. "I'd be interested to know what you two talked about."

"Did you ask your father about the argument with Harrison?" Monica adjusted the oversized glasses.

Rachel found it hard to breathe.

"What argument?" Boone turned to Rachel again and questioned her with his eyes.

Monica glanced at Boone, then back to Rachel. "You haven't told him? I thought surely you had. I'm sorry."

Rachel doubted that.

"What is she talking about?" Boone demanded.

Pressure built in her chest until Rachel thought it would explode. "We, ah . . ." She couldn't get the words past her lips.

Boone turned to Monica. "Would you mind explaining?"

The older woman glanced toward Rachel and then shrugged. "After Gabby Winslow's funeral, I overheard Harrison and Judge Winslow arguing. Harrison threatened to go to the police, said he had proof that the Judge killed his wife."

"He didn't have any proof because there wasn't any," Rachel said, turning to Boone. "Foxx was trying to blackmail him, though. But my dad wasn't having any of it."

"Maybe so," Monica said, "but he threatened to kill him. I heard him."

"No, he didn't. He just said he should have gotten rid of him years ago, meaning he should have gotten him out of my mother's life."

"Is that what he told you?"

Why was Monica pressing this issue? "Maybe you made the whole thing up. Where were you the night Foxx was killed?" Rachel stepped into Monica's space.

"What?" She took a step back.

"Maybe you killed my mother, and now you're trying to pin the murders on my dad."

"That's enough, Rachel," Boone said, stepping between the two.

"But—"

His look silenced her, and then he turned to Monica. "You better go for now, but I'd like to discuss this with you further. Can I reach you tomorrow?"

"Sure, I'll be at my condo until five. Then I'm going to the candlelight vigil at Graceland."

Silence filled the room once Monica left. Boone was furious. She could tell by the way his jaw muscle twitched and the icy glare he gave her.

He planted his feet on the slate floor and crossed his arms. "You want to tell me why I had to learn your father had motive to kill Foxx from Monica Carpenter instead of you?"

"Not really. I'm still investigating what she told me."

"And you didn't think it was important to tell me?"

"I wasn't aware I had to run every little thing by you."

Boone tapped his fingers on his arm, apparently waiting for a better explanation.

"Look, I was going to tell you once I knew more," she said, desperate to make him understand. "But if reporters got ahold of it, even if he was cleared, the hint of a scandal would ruin Dad. I thought if I could disprove it, no one would ever have to know."

"You didn't trust me?" Hurt sounded in his voice. "You thought I'd give that information to reporters?"

Miserable, she stared at the floor. "It wasn't that I thought you'd purposefully tell anyone, but information like that gets out. If it does, you know what will happen."

"It never occurred to you that Monica might go to the reporters?"

"She said she wouldn't, not until the Supreme Elvis contest was over."

"I see."

There was such finality in those two words. Rachel risked a look at him. He'd walked to the window and stood with his back to her, staring out. If only she could go back to earlier in the day. But if she had it to do over again, would she tell him? She dug deep, looking for the answer, and didn't like what she found.

No. Because if she did, she'd lose control of the case.

He turned. Resignation was written all over his face.

"This is why officers don't work on cases involving their family." Boone paused and took a breath. "I think you need to take a couple of days off. And when you come back, I'll assign you to another case."

He couldn't take her off the case. "No! I—"

"You're too close to the people involved. You know it, I know it. Just like with your friend Terri. You would not have waited for a dinner chat to question any other person of interest about their husband. And if it'd been anyone other than your father, you would have told me about the threat to Foxx the night he died."

"I . . . I just wanted to check it out first."

"No. You didn't trust me," he said. "And I can't work with someone who doesn't trust me."

Her heart plummeted. "I'm sorry."

"So am I."

Rachel ducked her head, not able to stand the pain smoldering in his eyes. Perhaps if he understood why. She felt his presence as he walked to where she stood, and she raised her gaze, his image blurred by the tears that never got past her eyes. "You don't know what it's like. I lost my mother and Corey . . . because I let them down. If I'd been with them, they would still be alive. I couldn't lose my dad too."

His eyes softened. "You're right. I haven't been where you have." He lifted his hands as though to take her in his arms, then dropped them to his side. "But I can't compromise the case."

Why couldn't things be different? "Do you want me to resign?"

He shook his head. "I'll assign you to another case, and I won't put anything in the report about your dad just yet."

She nodded, not trusting her voice.

"Go home and get some rest. We'll talk tomorrow."

Rachel took a shaky breath. She had to try one last time. "Let me stay on the case. I won't hold anything else back."

"Oh, Rachel." He groaned. "I can't. If it'd been anyone but you, I would have already taken them off the case. Leave it to me. I promise, I'll get whoever is responsible."

❖

Rachel shivered even though heat wrapped around her as she exited the CJC and walked across Washington Street to the parking garage. She'd failed her mother once again. Her jaw ached from clenching it so hard. She was so close. Her phone chirped and she started to ignore it. But it could be Boone, changing his mind. A quick look at her phone told her otherwise. Terri.

*Call me.*

She didn't want to talk to anyone. But her conscience would not let her ignore her friend. She stopped outside the garage and dialed Terri. "What's up?" she asked when Terri answered. "How's your headache?"

"Killing me, but what's wrong? You sound like you've lost your best friend."

"Boone took me off the case."

"He found out about your dad and Harrison, and you hadn't told him."

"Yeah. Monica Carpenter was all too happy to tell him. He doesn't trust me now."

"I'm sorry. But you should have—"

"I don't need a lecture."

"You're right. But I remembered a couple of things from just before your mom died."

"Really? What?"

She hesitated. "I don't like gossip, but . . . well, when I choreographed the St. Jude event, I kind of blended into the background. I wasn't important like your mom, so people didn't really see me. But I saw them. Foxx was juggling three women around the time he died. Lucinda Vetch, Monica Carpenter, and Donna Dumont. I think he was getting money from all three."

"Donna loaned him money?" She'd mentioned dating Foxx, but not loaning him money.

"Yes. Donna was obsessed with him, hanging around backstage, slipping into his dressing room. She can be very conniving." Bitterness rang in Terri's tone.

"How do you know her so well?"

"I'll tell you someday, but I'm not up to it tonight. I know she's your friend, but watch yourself around her."

"Thanks. I'll pass this on to Boone." Once she hung up, Rachel dialed Boone. "I talked to Terri and you might want to take a closer look at the three women Foxx was dating when he died."

Rachel conveyed Terri's information, hoping he would change his mind about her staying on the case. Instead he thanked her and told her to pass along anything else she learned.

She slipped her phone back into her pocket and entered the garage just as a car drove onto the exit. Monica. *Let her just drive on.*

Instead Monica lowered her window. "Didn't mean to cause you any trouble tonight."

"I'm sure you didn't. If you have any more information, just take it straight to Boone."

"Why?"

"I'm not working the case anymore."

"I didn't—"

"Yeah, you did. And if you're involved in Vic's murder, Boone will find out." She left Monica sitting in her car with her mouth gaped.

# 44

TUESDAY MORNING Boone tried to reach Terri Morrow, but again the call went straight to voicemail. He wrote her name at the top of his list of people to interview, and then he scanned the reports from the uniformed officers. They had stopped at every storage facility in the city looking for a rental in Vic Vegas's name and had come up empty. Where else could Vic have hidden his files?

He missed having Rachel to bounce ideas off of. He should still be angry with her, and on one level he was. Deeply disappointed too, even if he understood why she hadn't told him about her father and Foxx. He hadn't ruled out Carpenter as a suspect, either.

He turned as Donna came into the conference room. "A fax came for you from Crockett Cancer Institute."

"Thanks," he said, taking the papers from her. "When you were dating Foxx, did you ever loan him money?"

She took a step back. "Loan him money?" She shook her head. "When I knew him, I didn't have any money to loan. Why did you ask that?"

"Several of the women he dated did, and I wondered if you might have."

"Well, I didn't." She glanced past him. "Where's Rachel?"

"Taking a couple of days off," he said.

"Oh. For her birthday?"

He'd completely forgotten today was Rachel's birthday. "No."

When he didn't comment further, she nodded. "Let me know if I can help you in any way."

"I will." He scanned the report and quickly dialed Ms. Patterson from the Cancer Institute.

"I was expecting you to call," she said.

"How did a vial of ricin go missing?"

"I don't know. It wasn't discovered until after Bobby Morrow's death, and there was no one to ask. At that time, he was the only one who used ricin in the labs."

"Was it reported to the police?"

She paused a long moment. "I'm afraid not. It was an oversight on the part of the administrator. Unfortunately, he is no longer with us."

"Was there even an investigation?"

"Yes, but about that time, we lost a rather large grant and several people were let go. I don't believe any of the released employees were questioned."

"I see. How about the woman Morrow had an affair with? Do you remember her name?"

"I'm pretty sure it was Irene Baker, but I scanned the employee records and the only Baker I found was a Shirley, and that name doesn't ring a bell. I'm still looking."

"If you think of anything else that might help with this investigation, please give me a call," he said. After he hung up, he dialed Steve Lock and filled him in on the missing ricin. "I'll fax you what the cancer center sent me this morning."

"Thanks," Steve said. "I received the toxicity report on the ricin sent to Judge Winslow last night. Like the note indicated, it's inactive."

"So it could very well be the ricin in question."

"That's what I'm thinking."

"Why would someone send an inactive poison to him? If the

sender didn't know in the beginning, he or she had to know after the news reports."

"I've been looking at the case he's presiding over. A witness was supposed to give incriminating evidence against the defendant today, but after the delay, he's suddenly changed his mind and refuses to testify. I think someone used the poison threat to delay the trial and get to the witness."

That was better than thinking it was personal against the Judge or Rachel.

"How's your case with the Elvis impersonators coming?"

"Dead ends everywhere we look."

"I wish you luck on it."

As soon as he ended the call, Boone dialed Rachel's number. He wanted to touch base with her and wish her a happy birthday. "Come on, Rachel, answer."

When it went to voicemail, he clicked off his phone. She wasn't going to answer his calls. He'd let her stew a while. He picked up her original report on Vic Vegas's request that she investigate Harrison Foxx's murder and skimmed it. At the bottom of the page was a note. Original name—Phillip Grant. Legally changed to Vic Vegas in 1995.

Boone dialed the head of the uniform division and asked if his people could check the storage rentals again, this time under the name of Phillip Grant. When he agreed, Boone thanked him and hung up. Then he glanced at the computer with the surveillance videos on it, wishing Rachel were here to look at them. Maybe he'd been too hasty in taking her off the case.

*It's against the rules.* But the department was shorthanded. He could bend the rules slightly—give her a desk job—but he'd have to keep her out of the field. Boone stared at the computer. Why not test the waters, see if she'd be willing to come back under those circumstances. It would give him the opportunity to at least check and see how she was doing.

Before he could change his mind, he dialed her number. When she still didn't answer, he sent her a text, requesting she call him. Five minutes later, she hadn't answered. Where could she be? It wasn't like her not to answer. Maybe her father might know. The Judge picked up on the first ring.

"Boone, I was just about to call you. Is something wrong?"

"I'm trying to reach Rachel. Is she with you?"

"No. Why isn't she with you?"

"I gave her a few days off."

"What's going on, Boone?"

"It's not anything I want to discuss over the phone."

"I'm coming downtown later this afternoon and planned to stop in—that's why I was about to call you. Will you be there around four?"

"Yes, sir. And could you check with Rachel's grandmothers and see if she's with one of them? If you find her, ask her to call me."

The Judge assured him he would. Boone tapped the phone in his hand. He didn't know anyone else to try except Terri Morrow, and she hadn't answered any of his calls. He'd barely punched in two numbers when a text from Rachel dinged on his phone. His taut muscles turned to Jell-O, surprising him.

---

What do you want?

---

Would you answer your phone, please?

He dialed again.

"Where are you?" he asked.

"My phone was in the other room, and I didn't hear it ring."

"Well, you scared me to death. I thought . . . never mind what I thought. Happy birthday, by the way."

"You went to all that trouble just to wish me a happy birthday?"

"Not exactly."

"Well?"

"I thought you might like to come in and view the surveillance videos."

"What made you change your mind?" Her voice was guarded.

"Maybe I missed you." With a jolt he realized he did miss her. "And it's only a desk job—you can't go out into the field."

"I see."

When she didn't say anything else, he said, "Look, I'm bending the rules. Do you want it or not?"

"Yes. I'm just trying to understand why you're doing this."

"Consider it a birthday present."

"You've never given me one before."

"I didn't know you last year." When she appeared to be waiting for him to continue, he said, "Okay, because I need your help. Satisfied?"

"Yeah." The grin in her voice came through the phone clearly. "I'll be there in half an hour."

"Good. Oh, and call and let your father know you're okay."

"You called him?"

"When I couldn't find you." When she groaned, he added, "You should have answered your phone."

Humming, he hung up. The day just got a lot brighter.

# 45

RACHEL WAS OFF THE CASE, and now Shirley wouldn't be forced to kill her. And Randy hadn't remembered a thing about the necklace. He'd soon be home, where she could keep tabs on him. But if he hadn't remembered by now, he wasn't likely to.

Relief spread through her body. Maybe no more deaths. She didn't like killing. After all, she wasn't a monster. Not killing Rachel and Randy proved that. She never would have killed anyone if they hadn't pushed her to it.

*Rachel wouldn't have been an issue if you hadn't stolen the necklace that night. You're not good for anything.*

"Shut up." There had to be a way to silence her father's voice. She pressed her thumbs against her ears.

*The necklace is still out there.* His voice taunted her. *Vic hid it somewhere.*

"It doesn't matter!" The words tore from her lips. "Do you hear me? As long as Rachel doesn't see it, no one will ever know I took it from Gabby that night."

Of course he couldn't hear her. He was dead. She'd cut his throat with a razor . . . Shirley closed her eyes, reliving that night so long ago.

*The fireball had lit up the night sky, but darkness had hidden her as she crouched behind a huge oak. Her legs would not move as she stared, mesmerized by the flames. Men poured out the tavern door, shouting for someone to call the fire department.*

*Home. She had to be there when the law came.*

*Forcing her legs to carry her, she slipped away from the scene, arriving at the back door of the small bungalow half an hour later. Drops of blood were splattered on the kitchen floor. She had to clean it up before anyone arrived. Shirley grabbed a bottle of Clorox and twisted the top off. No. The smell was too strong—the law would wonder why she'd used bleach on the floor. There'd be time for that later. She would mop the floor with water now.*

*Her gaze fell on the razor. She grabbed it and hurried to the bathroom with it and sprinkled Old Dutch Cleanser on it, scrubbing it with a brush.*

*Where was the strap? She found it on the kitchen floor where her father had dropped it*

*"They're going to catch you, girlie."*

*No! How could she hear his voice? He was dead. She'd seen him take his last breath.*

*"I'll come back to haunt you. You'll never get away from me."*

*She sank to the floor. No . . .*

Thinking back now, the memories made Shirley's skin crawl. She didn't know how her father did it, but his voice had haunted her all her life. Still, she'd gotten away with his murder.

What she hated most was burying him beside her mother in Elmwood Cemetery in Memphis. Being next to her was too good for him.

*Rachel will find out you spent time in the mental institution at Bolivar.*

"You're crazy! I did not go to a mental institution."

*You're lying, girl. You were there three years. And Rachel's smart. She'll find out.*

"She's not as smart as I am. Just leave me alone." Was it true? Did they really put her away for three years? And her father. If he was dead, why did she keep hearing his voice?

# 46

By FIVE O'CLOCK, Rachel had reviewed every frame of surveillance video taken from Friday night until after Culver's collapse on Saturday. Nothing stood out. She might as well have been at home, for all the good she'd done. Her cell phone rang and she answered.

"I-it's m-me, Erin."

Erin never called her. "Honey? Are you okay?"

A muffled sob came through the line. "Terri can't take me to Elvis's house to light my candle tonight. Can you?"

Rachel's heart sank. Erin had been looking forward to this for weeks. "Why can't she take you?"

"She's sick."

Another call beeped in. Terri. "Hold on a sec. I think she's calling me now." Rachel switched over to the other call. "Terri?"

"Yeah. Look, can you take Erin to Graceland tonight? That migraine last night? It's had me with a vengeance, and while it's easing, it'll be another hour before I can function—too late for the vigil."

"Hold on a second, let me check." Rachel looked around for Boone. He was looking through a file. "I'm done here. Do you need me any longer?"

He looked up. "No, there's nothing else for you to do."

She gave him a thumbs-up. Maybe this desk job wasn't all bad. "I can take her. But don't forget, Boone wants to speak to you."

"I know. He's called a dozen times, but I just couldn't answer the phone."

"Call him as soon as you can. Let me tell Erin I can take her."

She switched the call again and was surprised Erin was still there. "I'll come pick you up in half an hour, okay?"

"Really?" Her voice brightened. "Can I wear my new red shoes?"

"Of course." Rachel smiled. It took so little to make Erin happy. "See you soon."

After she hung up, she grabbed her keys. "I'll see you in the morning."

"Where are you going?"

"You said you didn't need me so I'm taking Erin to Graceland. Oh, and Terri is in bed with a migraine. I told her to call you."

Boone frowned. "Are you certain you want to get in that crowd?"

"I don't have any choice now. I told Erin I'd be there."

"I don't like it."

"It will be fine. We'll be out there with thirty thousand other people." Thirty thousand? She hadn't thought this through.

Donna stuck her head in the doorway. "I didn't know you were here. Happy birthday."

"Thanks."

The office manager turned to Boone. "I'm leaving a little bit early. Going to get my place at Graceland's candlelight service."

"You too?" Rachel said. "Wait and I'll walk out with you."

"Wait—" His cell phone rang, cutting him off.

She waved him off. "Donna and I will hang out together. We'll be fine."

Rachel left him talking on his phone and walked to the elevator with the office manager. She glanced at the cropped palazzo pants and the loose-fitting top her friend wore. "Love your outfit," she said. Then she noticed the umbrella Donna carried. "Is it supposed to rain?"

"The weatherman said there might be thunderstorms, but they should hold off until after the vigil," Donna said. "I didn't know you ever went to this."

"I don't usually. But I just now promised Erin I'd take her. There are some perks to not working the case." She let Donna go first on the elevator. There were several people riding down with them and neither of them spoke until they'd exited the elevator.

"So you have to pick up Erin?"

Rachel nodded. "But I'd like for us to hang out with you. Where do you want to meet?"

Donna smiled. "I have an idea. Parking is going to be murder as well as finding you two in that crowd. Why don't I just follow you to Erin's and we'll go in my car from there? You can pick your car up when we take her home."

She hadn't been looking forward to driving in all the traffic that was sure to be near Graceland. "You don't mind?"

"Of course not. It'll give me a chance to get to know Erin better. Your father acts really fond of her."

"Yes, he is. How is it going with you two?"

"Really well. Of course, he's preoccupied with the ricin deal. He had to call a mistrial, you know."

No, she didn't. Maybe the whole ricin thing had been about getting a mistrial. "Just remember he's been single a long time. Don't set your sights on marriage."

Donna grinned at her. "Don't worry about me. But if I do, he'll come around. Everyone usually does, one way or the other."

# 47

BOONE HURRIED UP THE STEPS to the Med. Randy Culver's nurse had called with the message that Culver had remembered something and wanted to see him. Boone started to call Rachel and decided to wait until he knew if the information was important.

Culver was dressed and sitting on the side of the bed. "Are you being discharged?" Boone asked.

"Tomorrow," he said. "Doc says I'm going to be fine."

And he looked much better. "Do you have anyone to stay with you?"

"He didn't think I needed anyone." Culver pinned him with a hard look. "Do you have any leads on who switched my bottle of insulin? Still can't figure out why anyone would do something like that."

"I believe it has to do with Vic Vegas's death. I think his killer saw him tell you something Friday night."

Culver pressed his hands to his head. "I started getting bits and pieces of what happened this weekend earlier today, but I don't see how anything we talked about could be that important."

"What do you remember?"

He looked up. "Vic asked me again about Harrison Foxx. Had I ever heard that he gambled a lot—that was the first time we talked.

297

Told him I barely remembered Foxx. The next time, Vic showed me this necklace and asked if I remembered seeing it. I thought he was crazy, but he said it was important. That it belonged to some woman who had died. Then he said something about Harrison Foxx, but I can't remember what."

Could the woman be Gabby Winslow? "Can you describe the necklace?"

"It was either platinum or white gold and shaped like a guitar. And it had diamonds in it. Really nice. Told him I'd never seen it before, and believe me, I would have remembered if I had. That thing cost some money."

"Did he say where he got it?"

"If he did, I don't remember, but that conversation didn't last over thirty seconds," Culver said. "I had to go on stage and I was concentrating on my song anyway. When I finished, Vic was gone. And the next day, I learned he was dead."

"Do you remember anyone he talked to? Especially a woman."

"Let me think." He scratched his jaw and looked down at the floor. "Everything is such a blur, and he was always talking to someone . . . but I do remember this woman with dark hair . . ." He looked up. "Yeah, I remember now. Vic was talking to her . . ." He shook his head. "Wait. Monica. He stopped and talked to her just before I went on stage."

Monica could have easily switched Culver's insulin, and she had been at the hospital every day. Checking to see what he remembered? "Did he have the necklace when he talked to her?"

"I don't know. It's all jumbled in my mind."

"Do you think you could describe the necklace and the other woman to a sketch artist?"

"The necklace, yeah, but I'm not sure about the woman. They were sitting in a dark corner of the room. Mostly what I remember is the hair."

Boone took out his phone and dialed a forensic sketch artist he knew. She agreed to bring her sketchpad to the hospital. He hung up and turned to Culver. "Someone's coming by in the next hour. Just do the best you can."

When he returned to the office, Lucien Winslow was waiting for him in the conference room. "Hello, sir. Don't get up," he said as the older man started to stand. After shaking hands with the Judge, Boone sat behind his desk.

"Sorry I'm late," the Judge said. "Is Rachel around? I have something to say and wanted her in on it."

"She just picked up Erin to take her to Graceland."

"I'd forgotten about that. It's just as well, I guess. I doubt she's told you, but I had an argument with Harrison Foxx the night he was murdered. She learned about it yesterday, and I'm afraid it's put her in a hard place."

"Yeah, I know about the argument."

"Then you know Foxx tried to blackmail me." He tilted his head. "I'm surprised she told you."

"She didn't. It came out during a conversation with Monica Carpenter."

He leaned forward. "And that's why you took her off the case?"

"Yes. She's too close to it. Although I did assign her some desk tasks."

"I should have called you as soon as I knew she had the information," he said.

Boone leveled his gaze at the Judge. "I don't know all the details. Would you like to explain?"

# 48

Rachel looked in the rearview mirror. Erin fidgeted as she stared out the window. She should've had Donna meet them closer to Graceland. Erin didn't do well in the back seat by herself. And it didn't help that Donna practically ignored Erin as Rachel complimented Erin's heart pendant and new shoes. Just now they'd finished discussing Rachel's sandals, and she was about out of topics to talk about.

A traffic light turned red, catching her as she shifted lanes to avoid a slow-moving car. While she waited, Rachel drummed her fingers on the steering wheel and tried to puzzle out how they ended up in her car. When she had returned to her car after signing Erin out of the group home, Donna was sitting in the front passenger seat of Rachel's Honda. And the office manager had been very quiet.

"You okay?" Rachel asked her as they pulled away from the light.

"My stomach is bothering me. Must have been something I ate."

Erin leaned toward the front seat. "Donna has an Elvis necklace. Do you think she would let me wear it?"

"An Elvis necklace?" Rachel said and glanced toward Donna with an apologetic smile. Since she wasn't wearing a necklace, where had Erin come up with that question? "I don't know, but *you* can ask her—she's sitting right there. Although if she has one, it's probably at her house."

"No, you ask her."

Rachel sighed. Sometimes her friend's social graces needed work.

"What are you talking about?" Donna snapped. "I don't have an Elvis necklace."

The older woman's sharp tone made Rachel flinch. Evidently Erin wasn't the only one who lacked tact. She checked the rearview mirror, hoping Erin would let the matter drop. She could get so obsessed with a subject sometimes, especially when it came to jewelry, but Erin stared out the backseat window, fingering the small heart pendant hanging from the chain around her neck, and Rachel relaxed a little. Her cell phone rang, and she grabbed it off the dash and thumbed the answer button. "Hello?"

Then she frowned as she noticed that the fuel gauge was almost on empty. She'd forgotten to fill up this morning.

"Where are you?"

Boone's voice blasted into the car, jolting her. She'd accidentally put the call on speakerphone. "Just picked up Erin at the group home and we're on our way to Graceland. Hold on a sec." She managed to take the call off speaker.

"Is that Boone?" Erin said, unbuckling her seat belt and leaning between the front seats.

"Erin, you have to keep your seat belt fastened. Okay?"

"I don't want to. I want to talk to Boone!"

"Buckle up or we'll turn around and go home."

"No!" But she complied, albeit with a frown.

"Okay, I'm back. What's up?" she asked.

"I talked earlier with Randy Culver, and he's starting to re-member this weekend. Said Vic Vegas showed him a guitar-shaped necklace with diamonds."

Adrenaline shot through Rachel's body. A guitar-shaped neck-lace? That was the necklace Culver couldn't remember? She'd only seen one like it in her life. The one Harrison Foxx had given her mother the night she died. How had she forgotten it?

In her peripheral vision, Donna sat up straighter. Then Rachel had to concentrate on traffic as a car cut in front of them, and she almost rear-ended it.

"Are you still there?" Boone asked.

"Yes. Traffic is awful. I'll call you as soon as I can." She dropped her phone in her bag, her mind whirling. Was it possible? There couldn't be that many diamond guitar pendants around. She wished she'd asked if he knew where Vic got it.

In the back seat, Erin leaned forward. "I want to go to Donna's house and get her Elvis necklace," she said. "So I can wear it."

"I don't know what you're talking about. I told you I don't have any such necklace."

Rachel glanced toward Donna and stiffened. Donna's face had turned dark and brooding. And her eyes . . . What was going on with her? "I'll handle this," she said quietly. "Erin, sweetie, we don't have time."

Erin crossed her arms. "But she's telling a fib, and you're not supposed to do that. She had it on when I saw her with Elvis."

Terri had said she'd taken Erin to the Elvis tribute contest at Blues & Such Friday night. She must have seen Donna then.

Donna snorted. "Elvis is dead." She fidgeted with something in her pocket. "Let's talk about something else."

"No! I saw him Friday night. He gave me his shiny tie."

Erin was talking about Vic. She looked in the mirror again, and Erin's face had turned red. A meltdown was coming if Rachel didn't divert her attention. "You can wear my necklace," she said. "As soon as we get parked."

"No! I want that one. It's pretty." She pulled against the seat belt as she leaned toward the front seat. "I know why she won't let me wear it. Elvis took it when he yelled at her.

"'Give me that necklace!'" Erin lowered her voice in a good

imitation of Vic's Southern drawl. "'This is the necklace Harrison gave Gabby! You killed her and then you killed Harrison when he found out.'"

Rachel's world upended. She tried to get her breath, but it was frozen in her chest.

Erin spoke in Vic's voice again. "'I'm taking this to Rachel Sloan and—'"

"Shut. Up." Donna jerked her seat belt off and reached over the seat for Erin. She was surprisingly fast.

"Leave her alone!" Rachel swerved, dumping Donna back in the seat. Then she saw the small pistol in her hand. "What are you doing? Are you crazy?"

"Shut up and keep driving. Turn right at the next corner."

"I want to go home," Erin whimpered in the back seat.

Donna poked the gun in Rachel's ribs. "Either you find a way to keep her from talking, or I will."

"I'm pulling over. We need to discuss this."

"There's nothing to discuss. Keep driving or I'll shoot her."

"Ra-chel!" Erin wailed. "Take me home!"

"I'm warning you. Keep her quiet . . ."

Rachel's mind raced. Erin hadn't made up what she heard. Donna had killed Vic. And the only way she could have had the necklace . . . Rachel was going to be sick.

*Focus.*

She tried to recall what she'd learned in the hostage negotiation classes she'd taken and tried not to let her mind go to the fact that the woman she thought was a friend had killed at least two people. *Focus. Keep the hostage-taker calm.* That started with not letting Erin irritate her.

"Erin, honey," she said, keeping her voice soft. "I need you to be really quiet. Okay? If you are, I'll find you a pretty Elvis necklace."

"Promise?"

"Promise."

She took her eyes off the road long enough to look in the mirror again. Erin had settled back against the seat. Good. Now Rachel had to find a way out of this. She glanced at the gas gauge again. It was past empty. They couldn't go far. Maybe if they stopped she could get someone's attention.

"We're almost out of gas," she said.

"Drive," Donna commanded. "What did you do with your cell phone?"

Rachel did not want to give up her phone. She flinched when Donna poked her in the ribs again with the pistol. "In my bag. Why are you doing this?"

"I don't have any choice. All you had to do was drop Vic's case, but you wouldn't do it." Desperation had crept into Donna's voice. That was never good.

"I don't understand."

"Just keep your eyes on the road." With the pistol still trained on Rachel, Donna pulled the phone from Rachel's purse and stuck it in her pocket.

She had to get the phone back. It was the only way she could contact Boone for help. Wait. She still had her automatic. Back at the garage, she'd taken it off and put it under her seat. If she could find a way to get her gun, she would have a fighting chance to save them.

Rachel licked her lips. "There's no need for this to go any further. I'll pull over and let you get out."

"You don't understand. I'm not going anywhere. Not until I take care of you." She slammed her fist on the console. "This is all your fault!"

Another traffic light caught them, and she risked a glance at Donna. Their gazes collided. The wild look in her eyes made Rachel's blood run cold. This couldn't be happening. And especially not with Erin in the car. She couldn't let anything happen to her. *Get your automatic.* She couldn't. Not with Donna holding a gun and looking at her like she'd seen a ghost.

"G-Gabby?" Donna drew back against the door. "Go away."

A horn blew behind them, and with a start Rachel realized the light had changed. With another glance at Donna, Rachel gunned the motor. She didn't know whether to pretend to be her mother or not. It might push Donna all the way over the edge. "It's me. Rachel."

Donna blinked, and her eyes cleared. "Of course it's you, Rachel. Why did you say that?"

"You called—it doesn't matter. What matters is we can end this now. There's no need for anyone to get hurt. Just hand me the gun."

"But I can't let you go. It—it's too late."

"No, it isn't. I won't tell anyone."

"Don't you understand? You're the only one who knows the necklace belonged to Gabby, that Harrison gave it to her and she was wearing it the night she died. That's why you have to die."

How could anyone say those words so calmly? Rachel tried to follow Donna's logic and at the same time drive in the heavy traffic. "No one knows you stole it."

"*He* said they would know. And Vic knows. Erin heard him accuse me of killing Gabby. And that the necklace was proof."

"Is that why you killed him?"

Confusion crossed her eyes. "Vic's dead?" She frowned and shook her head. "Yes, of course, Vic's dead. He wouldn't give me the necklace. He laughed at me. Just like Harrison."

Donna had killed Harrison too? How many others? Rachel glanced at the fuel gauge again. They had to be coasting on fumes now.

"I don't want to talk about Vic."

"Then let's talk about you killing my mother."

"That was an accident. And I don't want to talk about that, either."

Rachel's stomach lurched at hearing her confession. She gripped the steering wheel to keep from doing something foolish.

"Pull in at the station on the corner."

"I have to go to the bathroom," Erin said, raising her voice.

Evidently Donna had forgotten anyone else was in the car. Her eyes widened, and she jerked her head toward the back seat. Rachel wheeled sharply into the service center and slammed on the brakes, throwing Donna against the dash. Rachel grabbed for the pistol.

Donna elbowed her in the throat and then slammed the pistol against the side of her head. Stars blinded Rachel.

"Do that again and I'll shoot your friend without a second thought. Do you understand?"

Rachel closed her eyes to keep everything from spinning and drew a ragged breath. A spasm gripped her throat and she rubbed it.

"Do you understand?"

Rachel looked around and stared into the eyes of death.

# 49

BOONE WAITED while the Judge studied his clasped hands. This man had not killed Harrison Foxx, and if there were any way possible, he would keep Monica's statement out of the press.

Lucien raised his gaze. "My wife had been funding Harrison Foxx for several years. Loans, she called them, that he would repay when he hit it big. She believed in the man, but I knew better. He was never going to be more than he was. It was her money, though, inherited from her grandfather. If that's what she wanted to do with it, I couldn't stop her.

"At the cemetery, Foxx approached me and asked for a loan. When I turned him down, he got angry, threatened to tell the police he heard Gabby and me arguing the night of the Elvis contest. And that I shoved her. I'm afraid I lost my temper with him. Evidently Monica Carpenter happened along right about the time I told Foxx I should have gotten rid of him years ago."

"Did you and your wife argue that night?"

"No. A discussion, yes. She and Rachel had a lulu of an argument, though."

Could that be what was eating at Rachel? But why wouldn't she have told him about it? "Why did they argue?"

307

"I asked to come home, but Gabby wasn't ready. Rachel blew up, but I don't think she remembers the argument."

If she didn't remember it, that meant she hadn't dealt with it after her mother died. "Why didn't your wife want you to come home?"

"She thought we should go through another month of counseling. And she wanted to see more evidence that I was backing off the long hours." He crossed his arms. "I did not kill my wife or Foxx."

Boone looked up as a uniformed officer paused outside his cubicle.

"Lieutenant Callahan?"

"Yes. Can I help you?"

"I've been canvassing the storage rentals, looking for one registered to a Phillip Grant, and I've found it." He tore out a sheet from his notepad and handed it to Boone. "It's located on the south end of Getwell."

So Vic had rented a space under his original name. "Thanks."

After the officer left, Boone took a warrant from his desk and filled it out. "I don't know that I need this," he said, handing it to the Judge, "but in case the key I have doesn't work, would you mind signing this warrant for me to open Vic Vegas's storage space?"

The Judge looked over the warrant and then signed it. "Rachel mentioned Vegas to me last week. What kind of files do you think he has?"

"I'm not sure. Rachel said he'd documented everything he'd learned about Foxx's murder. Want to ride along?"

"Absolutely."

Boone retrieved the key from the evidence room, and half an hour later, his muscles tightened as he inserted it into the lock on the storage room door. It turned easily, unlocking the door. They would either hit the jackpot or bust.

Inside were several trunks and at least six cardboard boxes. Somehow he'd expected once he had the storage room, it would be easier. He turned to Winslow. "Do you mind helping me go through these boxes?" he asked.

The Judge sat on one of the boxes and pulled another to him. "What am I looking for?"

"Journals, I imagine."

By the time Boone had gone through the two trunks and several of the boxes, he feared they were wasting time. His cell phone rang just as he opened another box. Terri Morrow. He quickly answered. "Terri, thank you for calling."

"Have you heard from Rachel? I can't reach Erin or her." Panic rode her voice.

"Last time we talked, she had just picked up Erin on her way to Graceland." He checked his watch. "They should be there now. Probably can't hear their cell phones in that crowd."

"But you don't understand. I have an app on Erin's phone that tells me where her phone is at all times. And it's not working."

"That many cell phones in one place will overload the circuits, crash everything. Let me try calling Donna Dumont—they're riding with her."

"What? What are they doing with that woman?"

The venom in her voice took him aback. "I—I don't understand. She's our office manager and Rachel's friend."

"She is no one's friend."

"Just how well do you know Donna?" he asked as he lifted the top on the box in front of him.

"Well enough to know she almost broke up my marriage."

"Wait—are you saying she was the woman your husband had an affair with at Crockett Cancer Institute?" He hadn't seen Donna's name on the list of employees.

"Yes." She spit the word out. "At that time, she was going by Irene Baker. She married the Dumont man, and after he died, she changed her first name to Donna."

"I didn't know she'd ever been married."

"Yes, to an older, wealthy man. They hadn't been married a year when I heard he was about to divorce her. And then he conveniently died, leaving her a nice income," Terri said. "But evidently not nice enough, since she's working again—she quit the Institute right after his death."

Boone tried to remember everything he knew about Donna. She'd come to work at the police department seven or eight years ago, but other than that, he knew little about her. Except she liked Elvis. His heart dipped. She'd been at Blues & Such Friday and Saturday night. "She knew Foxx, but did she know Vic Vegas?"

"Oh yeah, she knew him, and as far as Foxx is concerned, that's probably where her inheritance went. Rachel said you wanted to question me about Bobby. Can it wait until tomorrow? I want to try and reach Erin again."

"Sure, but just tell me what you know about ricin missing from his research project after he died."

"I didn't know anything about it until Rachel mentioned it. And I didn't work anywhere near his lab. Gabby Winslow got me a job in her department. I met Bobby at a company picnic that summer and we married in six months. I never went back to work there after he died." She was silent for a second. "I wouldn't put it past Donna to steal a vial—even though she was married, she was still going by Irene Baker. Her husband supposedly died of food poisoning from a restaurant in town, but nobody else got sick. Maybe she killed him with it."

It bothered him the way she pointed the finger at Donna. "Thanks for your help. I'll be back in touch."

He disconnected and turned to the Judge, who had been listening to his side of the conversation. "Did you follow our conversation?"

"And heard parts of hers."

"What do you think? Talk to me about Terri. And Donna."

"Terri was a friend of Gabby's, my friend since my wife's death. She's just always been there."

"Nothing romantic?"

"No. At least not on my part. I get the sense sometimes she'd like it to be more. I knew that her husband had cheated on her, but I had no idea it was with Donna." He shook his head. "I wouldn't have thought that of her. And I can't see either of them being behind the ricin attack. I certainly don't see either of them killing Vegas or Foxx."

Boone didn't either. "Let's go through the rest of the boxes so we can get out of here."

He opened the one closest to him, picked up a packet of photos, and looked at the date. August 2000. His pulse kicked up a notch, and he thumbed through the photos, stopping at one of Gabby Winslow.

"What's this?" the Judge asked, lifting a necklace from a clear plastic bag.

"I do believe you just hit the jackpot. That's the necklace Randy Culver described. And here's a photo of your wife wearing it."

# 50

Donna braced her hand on her knee to keep the gun from shaking. She glanced out the window to see if they'd drawn anyone's attention. So far, no one was staring.

"Why don't you just go ahead and kill us," Rachel said.

*Yes! It'd be better to get rid of them right now. They're more trouble than they're worth.*

"No!" She had to take them to the cemetery. She'd kill them both there at his grave. "You'll shut up then."

"Who are you talking to?" Rachel asked.

"No one." She glanced at their surroundings. Cars whizzed by on Poplar, and there were three vehicles at the pumps with more people inside the store.

*You're in a fine mess now. But what did you expect?*

"Shut up!"

Rachel flinched, and in the back seat, Erin moaned.

*Now you've done it. You get that woman to crying and somebody will come see what's wrong. You never learn anything. And just how do you expect to get away with this? You're so stupid. You deserved every beating you made me give you.*

Breathe. Just breathe. In. Out. She couldn't let him get to her. But he was right. She would be Boone's number one suspect. A plan. She had to come up with a plan. But first things first. "Pull the car to the pumps and get the gas. And remember I'll have the gun on Erin."

"Let me get my credit card." Rachel reached for her bag.

"No. Use cash." Boone Callahan would run a check on Rachel's cards when he realized she was missing. Hers too.

*See. You'll never get out of this alive. He'll know you took them.*

She rubbed her temple. "No. He'll think you did it."

"You're talking to someone. Who is it?" Rachel stared at her, a strange look in her eyes.

Donna shook her head. "Just put the gas in the tank."

"With what?"

"Cash," Donna snapped. "Do I have to spell it out? Maybe a taste of the strap will get your attention. And stop looking at me that way."

Rachel turned her head and stared through the windshield. "I don't have any cash."

Donna's head hurt. Did she have any money in her purse? She raked her fingers through her hair. Cash wasn't something she carried. But they had to have gas. There wasn't enough in the tank to get to Elmwood Cemetery.

Donna pulled her wallet from her purse and handed Rachel a credit card. "Roll the window down so I can hear if you say anything. Don't do anything stupid."

Rachel lowered the window, then climbed out of the car. "I hope you won't either."

Erin stirred in the back seat. "I have to go to the bathroom."

Donna ground her teeth. If Erin didn't shut up . . . "You'll have to wait."

Rachel put her head back through the window. "I'll take you in a minute."

As soon as the pump clicked off, Donna said, "That's enough. Get back in the car." Once Rachel was in the driver's seat, she said, "Take a right out of the lot."

"But she has to—"

"I need—"

Donna nudged Rachel with the pistol. "Too bad. Now drive."

"Come on, the restroom is on the outside," Rachel said. "You can come with us to get the key and stand guard. I won't even take the key back. We'll leave it in the restroom."

*Don't do it. Just drive away.*

"Leave me alone." She was so tired of him telling her what to do. She could make her own decisions. And if she didn't let them go, Erin would keep whining and she couldn't take that. "All right, get out."

"Thank you," Rachel said and opened the car door.

*See how Gabby is smirking? You're playing into her hands. Don't do it.*

"No! Stop telling me what to do!"

Gabby closed the door and stared at her. "You need help, Donna. Let me call Boone, so he can find you a doctor."

"Stop talking. They're not locking me up again." Donna's head buzzed with tangled thoughts racing through her mind. She pressed her left hand against her temple. She was done letting him boss her around. She was in control now, and she knew how she was going to fool Boone. Such a simple plan, she should have thought of it earlier. She'd tell him the man who carjacked them made her do it.

Motioning with the gun, she said, "Once we're out of the car, you'll go in first, but I'll be right behind you with Erin. And Gabby, if you make one wrong move, your friend here is dead."

# 51

Back at the Criminal Justice Center, Boone spread the contents of the box on the conference room table. Photos, a journal, and several file folders.

The Judge had taken a seat at the end of the table, and he picked up one of the folders and looked inside. "This is a dossier on Terri Morrow." He scanned it. "And it's pretty accurate. He even has an article about her husband's fall at Big Sur." He handed it to Boone.

He flipped through it as Lucien picked up another file.

"This one's on Monica Carpenter, but I don't know anything about her. You probably need to read it."

Boone took the folder and scanned the papers in it. The information matched what he'd gleaned from interviews with Monica. He picked up the last folder. It was thicker than the others. "This is on Donna Dumont. Says here her real name is Shirley Irene Baker and her father died in 1980 when she was fifteen. Then her husband, Chandler Dumont, died when she was twenty-one. Food poisoning, so Terri was right."

Then Boone frowned. "Why didn't she use her married name at the Institute?"

He pulled the records Ms. Patterson had given him and found the name Irene Baker. "She started to work there in 1983. She would have been eighteen. Is there anything in the articles indicating when she married?"

The judge sorted through the file. "Here's something."

He held up a *Memphis Commercial Appeal* clipping titled "For the Record: Marriage License Issued in Shelby County." A red line circled two names. "Says here Shirley Irene Baker, 20, and Chandler Evan Dumont, 54, applied for a marriage license on June 21, 1985."

"So her name was Baker when she started work at the Institute," Boone said, then thinking out loud added, "Maybe she never went to the trouble of changing the records."

The Judge looked over Boone's shoulder. "What's that question mark beside food poisoning? And the note beside the information about her father that says see articles?"

"I don't know." He laid the folder on the table and shuffled through it, looking for newspaper articles.

The Judge rubbed his chin. "I've been doing research on ricin poisoning, and when it's ingested, it mimics food poisoning. And didn't she work with Robert Morrow?"

"Yeah, but to plan a murder like that . . . If she stole the ricin and either injected her husband with it or put it in his food, that's premeditated murder." Boone couldn't see the Donna he knew being a cold-blooded killer.

He paused to read a page Vic had typed. "Oh my word. Vic indicates here that Donna spent time in a mental facility when she was fifteen for killing her father." He looked up. "At the facility she confessed she had cut his throat with a straight razor."

The judge paled. "How did she get a job with the Memphis Police Department?"

Boone scanned another folder. "It looks like she was never charged with his death, so she was never fingerprinted. If no red

316

flags showed up on a basic background check, the department wouldn't go much deeper, not for an office assistant job." He sorted through the other papers in the folder. "Here's a photocopy of a *Commercial Appeal* article dated the time of her father's death. And an obituary," he said, reading the paper stapled to the article.

"So it happened here in Memphis?"

"No, in a small town outside the city, but he's buried in Elmwood Cemetery." He quickly scanned the article and handed it to the Judge. The fact she killed her father did not necessarily mean she was their killer. "It was ruled justifiable homicide. She was catatonic when the deputy sheriff came to tell her he'd been killed in an accident, and he found blood on the kitchen floor. Her eyes were blackened, and bruises and contusions covered her body . . . and there was evidence of prior beatings—broken bones that had healed without being set. The article doesn't give her name, but does the father's. Alfred Baker. That's consistent with the name Irene Baker she used at Crockett Cancer Institute."

"I wonder where the mother was?" the Judge asked.

"Here's another article, a couple of years later. Still doesn't name her, just calls her the victim, but says the mother had died when she was fourteen," Boone said, reading from the article. "Again it indicates Donna remained in the mental hospital for three years—until she turned eighteen."

The skin on his neck prickled. Scenarios ran rampant through his mind. He took out his phone and dialed Rachel's number, his stomach clenching when she didn't answer. He realized he should have gotten Erin's number, and found her sister's number on his recent calls. Terri didn't answer, either.

Boone tapped his phone on the table, then stood and walked to the whiteboard in the room. "Let's look at this rationally."

He wrote Donna's name on the board, then listed the people in her circle who had died.

Alfred Baker—father

Robert Morrow—affair

Gabby Winslow—friend?

Harrison Foxx—affair?

Vic Vegas—Boone wasn't sure of Vic's connection to Donna yet.

The Judge picked up the file. "You forgot her husband—Chandler Dumont."

Boone added his name. "Did it say what the mother died from? We might need to look at that."

"Fell down the basement stairs," he said. "While there's no proof Donna was connected to any of those deaths other than her father's, that's a lot of deaths in one person's life." Lucien picked up the guitar pendant. "What does the necklace signify?"

"Culver said Vic was arguing about it with a woman. But Vic never mentioned her name."

"You indicated it belonged to my wife, but I've never seen it before."

Boone walked back to the table and found the photo of Gabby Winslow wearing the necklace. "Here she is wearing it the night of the St. Jude charity event. You're sure you've never seen it?"

"I'm positive." The Judge turned the necklace over. "She didn't have it on when I saw her that night, either. I would have remembered something like this. Although I did leave before the gala was over, so Harrison could have given it to her after I left."

"Could she have bought it?"

"If she did, Gabby would have charged it—she charged everything—and I don't remember seeing a bill for a piece of jewelry after she died. This would've cost at least a couple of grand, even seventeen years ago."

"Lucien, thank goodness you're here!"

Boone turned. Terri stood in the doorway, pale and hollow-eyed.

"What's going on?" the Judge said.

"Rachel and Erin. They're not answering their phones."

"I know, I just tried to call Rachel."

"Donna has them. I know she does."

# 52

DONNA HAD CALLED HER GABBY. Once again she'd slipped over the edge, and from the look in her eyes, she might not come back. Rachel was dealing with an insane person, and there was no way to predict how she would react to any situation. Whatever Rachel did, she had to be careful. One wrong move could cost Erin's life, as well as her own.

Donna turned and glared at Erin. "All right, get out and stand by my door until I get out. And if you so much as look at anyone, I'll shoot Gabby. Do you understand?"

Erin's eyes widened as big as saucers. She nodded and then did as she was told.

Rachel wasn't worried about Erin doing or saying anything. She'd gone silent now and appeared to understand the danger.

Donna turned to Rachel. "Sit there until I get out, and then we'll go inside."

A minute later, Rachel walked inside the service center on legs that felt like noodles, conscious of Donna following close behind with her hand on Erin's elbow. The other hand held the gun hidden in her pants pocket. At the cash register, Rachel said, "May I have the key to the restroom?"

The clerk handed her a key attached to a small wooden paddle. If he thought it was odd that all three of them came inside for the key, he didn't say anything. But then they probably looked like any other mother and daughters traveling together. Normal.

Inside the restroom, there were two stalls.

"One at a time," Donna instructed.

"I'll hold your purse," Rachel said, pointing at the red bag Erin gripped to her side. Somehow she had to get the purse. If it held Erin's usual lipstick, she could at least leave a message. Once Erin was out, Rachel ducked into the stall and opened the purse. *Yes!* Erin's phone was in the bottom. But it was turned off, and she didn't have enough time for it to power up and send a message.

She made sure the ringer was silent and turned the phone on before slipping it in her back pocket. Now Terri would be able to track their location—if she checked. Surely she'd check when they didn't show up at the group home after the candlelighting service. Rachel might even get an opportunity to use the phone herself.

"Hurry up," Donna snapped.

"Coming." She found the tube of lipstick and quickly scribbled "Help!" Suddenly the stall door flew open and Donna snatched the paper from her hand.

"What are you doing?" she yelled and jerked Erin close, pressing the gun against her side. "Get out."

Gritting her teeth, Rachel did as she was told, her fingers itching to attack Donna. But not while she held the gun on Erin. Donna turned and pushed Erin toward the door, and she stumbled to the floor.

Rachel dove for the pistol, but Donna was faster. She jerked back, and then slammed the pistol against Rachel's cheek. Rachel reeled against the wall and pressed her hand to her throbbing face.

The gun shook in Donna's hand. "I ought to kill you now."

"No!" Erin cried.

Rachel's cheek throbbed. Donna was surprisingly strong. "You won't get out of here alive if you fire that gun."

For a minute, she wasn't sure if reason would win out, but gradually the gun stopped moving and Donna took a breath.

"Get in the car, and if you try something like that again, I promise you, I don't care where we are, I'll kill you both."

Rachel opened the bathroom door, and Donna shoved her forward. Right away Rachel noticed that dark clouds had formed to the west. She didn't know if that would be a good thing or not.

Once they were in the car, Donna said, "Take a right out of the lot and stay on Poplar until I tell you to turn."

They were nearing I-240 when she noticed Donna had Rachel's phone out and was typing.

"What are you doing?" Rachel asked when her phone whooshed with a sent message.

"You just told Boone we've been carjacked."

Why would she do that? Goose bumps raised on her arm. If Donna thought Boone would believe that, she had totally lost contact with reality. The *Dragnet* ringtone she'd assigned Boone rang from her phone. Donna lowered the window, letting the wind whip through the car as she tossed the phone.

"No!"

Donna laughed, and the eerie sound sent shivers down Rachel's back. "You won't need your phone where you're going. Now go west on I-240 and drive toward downtown."

Rachel's mind raced as she gripped the steering wheel and took the ramp onto the interstate. Short of crashing the car, she had no option other than to do as Donna said. For now.

This was more than she could handle on her own, and she wished she was on better terms with God. She could really use his help now. *"When you pass through the waters, I will be with you."* The verse she'd memorized in childhood popped into her mind. It was the verse she'd comforted herself with after her mother died.

Hope crept into her heart. *Focus on the positive.* Boone would put out a BOLO—be-on-the-lookout alert. And he'd call Terri. She could track them on Erin's phone. For the first time, she had hope they might get out of this.

# 53

"Where do you think Donna took them?" Boone asked as Terri collapsed in a chair at the table.

"Who knows? She's crazy." She buried her face in her hands. "If only I'd gone to the police back when I thought she killed her husband. But I didn't have any proof."

"You have proof now?" Lucien asked.

Terri lifted her head. "Nothing I could bring to you, Lucien. Just my gut feeling, and it's rarely wrong." She turned to Boone. "She was my husband's lab assistant and had access to everything he did. If ricin went missing from his lab, she took it. My husband would never have stolen it or misplaced it—research was his life and he prided himself on his work. He wouldn't have risked his reputation for anything."

Boone showed her the pendant. "Have you ever seen this before?"

Terri shook her head.

He handed her the photo of Gabby with Harrison. "Could he have given it to her?"

"I don't know." She brought the photo closer to her face. "But that's Donna in the background."

"What?" He examined the picture. The scowling person she

pointed out was heavier than the office manager he knew. But if he looked close, he could see a resemblance.

"Is that a list of people you think she killed?"

He turned, and she was staring at the whiteboard.

"Not exactly. Except for the father. The rest of them had contact with her."

"What happened to her father?"

Boone handed her the two articles. Her eyes widened as she read. When she finished, she dropped the papers on the table.

"Earlier when I called her crazy, I was using a figure of speech. But she really is." She swallowed hard. "There . . . is something I've never told anyone. When Bobby broke it off with her, she threatened to kill him."

"You didn't tell the police about her threat when he died?" Boone asked.

She shook her head. "I believed it was an accident, and I never dreamed she'd actually do it . . . except I never understood why he was that close to the edge of the cliff. He was always so careful. It wasn't like him . . ." She pressed her hands together and touched them to her lips and looked at the board again. "What if Donna followed us to Big Sur? Bobby told me when he was confessing their affair that he and Donna had hiked it. That's why we went there. To overlay his memories of being there with her with memories of the two of us. And he died instead."

A text dinged on Boone's phone. They all stared at his phone as though it'd grown wings.

"It's from Rachel." He couldn't believe the message. "They've been carjacked."

Immediately he tried to call her, but it went to voicemail.

"Maybe Donna has her phone," Terri said.

The Judge leaned forward. "What purpose would it serve for Donna to send a text saying they'd been carjacked?"

"Good question." He exchanged glances with the Judge. "I

think we've been looking at this all wrong. We've been going on the assumption we're dealing with a normal person." He looked at Terri. "Did you say you had a tracking app on Erin's phone?"

Terri yanked her phone from her pocket and clicked on an orange and white app. "Come on," she muttered. Then she gasped. "It's working now. They're on Lamar! Right at Airways, it looks like."

"Do you suppose they're still headed to Graceland?" the Judge asked.

"I doubt it. Figure she's headed out of the state. Maybe on the way to Mexico." Boone rubbed his jaw.

"You really think she'd try something like that?" the Judge asked.

"If Donna has kidnapped them, she's crazy and there's no way to predict anything she'll do. But eventually, they'll have to stop for fuel. Maybe then Rachel will get an opportunity to get away."

"Rachel won't leave Erin," Terri said.

He picked up his office phone and dialed the dispatcher. "I need a BOLO for Donna Dumont's vehicle—you'll have to get DMV to look up her tag number. And add a 2005 or 2006 dark gray Honda Civic to the BOLO. It's registered to Rachel Sloan. You can get her tag number from DMV as well."

He disconnected and then dialed the Financial Crimes Unit. If anyone could quickly track either of their credit cards, the FCU officers could. He explained what he wanted and that they could get Donna and Rachel's personal information from their personnel records.

"They'll let us know as soon as they know something," he said after he hung up. Then he turned to Terri. "Check their whereabouts again."

She refreshed the app and then groaned. "It says location not available. Why did it quit working?"

Boone brought Google Maps up on his computer. "Where did you say they were?"

"Airways and Lamar. Could they be going to the airport?"

"I don't think so. No tickets, too many people." But he typed in the Memphis, Tennessee, airport. The area around it was a good place to start. Nothing spoke to him and he zoomed out, following Lamar toward downtown. Boone caught his breath. "What was that cemetery her father is buried in?"

"Elmwood," the Judge said. "Same one Gabby is buried in."

"I think that's where she's headed." The cemetery was huge, and in another hour it would be dark. What if Donna made a break for it when they confronted her? They'd never find her in the dark. Boone grabbed his phone and called for a chopper. They would need the lights the helicopter would provide. Thunder rumbled, and he glanced toward the window and frowned. It was too early to be this dark. When someone in the Air Support Division answered, he explained what he wanted. "But don't deploy unless I ask for assistance."

"Sorry, Lieutenant, but we're about to get hit with a powerful thunderstorm in the next thirty minutes. We're grounded."

His muscles tensing, Boone quickly hung up and called the dispatcher again. "I have a possible hostage situation, and I need every available car to invisibly deploy toward Elmwood Cemetery and remain on standby. Do not attempt to apprehend the occupants in the vehicle. I repeat—do not apprehend."

He grabbed his keys and rushed toward the door.

"Hold up," the Judge said. "I'm coming with you."

Boone turned to refuse, but the determination in the Judge's face stopped him. It was plain he was coming with him or in his own vehicle. It was the same with Terri. "Okay, but once we get there, you'll have to remain in the car."

He half trotted across the street, keeping a wary eye on the low-hanging clouds in the sky. A thunderstorm was the last thing they needed. "What's the quickest way to Elmwood?" he asked as he peeled down the garage ramp and out on to Washington.

Terri waved her phone. "I'll check." A minute later, she said, "I-40 to I-240 South, come off on exit 29. ETA is eight minutes."

"Check and see the time from Airways and Lamar." Boone flipped on his flashing lights and siren as he turned right on Poplar. At least downtown traffic had cleared out. "And while you're at it, see if you can find anyone who can tell us where Alfred Baker's grave is."

"Seven minutes, but they've been traveling since I checked. They're probably already there." Then she said, "It says here the cemetery closed at four thirty."

"Let me alert the Uniform Patrol. We might have a situation if she can't get in."

Terri took out her phone. "I'm going to try Erin one more time. Maybe someone will pick up."

# 54

THEY WERE NOW TRAVELING down Lamar toward downtown Memphis. Rachel took her eyes off the road for a second to check on Donna's stability. She was no longer calling her Gabby, and in spite of the laugh, she acted calmer. Not so close to the edge of madness.

Donna caught her looking, and for half a second, her eyes softened. "I didn't mean to kill your mother."

"What happened that night?" She kept her words soft, non-accusing, in spite of the fact she wanted to rip into her.

Donna pressed her lips together so tightly they almost disappeared.

"I won't be angry," Rachel said. "Was it an accident?"

"Yes!" She said the word eagerly. "That's exactly what it was. It wasn't my fault. You've got to understand that. All I asked Gabby to do was just break it off with Harrison."

Rachel frowned. "My mother wasn't in love with Harrison."

"I know." Donna slapped her hand on the console.

Rachel flinched and glanced in the mirror to check on Erin. Thank goodness, she'd dozed off. Shut down, most likely.

Donna continued, her voice rising. "Gabby didn't care about

329

Harrison, but she wouldn't leave him alone. And as long as she was hanging around, he wasn't going to marry anyone else."

Anger radiated off her like a blazing fire. Maybe they should talk about something else. Heavier clouds loomed on the horizon. The weather. That was always a normal topic. "Looks like we might get that rain they promised." Silence. "I hope it waits until after the candlelighting."

Again, no response. Maybe if she could make an emotional connection to Donna, she could reason with her. Once when they were working out, she'd mentioned how hard her life had been, and how her father had died when she was fifteen. "We have a lot in common, you know."

"What makes you think that? You're just a kid, compared to me."

"I may be younger, but I lost my mother at the same age that you lost your dad. I know how hard that is."

"It wasn't the same situation." Donna shifted in the front seat, and tapped her foot against the floorboard. "We argued all the time."

"Yeah, most families do that. I don't think Mom and I ever did, though."

That horrible, eerie laugh erupted from Donna's lips again. "Of course, you did. That night at the charity contest. You had a horrible fight."

"No, we didn't." Something inside Rachel twisted, and bits of memory surfaced. *"I hate you."* Had she said that? Her chest tightened. They couldn't have argued. It was her dad. He was the one. Anger flared, searing her heart. He hadn't been there because he had someone else. *No. There wasn't anyone else. Just his work.*

A low buzzing jerked her thoughts from the past. Erin's cell phone vibrated against her hip. *No!* Why hadn't she checked to see if vibrate was turned on?

330

"What's that noise?"

Rachel willed the phone to stop buzzing. Had to be Terri. Or Boone.

"That's a cell phone!" Donna stuck the gun in her ribs. "Hand it over."

"No! And I don't think you'll shoot me since we're traveling fifty miles an hour—unless you want to die in a car wreck."

Donna swung the gun toward the back. "No, but Erin's not driving. So hand it over."

The buzzing stopped, leaving dead silence in the car. "Say goodbye to your friend," she said in a singsong voice.

"I'll give it to you." Rachel fished the phone from her back pocket and handed it to her. At least she still had her gun under the seat. As she expected, Donna lowered the window and threw the phone out.

"I hope you don't do anything else stupid," Donna said.

Rachel gripped the steering wheel. A patrol car going in the opposite direction caught her eye. Did he speed up? Maybe he recognized her car.

"Did Harrison figure out you killed my mother?" she asked to distract Donna.

She didn't answer but instead twisted to follow the police cruiser. "Stop asking questions. I can't think."

Another wall of clouds rolled in, darker than the first, reminding Rachel that their chances of surviving would diminish with nightfall. She willed the police cruiser to catch up with them, but in case it didn't, she needed a plan for when they got to wherever they were going.

"How long do you want me to stay on Lamar?"

"Until you get to South Dudley, and then take a left to Elmwood Cemetery."

Elmwood Cemetery. Was she taking them to her mother's grave? To kill them there?

Memories slammed her heart. Backstage at the Cook Convention Center. Her dad. Wanting to come home. Looking so hurt.

*"You have to let him move back, Mom! You should forgive him! Think about me!"*

*"Oh, honey, you don't underst—"*

*"Yes, I do! I need my dad! Let him move back home!"*

*"Rachel, that's enough. He's not moving back home now and that's final."*

*"You're so selfish! I hate you!"*

It was all clear now, and unshed tears burned her eyes. Rachel had stormed away, left her mother standing backstage. Later she'd called a friend to come get her and had spent the night at her friend's house. When she finally returned home the next morning, she found her mother dead.

A band squeezed her heart. If she'd just gone home with her . . .

Rachel never got the chance to tell her she was sorry.

"Turn left at the next block," Donna said suddenly.

"The cemetery is closed. You won't be able to get in." Rachel glanced in the mirror. Erin was awake and staring at her like a lost puppy. Rachel could not let her die in this cemetery.

"It's open. Saw in the paper it's some anniversary and they're having evening tours all this week."

The 165th anniversary. Rachel had forgotten about seeing the poster when she and Erin were here.

The entrance to Elmwood Cemetery came into view too soon, and memories she'd suppressed for so long flooded her mind again. For seventeen years she'd buried the truth—she'd argued with her mother and then ran away, leaving her to go home alone. To die. But she hadn't been able to just blame herself and had self-righteously blamed her father as well, because if he hadn't had an affair, he would have been home. She'd gotten it all wrong.

It hadn't been his fault. The truth speared her heart. And it hadn't been her fault either. Rachel gripped the steering wheel. Donna had gone to their house that night to kill her mother. Resolve swelled in her chest.

She would not let her get away with two more murders. Rachel had to stop her. If she didn't, Donna would be free to kill again.

# 55

HALF-DOLLAR-SIZED RAINDROPS splattered the windshield as Boone's cell rang. He quickly answered. It was dispatch.

"Elmwood is still open. They were supposed to have tours this evening, but they've been canceled. I advised the administrator to evacuate but leave the gates open until you arrive."

"Good." At least Donna wouldn't be locked out. He really wanted to contain her in the cemetery.

"Any sightings of either car?" he asked.

"Yes. The gray Honda was seen on Lamar near E. H. Crump Boulevard. Appears to be two people in the front seat. No sign of a third person. The officer is keeping the car in sight, but not approaching. Looks like it's headed to the cemetery."

Had they left Erin somewhere? He certainly hoped so. Boone pictured the entrance to the cemetery. He'd been to Elmwood in the past, and the main access was a narrow bridge over the railroad tracks. There was a fence around the perimeter, but he couldn't remember if there were other entrances on the bordering streets. "Once the Honda enters, block the main entrance and secure all other points of access." He hung up and glanced in the rearview mirror. "Any information on Alfred Baker's grave site?"

"No," Terri said. "No one is answering at the office."

Hopefully that meant they were no longer there. At exit 29, he swung off I-240 at Lamar and shut his siren off. The cemetery couldn't be over five minutes away.

# 56

As THEY APPROACHED the narrow bridge leading into Elmwood, Rachel glanced to the right and made herself breathe normally. There. Parked in a lot with tombstones for sale. One of MPD's unmarked cruisers.

Did Donna see it? A quick glance. No. She leaned forward, focused on the bridge ahead. Was Boone here? Inside the cemetery, waiting? To the west, a bolt of lightning arced across the dark sky, followed by a boom of thunder.

"Rachel," Erin cried from the back seat. "I don't like thunder."

"It's going to be okay."

Donna didn't appear to hear them.

"Where are we?" Erin asked.

"At Elmwood." They were on the bridge now. "You remember crossing this bridge when we were here Saturday?"

"Mmmhmm. It's where the angels are."

"Do you remember the cottage and how we got there?" she asked as they passed the office. A tan car sat parked in front of the building. She recognized it as another unmarked cruiser.

"Yes. We walked from over there." Erin pointed in the direction of her mother's grave.

"Good." Erin had an uncanny sense of direction. If Rachel

could distract Donna somehow once they were out of the car, maybe Erin could make a run for the cottage. "Pay attention now."

"What are you talking about?" Donna demanded. "And turn left at the next crossroads."

"Just trying to distract her," she said quietly. They were not going in the direction of her mother's grave. Another bolt of lightning zigzagged in front of them. "Where are we going?"

"You'll see."

The cemetery was a maze of winding roads. Her headlights caught the bending trees as the wind whipped ahead of the approaching storm.

"Stop there at that black obelisk, and park so the lights are on the small monument to the right of it."

Rachel stopped the car in front of a tall three-sided monument and backed up, lighting the smaller stone. "Who is Alfred Baker?"

"My illustrious father. Get out and I'll introduce you."

She had to get Donna's gun. Or hers. It was their only chance. But how? It was so close in her little car, Donna could see every move she made. *Stall for time.* She unfastened her seat belt. "Why do you think you'll get away with this?"

"I just will." She turned her head toward the grave. "I always have."

Rachel lunged over the console for Donna's gun. "Run, Erin! Run!"

The back door flew open as they struggled for the automatic. Donna pummeled Rachel. Rachel balled her fist and slammed Donna right above the elbow. The gun clattered to the floor. No way to get it. Rachel reached under her seat for her own automatic.

# 57

THE ROAD TWISTED YET AGAIN, and no sign of Rachel's Honda. "We must have taken a wrong turn."

"There are so many crossroads," Terri said.

"Maybe I can hear something if I get out of the car." Boone shifted the gear to park. "You two stay here. There may be gunfire, and I don't want you caught in it."

A wind gust caught the door when he opened it, almost jerking it loose from his grip. Cloud-to-ground lightning lit up the area, illuminating the trees as they bent against the coming storm. He pulled his gun. Was that a light up ahead? He jogged toward it, hearing nothing but the roar of the wind as the rain moved in. More lightning lit up the area, silhouetting a figure running toward him in the distance. Too small to be Rachel or Donna.

"Erin!" The wind snatched her name from his mouth, carrying it away from her. He ran toward her and caught her in his arms. "Erin, where's Rachel?"

Her eyes were huge. She pointed behind her, toward a faint glow. "D-Donna. Sh-she ha-has a g-gun!"

Suddenly Terri was there, wrapping her arms around her sister. "Go," she yelled. "Find Rachel!"

Boone sprinted toward the light.

◆

Blood gushed from Rachel's nose. She felt for her gun under her seat. Gone. *Run!* She fumbled for the door handle.

"Hold it right there."

The barrel of the pistol pressed against Rachel's temple.

"You think I'm stupid enough to leave your gun in the car?" Donna's breath came fast as she kept the automatic pressed to her skin.

"I don't think you're stupid at all." Her voice shook. "I never dreamed it was you. You're quite brilliant."

"I know. And I know you're just saying that to make me relax." Even so, she backed the gun away from Rachel's head. "Put your hands on the steering wheel where I can see them and don't move." Keeping the weapon on Rachel, Donna scrambled out of the car and came around to the driver's side. "Get out."

As she crawled out of the car, Rachel searched for any sign of Erin, fearing she might have hung around instead of running to the office. "You won't get away with this."

Lightning arced across the sky and the skies opened, releasing a torrent of rain, stinging her body in the electrically charged air.

"It's over," she yelled over the roar of the storm. "Boone's here, in the cemetery. He's found Erin by now."

"Doesn't matter!" Donna pushed her toward the monument.

"You don't have to do this."

"Yes, I do. It's the only way I can shut him up. And shut Gabby up. They won't leave me alone."

Another bolt of lightning split the air. The oak by the side of the lane exploded, and Donna jerked her head toward it.

Rachel charged her. She was not dying on this hill in this cemetery tonight.

"No!" Donna swung the gun toward her and fired.

◆

Boone heard the scream as he rounded a curve in the road. Two people, struggling in the light from the car headlights. A gunshot rent the air, and Rachel stumbled.

Donna lifted the gun again.

"No!"

He saw Lucien Winslow in his peripheral vision. Boone took quick aim and fired.

Donna's arm dropped, and she stumbled to her knees.

Boone rushed her and picked up the gun she dropped. Then he turned to Rachel lying on the ground. Police cars converged on the scene. He turned her over and felt for a pulse. She was alive. "Call for an ambulance," he yelled and ripped her shirt away from the wound.

The judge knelt beside him. "Is she alive?"

The rain beat down, soaking him, and he wiped water from his eyes. "Yes. Looks like a shoulder wound."

"Thank the Lord."

Rachel's eyes fluttered open. "You made it," she whispered. "Both of you."

# 58

SIX WEEKS LATER

At the police academy gym, Rachel knelt and tied her shoelaces. It felt good to be back in the swing of things. Yesterday she'd passed the physical fitness test, and Monday morning she would officially be back on duty.

"You sure you're up to this?"

She looked up. Boone, dressed in a black MPD T-shirt that emphasized his broad shoulders, stood with his feet planted. Warmth spread through her chest. He'd come to see her every day in the hospital and then brought her meals by the house. Not to mention flowers. She had enough to start a shop of her own.

"You afraid I'm going to beat you again?" she asked. He offered his hand, and she took it to steady herself as she straightened.

"Nah. I've been practicing. And we can celebrate my victory at your dad's barbecue tonight."

"Pretty sure of yourself." She couldn't keep from teasing him.

He lifted his shoulder in a half shrug and gave her a devilish grin that sent her heart rate soaring. "I've heard my number one competitor isn't quite at 100 percent."

He was right about that, and she would probably have trouble with the four-foot cube since her shoulder was still tender. Maybe even with the beam.

"Why don't you give the competition another month? I want you to be 100 percent when I beat you."

She rolled her shoulder, wincing at the short jab of pain that shot through it. "Okay. I'll wait."

"Whoa! You're actually going to listen to me?"

Rachel simply grinned at him. She'd come a long way in the last six weeks. From mending the breach with her father and agreeing to go to counseling with him, to finally remembering the argument with her mother and accepting that she couldn't undo what happened. She'd even been able to cry at her mother's grave.

"Let's get out of here," he said.

He held her hand as they walked to his pickup.

"Have you finished your sessions with the department psychiatrist?" she asked. Donna Dumont's death had hit Boone hard, and Rachel was glad that counseling was mandatory after an officer killed someone in the line of duty.

"I have one more session. How about you? Nightmares last night?

"No. None since the first of the week."

"Good."

Peace wrapped around her heart. Boone made her feel cared for, safe. Rachel didn't know where their relationship was headed, but once her stint in Homicide was up, she was ready to give love a try.

"By the way," he said, swinging in front of her. "My transfer came through today."

"What transfer?" Boone couldn't be leaving Homicide. He loved it almost as much as she did.

"To David Raines's Cold Case Unit."

Her eyes burned, and a lump lodged in her throat as she looked at the ground. "Are you sure you want to do that?"

He cupped her chin and lifted it until she was gazing in his eyes.

"You probably aren't aware of it," he said as he traced his finger down her cheek, "but I applied last year when Brad did, and he got it."

Her heart beat so fast she could hardly breathe. "But I thought—"

"You're always thinking, and sometimes you're wrong. That's what I meant a long time ago when I told you we could work things out." Boone's eyes darkened as held her gaze. "Just in case you don't know, I love you, Rachel," he said, his voice husky. "More than the job, more than . . . *anything*."

She thought her heart would burst. He loved her. She closed her eyes, savoring the moment. Slowly she opened them and sighed. "I love you too."

He bent his head until his lips were inches from hers. She slipped her arms around his neck and pulled his mouth to hers. Boone kissed her gently and then pulled her closer. She melted into his arms and lost herself in his kiss.

She wasn't ready to stop when he released her, but then she suddenly realized what his transfer meant. "That means we can do this and not get in trouble?"

"You got it," he said, grinning. Then his eyes widened. "I didn't mean to make you cry!"

She wiped her cheeks with the back of her hand. "It's okay," she said. "These are happy tears."

# ACKNOWLEDGMENTS

As always, to God, who gives me the words.

Thank you to my readers. Without your support, I wouldn't be here.

To my family and friends, who believe in me.

To my editors at Revell, Lonnie Hull DuPont and Kristin Kornoelje, and Julie Davis—thank you for making my stories so much better.

To the art, editorial, marketing, and sales team at Revell—Michele Misiak, Karen Steele, Erin Bartels, Hannah Brinks, and Cheryl Van Andel, thank you for your hard work. You are the best!

To Julie Gwinn, thank you for your direction and for working so tirelessly with me and for being my friend.

To Sgt. Joe Stark, MPD, thank you for always answering my questions, even when I shoot them over to you in the middle of the night. And because what you said and what I heard may not always be the same thing, I apologize for not getting it right sometimes.

To Susan Buske, thank you for finding and correcting my medical errors.

Patricia Bradley is a published short story writer and cofounder of Aiming for Healthy Families, Inc. Her manuscript for *Shadows of the Past* was a finalist for the 2012 Genesis Award, winner of a 2012 Daphne du Maurier Award (first place, Inspirational), and winner of a 2012 Touched by Love Award (first place, Contemporary). When she's not writing or speaking, she can be found making beautiful clay pots and jewelry. She is a member of American Christian Fiction Writers and Romance Writers of America and makes her home in Corinth, Mississippi.

Meet
# Patricia
# BRADLEY

www.ptbradley.com

 @PTBradley1

 Patricia Bradley Author

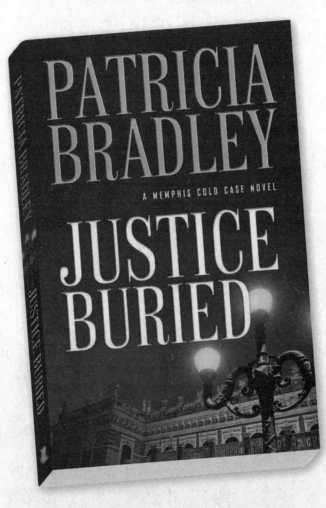

Sparks fly when security specialist Kelsey Allen and cold case
detective Brad Hollister work together to find a murderer—
until their attention must turn to keeping themselves alive.

Revell
a division of Baker Publishing Group
www.RevellBooks.com

Available wherever books and ebooks are sold.

In one week, the wrong man will be executed for murder.

# LET THE CHASE FOR THE REAL KILLER BEGIN.

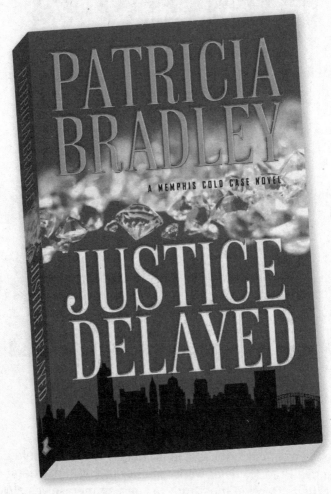

PATRICIA BRADLEY

A MEMPHIS COLD CASE NOVEL

JUSTICE DELAYED

Revell

a division of Baker Publishing Group
www.RevellBooks.com

Available wherever books and ebooks are sold.

# Also by
# PATRICIA BRADLEY . . .

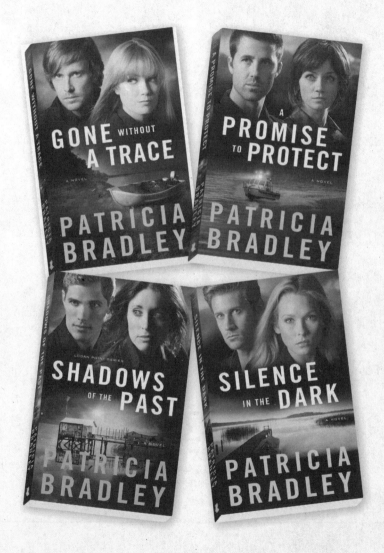